DRONE

DRONE

MIKE MADEN

G. P. PUTNAM'S SONS

NEW YORK

PUTNAM

G. P. PUTNAM'S SONS
Publishers Since 1838
Published by the Penguin Group
Penguin Group (USA) LLC
375 Hudson Street
New York, New York 10014

USA · Canada · UK · Ireland · Australia
New Zealand · India · South Africa · China

penguin.com
A Penguin Random House Company

Library of Congress Cataloging-in-Publication Data

Maden, Mike.
Drone / Mike Maden.
p.   cm.
ISBN 978-0-399-16738-6
1. Drone aircraft—Fiction.   2. Vigilantes—Fiction.
3. Suspense Fiction.   I. Title.
PS3613.A284327D76   2013   2013025096
813'.6—dc23

Printed in the United States of America
1   3   5   7   9   10   8   6   4   2

BOOK DESIGN BY MEIGHAN CAVANAUGH

This book is dedicated to you, Tom Lavin, my magnificent father-in-law, a combat-wounded, combat-decorated Marine. In 1952 you were just a kid hunting the enemy on night patrols with nothing more than a .45 in your hand and your head on a swivel, the point man on a zeroed-in path between rice paddies forward of the MLR. Overrun on the Yoke, bombarded on X-Ray, ambushed on Irene, you and your friends were outnumbered and outgunned, but you prevailed, unyielding in blood and valor. You did your job well, Pop, and so did your friends, the ones who came home from Korea and the ones who didn't. You believed, and that made all the difference.

CHARACTER LIST

PEARCE SYSTEMS

Troy Pearce	CEO, Pearce Systems
Udi and Tamar Stern	Husband-and-wife team; field operatives
Stella Kang	Former U.S. Army drone pilot; field operative
Judy Hopper	Pearce's personal pilot
Johnny Paloma	Former LAPD SWAT; field operative
Ian McTavish	Director of IT operations/research specialist
Dr. Kirin Rao	Head of research and development
Dr. Kenji Yamada	UUV research and operation; oceanographer (whale researcher)
August Mann	UGV specialist; head of nuclear deconstruction division

MYERS ADMINISTRATION

Margaret Myers	President of the United States
Bill Donovan	Secretary of the Department of Homeland Security
Jackie West	FBI Director

Dr. Karl Strasburg	Foreign Affairs/Security Advisor
Frank Romero	U.S. Ambassador to Mexico
Faye Lancet	Attorney General
Mike Early	Special Assistant (Security) to the President
Nancy Madrigal	DEA Administrator
Pedro Molina	Director of ICE
Robert Greyhill	Vice President
Roy Jackson	Head of DEA Intelligence
Sandy Jeffers	President's Chief of Staff
Sergio Navarro	DEA Intelligence Analyst
T. J. Ashley, Ph.D.	Head of Drone Command
Tom Eddleston	U.S. Secretary of State

OTHER NOTABLES

Antonio Barraza	President of Mexico
Hernán Barraza	The president's brother and chief advisor
César Castillo	Head of the Castillo Syndicate
Ulises, Aquiles Castillo	César's twin sons
Colonel Israel Cruzalta	Battalion Commander, Infanteria de Marina Mexicana
Victor Bravo	Head of the Bravo Alliance
Dmitry Titov	President of the Russian Federation
Konstantin Britnev	Russian Federation Ambassador to the United States
Ali Abdi	Quds Force Commander

ACRONYMS

AMISOM	African Union Mission in Somalia
AUMF	Authorization to Use Military Force
ARGUS-IS	Autonomous Real-Time Ground Ubiquitous Surveillance Imaging System
ARSS	Autonomous Rotorcraft Sniper System
BMI	Brain-Machine Interface
DARPA	Defense Advanced Research Projects Agency
DAS	Domain Awareness System
FISA	Foreign Intelligence Surveillance Act
JDAM	Joint Direct Attack Munition
JSOC	Joint Special Operations Command
LATP	Lima Army Tank Plant
RIOT	Rapid Information Overlay Technology
UAV	Unmanned Aerial Vehicle
UGV	Unmanned Ground Vehicle
USV	Unmanned Surface Vehicle
UUV	Unmanned Underwater Vehicle
WPR	War Powers Resolution

Anything one man can imagine, other men can make real.

— Attributed to Jules Verne

AUTHOR NOTE

All of the drone systems described in this book are currently deployed or in development. I have taken the liberty of simplifying and, in some cases, amplifying their performance characteristics for the sake of the story. However, I am confident that the "new and improved" versions I have described will soon be widely available.

MAY

1

___

El Paso, Texas

Cinco de Mayo was cooler than usual in the sprawling border city of El Paso, one of the poorest in America. In one of its grimmest barrios, a pink stucco house thrummed with life on a dark, narrow street. A crowd of teenagers from the nearby arts academy high school danced to throbbing music in the frame of its big picture window, their faces all smiles and laughter. The first graduation party of the year.

Out on the front porch, a knot of young men in hoodies and drooping pants stood guard, drinking beer out of Solo cups and smoking cigarettes, trying to look tough in a brutal part of town. To anybody passing by, they looked like somebody's crew, but they were just teenagers like the kids inside, their young bodies rocking unconsciously to the beat of the music behind them.

An obsidian-black Hummer on big custom wheels slowed as it passed the house. The windows were blacked out. Death-metal music roared inside. No plates on the bumpers.

The hoodies out front pretended not to notice, playing it cool but keeping careful watch out of the sides of their bloodshot eyes.

Four houses up, the Hummer's red brake lights flared as it slowed to a stop, then its white back-up lights lit up. The big black box of steel rolled backward. The gear box whined until it stopped in front of the pink stucco house.

It just sat there, idling.

The death-metal music still thundered behind the Hummer's blackened glass, muffled by the steel doors.

Now the boys turned in unison, stared at it, starting to freak out. The oldest kid nodded at the tallest.

"Yo. Go check it out."

"Me? *You* check it out."

No need.

The Hummer's doors burst open, death metal exploding into the night, drowning out the music inside the house.

Two men leaped out, strapped with shoulder-harnessed machine guns. Balaclavas hid their faces. They wore black tactical gear and Kevlar vests stitched with three letters: ICE.

The ICE men advanced in lockstep as they raised their weapons in one swift, synchronous motion, snapping the stocks to their cheeks, picking their targets through their iron sights.

The boys bolted toward the back of the house.

Too late.

Machine-gun barrels flashed like strobe lights in the dark. The air split with the roar of their gunfire.

The first rounds tore into the lead runner, then raked into the backs of the guys right behind him. They tumbled to the pavement in a heap like broken marionettes.

The gunmen advanced toward the porch, firing at the big picture window. The plate glass exploded. Panicked shouts inside.

In sync, the shooters loaded new fifty-round drum mags and fired at the house. Steel-jacketed bullets sliced through the walls, throwing big chunks of soft pink stucco into the air. One of the rounds smashed the party stereo, killing the music inside.

The shooters dropped their empty mags again and loaded two more. They advanced shoulder to shoulder onto the porch, the machine-gun stocks still tight to their faces. Gloved hands tossed flash bangs through the shattered picture window. The concussion grenades cracked like lightning.

Bodies on the floor writhed in blood and glass. The killers jammed their machine guns through the window frame and cut loose until the ammo gave out and the barrels smoked with heat.

Three hundred rounds. Eighteen seconds. Not bad.

Grinning behind their masks, the two shooters high-fived each other, then scrambled back into the Hummer. They slammed the doors shut as the vehicle rocketed away, tires screeching. The roar of the machine guns and the shrieking death-metal music disappeared with it. The night was finally quiet around the little pink house.

Except for the screaming inside.

2

Mogadishu, Somalia

Colonel Joseph Moi took his daily afternoon nap from exactly 3:15 p.m. to 3:45 p.m. It kept him sharp late into the evening when he usually did his whoring. It also gave him a reason to stay out of the withering sunlight boiling his troops in the compound outside.

The colonel's sleep was abruptly interrupted when his silenced cell phone vibrated on the nightstand like a coping saw on a piece of tin. His conscious mind rose through the thick waves of REM sleep just enough to guide his hand to the phone and shut it off. Gratefully, the practiced maneuver spared him any significant mental effort and he was able to slip back down into the depths of perfect slumber, noting the faint breeze beating gently on his face from an overhead fan.

Then his cell phone rang.

Pain furrowed his angular face. Once again, his mind had been dragged into semiconsciousness, but now it was attended by a splitting headache. He'd been robbed of precious sleep. Rage flooded over him.

Who the hell is calling?

He forced his heavy eyes open.

It suddenly occurred to him that it wasn't possible for the phone to be ringing like this. He'd put it on silent, as always, just moments before he lay down, and when it vibrated earlier, he'd silenced it again.

Strange.

Moi rolled over and snagged the phone off of the nightstand. The number read UNKNOWN.

That was stranger still. Only two people had the number to this particular phone and they were both well known to him.

The first was General Muwanga, the overbearing Ugandan army officer in charge of the African Union military district to which Moi's command theoretically reported. That was a phone call he would have to take despite its inevitable unpleasantness.

The other was Sir Reginald Harris, the English lord and bleeding-heart administrator of a charitable family trust, but that would have been a very enjoyable phone call to receive. Harris would have rung him up only if he was ready to pay the additional "security fees" Colonel Moi demanded in order to release the shipment of corn soya blend (CSB) the trust had shipped to Mogadishu two weeks ago. Harris's CSB shipment was intended for three thousand starving Somali children at a refugee camp one hundred kilometers toward the northwest.

Colonel Moi's compound was strategically located in one of the least inhabited suburbs of Somalia's capital city. As the commander of a unit of Kenyan troops assigned to AMISOM (the African Union Mission in Somalia), Colonel Moi's responsibility was to ensure the safe transport of much-needed foodstuffs from Mogadishu's revitalized deepwater port to the hinterland where famine had once again displaced over one million starving Somalis.

The Islamist al-Shabaab militia had reinfiltrated Mogadishu recently despite the best efforts of the African Union forces that battled against them in an attempt to give the Somali Transitional Federal Government time to reestablish functioning democratic institutions in the world's most infamous failed state. At the moment, the Shabaab militia posed the greatest threat to the safe delivery of food.

But not in Moi's sector. His command had completely cowed the Shabaab, thanks to Moi's aggressive tactics. Or at least that's what Colonel Moi reported to the Western aid organizations that coordinated deliveries

through him. Moi cultivated the extremely profitable fiction for naive
outsiders. The Shabaab left Moi alone because he paid them in hard cur-
rency, not because they were afraid of him.

Since it was likely neither Muwanga nor Harris calling him, Moi
snapped off the phone again, but now he was wide awake.

Damn it. It was only 3:22 p.m. He decided to fetch a cold beer from
his refrigerator. He padded barefoot across the silken, handwoven carpet
toward the tiled kitchen area. The cold marble felt good on his aching
feet. He flung open the stainless-steel Bosch refrigerator and yanked out
a frosty cold Stella Artois. As he was twisting off the bottle cap, the phone
rang again. He took a long swig and marched back over to the phone,
slamming the glass bottle down on the nightstand. With any luck, he'd
have the fool on the other end of the line in chains before nightfall and a
twelve-volt car battery clamped onto his balls.

Moi snatched up the ringing phone.

"Who is this?" As an educated Kenyan, Moi spoke excellent though
heavily accented English. Like many Africans, he was conversant, if not
fluent, in several tribal languages, but in the polyglot world of Mogadishu, the English tongue was the most commonly employed, particularly
among African troops. "This is an unlisted number."

"Colonel Moi, turn on your television set."

Moi cursed under his breath. The voice was a white man's. An American, he guessed. Moi stared incredulously at the phone. "My television
set?"

"Yes, the big eighty-inch LCD hanging there on the wall in front
of you."

Moi glanced at his eighty-inch Samsung LCD television, a gift from a
local Somali government official in his debt.

"How in the blazes do you know about my television?"

"I know a lot of things about you, Colonel Moi. Why don't you turn it
on, and I'll tell you all about yourself."

"When I get my hands on you, you shall learn things about me you wish you did not know."

"Keep yammering and it's gonna cost you one million pounds sterling."

That caught Moi's attention. "What are you talking about?"

"I'm talking about your bank account in the Cayman Islands. Do you want me to tell you the account number?"

Moi frowned. *How could he possibly know about that?* "Fine. I will turn it on."

Moi picked up the remote control and snapped on his television. It was linked to a satellite service. What he saw made him nearly crap his camouflaged pants. It was a crystal-clear infrared image of his compound from several thousand feet above.

The colonel quickly pulled on his combat boots and laced them up without taking his eyes off of the screen. When he finished, he approached the television and studied the image closely from just inches away. It was a live feed and he could make out each of his twenty soldiers at their various stations around the compound, even the ones loafing in the barracks. There was even a glowing gray image of him located in his second-story penthouse.

"Satellite imagery. Impressive," Moi acknowledged. Obviously, the white man had some sort of satellite reconnaissance capability at his disposal. That likely meant he was with the American government.

"What does the CIA want with me? And what is your name?" Moi asked again, but in a less threatening tone.

"I'm not with the CIA. I'm a private citizen. A businessman, to be specific. As far as you're concerned, my nationality is money, and my name isn't important." This time the American's voice boomed out of the television's surround-sound system. "And you can turn your phone off now. No point in running up your bill."

Moi shut his phone and pocketed it. "Then what do you want, Private Citizen?"

"I've had my eye on you for a while, Colonel," the voice on the phone said. "You're a man of routine, like most military men are. Routine makes men predictable. It also makes them targetable."

Red target reticles suddenly appeared on each of the men visible in the high-definition video image and tracked them as they sauntered through the compound. Fortunately for Moi, no reticle appeared over his image, at least not yet.

"Not satellite. Predator," Moi confidently concluded with a smile. Satellites couldn't target men on the ground like that.

"Bingo. And what I want from you is to deliver the CSB shipment to the refugee camp as you promised, and I want you to do it right now."

"Oh, so you are a Good Samaritan as well?"

The American laughed. "Me? Hardly. The Good Samaritan gave his money away."

"It sounds to me like you want the CSB for yourself, Private Citizen. It is worth quite a bit of cash."

"I was hired to make sure you fulfilled your contract, nothing more. One way or another, the CSB will be delivered today."

"That is not possible. The Shabaab militia would like nothing more than for me to expose this shipment to one of their terror squads who would either steal it or burn it."

"There hasn't been a Shabaab militia unit in Mog in over six months. You know that better than I do."

"African politics are quite complicated. Since you are a foreigner, I can hardly expect you to understand," Moi insisted. He kept his eyes glued to the television set. He was glad that his image still wasn't targeted.

"To tell you the truth, I hate politics, African or otherwise. I've lost way too many friends because of it. And we both know you're stalling. You're holding the CSB shipment hostage. My employer wants to know why. He's already paid you to ensure safe delivery of each shipment."

"I have broken no agreement. The food is safe here with me and will be shipped out when the conditions warrant."

"What conditions? And don't hand me any Shabaab bullshit either."

Moi quickly weighed his options. He could bolt out of the room, but then what would he do? His unit didn't have any antiaircraft weapons to speak of. If he entered the compound, there was a chance he'd be targeted and taken out by a Predator. But if he could get to his Land Rover, he might be able to escape, but then again, a Predator could easily track that, too.

"Colonel, you're pissing me off. The clock's ticking."

"My apologies." Moi swallowed hard. He hadn't apologized to any man in over twenty years, even when he was in the wrong. "My expenses have gone up. There are more government officials to bribe. And the roads are increasingly dangerous. Not from Shabaab, of course, but from street gangs and even those filthy Djiboutis." He was referring to one of the other AU peacekeeper nations with forces stationed in the sprawling city.

"So you want more money? Jeezus. How much is enough?"

"A question for the ages, Private Citizen. But I might ask you the same. What is Harris paying you? I shall double it."

"With what?"

"With the money I have in the Caymans account."

"You mean the one million?" the American asked.

"Yes, of course."

"Or did you mean the three million? There are three accounts in three separate Cayman banks, each worth just over a million. Look."

Moi gulped when his three separate account statements were displayed on the big plasma screen.

"The only problem, Colonel Moi, is that you don't have any money. At least not anymore."

Moi watched the balances of each account zero out.

"You are no businessman. You are a thief!"

"I only returned the money to my employer for your failure to abide by the terms of your contract. He'll use it to buy more food supplies, which will probably be stolen by some other petty tyrant."

"Tell Lord Harris that if my money is not returned immediately, I shall order my men to dump the CSB into the ocean, and I shall not let one grain of food pass on to the camps in the future."

"You drive a hard bargain, Colonel."

Moi smiled. "Thank you. I take that as a compliment."

"You shouldn't."

Muffled thunder boomed overhead. Moi instinctively flinched. He recognized the sound of large-caliber rifle fire and the whir of rotor blades. Moi watched in horror as the plasma screen switched to multiple live video images from several overhead cameras, all of them at much lower altitudes, swooping and careening over the compound.

One by one, Moi watched his men fall, each dropped by a single shot fired from a laser-targeted sniper rifle mounted on one of several Autonomous Rotorcraft Sniper Systems (ARSS)—small, unmanned helicopters. Within moments, all of his men were dead, down, or fleeing for cover.

"Not Predators. ARSS. Impressive," Moi admitted. He was, after all, a military man. Sniper rounds continued to fire.

"Hellfire II missiles cost a hundred thousand dollars apiece. Lots of collateral damage, too, which is also expensive. I took out each of your men with a single .338 Lapua Magnum cartridge at a cost of just four dollars apiece. It's important to control costs in business operations, don't you think?"

Moi stared at the plasma television. He was numb with disbelief. His entire command had been effortlessly destroyed by remote control. Chopper blades beat in the humid air outside of his penthouse. He glanced over just in time to watch a gray-skinned ARSS lower to the level of his balcony. The hovering unmanned helicopter was the size of a pickup truck and it pointed a suppressed RND 2000 sniper rifle directly at him from a turret fixed to the starboard runner. The roar of the rotor blades was barely muted by the thick double-paned glass of the penthouse's sliding glass doors.

Another image suddenly appeared on the television. Moi watched himself being watched by the ARSS targeting camera. It almost amused him.

"And now it is the paid assassin's turn to kill me," Moi lamented.

"I told you, I wasn't hired to kill you."

Moi shook his head. "What is to become of me then?"

Another overhead image popped up on the big screen: a convoy of AU vehicles racing through the streets of Mogadishu.

"General Muwanga will be here shortly to take you into custody. I don't need to tell you what kind of reception you're likely to receive in his interrogation facility. He'll also supervise the delivery of the CSB."

"That fat meddler. Why did he not have the guts to assault me himself?"

"The AU can't afford another fiasco. Neither can the Western aid agencies. Their donors are getting fed up with all of the corruption. And a pitched gun battle between African peacekeepers over stolen food would only embolden Shabaab and their al-Qaeda masters. So I was hired to clean up the mess."

"I may yet be able to afford General Muwanga a surprise or two," Moi boasted. He stormed over to a nearby closet and pulled out his personal weapon, an Israeli-built TAR-21 bullpup assault rifle. He favored the futuristic compact design over the dated but reliable Heckler & Koch G3 weapon system that was standard issue in the poorly funded Kenyan Defence Forces.

The ARSS yawed a few degrees. Moi froze. The giant sniper rifle's suppressed barrel seemed to be pointed at his head.

BAM! The sliding glass door shattered as the sniper rifle fired. Chunks of glass rained down on Moi as he dropped to the ground with a thud.

"Sorry about that," the American said. "Had to clean up one last item."

Moi was confused. He turned around. A splintered bullet hole was carved in the door. Thick red blood oozed beneath it and seeped into the fringes of the handwoven silk carpet. Moi's last surviving soldier had crept up into the stairwell to hide—and die.

Moi scrambled to his feet, embarrassed, and snatched up his rifle. He detached the magazine from the butt stock and checked it to make sure it was fully loaded.

"How long until the general arrives?" Moi asked.

"Six minutes, judging by his current speed. But there's an alternative."

"I look forward to putting a bullet in his fat, ugly face." Moi racked a round into the chamber.

"If General Muwanga takes you alive, the Ugandan government will humiliate your prime minister, and your uncle will no doubt be dismissed from his cabinet position and will most likely be arrested and executed after a show trial, along with several other members of your family, all of whom have profited from your misadventures. Your name will live in infamy, your family will bear unforgivable shame, and your nation will suffer a loss of prestige it can ill afford."

Moi frowned with despair.

"However," the disembodied voice continued, "an arrangement has been negotiated. If General Muwanga finds you and your entire command killed, it will be reported that you and your soldiers bravely died to a man defending a humanitarian food shipment from a Shabaab assault. You'll be buried with full military honors, and the surviving members of your family will enjoy the everlasting fame of your exploits."

"My uncle will see through this charade. He will demand retribution," Moi insisted.

The voice laughed. "Your uncle is the one who suggested it."

Moi's shoulders slumped with resignation. He glanced at the ARSS still hovering outside of the shattered glass door. He calculated that a headshot from this range should be easy for the American. Moi's back stiffened, as if he were suddenly on parade.

"I should be grateful if you would do the honor, Private Citizen. I prefer to die as a soldier."

"Then you should have lived like one, Colonel."

Moi wilted again.

"Yes, I suppose I should have."

He crossed over to his bed. He was tired now. He wished he'd been allowed to have his nap. "You have thought of everything, Private Citizen. I commend you on your efficiency. Your employer should be satisfied with the services you have rendered today."

"We aim to please."

And with that, Moi lifted the short barrel of the TAR-21 and placed it in his mouth. He began taking deep breaths to gather his courage. On the fourth inhalation, he found it. The rifle cracked and the top of his skull exploded, spattering blood and brain tissue onto the spinning fan blades above his bed.

Near the Snake River, Wyoming

Troy Pearce was still lean and cut like a cage fighter despite the strands of silver in his jet-black hair. His careworn face and weary blue eyes belonged to a combat veteran who'd seen too much trouble in the world.

"Satisfied, Sir Harris?" Pearce asked.

Sir Harris had watched the entire Somali operation unfold in a live feed while sitting in his country manor outside of London. They spoke via an encrypted satellite channel.

"Perfectly, Mr. Pearce. I trust you had no casualties on your end?"

"That's why I use drones, sir. The safety of my people is my top priority. Accomplishing the mission is second."

"Outstanding. Your team has accomplished the mission brilliantly, as expected. I don't suppose you'd be kind enough to upload that final footage to my intranet server?"

"Did you get that, Ian?" Pearce asked.

A thick Scottish brogue rumbled in Pearce's earpiece. "On its way now." Ian McTavish was Pearce's IT administrator and a certified computer genius.

"Of course." Pearce was running this mission out of a specially equipped luxury motor home he used on occasion. It was parked on one hundred acres of secluded woodlands next to a rough-hewn cabin hand-built by his grandfather sixty years ago.

Pearce added, "The CSB is scheduled to arrive at the camp by midnight, local time. General Muwanga will contact you directly when it's delivered. I assume you've already made the financial arrangements with him?"

"Yes. I just hope we won't be employing your services again, Mr. Pearce. Heaven knows the Western powers committed their share of crimes in the past, but it seems that the greatest challenges too many Africans face these days come from the hands of other Africans."

"I wouldn't worry about Muwanga. When he finds Moi's command torn to pieces, he'll understand the true cost of breaking his contract with you. With any luck, the word will get around to the other pirates and piss-ants and they'll leave you alone."

"Yes, quite." Sir Harris chuckled.

"My people will be providing top cover for the relief convoy, and then our contract is fulfilled."

"Splendid. Thanks again for your service, Mr. Pearce, and your discretion. And please congratulate your team on my behalf."

"I'll pass it along. Now if you'll excuse me, I have another matter to attend to."

Pearce broke the satellite connection and shut down his computer. His highly trained team of professionals on the ground in Somalia already had their orders and didn't require any further supervision from him. Pearce had other fish to fry.

Literally.

It was just after sunrise. The trout would already be biting. Time to break in the new fly rod.

3

It was nearly midnight and they were still an hour away from landing in Denver. Despite objections by the Secret Service over the enormous security risks, President Margaret Myers had attended the memorial service for Ryan Martinez and the Cinco de Mayo massacre victims and their families in El Paso earlier that day.

The galley steward had just cleared away her half-eaten Cobb salad and remained below deck to give her privacy. Her closest advisors were gathered in the West Wing conference center back in Washington. She was currently linked to them on a live video feed.

Myers stood, her glass empty. She had just finished two fingers of Buffalo Trace, her favorite Kentucky bourbon. She was fifty and tired, but didn't look much of either, even tonight, still dressed in black. Years of swimming and Pilates had kept her frame strong and lean like she'd been as a young girl growing up on a cattle ranch. She still hardly needed makeup, and her dark bobbed hair was colored perfectly.

"Anybody need to freshen up their drinks?" Myers asked as she crossed to the bar.

"I think we're all fine here, Madame President," Sandy Jeffers said with a tired smile. Despite his obvious fatigue, his salt-and-pepper hair was still perfectly coiffed, and his hand-tailored suit as crisp as the day he'd bought it. As chief of staff, he answered for the group.

Myers poured herself another bourbon.

"I want to thank each of you for picking up the slack in my absence. And, Bill, I'm also grateful for the security arrangements you and your team put together on such short notice."

Secretary Bill Donovan ran the Department of Homeland Security. He nodded in reply, stifling a yawn behind a beefy hand. He hadn't slept in three days. "We owe a great deal to our friends at Fort Bliss and the governor of Texas. We couldn't have done it on such short notice without them."

Myers smiled a little. "From where I sat, El Paso looked like the Green Zone with all of the tanks and helicopters you moved in there. I'm sure the press will make a lot of hay with those photos."

"Better safe than sorry," Donovan offered. Despite his morbid obesity, he'd proven to be an effective and energetic DHS secretary.

Myers nodded. "Of course. Now, for the business at hand." Myers returned to her chair.

The media had jumped on the first witness's statement that ICE agents had perpetrated the massacre. The witness had seen black military uniforms, military-style machine guns, and "ICE" emblazoned on their tactical vests, which accurately described ICE combat teams.

The idea that rogue ICE agents had perpetrated the crime fit the mainstream media metanarrative perfectly—Myers's ruthless budget cutting was causing chaos across the government. Only in Washington, D.C., could freezing future increases in spending be counted as a "cut."

But within a few hours it became apparent that the killers had merely impersonated ICE officers. All of the gear they wore was available for purchase on a hundred websites. The Hummer they'd used had been stolen two hours before the attack and later found abandoned and burned up in a vacant lot just across the Mexican border. Most important, every ICE agent's location and activity that night had been accounted for.

Responsible media began reporting the new facts as soon as they became available, but Myers's staunchest opponents resorted to a variety of conspiracy theories and began alleging a cover-up.

"Faye, why haven't we made any progress on the shooters?" Myers asked. Faye Lancet was the attorney general of the United States and thus the head of the Department of Justice and one of its subsidiary agencies, the FBI.

"Our most reliable informants on the street are suddenly either deceased or irreparably mute. Snitches have an extremely short life expectancy in that part of the world."

"You make it sound as if South Texas is a Third World country," Myers said.

"In some ways, it is," Lancet replied. "The border is still pretty porous these days."

"Maybe this was just a local neighborhood gang," Myers said.

Mike Early, Myers's special assistant for security affairs, spoke up. "Possibly, but not likely. According to witnesses, they were firing machine guns, probably German HK21s."

"How do you know that?" Myers asked.

"We found six proprietary HK ammo drums on-site, each with a fifty-round capacity. The Mexican army uses HK21s. They even manufacture their own under an HK license."

"You think the Mexican army is connected to this?" Lancet asked.

"No. But Mexican army guns have a funny way of turning up on the streets, whether stolen or sold." Early scratched his five o'clock shadow. "Hell, the Mexican army itself has had over a hundred thousand desertions in the last decade. God only knows how many weapons they take with them."

"The forensics point to two weapons used that night, which is corroborated by at least three survivors who thought they saw or heard two machine guns being fired," Donovan said.

Myers frowned. "Why couldn't local gangs purchase some of those weapons?"

"Possible, but highly unlikely. Mexican guns don't usually travel north. It's American guns moving south that causes problems down there. Even if a couple of street punks could find a high-end gun seller that wasn't a Fed, or a Fed informant, it's clear to me the shooters knew what they were doing. They weren't a couple of gangbanger lowlifes hosing down the neighborhood like Tony Montana," Donovan said.

Early added, "They discharged three hundred large-caliber, armor-piercing rounds in less than a minute in controlled bursts—and on target. The bastards were definitely trained."

"So who wanted to send a message? Why attack a house full of teenagers having a good time? And who's the message for?" Myers asked.

"Too soon to say who the message was for with certainty," Donovan said. "Word on the street is that it was a turf issue, and given that El Paso is Castillo Syndicate territory, it's not too big of a stretch to say that Castillo was the one pulling the trigger."

Myers fumed. "Castillo territory? El Paso is *American* territory, damn it. Who does that son of a bitch think he is?" The Castillo Syndicate was the most powerful drug cartel in Mexico, based out of the state of Sinaloa where it originated. Its power was exerted over the western half of Mexico and had extended itself steadily north into the United States and south into Central America for the last decade. Its main competitor was the Bravo Alliance, which controlled the eastern half of Mexico. Both cartels had effectively absorbed all of the other smaller cartels in recent years. It was a classic bipolar system, a vicious stalemate between two equally powerful enemies, like scorpions in a bottle.

"Madame President, if I may." The deep, resonant voice of Dr. Karl Strasburg chimed in. An old-school cold warrior, Strasburg was the elder statesman of the group, having served as a security advisor to every president since Nixon in one capacity or another. His opinion still exerted a powerful sway on Capitol Hill, and his views were deeply respected in the corridors of both power and academia around the world. His impeccable style and self-effacing manners, coupled with his faint Hungarian accent, gave him an Old World charm that few could resist.

"Please, Dr. Strasburg, share your thoughts."

"I am embarrassed to say this, Madame President, and I certainly do not ascribe to the idea personally, nevertheless I must point out that you are already seen as a weak president because you are a woman. One thing you must consider is this: if you fail to respond to this vicious and unprovoked attack with vigor, you will only strengthen the unfortunate stereotype associated with your gender in the Latin culture."

"I have never lived my life according to other people's views of me, and I will certainly not do that as president, either. If I start overcompensating for the expectations of my gender, I'm only playing into their idiotic stereotype."

From both a moral and fiscal perspective, Myers was adamantly opposed to any suggestion of going to war if it could be at all avoided. But Strasburg's line of thinking threatened to undo everything her administration had accomplished so far.

Myers narrowly won both the Republican primary and the general election on a platform of "pragmatism above ideology." Her primary campaign issue was to institute an immediate budget freeze once elected, and then to pass a balanced budget amendment. She managed to accomplish both in the first one hundred days of her tenure by promising progressives to keep American boots off of the ground in any new foreign conflicts, to close as many foreign bases as was practical, and to bring as many of the troops home as quickly as possible without endangering American lives left behind. Vice President Greyhill's establishment credentials had also helped her forge the coalition with right-of-center moderates in both parties who feared new runaway social spending at the expense of defense.

Unlike many of her fellow Republicans, Myers viewed big defense budgets as just another example of out-of-control government spending. She knew that defense was necessary; she was no pie-in-the-sky Pollyanna. But how much defense spending was enough? *If one new weapon system makes us safe, then two must make us even safer* seemed to be the irrefutable schoolyard logic of the hawks.

As a private-sector CEO, Myers had dealt with the armchair bureaucrats in the Pentagon who were as self-interested as any Wall Street investment firm, and just as guilty of "waste, fraud, and abuse" as any welfare department in the federal government.

America's economic malaise was being fueled by out-of-control government spending of all kinds, including the supposedly untouchable "entitlement" spending programs. As a businesswoman, Myers understood that the national debt was a millstone around the nation's neck. It was drowning the economy and would ultimately lead to America's systematic decline. Avoiding unnecessary wars and bloated defense budgets would actually make the nation stronger in the long run.

"The bottom line, Dr. Strasburg, is that I'm not interested in bolstering my street cred with Latin tinhorn dictators. What I want is what's best for the American people." She leaned forward in her chair. "What I *really* want is justice, especially for those grieving mothers in that gymnasium tonight. The question I'm putting on the table right now is, how do we get justice without putting American boots on Mexican soil?"

"I suppose that depends entirely upon your definition of justice, Madame President," Donovan suggested. The dark circles under his eyes were proof that the secretary of DHS hadn't slept in days while he sweated the details of the El Paso security setup. He fought back a yawn. "I don't mean to start a midnight dorm-room debate, but in the end, justice for most people means getting what they think they deserve, and they seldom get it unless they have the power to acquire it from the people who stole it from them in the first place. So for the sake of our discussion, what exactly do you want? What does justice look like?"

Myers nodded. "Fair enough. I want the men responsible for the killing arrested, tried, convicted, and punished for their crimes in either an American or Mexican court of law."

Lancet jumped in. "Forget extradition. We have the death penalty, and Mexican courts are reluctant to return Mexican nationals to American courts if there's the possibility of a death sentence. So you're definitely talking about a Mexican trial if the suspects are apprehended in Mexico."

"I can live with that," Myers countered.

Lancet continued. "It may well be possible for the Mexicans to arrest them and put them on trial. But given the lack of witnesses at the present time, let alone the current political and social crises that Mexico faces, I wouldn't count on a conviction. And even if the Mexicans do manage to convict on what would have to be circumstantial evidence, there's no guarantee of a punishment commensurate with their crimes."

"If you want American justice, you'll have to snatch them up and haul them here in irons," Strasburg said. "SEAL Team Six can do the job."

"And what if things go south? Do we really want American troops burned alive in an oil-drum soup?" Early was referring to the horrific cartel practice of melting people down in oil drums filled with boiling oil and lead. "These guys are batshit crazy. They're not playing by Marquess of Queensberry rules down there."

"Excuse me, but there are other issues to be considered here," Vice President Greyhill said. He'd served on the Senate Foreign Relations Committee for eighteen years before he had been shoehorned onto the Myers ticket. He was seen as a reliable "old hand" to steady her uncertain rudder. He relished the role, partly because he knew how deeply Myers resented it. As one of the Senate's elder statesmen, the wealthy, patrician Greyhill had been the GOP's hand-selected candidate in the primary, but the outsider Myers's populist, commonsense message had killed his one and only chance to be president. "You can't start invading countries because you don't like the way their court systems work, Margaret. You'd be in violation of a dozen international laws and treaties."

Myers bristled at his accusatory tone but chose to ignore it—for now. "It seems to me that breaking the rule of law in order to enforce the rule of law is a moral hazard. I don't want a war, legal or otherwise; I want justice. Let's give the Mexicans a chance to give it to us. They have a vested interest, too." Myers took another sip of bourbon. "Sandy, I want you and Faye to coordinate with Bill on this, and with Tom Eddleston when he gets back from China. When does he return?" Myers rubbed her forehead. A massive headache was coming on fast.

"The secretary of state will be back in town the day after tomorrow. But we can video-chat with him before then, of course," Jeffers gently reminded her. He knew she was at the end of her rope, physically and emotionally.

"Then what I'd like the three of you to do is put together a memo for Ambassador Romero and tell him what he needs to communicate to President Barraza. Something along the lines of affirming our support for his newly elected administration, our desire for swift and certain justice, well, you get the idea. But run it by Tom first. I don't want to step on his toes."

"Will do," Jeffers said.

Myers set her empty glass down. "Let's give our friends south of the border a chance to do the right thing. We can always step up our game later, if need be. Who knows? They might even surprise us. Are we clear?"

The heads on her video screen nodded in unison. "Good. It's very late and I have another long day tomorrow. Good night." Myers snapped off the video monitor and rang for the white-coated steward, who appeared a few moments later.

"What can I get for you, ma'am?"

"A couple of Excedrin and a club soda would be helpful. Have Sam and Rachel had something to eat?" Myers was referring to the two Secret Service agents who were accompanying her to Denver.

"Yes, they have, and they asked me to thank you." Normally, Secret Service agents didn't eat while on duty, but it had been a long day for them as well, and Myers insisted that they order from her kitchen galley.

The steward slipped away to fetch Myers's club soda and aspirin.

Myers sat alone in the empty cabin, drained. She turned around in her chair and stared at the aft compartment door. She rose and crossed over to it, then stood there for a moment gathering her courage, then went in, careful to shut and lock the door behind her.

Ryan Martinez's sealed casket lay on the center of the floor, lashed down with half-inch cargo polycord. The casket had been removed from the wheeled transport dolly for fear it might fall off should they experience any turbulence. The room wasn't designed to carry cargo, and the casket was heavy, posing a possible danger during takeoff and landing if it should start sliding around. Myers hadn't cared. She'd have flown the damn plane herself if the air force pilot objected. He hadn't. His own son had been killed in Afghanistan last year. A half hour later, the plane's chief master sergeant had bolted right-angle flanges into the aluminum floor with a pneumatic drill and secured the load with the cords. It was the best he could do on short notice, but it worked. Myers was grateful.

She kicked off her shoes and sat down on the floor next to the polished aluminum casket. It was just like all of the others. Myers had paid for the funerals of all of the kids killed that night—anonymously, of course, and out of her own personal funds. The El Paso families were mostly working poor. Myers saw no need to add crushing debt to their inconsolable grief.

Ryan's status as a hero on that fateful night was confirmed by both surviving witnesses and the county coroner's autopsy. Rather than running away from the gunfire, Ryan had run toward it, and thrown himself on top of two of his students, shielding them from the hail of deadly bullets with his own body. Miraculously, both girls had survived, though badly wounded. They were still in intensive care and unable to attend the memorial service for Ryan and the others.

She laid her hand gently on the lid. It had been three months since she'd spoken to Ryan on the phone. Years since they'd had a real conversation. She hadn't seen him since the inauguration earlier in the year, but even that reunion had been brief. At least it had been civil. God knows they knew how to push each other's buttons. She had to hit the ground running on the first day. Hadn't stopped running since.

Until now.

Myers's mind replayed a dozen conversations she'd had with the mourners before the memorial service. A pretty young math teacher introduced herself as Ryan's girlfriend. Her lovely green eyes were red with tears. Myers hadn't known that Ryan had a girlfriend. *But of course he did. That was normal, wasn't it? Normal people have relationships*, she reminded herself.

The girl's name was Celia. Or was it Celina? Myers couldn't remember. The girl was nice. Very pretty. No wonder Ryan fell for her. Myers felt sorry for her.

Myers's hand stroked the brushed-aluminum casket, but she was so lost in thought she wasn't even aware she was doing it.

The mother of one of the slain students handed her a slip of folded paper scrawled with a recipe for chile rellenos. "Señor Ryan asked me all the time for the recipe, but I never got around to it. He said it was his favorite. *Lo siento mucho, señora.*"

Myers thought Ryan didn't like chile rellenos. Maybe he still didn't like them. Maybe he was just being nice to this lady. Or maybe he really did like hers. Or maybe he did like chile rellenos. Maybe it was tamales he didn't care for. She wasn't sure now. They hadn't had a sit-down meal together for quite a while now. Years, actually. Myers was never much of a cook. Never had the time. Too busy building a business, then too busy running a state. She accepted the recipe from the grieving mother. "Thank you," Myers told her. "I'll have to try it sometime myself." But she knew she wouldn't. She didn't like Mexican food at all.

Myers sighed. Tomorrow was going to be a long day, indeed. She would bury her son in the family plot outside of Denver next to his father, John Martinez, with no one to stand beside her.

———

The steward reappeared in the empty conference room with a tray carrying the club soda on ice and a brand-new bottle of aspirin. He set the tray down on a small table and began to leave, but something in him made him pause. He knew she had a terrible headache. And he knew without a shadow of a doubt that she was in the room with her only child. Myers hadn't told him she wanted to be left alone. And she needed the aspirin. So he stepped over to the aft door.

Just before the steward knocked, he paused. He heard a sound. He leaned his ear as close to the door as he dared and listened.

Myers was weeping.

The steward stepped softly away from the door and headed back down to the galley.

4

Idaho Falls Airport, Idaho

The sun had just crept up over the horizon.

Pearce kept his hands thrust in his jeans against the chill as he stood near the tarmac. He watched the Pearce Systems HA-420 HondaJet touch down effortlessly, its wheels kissing the asphalt without a sound. Crisp sunlight glinted on the gray and white carbon fiber composite fuselage as the unusual over-the-wing pod-mounted engines began to cycle down. The sleek corporate jet taxiing toward Pearce reminded him of a completely different plane on a distant tarmac in a previous life he wished like hell he could forget.

Baghdad International Airport, Iraq
March 5, 2004

"What kind of name is Pentecost anyway?" Early asked. Like Pearce, he was dressed like a local and wore a three-day growth of beard on his chin beneath a bushy black mustache. He and Pearce leaned against a Humvee as they waited for the big C-130 to cut its engines in the pre-dawn light.

"Beats me."

"Sounds religious. Tongues of fire and all of that."

"You should ask her," Pearce said. "Maybe she's a fanatic."

"Don't need any more of those around here," Early grunted. "What else did Connor say about this hotshot?"

"Straight off the Farm but first in her class. A premium Core Collector by all accounts." The air was cool. The slight breeze coming out of the south put a chill on him.

"Is that why she rates her own plane?"

"Connor said she was eager. Wanted to get deep in the shit fast."

"She's probably a Poindexter with a pocket protector."

"Connor knows what he's doing," Pearce said.

The Joint Special Operations Command (JSOC) had authorized a special task force to deal with the recent wave of devastating IED attacks by Iraqi insurgents around the country. Connor had picked Pearce to lead a small hunter-killer team in Baghdad. Pearce chose Early, a first-rate gunfighter from the 10th Special Forces Group he had met during Operation Viking Hammer in 2003, along with an S-2 from Early's unit. But after the intel officer was killed by a sniper, Connor selected Pentecost to fill the slot.

The big four-bladed props on the C-130 finally spun down and the rear ramp lowered.

"Here she comes," Early said.

The woman coming down the ramp could have stepped out of a recruiting poster for Southern California surfer girls—lean, blond, and blue-eyed. But apparently she'd swapped out her flip-flops and bikini for combat boots and black tactical gear on the ride over.

Early's jaw dropped. "Whoa."

"You must be Early." She stuck out her hand. "Name's Pentecost. Annie Pentecost." She smiled. "Connor described you perfectly."

Early grinned, not sure if she was complimenting him or not. "Mike Early. Real nice to meet you, too."

Annie turned toward Pearce. Looked right through him.

Those eyes.

"Troy Pearce," he said, offering his hand.

She had a firm grip. Held his hand just long enough to feel the heat. "Annie Pentecost."

"Welcome to the shit," Early said, trying to get her attention.

"I think he meant 'team,'" Pearce corrected.

"Thanks. I've heard good things."

"So have we. How was the flight?" Pearce asked.

"Hard seats, cold coffee. The usual. The pilot just told me another IED ripped inside the Green Zone an hour ago."

Pearce nodded. "Police station. Three Iraqi policemen killed. One of our guys wounded, too. A contractor. Critical."

"We're supposed to find you a hot and a cot." Early yanked open the rear Humvee door. "We can check it out first thing tomorrow."

"It already is tomorrow," Annie said. "Let's go find us some bad guys." She tossed her duffel through the door and climbed in after it.

Pearce and Early exchanged a glance. Maybe Connor was right about this one.

And those eyes.

Idaho Falls Airport, Idaho

Pearce made his way into the state-of-the-art cockpit and dropped down into the plush leather passenger seat and buckled in. With the HondaJet's flat-panel displays and touch-screen controls, Pearce felt like he was trapped inside of a video gamer's wet dream instead of an actual airplane.

Pearce pulled the headset on and adjusted the mic.

Judy Hopper sat in the pilot's seat with an unreasonably radiant smile for such an early morning. "Fresh coffee in the thermos," she whispered in his earphones. She was a decade younger than Pearce, with a plain, honest face and clear eyes. She kept her hair pulled back in a ponytail and never wore makeup.

"Good flight over?" Pearce asked.

"Easy as pie. You ready?"

"Let's go. Sooner we get there, the sooner I can get back to the fish."

"ETA to Dearborn, ten-fifteen, local," Judy said. Their cruising speed was close to five hundred miles per hour.

Judy reached over and tapped the brightly lit glass touch screen in front of Pearce, part of the Garmin G3000 avionics package. The only thing analog about the glowing digital cockpit was the faded Polaroid taped to the instrument panel. It was ten-year-old Judy flying her father's missionary bush plane. She claimed it was her good luck charm.

After confirming GPS coordinates, weather patterns, and nearby traffic, Judy radioed in to the tower. She was cleared to taxi back to the runway for takeoff. The flat panel in front of her displayed a 3-D graphical terrain rendering and a simulated cockpit view. Pearce Systems had purchased one of the first HondaJets to roll out of the North Carolina assembly plant earlier that year.

There was no airport traffic that morning so Judy was able to taxi quickly into position. In a few minutes, they stood poised for takeoff. Judy quickly ran her preflight checks, then pointed at the yoke in front of Pearce. "You want to give it a whirl today?" she asked.

Pearce wasn't rated to fly the twin-engine turbofan jet, but he'd practiced on the simulator a half dozen times. He was also pretty good at flying single-engine props and had gotten better at it thanks to Judy's patient instruction. But he didn't have a fraction of the natural skill that Judy possessed.

Judy sensed his hesitation. "If you're not ready, that's okay. She's a handful, for sure."

"Just like every other woman in my life," Pearce said. He knew it was foolish to not let the far superior pilot take control of the aircraft, but Pearce couldn't resist the rush of controlling a four-thousand-feet-per-minute climb. Besides, it was his damn plane. "Let's rock and roll."

Judy winked. "That's what I wanted to hear." She called in to the tower one last time. They were cleared for takeoff. Pearce fired up the Stones' "Gimme Shelter" on the comm, then slammed the throttle home, rocketing the HondaJet down the tarmac. The plane leapt off the runway, blasting into the crisp morning sky like a mortar round, grins plastered on both of their faces.

Pearce Systems Research Facility, Dearborn, Michigan

Pearce's main research facility was located in an abandoned Mercury auto plant just south of I-94, a stone's throw from the General George S. Patton memorial. Pearce and his mysterious investing partner had purchased it just after the '08 crash to house their expanding research operations, which provided a significant revenue stream for the company beyond the various civilian and security services they provided.

For most of his missions, Pearce purchased off-the-shelf operational systems from legitimate vendors, often modifying them to his own specs. If particular drone systems weren't available for purchase, he was able to emulate their capabilities by manufacturing his own either by original design or by purchasing widely available airframe, power plant, and avionics components.

But Pearce Systems was also pioneering some of the latest drone technologies by partnering with or building upon the efforts of other bleeding-edge research organizations. Pearce and Judy had made the flight to the Dearborn lab that morning at the fevered request of Dr. Kirin Rao, the head of the research division.

"Thank you both for coming," Rao said. "Please follow me." With her long legs, soft curves, and cloying eyes, Dr. Rao looked more like a Bollywood movie star than a Ph.D. in robotics engineering. Pearce and Judy followed her to one of the computer labs.

"This is Jack," Dr. Rao said. She pointed at a Rhesus monkey seated in a miniature pilot's chair, nibbling on an apple slice. A square of hermetically sealed titanium was attached to the top of his skull—a brain-machine interface (BMI) device hardwired into his cortex. A large LCD TV was on the wall three feet directly in front of him, but no picture was present.

"Is that the wireless BMI?" Pearce asked.

Dr. Rao nodded enthusiastically. "Three months ahead of schedule."

There was a knock on the door.

"Come in," Rao said.

The door swung open.

"Ian. Good to see you," Pearce said. They shook hands. The wiry Scot had a kind, expressive face beneath two high arching eyebrows and a great shock of hair. Dark eyes betrayed his fierce intelligence.

"Come here, you," Judy said, wrapping Ian in a bear hug. They were close friends, though Ian preferred something more.

"I see you've all met our wee friend Jack."

"How are the legs these days?" Pearce asked.

Ian lifted one of his Genium bionic legs. His own legs had been amputated above the knee after he was cut down in the 2005 7/7 bombings in London. The new high-tech knee joints were controlled by a microprocessor that allowed for nearly perfect mobility. "Never better. I'll be sword dancing before too long."

"Shall we begin?" Dr. Rao shut the lights off. Instantly, the LCD panel lit up with a computer program.

"Looks like a flight simulator," Judy said.

"It is," Rao said.

"Where's the joystick?" Judy asked.

"There isn't one," Ian said.

A wire-framed Predator was centered in the screen, swooping low over a vast virtual desert, following a black ribbon of asphalt highway.

"Jack's flying it with his mind," Pearce said to Judy. "Dr. Nicolelis did something similar to this a few years ago." He tried to hide his irritation.

He could've watched this demonstration from the comfort of his cabin instead of flying all the way here. In fact, he'd seen Nicolelis's work on YouTube months ago after Rao sent him a link.

"Similar, but not exactly the same," Rao said. "Watch."

Moments later, an animated flatbed truck with a mounted machine gun appeared on the highway, surrounded by three other unarmed cars. The armed truck began firing at Jack's drone. Jack swooped and swerved to avoid the antiaircraft fire.

"Dr. Nicolelis's monkey could only track targets with his mind. Jack can avoid being a target. He can also do this."

The truck continued firing, but the other three cars fell away. Suddenly, a missile shot out from beneath the drone's wings. A moment later the truck disintegrated in a ball of digital fire, leaving the three other cars unscathed.

Rao beamed. "I bet my monkey can blow up his monkey."

"And you'll notice, little Jack isn't just using his motor skills to track a single target. He's making target *choices*," Ian said.

"How?" Pearce asked.

"We hacked into the deeper cognitive functions of his cortex," Rao said. She turned the lights back on, ending the game. "So what you're seeing is not only a brain-machine connection, but also a true mind-machine interaction."

Pearce nodded. It was impressive. One of the biggest challenges to achieving true autonomous drone capacity was artificial intelligence programming. If a computer program could ever simulate a sentient brain—and there were plenty of arguments against that eventuality—it would still be years away before that goal would be achieved. But why try to emulate a human brain with software if an actual brain could be used instead through BMI?

"Can you imagine the possibilities? Artificial limbs, exoskeletons, blindness . . . the medical applications are endless," Ian said.

"So are the military ones," Judy said. A rare scowl.

"Do you understand now why I wanted you to be here in person?" Rao asked. She had just made Pearce Systems one of the most important players in the field of neuroprosthetics.

Pearce nodded, trying to hide his excitement. "If you really want to impress me, next time have Jack fly me up here himself."

"Then what will *I* do?" Judy asked.

Pearce shrugged. "Sit back and enjoy the ride, I guess."

5

Isla Paraíso, Mexico

César Castillo's Roman villa–styled mansion stood at the peak of the six-hundred-meter mountain in the center of his private island ten miles east of the Baja California Peninsula. Locating his palatial home on the highest point had certain strategic disadvantages, certainly, but it was his dream of witnessing the ineffable beauty of the daily rising and setting of the sun that had caused him to build it there. He had not been disappointed with his decision.

Castillo stepped out of the civilian MD 500 helicopter onto the helipad almost before the landing skids had hit the ground. He made a beeline for the house. His security chief, Ali Abdi, waited for the pilot to land before jumping out and scrambling to catch up with his boss. As usual, the Iranian wore a brimmed hat and dark sunglasses in order to keep his face hidden from the ubiquitous American electronic surveillance devices that might be circling overhead. He hadn't survived this long without taking extreme precautions.

César stormed into the courtyard with the massive pool complex. The architect had replicated the expansive marble-and-tile Neptune Pool at Hearst Castle. But César had added Greek and Roman statuary depicting various gods and heroes with tridents, swords, and spears to stand guard around the crystal-blue waters of the Olympic-size pool. The face of Zeus bore an uncanny resemblance to César's with its fierce, cruel eyes and wicked grin.

Stretched out on chaise longues near the pool were his two strapping twin sons, Aquiles and Ulises Castillo, who were even more sculpted than the statues. Naked and tan, their muscled bodies glistened with sweat. Each was six foot three inches tall, nearly a foot taller than their father, who was a squat, barrel-chested man with enormous hands attached to abnormally long arms. César was built exactly like *his* father, Hércules Castillo, a Sinaloan tomato farmer long since dead. Hércules told his teenage son that God must have designed the Castillos to pick tomatoes since he gave them such long arms that they barely had to bend over to gather the fruit up. César Castillo had built the world's most powerful drug cartel just to prove both God and his father wrong.

Without a doubt, the two young men in their early twenties had emerged from the deep end of their mother's gene pool, an Argentine beauty of German, Italian, and Spanish descent. Broad shoulders, narrow hips, green eyes, and long, thick chestnut hair made the twins irresistible to women. Men, on the other hand, either admired or feared them. The few who had ever crossed them had long since disappeared.

"Who ordered the hit in El Paso?" César demanded as he stormed into the pool area. Ali had finally caught up. He took a position in the shade underneath the portico, a short but discreet distance away. Acoustical guitar music poured out of the hidden speakers located around the pool area.

Neither Aquiles nor Ulises stirred from beneath their Ray-Bans. They were fanatical sun worshippers.

"Welcome home, Father. How was your trip?" Aquiles asked.

César whipped around and snapped his fingers at Ali. The Iranian found the remote control and killed the music. A .40 caliber Steyr printed against Ali's back beneath his Cuban guayabera. Dark-haired and olive-skinned, the brown-eyed Iranian was fluent in Spanish. He shaved his beard but kept his mustache and easily passed for a Hispanic anywhere he traveled in Latin America or the United States.

"Answer my question." César stood directly over his naked son.

Ulises lifted his sunglasses. "You're blocking the sun, Father."

Aquiles laughed. How could such a short man block anything, let alone the sun?

"Why are you laughing?" César asked.

"No reason, Father. I'm sorry. It just struck me as a paradoxical thing for Ulises to say."

"'Paradoxical.' That's a big word. I suppose that's why I paid all of that money to send you to university, so you can use big words with me, eh? Put some clothes on, both of you. You should be ashamed to lie around here like a couple of *putos*."

Ulises's green eyes, which had been mockingly coy until now, flashed with rage, but only for an instant. "Yes, you're right. We should dress." Ulises stood up from the lounger, towering over his diminutive father. He yawned and stretched his muscular arms high over his head, fully displaying his powerful physique. It was a threat display worthy of a silverback gorilla.

César grabbed his son by the testicles with his left hand and crushed them as hard as he could while clutching his son's throat with his right hand. The pain exploded in Ulises's scrotum, but his scream only came out as a yelp because his windpipe was blocked. César charged into his son like a bull, toppling the bigger man backward until they reached the edge of the pool, where he tossed the boy into the water with a splash.

Ali watched the battle intently. He redistributed his body weight so that he was equally balanced on both feet as he slowly, carefully, slipped his hands behind his back, clasping them together just above the pistol holstered in his lower back. He had never seen either son raise a hand to their father, but he was prepared for anything with these two wild wolves. He knew exactly how dangerous the boys were in hand-to-hand combat because he had trained them himself. It had taken Ali over eight months to work his way into his current position as Castillo's head of security, the first step of many more to come. Ali wasn't about to let either boy derail his plan by killing their father, even if he deserved it.

Aquiles watched the lopsided battle in amused horror as he yanked on his swim trunks. He stifled the urge to laugh at his brother.

"To answer your question, Father, we put a hit on Los Tokers," Aquiles said, tying the string on his bathing suit. "They were throwing a party on our turf. Those punks are like roaches. If you don't squash them, they just keep spreading. Isn't that what you taught us to do?"

"Who told you it was Los Tokers?" César asked as he stomped back over to Aquiles.

"We got a phone call. A Mara named Hater," Aquiles said. "He's one of our meth dealers and an enforcer."

"And you trust this Hater guy?"

"Yes. Why?" Ulises asked.

"Because either he got it wrong or he screwed us," César replied.

"What are you talking about?" Aquiles asked.

"Because there weren't any Tokers at the party."

Aquiles frowned, thoughtfully. "And why is that a problem?"

César suppressed the urge to strike his son across the face. He'd killed better men for less offense. "Tell me how it's not a problem."

"A hit is a hit, Father. We put the word out on the street that we thought Los Tokers were muscling in, so we smashed them. The message was sent. Mess with us and you die. And the message still makes sense even though Los Tokers weren't there. People died just because we *thought* Tokers were there. Nobody's even going to think about setting up shop on our turf again, at least not for a while," Aquiles bragged.

César slapped his son's grinning face. The sound echoed around the courtyard like a gunshot. Aquiles didn't flinch, but his eyes watered. Whether from rage or pain, Ali couldn't be certain. Probably both.

Ulises tread water in the pool, remaining a safe distance from his father's reach. "Why are you so upset with us, Father? You told us to mind the store while you were away. We did."

César wagged a thick finger at both of them. "You lazy bastards. You think all you have to do is pick up a phone and order people killed? You should have done the advance work yourselves. You never want to get your hands dirty yourselves, do you?"

Ulises glared at his father. He'd grown up with the endless stories of his grandfather's backbreaking work in the tomato fields. To be accused of not wanting to get his hands dirty was the moral equivalent of accusing a soldier of cowardice in the face of battle. The verbal jab was worse than his father's physical slap.

"But you're wrong, Father. We did get our hands dirty." Ulises glanced at his brother for moral support. Aquiles nodded for him to continue. "We're the ones who pulled the trigger. We're the ones who sent the message."

César fell into a lounger. He buried his head in his massive hands and moaned aloud. "What have you two idiots done?"

"We took care of business. Those punks were just collateral damage. It happens." Aquiles had lowered his voice to a near whisper, fearing another slap by his father. He sat down on the lounger next to him.

César looked up. "Collateral damage? Are you insane? You think Ryan Martinez is just 'collateral damage'?"

"Who's that?" Ulises asked.

César howled with laughter. "How paradoxical! A stupid tomato picker like me knows more than a college-educated fairy. Don't either of you listen to the news?"

"Only ESPN," Ulises said. "And hardly that."

"So who *is* Ryan Martinez?" Aquiles asked.

"Ryan Martinez was a schoolteacher at that party you shot up," César said. He wiped his thick mustache with one of his monstrous hands.

"And . . . ?" Ulises asked, cringing, half expecting another blow.

"Ryan Martinez was the son of the president of the United States! And now she is going to unleash holy hell on us for murdering her only child."

The boys glanced at each other, frightened and confused. "We didn't know," they said to each other, as if talking to themselves in a mirror.

César leaped to his feet, reaching for the chromed .45 caliber Desert Eagle in his waistband. Screaming with maniacal rage, he opened fire at the nearest statue, a goat-legged Pan with a great golden phallus thrusting up to his midsection. Pan's marble head exploded with the first hit. The next rounds tore away the god's massive pectorals and mashed his silver shepherd's flute. César kept firing until he emptied the magazine. He dropped the clip and slammed a new one home, then chambered the first round.

César pointed the gun at each of his sons like an accusing finger.

"Tell me, smartasses. What should I do with the two of you now?"

6

The White House, Washington, D.C.

Ambassador Konstantin Britnev was ushered into the Oval Office where he was greeted by the warm smile and firm handshake of President Myers. A White House press camera flashed three times.

"I hate having my picture taken," Myers whispered to Britnev under her breath.

Britnev nearly laughed as he widened his alluring smile. "You should see my passport photo. It's terrible." They held hands as several more shots were snapped.

"That will be all. Thank you," Myers said to the photographer.

"Thank you, Madame President, Ambassador Britnev. Excuse me." The female photographer cast a brief, leering glance at the handsome Russian as she exited through the secretary's office door.

"Dr. Strasburg, so good to see you again." Britnev nodded cordially as he extended his well-manicured hand. Strasburg was on the couch. He struggled to rise.

"No, please, Doctor, remain seated." Britnev stepped closer to the couch and shook Strasburg's veiny hand. The Russian, thirty years younger than Strasburg, had studied the famed security advisor's illustrious career at the Institute for USA and Canadian Studies years ago. Now

Britnev was one of the key players in the Titov administration, hand-picked by the Russian president personally for the Washington post.

"It's good to see you as well, Ambassador Britnev. At my age, it's good to see anybody."

Britnev politely laughed at the old man's threadbare joke.

"What would you like to drink, Konstantin?" Myers asked. She'd dismissed the waitstaff for this morning's private meeting.

"A coffee, please, black, no sugar, if it's not too inconvenient." What he really craved was a cigarette.

"No, not at all." Myers crossed over to a credenza. She poured him a cup of coffee from a freshly brewed pot. Britnev was a huge coffee fan. He had even helped broker the first Starbucks franchise in Moscow. She handed him a cup and saucer imprinted with the presidential seal.

"Thank you, Madame President." Britnev took a sip.

"How about you, Karl?"

"None for me, thank you. Doctor's orders."

Britnev's eyes drifted over to a side table. An antique chess set was on it. He stepped over to it.

"It's a lovely set. May I?" Britnev asked.

"Yes, of course," Myers said as she poured herself a cup of coffee.

Britnev set his cup down and picked up a white knight, faded to yellow. "Hand-carved ivory?"

"Yes, elephant tusk, unfortunately. It's actually a set that belonged to President Jefferson. He was quite an avid player."

"He was a very talented man. Many gifts." Britnev gently returned the piece to its position. "It appears as if White has opened with a queen's gambit."

Myers crossed over to Britnev, coffee in hand. She glanced at the board.

"You're very observant. Do you still play?" She took a sip of coffee.

"Not with any real skill," he said. He exuded a boyish charm, despite

having just turned fifty. His hand-tailored Italian suit perfectly comple-
mented his athletic frame, though a back injury at university had ended a
promising ice hockey career.

"You were a grandmaster at the age of sixteen, Mr. Ambassador. That
sounds pretty good to me," Myers said.

"But never a world champion. As I recall, that's about the same age
you were when you wrote your first AI program, isn't it?"

"Hardly an AI program. Just a program for playing chess. Please, shall
we sit?"

"Yes, of course." Britnev took the couch opposite Strasburg while
Myers took a chair.

"Where did you learn to play the game, Mr. Ambassador?" Strasburg
asked.

"My father taught it to me when I was a boy while he was stationed in
Tehran. We used to play every evening together. I suppose it's why I have
such a strong emotional bond to the game. You know, chess was invented
by the Persians, but the mindless *mullahs* banned it for years after the
revolution. Do you play, Dr. Strasburg?"

"On occasion, but poorly. I believe it was Bobby Fischer who said that
one only becomes good at chess if one love the game."

"I do still love it, but I seldom have the time," Britnev said.

Strasburg paused, lost in a painful memory. "My brother loved the
game. He said that he could tell a lot about a man after he played three
games of chess with him. Do you find that to be true, Mr. Ambassador?"

"I find that one match is usually enough." Britnev chuckled. "But perhaps that is because it is a Russian's game. We understand the virtues of
sacrifice and taking the long view. You Americans have no patience for
such things. That's why the Russian players are the best in the world."

"Until IBM's Deep Blue defeated Garry Kasparov." Strasburg smiled.
The old cold warrior couldn't resist the dig. "Of course, there are other
ways to defeat a grandmaster." Both men were well aware that Kasparov

had been a vicious opponent of President Titov and had been recently arrested for his political activities.

Britnev turned back to President Myers. "Is it true you never actually played chess in your youth?"

Myers nodded. "Never a full game, no."

"Remarkable. Then how in the world did you manage to write a piece of chess-playing software?"

Myers shrugged. "Chess is a function of finite mathematics: sixty-four squares, thirty-two pieces, and a maximum of five million possible moves. The longest championship game ever played was under three hundred moves. It was simply a matter of finding the right decision algorithms."

Britnev smiled playfully. "I suppose, then, that everything you need to know about a person is contained in the software programs he writes?"

"Depends upon the person. Or the software." She flashed her most charming smile back at him.

Strasburg shook his head. "The whole subject is depressing to me. Computers are taking over everything. The 'singularity' is nearly upon us, and humans will soon no longer be the highest form of intelligence on the planet."

"The highest form of intelligence? I'm afraid we lost that title the day the first human invented the war club," Myers said. "Maybe computers will do a better job at politics than we have."

"Unless it's the same politicians who are writing the software. As a trained software engineer, Madame President, I'm afraid you possess a distinct advantage over the rest of us." Myers had been the CEO of her own software-engineering company before she ran for governor of Colorado.

"Hardly. It won't be long until we've developed software that can write its own software, so we poor humans will soon be out of the loop."

"That's a frightening thought, Madame President," Strasburg said. "I'm glad I won't be here when that happens."

"It probably already has, Karl. They're just not talking about it." Myers took another sip of coffee, then set the cup down on the table in front of her. "So, Ambassador Britnev, to what do we owe the pleasure of your visit today?"

Britnev set his cup down, too. "First of all, President Titov asked me to send his personal condolences to you at your time of loss. The Russian people grieve with you."

"Please thank President Titov for me for his kind thoughts."

"He also pledges any assistance he can give you in your search for the murderers. We are not without some influence in Mexico and President Barraza seems to be a reasonable fellow."

"We would greatly appreciate any assistance he can provide," Myers said.

"We also understand borders. Unlike you, we have a thousand-year history of enemies violating ours."

"An ocean on either side is our distinct advantage." She grinned. "And Canadians to the north. Couldn't be better neighbors."

"Yes, Canadians. An amiable folk. Not like the Azeris."

Myers and Strasburg shared a glance. *So that's why he asked for this meeting.* Oil-rich Azerbaijan had just changed regimes.

"I should think you would welcome a peaceful, nonviolent, and secular revolution on your periphery," Strasburg said.

"With a curiously pro-democracy, pro-Western, and pro-NATO orientation," Britnev countered. "They almost sound Canadian, don't they?" He chuckled at his own joke. "But maybe they're more like the Mexicans, also swimming in oceans of oil and instability."

"We'll have to wait and see, won't we? But so far, the Azeris don't seem to pose any problems for your government, or am I missing something?" Myers asked.

"I believe Khrushchev said much the same thing to Eisenhower when Castro first came to power," Britnev said.

"It was the Soviet missiles Castro allowed onto his island that caused the problem, as I recall," Myers said.

"Ah, yes. I believe that is a correct understanding of the history, Madame President." Britnev smiled.

Myers held his gaze. *Is he worried about NATO missiles being deployed in Azerbaijan?*

"And as I recall, the United States has a history of resolving its border issues with Mexico in a very direct way," Britnev added. "Should I inform our government to expect a few fireworks? Frankly, we wouldn't blame you. Sometimes the iron fist is the only solution. Don't you agree, Dr. Strasburg?"

"This administration is pursuing other options. As the proverb says, 'If all one owns is a hammer, then every problem looks like a nail.'"

"We're committed to reducing our military footprint around the world," Myers said. "The global community is becoming an increasingly complex and finely tuned mechanism, but war is a blunt-force instrument. We're also trying to get our financial house in order. Our spending has been out of control and maintaining the Pax Americana is proving to be too expensive."

"Weakness is even more expensive, Madame President. As victims of international banditry ourselves, we can perfectly empathize with your dilemma. This is why we believe that the ultimate way forward is through mutual cooperation and understanding between our nations whenever it is possible."

"I quite agree, Ambassador. The United States is fully committed to mutual cooperation and understanding with the Russian Federation. How can our meeting today facilitate that process?"

"As you are both well aware, there is a growing Islamist threat all over the world. So-called Arab Springs."

So it's not about NATO missiles. "The world is changing," Myers said. "The dialectic of history, I suppose."

Britnev shrugged. "But such uprisings don't emerge victorious without intervention, particularly without modern weapons and military advisors, usually from the West. And unfortunately, the uprisings have been usurped by forces even more despotic than the regimes they have replaced, wouldn't you agree?"

"We're no longer in the nation-building business, Mr. Ambassador, I assure you. We can't control outcomes when regimes change," Myers asserted. "But we can't stand in the way of natural forces, either."

"But the West has played an active role in the toppling of several regimes in the past decade and continues to meddle in the Syrian civil war. Our fear is the Caucasus. Islamo-fascism is rearing its ugly head again on our borders."

"That is why you should welcome the Azeri revolution. Democracy is your best buffer," Strasburg said.

"Hitler was democratically elected," Britnev countered, "which is why we're not as confident as you are in the benevolence of democratically elected governments. We prefer reliable allies bound to us with mutual strategic interests. Syria, for example."

Syria had been Russia's last great ally in the Middle East. The recent events there upset Russia's security policy in the region.

"We assure you that past Western support for emerging democratic movements against dictatorships has never been an attempt to undermine the strategic security of the Russian Federation. It was due strictly to humanitarian concerns."

Britnev set his coffee cup down as he gathered his thoughts. "In your inaugural address, Madame President, I believe you expressed your commitment to the rule of law."

Myers stiffened. "Of course I did. We are a nation of laws, and we have tried to help build a just social order by supporting the rule of law both within and between nations. It's the only alternative to war."

Britnev nodded and softened his voice. "How then did violating the sovereignty of a nation like Libya logically cohere with that sentiment, if I may be so bold?"

"I believe President Obama was supporting European efforts to enforce a UN resolution. Despotic regimes like Gaddafi's Libya do not respect the rule of law and they violate the civil rights of their citizens. By helping to facilitate the demise of dictatorships like his, the United Nations is ultimately affirming the universal rights of the Libyan people to live in a nation and world of just laws."

"Yes, of course. That seems perfectly logical." Britnev paused. "I remember during the financial crisis that President Bush declared that he had to abandon free-market principles in order to save the free market. I suppose that is the same sort of idea?"

"All of that is in the past. I assure you, Mr. Ambassador. My administration has set a new course. The United States is out of the business of picking winners and losers. It's a fool's errand, at best, as recent history has demonstrated," Myers said. "Without putting too fine a point on it, we can assure you that this administration is committed to refraining from any destabilizing activities in the Caucasus."

Britnev turned his gaze toward Myers. "We have your word on this?"

"You do," she assured him.

Strasburg leaned forward. "I trust that your government appreciates the wisdom of the American people for having elected such a thoughtful and logical chief executive?"

"Indeed we do, Dr. Strasburg." Britnev turned slightly to face Myers. "Madame President, you have exercised remarkable restraint in regard to the Mexican crisis. I'm not sure I would have been as rational as you had I been in your place."

"The biggest problem we face in our country today, Ambassador, is that we're governed by feelings more than by our minds. I mean to change that." Myers shifted in her chair. "I want to respect both the laws and borders of other nations, including Mexico. I trust that President Barraza's government will deliver what justice it can."

Myers checked her watch. "Forgive me, but we have another engagement." She stood up, ending the meeting. Britnev stood as well.

"Thank you for taking the time to meet with me today on such short notice. I will convey to President Titov your assurances regarding the Azeris."

Myers extended her hand. "Please convey to President Titov our warmest regards."

Britnev took her hand in both of his and lowered his voice. "And please, all formalities aside. If there's anything I can do, don't hesitate to contact me." Her grip relaxed in his warm, soft hands.

"Thank you, Mr. Ambassador." She felt a tingle on the back of her neck and suddenly realized she was grinning a little too broadly for her own liking.

Myers watched him turn and leave, shutting the door behind him. She turned to Strasburg. "Eddleston was right. He's quite the charmer."

Strasburg shrugged, a thin smile on his face. "Cobras often charm their victims before they strike."

7

Later that afternoon, Senator Gary Diele, the senior senator from Arizona, was huddled together with General Winston Winchell, the current chief of staff of the United States Air Force (USAF). The two silver-haired men were devouring thick porterhouse steaks at Ernie's, one of the oldest watering holes in the District. Dark lighting, leather booths with thick oaken tables, and discreet waiters had made this place a favorite of the Washington power elite for decades.

"Her own damn kid. Can you believe it? I'd carpet-bomb Mexico City if they'd done that to my boy," Winston grumbled as he chewed his steak.

"The president is vulnerable. She ran on a promise to scale back American foreign intervention. She can't exactly run across the border with General Pershing in order to chase down Pancho Villa now, can she?" Diele cut himself another bite.

"Her failure to act makes us vulnerable. It makes us look weak."

Diele grunted. "Who cares what the Mexicans think?"

"I'm talking about the Chinese. Do you remember back during the Clinton administration when a couple of our JDAMs accidentally hit the Chinese embassy in Belgrade? The Chi-Coms went absolutely apeshit. I was visiting the U.S. embassy in Beijing at the time. Tens of thousands of protestors surrounded the compound, throwing rocks and raising a ruckus. It looked like the damn Boxer Rebellion all over again. We were all trapped in there for days, including the ambassador."

Diele chuckled. "I remember the picture of Jim Sasser's face peering through the broken door glass. Looked like a scalded cat."

"Of course, the Chinese government had organized all of that. They would no more allow a spontaneous riot in the capital than they would authorize a gay pride parade in the Forbidden City. The hell of it is, poor old Clinton kowtowed to the State Department China hands and taped a slobbering apology to the Chinese for allowing our 'smart bombs' to turn dumb all of a sudden. And you know what? The Chi-Coms wouldn't let it air on Chinese television! Do you see my point? What we see as restraint, they see as weakness. What we view as an accident, they view as a direct assault. If they think they can get away with something, they will. They have the long view and the will to chase it. How do you think the Chinese government would have responded if the premier's son had been the one gunned down in El Paso? There'd be Chinese paratroopers goose-stepping in the Zócalo before the week was out, and they'd dare us to do something about it."

"Calm down, you'll spoil your lunch," Diele said. He took another bite of his porterhouse. "You and I are in complete agreement. But what can we do?"

The general cut a piece of bloody red steak and forked it into his mouth. "We're going to lose air supremacy to the goddamn Chinese within ten years, maybe five, if we don't keep pushing on the new ATF systems." Winchell was referring to the Pentagon's enduring pursuit of the world's most advanced tactical fighters. "The F-22 was killed in 2011 under Obama, now this administration is threatening the slowdown of the F-35s."

"Can't be helped, Winston. Myers is a grocery clerk masquerading as a commander in chief. It's the times we live in." Diele took a sip of his Seagram's 7 and 7. "It's all about the pennies with this woman. She fails to see the big picture. That's what you get when you elect a businesswoman to the White House instead of a strategic thinker. And I can't muster enough senators on either side of the aisle to filibuster her sweet ass. It's the damn Tea Party tyranny. Do you know, we've lost six thousand defense-related jobs in just the last month because of her? It's insane. Defense work is the best kind of manufacturing job there is these days. It's good, solid, middle-class work, whether you're blue collar or white collar." Diele cut another slice of beef.

The two men chewed in silence. There was no doubt that the defense budget was being ground down, though technically it was only frozen to last year's record level. But rising health care costs, automatic salary increases, and mandatory retirement payouts were consuming a larger share of the Pentagon budget every year. A defense budget freeze actually cut deeply into new weapons acquisition.

What neither man acknowledged was that the Pentagon's weapons acquisition programs were badly flawed and ill suited for the challenges of the twenty-first century. The F-22 Raptor fighter jets cost over $140 million apiece and still suffered a mysterious malfunction in the oxygen system. The problem was so bad that some air force pilots reportedly refused to fly the plane.

The F-35 series was the next fighter behind the F-22 that was designed to give America air combat superiority. Ironically, the F-35 was going to be sold to several nations, including Japan and Turkey, thus technically eliminating "American" air superiority. But the partnerships were considered necessary to help offset the astronomical expense of development and production, and yet it still cost American taxpayers over $300 million per plane. But the F-35 program continued to experience significant setbacks in production problems, cost overruns, and testing, including losing one computer-simulated combat scenario against fourth-generation Russian fighters.

The ultimate irony, of course, was that the United States hadn't fought a single air-to-air combat engagement since the first Gulf War twenty years ago. Seemingly, the U.S. was building fighters for future air battles it wasn't going to fight anytime soon. Defense analysts outside of the Pentagon had reached similar conclusions for other weapons systems in other service areas. Not only do generals and admirals prepare to fight the last war, they procure the weapons systems needed to fight them.

Of course, Americans weren't the only ones guilty of this. In the period between the world wars, few generals or admirals anywhere realized the potential for tanks, airplanes, submarines, or aircraft carriers as revolutionary weapons technologies. European and American defense budgets were squandered on outmoded technologies like giant battleships, the Maginot Line, and other weapons systems perfectly designed to fight and win World War I. Unfortunately, the Germans and Japanese had prepared for World War II and nearly won it.

But these history lessons were lost on much of the current Pentagon establishment. That was partly due to the culture. The very highest air force and navy ranks were only achieved by the men and women who wore pilots' wings or who had captained warships or submarines. Naturally, they favored the most advanced weapons systems and promoted the warriors who mastered them.

Unfortunately, history taught still another lesson the Pentagon hadn't learned.

The only wars America had lost since World War II were those fought against technologically inferior opponents. America's famous B-2 stealth bombers cost over $2 billion each, counting the entire cost of development and production, but the Afghanistan countryside was dominated by illiterate Muslim peasants carrying $200 AK-47s a decade after the invasion.

"I'm afraid for this country, Winston. I thank God every day for men and women like you who are standing guard over us. I just want to put the right tools in your hands so that you can do your job," Diele said. What Diele didn't say was that he wanted to hand him the weapons systems the big lobbyists wanted purchased, sometimes even over the protests of the generals and admirals. Congress was famous for buying unrequested weapons because they brought a direct material benefit to their home districts and states, and virtually every congressional district had at least one DoD contract of one sort or another in any given ten-year period.

Nearly all of the current pilots of the venerable B-52, first introduced in 1955, were younger than the airplanes they flew. B-52s were scheduled to remain in service until 2040. That meant, theoretically, a B-52 pilot in 2040 could be flying a plane his grandfather flew in.

"Gary, I'm just an old soldier. You tell me what I need to do, and I'll do it," the general said.

Diele laughed to himself. The general was about as political as they come. When Winchell was appointed the superintendent of the Air Force Academy, he stated that the primary purpose of the school was to promote racial and sexual diversity in the service, and its secondary purpose was to promote military preparedness. He did that knowing full well that one day he'd need that kind of politically correct gold star in his record if he wanted the Senate to confirm his appointment as a major general, which it recently did, thanks to Diele.

"Well, I'm no soldier, Winston, but I've read a little history, and it seems to me that patience is a virtue in both politics and war. We'll wait and see for now. I have a feeling that Myers will hand us the nylons we need to strangle her with."

8

Isla Paraíso, Mexico

The .50 caliber Barrett sniper rifle roared. Another massive brass casing tumbled onto the stony ground.

Water sprayed up a half meter to the left of an orange target buoy bobbing in the bright blue Pacific water five hundred meters away.

"¡Hijo de puta!" César barked. He lay prone on the ground as he fired the tripod-mounted weapon, Ali next to him. A pair of oversize earmuffs made the crime lord look more like a DJ than a sniper. Ali wore a similar pair. The Barrett's big-caliber rounds were designed to pierce armor and the blast was deafening, literally.

César stood up and pulled the muffs down around his neck. So did Ali.

"No, *jefe*. It was an excellent shot. The wind has risen."

The gusting wind on top of the island's mountain peak buffeted them, fluttering their hair and shirts.

"I'm worried, Ali."

"About Hater?"

"I have tried to reach out to him, but nobody can find the bastard."

"If he has gone to the Americans, they would already have been here and your sons killed—or worse. Trust me, there is no evidence linking your sons to the massacre. The fact that they are still breathing proves this."

"You seem certain," César said.

"I am, *jefe*. I trained your sons myself. I am certain they left no clues behind."

César stared hard into Ali's eyes, probing him for lies. He found none.

That was because Ali was supremely confident about Hater. He had ordered the Mara gangbanger crushed to death in a thirty-ton hydraulic press the day after the massacre. Hater's tattooed remains were scooped into a sealed barrel and sunk to the gulf floor where the drum settled in the middle of an abandoned dumping ground for American military ordnance. The Mara had to be killed. Hater was the only link anyone had to the massacre—and Ali.

But the inability of either the Mexican or American government to find other hard evidence against the Castillos and launch an attack had come as a complete surprise to the Iranian. *The boys really had covered their tracks.*

Now Ali wondered if the feckless Americans would ever seek their revenge against the Mexicans. If evidence was the problem, he'd have to provide it. Fortunately, he'd planned for this contingency, too.

César laughed. "Yes, you trained them well, didn't you?" He clapped Ali on the back, then turned the Iranian back toward the big sniper rifle. "So tell me, maestro, why can't I hit the fucking target with that thing?"

"It takes patience, *jefe*. You just need to practice. Trust me," Ali said, smiling.

Three hours later, the three Castillos and five premium escort girls were barricaded behind the gilded doors of the mansion's Fiesta Room, a sordid collection of vibrating beds, leather sex swings, exotic animal skins, glittering disco balls, thundering audio, and a bank of digital projectors looping porn on every wall.

When he was certain they were all passed out from copious amounts of Cristal, meth, dope, and perversion, Ali slipped into his own private quarters and locked the door behind him. He opened up his encrypted cell phone and dialed an untraceable number that bounced off of a series of satellites and cell towers, sending the signal halfway around the world and back again until someone on the other end of the line picked up.

"Yes, Commander?" a man asked in Farsi. The Western-trained computer specialist was speaking from Quds Force headquarters in Ramazan, Iran.

"The dog needs her bone," Ali said.

"It will be done within the hour."

Ali clicked off his phone. The technician he had spoken with was first-rate. By this time tomorrow, Myers should be howling with rage, and by the grace of Allah, tearing at Castillo's throat with her sharpest teeth.

9

Arlington, Virginia

Within the last fifteen minutes, there had been an explosion in tweets and retweets on a string of highly related, red-flagged search topics: #elpaso, #cincodemayo, #massacre, #myers, #killers, #aztlan, and others.

What was going on?

Sergio Navarro was at his computer workstation inside the Intelligence Division of the DEA headquarters building. It was 4 a.m., he was the shift supervisor, and he was bone-tired.

The twenty-six-year-old intelligence analyst had helped form the new Social Media Task Force organized around RIOT, Raytheon's new social-media data-mining software. Rapid Information Overlay Technology not only hoovered data on suspects using social networking sites like Twitter, Facebook, and Foursquare, it also predicted their future behavior. Drug dealers were as attracted to social media as the rest of the world was, and their desire for more human interaction through inhuman computers enabled the DEA to harvest terabytes' worth of vital intelligence information that they might not have otherwise acquired.

Navarro had been slumped behind his computer working on his master's thesis project, designing hardware and software for an open-sourced, Arduino-based crowdmapping device to locate and track drug dealers. Because it was all open-sourced, he could distribute the devices for free to poor communities victimized by drug violence all over the world. But with the budget freeze, the DEA couldn't pay for it, so Navarro had turned to Kickstarter and crowdfunded six figures for the project. When the RIOT software alarms rang, Navarro quickly pulled up the search window.

Tonight's automated search had focused on El Paso and the terrible massacre that had occurred just over a week ago. RIOT had just found the string of tweets, and they were all being generated by a single event: an uploaded video file. RIOT had found the video link as well, so Navarro opened it.

It was a cell-phone video of the Cinco de Mayo massacre.

Holy crap!

This was the smoking gun his division had been looking for.

The video was dark, shaky, and suffering the pangs of autofocus—the attack had been at night and the scene was lit primarily by a distant street lamp. Nevertheless, the video was generating quite a stir in the blogosphere. The video showed the two killers blasting away with their machine guns, death-metal music screaming in the background. Unfortunately, audio quality was poor because of the cheap microphone in the cell phone that shot the video.

Navarro located the video on the original Facebook post in question and dubbed a clean copy for the DEA's use. Navarro then reflagged the El Paso automated-search packages in order to catch the rising tidal wave of interest in the video, now surging to several hundred hits and climbing by the minute. It was about to go viral.

At the same time, the search bots were also sifting through the comments on the video posted on various web, Twitter, Tumblr, and Facebook pages. Just like old-school serial killers needed to keep physical trophies of their gruesome work, psychopaths in the social-media age often uploaded video of their crimes—a kind of digital trophy.

Navarro now had the time to fiddle around with the video clip he'd just copied to his own hard drive. He majored in computer science as an undergrad, but he had taken a couple of filmmaking courses as electives, including a class on nonlinear editing where he had learned to use Final Cut Pro.

Navarro opened his copy of FCP and dropped the video clip into the timeline. He played around with the filters to improve the quality of the image, slowing the shaking and enhancing the sound. He then experimented with the zoom feature. He played the newly edited clip a half dozen times, alternately slowing or speeding the clip. Something began to strike him as odd about the two shooters.

Navarro had avidly followed the El Paso massacre story. He had an aunt and uncle who lived in that city, and two cousins who had recently graduated from the Frida Kahlo Arts Academy. Navarro stopped the video clip loop. Rewound it. He put the two killers right in front of the open doors of the Hummer and paused it again. He studied the shooters. Examined the Hummer again.

That was it.

Navarro snatched up his phone and speed-dialed his supervisor.

10

The White House, Washington, D.C.

President Myers sighed. It seemed as if each new closed-door meeting was more crowded than the last.

Seated around the table were DEA Administrator Nancy Madrigal and Attorney General Faye Lancet, who was the head of the DOJ, under which the DEA operated. The director of ICE, Pedro Molina, sat next to his boss, DHS Secretary Bill Donovan, one of Myers's closest advisors. Bleary-eyed Sergio Navarro was also at the table seated next to his boss, Roy Jackson, the head of the DEA Intelligence Division. But the rest of Myers's trusted inner circle was also in attendance, including Mike Early and, of course, Sandy Jeffers, seated to her immediate right. Dr. Strasburg sat strategically across from her.

Protocol, not preference, put the vice president on Myers's immediate left. If it were up to her, Greyhill would have been seated in the men's room.

Everyone had hot coffee or bottles of water and iPads on the table in front of them. They listened intently.

Jackson adjusted his wire-rimmed glasses. He was a bookish, middle-aged African American just under six feet tall but well over three hundred pounds. He shifted in his chair, a nervous habit. The chair creaked under the enormous load. He picked up the video controller.

"One of my IAs, Sergio Navarro, brought this video to my attention just three hours ago. Whoever shot this was lucky they weren't killed in the attack. We estimate they were standing about one hundred yards south of the north-facing vehicle at an oblique angle of approximately forty-five degrees. That meant the camera operator was out of the shooters' line of sight, otherwise they likely would have been gunned down as well."

"Any idea who shot the video?" Greyhill asked.

Jackson nodded at Navarro. He knew his IA was not only racked with fatigue but also intimidated by this morning's briefing. The young analyst had never even met the DEA director before, let alone the president and other cabinet officials. But Navarro had made the discovery and Jackson wanted him to get the credit.

"The video was posted to Facebook under a pseudonym," Navarro said. "I ran the sensor pattern noise profile against SPNs in our database, but we came up short." SPNs were the unique digital fingerprint that every silicone chip embedded in a digital-camera image. "We're still working on that."

"Where was it posted from? Maybe that will give us a clue," Greyhill suggested.

Navarro leaned forward. "That's the interesting part. We can't locate the server. We can't even identify it. Pretty sophisticated firewall."

"Isn't that suspicious?" Myers asked.

"Not necessarily. Whoever posted it was smart enough to know that they would be the only material witness to the killing. They probably wouldn't have posted it if they weren't sure they couldn't keep their identity secret," Donovan said.

"Which makes them a prime target," Early added.

Myers referenced her iPad. "What do these comments mean?" She was referring to the viewer posts on the Facebook page.

"I'm sorry, but I don't speak Spanish. I came up through the Russian desk," Jackson said.

"You didn't get them translated? There might be a clue," Myers asked.

Jackson hesitated. "Actually, yes. Agent Navarro translated them for me. I have it on a separate report."

"What do they say?" she demanded.

Jackson shook his head. "Just a bunch of crackpot comments. Vile. Not worth the time."

"I'll be the judge of that, Mr. Jackson. Read them aloud, please."

Jackson reluctantly opened another file folder on his iPad and pulled up a sheet of translated comments. "Most of the names are nicknames or posted as 'anonymous,' but we're running them down." Jackson cleared his throat. "I'll just start at the top, the most recent posts. The first one reads: 'The whore's son deserves it.' Signed, RicoPico. The next one reads: 'Man, I wish I had a gun like that. I'd kill me some gringos, too.' Signed, PanchoVilla247. The third one reads: 'What was he doing there anyway? Probably hitting the bong and banging his students.' Signed, Azteca-Nacion. The next one reads—"

"Thank you, Mr. Jackson. I think I catch the drift. Please continue with your presentation."

Jackson gratefully closed the document and pulled up the original presentation file folder. "We estimate the person shooting the video was between five ten and five eleven, judging by the height of the image, which means that the camera operator was most likely a man," Jackson added.

"So I take it we have some good video footage?" Jeffers asked. He was growing impatient. He wanted to see the video.

"I'm afraid it's not like the movies, sir," Navarro said. "Most cell phones utilize poor-quality plastic lenses with a fixed focal length and no shutter, and this particular video was shot in extremely low resolution, only 480 dpi, probably because the cell phone was low on memory. The true cost for the whole camera on these phones is less than forty dollars, usually. So the overall image quality we have is very poor. I cleaned it up as best I could, but there just isn't enough data there for us to enhance the image any further at the moment."

"That's unfortunate," Greyhill said. "Maybe we can send the video on to the FBI lab and see what they can do with it." He saw Director Madrigal tense up at his suggestion. "You DEA guys have enough on your plate without going into the video business."

"I think we should see the video now," Jeffers suggested. He dimmed the lights with a remote control. Jackson hit the play button on his video controller.

Everybody in the room turned their focus to the far wall screen. A title card read REAL TIME, and then the clip began. The clip started with the Hummer already parked. The doors burst open immediately and the two killers leaped out, each cradling a shoulder-harnessed machine gun. The death-metal music blared in the room's flush-mounted ceiling speakers.

The assassins advanced in lockstep, shouldered their weapons, took aim, fired. The machine-gun barrels flashed in controlled bursts. The speakers roared overhead so loud it was jarring.

"Sorry," Jackson whispered in the dark as he thumbed the volume control down.

The cell-phone video camera had been in wide-shot mode. It caught the death of the first victims on the porch, the exploding plate-glass window, the house getting shot up. The camera tracked the killers marching onto the porch, then firing through the broken window until they were out of ammo, then high-fiving each other. The video clip cut to black. Total playing time was sixteen seconds and two frames.

Another title card appeared: HALF SPEED—MOS. Jackson froze the frame.

"In this clip, I would ask you to please observe the precision of the two shooters. Note the way they move, their target selection, their rate of fire."

Jackson hit play again. The second clip started with the Hummer already parked, but this time the doors burst open in slow motion. The sound was cut out in this clip because the slow-motion effect distorted it too badly.

The two killers exited the Hummer as if they were stepping out of a space capsule into a weightless void that made the flickering, grainy images even more gruesomely surreal. The slow-motion flashes exploded out of the machine-gun suppressor ports like flaming stars, bursting and collapsing and bursting over and over again. The assassins' slow, mechanical march toward the porch took forever, as did the emptying of the last rounds into the window. The video clip finally cut to black. Total playing time was thirty-two seconds and four frames.

"Mr. Jeffers, if you don't mind," Jackson asked.

The lights flicked on. Jeffers set the remote back down.

Jackson began to speak, but he noticed that the room sat in stunned silence. He realized this was the first time that any of them had seen the tape. He'd already reviewed it over a dozen times before the presentation so it no longer had an impact on him. He glanced around the room. It suddenly hit him.

He'd just forced the president of the United States to witness the murder of her own son. Twice. *And in slow motion.*

Jackson glanced over to his boss, Nancy Madrigal, for reassurance, but her eyes were focused on her hands clasped in her lap.

Myers stared at the blank screen. Her mouth was a thin scar on her emotionless face. Jackson saw the muscle flexing on her jaw line.

The other people around the table glanced mindlessly at their iPads, took sips of water, or pretended to take notes.

A few more agonizing moments passed.

"Madame President, I don't know what to say," Jackson stammered. "I'm so sorry."

Myers turned toward Jackson. Her face softened. "There's nothing to apologize for, Roy. I'm the one who asked to see the video. Your division has done an excellent job finding it and bringing it to our attention."

"We're just doing our jobs, ma'am."

"So tell us, please, Mr. Navarro, what is the takeaway from these clips, particularly the second one we were asked to observe carefully?" Myers asked.

Navarro took a sip of coffee to clear his throat. "What's clear to me is that these two men have received specialized training in weapons and tactics. These aren't gangbangers running and gunning wild on the street."

That was exactly Mike Early's take on the flight to Denver. "So these are military or ex-military?" Myers asked.

"Not necessarily," Navarro said. "I'm only suggesting they've received military-style training. I think they're civilians."

"Why?" Early asked.

Navarro pointed at his iPad. "If everyone will refer to the freeze-frame photo I pulled from the video—it's on the first page of the upload I sent out."

The others pulled up the photo in question. It showed the two masked assailants standing in front of the Hummer.

"The vehicle is a General Motors Hummer H2. The factory specs indicate that a stock H2 is 81.9 inches in height. But if you'll notice, the tires are oversize, which means there's a lift package on the suspension. Our best estimate is that another eight inches have been added to the overall height of the vehicle, so that puts it at just about seven and a half feet tall. Please notice where the heads of the two shooters are and that neither of them is standing fully erect. You can enlarge the photos on your screens, if you need to."

"Wow. That means these guys are pretty tall. I'd guess around six three or six four," Early offered.

"That's our estimate, too," Navarro said.

"So who are these men?" Donovan asked.

"They're masked, wearing gloves. Combat gear. No visible skin, which means no visible scars or tattoos, if any exist. There weren't any fingerprints or DNA on any of the shell casings or recovered bullets. It's almost impossible to make a positive ID at this time," Jackson said.

"You said 'almost impossible' to tell. I take it you have a hunch?" Myers asked.

"More than a hunch. As near as we can tell, these two men appear to be the same height and the same build, and their movements are highly synchronized, above and beyond any practiced training that they've had," Jackson said.

"Synchronized in what way?"

"Like they're used to doing things together a lot, or maybe even because they share the same build. Their movements are practically mirror images of each other."

"You mean twins?" Early asked.

"Yes," Jackson answered. "There are an estimated ten million identical twins in the world and one hundred and fifteen million fraternal twins."

"Well, that really narrows it down," Jeffers said.

"Technically, it does. That gets us down to less than three percent of the world's population. Less than half of that if you only count adults, and half again if you discount women, which is probably a safe bet. Of course, there really is no way of telling who these men are precisely, but since we're talking about El Paso, that's Castillo Syndicate territory, and as it turns out, César Castillo has identical twin sons by the names of Aquiles and Ulises. According to records we've obtained through our counterparts in Mexico, the Castillo brothers are each six foot three."

"And I take it we still don't have any witnesses at the scene who will identify the twins as the shooters?" Greyhill asked.

"No, but Mr. Navarro was able to put them in the vicinity at the time of the incident," Jackson said.

"How?" Myers asked.

"By pulling up traffic-camera images of both men in Juárez approximately three hours before and one hour after the incident."

Myers frowned. "But not in El Paso?"

"No."

"Were they seen inside the Hummer?"

"No. Nor were they in tactical gear. Either by accident or intent, they went to a location outside of traffic-camera range. There, they could have changed into tactical gear, stolen the Hummer, crossed the border, committed the shootings, crossed back over the border, ditched the Hummer and the tactical gear, then returned back to their own vehicle."

"That's a lot of ifs," Greyhill said.

Jackson shrugged. "It's not conclusive, but it's another straw on the camel's back."

Donovan leaned forward. "So do you think the Castillo twins are the shooters?"

Jackson hesitated. "At the very least, they're the prime suspects. And they certainly have the means, motive, and opportunity."

Myers glowered at Jackson. "You were asked a straightforward question. The answer is either yes or no. Which is it, Mr. Jackson?"

Jackson glanced back at his boss, Nancy Madrigal. *Are you sure you want to go through with this?* Madrigal nodded in the affirmative. "From an intelligence perspective? The answer is yes. No question in my mind. But without further evidence, it seems to me it would be difficult to obtain a conviction in an American court of law."

Myers turned to her attorney general. "Do you agree with Mr. Jackson's legal opinion?"

Lancet leaned back in her chair, processing the president's question. "A conviction would be difficult, yes, and probably impossible in an American court, based on the lack of hard admissible evidence. But the rules of evidence are one thing; the question of guilt is quite another. I agree with Mr. Jackson's intelligence assessment. As a former prosecutor, my gut tells me these two men are the shooters. I'm just not sure what that gets us. The question now is, what do we do with this new information?"

"Same problem, same solution. We'll hand our analysis off to the Mexican government and ask them to investigate further," Myers said. "At the very least they can bring them in for questioning."

"It's one thing to ask the Mexicans to arrest a dealer or a shooter. It's something else again to ask them to bring in the sons of César Castillo," Madrigal said.

"I'm the first to admit I'm no expert on Mexican politics, but it seems to me that they would want to cooperate on this matter, just out of a sense of human decency if nothing else. They've partnered with us on the drug war for years. All we're asking for is further investigation. What am I missing?" Myers asked.

All eyes turned to Dr. Strasburg, who'd been as silent as a Buddha until now.

"Madame President, your counterpart, President Antonio Guillermo Barraza, was also just recently elected to office. And like you, he narrowly won a hotly contested race, and he prevailed, in part, because he promised, like you, to give his people a respite. Mr. Molina, would you please tell the president about the AFI?"

The ICE director nodded. "The first thing President Vicente Fox did when he was elected in 2001 to combat the pervasive corruption within the Mexican law enforcement community was to form the AFI, the Agencia Federal de Investigación, the equivalent of our FBI, which actually trained and equipped the AFI. The AFI became the premier antidrug agency in Mexico. But the Mexicans recently dissolved the AFI, which sent a powerful signal to the drug cartels that Mexico intends to stop seriously prosecuting the drug war against them. We suspect cash was probably exchanged in the deal, and maybe even a truce brokered. President Obama's 'Dream' executive order also ended deportation of young illegals, which sent another powerful signal to the cartels: you can start sending your mules across the border again."

Strasburg continued. "The American people are tired of the battlefield deaths and casualties of our troops in the far-flung corners of the Middle East. The majority of Americans want an end to those wars and want our troops to come home and this is one of the reasons why you were elected. We've expended a great deal of blood and treasure on the wars in Iraq and Afghanistan, and with what result? As likely as not, people who don't like us will return to power—maybe under a different name or party or platform—and we're already seeing a return to the car bombings and suicide attacks of the previous years. And without putting too fine a point on it, the truth of the matter is, the vast majority of Americans paid far more attention to the box scores in the sports pages than they ever did to the war. Most American families didn't send soldiers to war. The war had very little practical or immediate effect on most people. And yet, as a nation, we became tired of the struggle."

Dr. Strasburg folded his hands on the table in front of him. "But consider the Mexican situation. At our urging, the Calderón administration went to war with the drug lords, and they fought courageously. But whereas we lost just over six thousand soldiers in our eleven-year War on Terror, the Mexican people have lost over fifty thousand people in about half that time. The number of Mexican dead is about equal to the number of soldiers we lost in combat in Vietnam.

"The only difference is, those Mexican casualties were mostly civilian casualties, and they all occurred in the hometowns and the city streets of Mexico itself, not off in some distant foreign land. If we are tired of our conflict, can you imagine how much more exhausted the Mexican people are? Of the stacks of human heads, the burned corpses in the streets, the bodies hanging from bridges?"

"I'm afraid Dr. Strasburg has a point," Donovan said. "I've spoken to my counterparts off the record, and there is a great deal of fatigue setting in among the men and women who are actually fighting the drug war down there."

"For all we know, there might be as many honest Mexican cops in witness protection with us here in the United States as there are in all of Mexico today," Lancet added. "There have been chiefs of police who have fled into our consulates with their families with nothing but the clothes on their backs, scared to death of being assassinated. About thirty mayors have been assassinated since 2008; even more journalists. It's a Wild West Show down there."

"Though in the last few months, the violence has calmed down a little bit now that Barraza has backed off," Molina said.

Madrigal raised a finger. "Violence is only part of the issue at stake. The Mexicans run annual trade deficits of around eight billion dollars a year, but we're exporting between twenty and sixty billion dollars of drug money a year down there."

"That's a big spread in the numbers," Myers said.

"The drug numbers are all over the place. It's not as if you can audit anybody's books. The best guess is that the drug trade accounts for three percent of their GDP. I've read one estimate that claims the cartels make three times as much profit as Mexico's five hundred biggest corporations combined and employ half a million people."

"What's your point?" Myers said.

"I'm merely suggesting that there are some Mexicans not connected to the drug trade who are conflicted over the issue."

"Sounds like you're picking a fight you can't win, Margaret," Greyhill said. "I'd let this one go if I were you." What he meant was *if I were president.*

"Sounds to me like you're throwing in the towel, Robert."

Greyhill's eyes narrowed at the thinly veiled reference to his concession speech to Myers at the convention last year.

Myers turned to the others. "And you all are giving up, too. Is that what I'm hearing?"

Strasburg shook his heavy head. "Not at all, Madame President. We understand your desire for justice and, in fact, share it. But consider Barraza's situation. Imagine if he had a son who was killed by an Iraqi terrorist and he asked you to reinvade Iraq in order to get justice for his murdered son. How willing would we be to open that wound all over again? It's a horribly unfair and hyperbolic comparison, I know, but my ridiculous question points to the anxiety the Barraza administration has regarding the cartels."

"I agree with you, Dr. Strasburg. It is a ridiculous comparison. I'm not asking Barraza to start a war. I'm asking him to make an inquiry."

"But to Castillo, that *will* seem like a declaration of war," Madrigal said.

Myers stiffened. "All I know right now is that the Castillo boys are the prime suspects—the *only* suspects—in a heinous crime committed on American soil. I would think the Mexican government would be interested in solving such a crime, that is, if the Mexican government is still committed to the rule of law. I'm not looking for scapegoats or a vendetta. I'm looking for a little cooperation and I mean to have it. Am I clear on this?"

The room sat in chastised silence until Jeffers finally spoke up. "Yes. Perfectly clear."

"Then call Eddleston and get him over here ASAP, and let's get Ambassador Romero on the line. I want this handled with kid gloves—but I want it handled now. And I don't want the press involved. No point in putting more pressure on Barraza. I want to give him every possible leeway to pursue the matter in a way that makes sense for him. But we're going to get to the bottom of this Castillo thing, one way or another."

Myers stood up. So did everyone else.

The meeting was over. Everybody filed out except Jeffers. When the room was clear, Jeffers asked, "Greyhill's going to be a problem, isn't he?"

"The vice president has decades of experience in foreign affairs, which I value greatly. I think a goodwill tour of our G-8 allies by the vice president would be greatly beneficial to the nation, don't you?" Myers said.

"The G-20 might be more . . . timely," Jeffers offered, smiling. "You might want to toss in a few base closings and a couple of funerals while you're at it."

"Agreed. Please make the necessary arrangements. I'll call Robert tonight with the good news. He always wanted to be somebody important."

11

Los Pinos, Mexico D.F.

In his offices in Los Pinos, the Mexican White House, President Antonio Guillermo Barraza sat on one of the couches in an elegantly tailored suit. Tall and athletic, the president of Mexico had been a leading man in a number of Spanish-language films before turning to a career in politics. With strong endorsements from the business establishment and several state governors, the gifted speaker with an affable smile was quickly dubbed the "Ronald Reagan of Mexico" when he first announced his candidacy.

Sitting on the same couch was his brother, Hernán. Though five years younger than his movie-star sibling, Hernán appeared to be a decade older. Short, pudgy, and scarred with acne, the younger Barraza lacked all of the outward physical gifts the gods had bestowed upon his brother, but he possessed a brilliant mind hidden beneath his pathetic comb-over, far eclipsing the president's limited intellect. While his older brother virtually fell into fame and fortune, Hernán battled his way through law school to become first in his class, then clawed his way to the top of his law firm, earning a well-deserved reputation as a ruthless and fearsome corporate litigator. This laid the groundwork for his ultimate ambition, politics, and over the last two decades Hernán had become Mexico's most accomplished political operative. It was only in the last few years that the two brothers' career paths came together.

On the couch opposite both of them sat the American ambassador to Mexico, Frank Romero. Ambassador Romero was a former pro golfer and heir to one of the largest private vineyards in Napa Valley. Romero had been the youngest lieutenant governor in California history and was a rising star in the Democratic party until he bucked his governor and endorsed Margaret Myers's candidacy for president. But the gamble had paid off in spades, and Romero won the coveted ambassadorship to Mexico, a country he and his family knew intimately.

All three men held snifters of Casa Dragones, a premium sipping tequila, clear as the cut-crystal decanter it came in. Hernán sat motionless, studying the glass in his hands through the thick lenses of his Clark Kent glasses, as the other two men talked.

"A 'discreet inquiry'? Is such a thing even possible anymore?" President Barraza joked.

"You can well imagine President Myers's desire to bring this issue to a swift conclusion. If the Castillos are innocent, an inquiry shouldn't be a problem," Romero said.

"It seems to me, Frank, that the case you've presented is unpersuasive. My attorney general has gone over everything you sent. She agrees with me that there is no conclusive evidence linking the Castillos to the massacre." President Barraza's English was flawless, but he added in Spanish, *"Donde no hay humo, no hay lumbre."* Where there is no smoke, there is no fire.

"Of course, Mr. President. We're not accusing anybody of anything. But it's precisely because we're in the dark that we're searching for any kind of lead we can find. All we'd like to do is to speak to Mr. Castillo and his two sons. Where's the harm in that?" Romero took another sip of tequila.

"César Castillo is a law-abiding citizen of Mexico. He also happens to be the CEO of Mexico's largest agricultural combine—our number one supplier of fruits and vegetables to the American market. As a vertically integrated concern, his company also manufactures fertilizers and pesticides for their thousands of acres of productive land, but he exports those chemical products around the world as well. Insulting Mr. Castillo is like insulting Mexico itself, and he's a very proud man. More important, he is a very private man. Personally, I've never met him. I don't think he's even appeared in public in over five years."

"Forgive me, Mr. President, but it almost sounds like he's in hiding. How is a legitimate businessman able to do business like that?"

President Barraza laughed. "The same way the American billionaire recluse Howard Hughes built his aviation empire, I suppose."

"But if the man and his sons aren't hiding anything, why not answer a few simple questions?" Romero asked.

"Because the very question itself is a veiled accusation and an implication of wrongdoing that is all the more damaging for the truly innocent. Right now, you say that you don't know who the real killers are. So tell me, Frank, in the interest of resolving the issue, should I instruct our attorney general to question President Myers as to *her* whereabouts on the night of the killings? And what would she say about us if we did make the inquiry?"

"She would be angry and insulted, certainly. But that would be a ridiculous request. There's no reason to suspect—"

President Barraza held up his hand. "No need to explain, Frank. I agree. But you get my point, don't you? Rightly or wrongly, César Castillo would feel as justified in his resentment as President Myers would in hers."

The president rose and crossed over to the credenza, making a beeline for the bottle of Casa Dragones.

"I hope President Myers understands how completely sympathetic I am to her situation, both in regard to the death of her son, as well as the political difficulties she now faces. I hope that she can appreciate my difficulties as well." Barraza flashed his million-watt smile.

"Unfortunately, Mr. President, there are members of our Congress who are very capable of stirring up trouble for both of our countries. The amnesty bill, the guest-worker program, the NAFTA renegotiation—all of these things that both of our governments want will be difficult if not impossible to achieve if your government is seen as the least bit hesitant to bring this case to a just and equitable conclusion."

President Barraza hovered over Romero and refilled his glass.

"This really is a marvelous tequila. Sweet pear and citrus notes with a pepper finish. I'm going to have to buy a case," Romero said.

"No need. I'll have one sent over this afternoon." The president crossed over to his brother and refilled his glass, then set the bottle down on the coffee table between them. He took his seat.

Hernán Barraza rolled the snifter between his stubby fingers, never lifting his eyes from it as he finally spoke. "My associates in the distillery business pray for the day you Americans make liquor illegal again—it would quadruple their profits." He swirled the liquor in the glass and sniffed the aroma. "Cartels make drugs, but it's your politicians who make the laws that make the cartels rich. The drug problem, as we all know, is a demand problem, not a supply problem. If you Americans had an insatiable lust for tomatoes, we wouldn't be having this conversation today, and maybe we would have been spilling tomatillo sauce instead of blood all these years."

Hernán finally looked up from his glass. He smiled at Romero with his sad eyes and a mouth full of small, crooked teeth. "I only see one flaw in your request, Frank. What happens if we do make a 'discreet inquiry' and Mr. Castillo and his sons insist they had nothing to do with the El Paso event? Will President Myers be satisfied with that answer?"

Romero set his empty glass down on the table. He cleared his throat. "Frankly, no."

Hernán took another thoughtful sip. "Thank you for your candor. Of course she wouldn't be satisfied. Neither would I, were I in her shoes. Officially, César Castillo is an upstanding Mexican businessman who donates millions to charitable work. His two sons earned their bachelor's degrees in business administration at the University of Texas at Austin, and MBAs at the IE Business School in Madrid. They, too, are legitimate businessmen working within their father's privately held corporation. Neither Mr. Castillo nor his sons have ever been convicted of a crime."

Hernán swirled the tequila again in his snifter. "And yet, *'Hijos de maguey, mecates.'*"

Romero nodded. "The sons of a hemp plant are going to become ropes." It was a clever variation on an old Mexican proverb.

Hernán leaned forward, his eyes locked with Romero's.

"Unofficially? I think we can all agree that César Castillo is the boss of the most powerful crime syndicate in Mexico, if not all of Latin America, which makes him a very dangerous man. He will not view a 'discreet inquiry' as anything less than a personal assault on his honor and his position, and he will likely retaliate. But a 'discreet inquiry' won't accomplish anything at all, as you yourself have just admitted."

Hernán leaned back in the couch, his head against the rear cushion. He was so short that the top of his head didn't reach to the top of the couch. "America is our strategic partner and our best trading customer. We share a common border and a common history and, increasingly, a common people, which means we share a common destiny. We want an end to the violence and destruction even more than you do."

Hernán turned toward his brother, his head still resting against the couch.

"What I recommend, Mr. President, is that we bring the two Castillo boys in for questioning, by force if necessary. If we suffer the consequences for this, so be it. It's the least we can do for our friends in the north, don't you agree?"

President Barraza frowned with confusion. That was the last thing in the world he expected his nationalistic brother to say. An oily smile greased Hernán's pockmarked face. *What was Hernán's game?* No matter. He would follow his brother's lead. The president smiled, too, and turned toward Romero.

"Yes, of course. We will do whatever it takes to get to the truth behind this terrible tragedy. You have my word on that, Frank."

Romero beamed. "Thank you, Mr. President. I will convey your heartfelt message to President Myers, and I can assure you she will be eternally grateful for your assistance in this matter."

Romero departed for his embassy, eager to convey the good news to Secretary of State Eddleston on a secure line. Antonio Barraza shut the door behind the American, then stormed over to his brother, who had retaken his seat on the couch.

"Are you fucking crazy? We can't arrest Castillo's kids. Next thing we know, he'll be stacking cops' heads in the Zócalo. Maybe ours, too."

Hernán leaned back on the couch, propped his stumpy legs on the hand-carved coffee table, and folded his hands on the curve of his round belly. He closed his eyes. "This Myers woman. She's not stupid. If she could handle this problem herself, she would. But she can't. So she needs us to do it. Or at least try to do it." His voice was calm, even soothing.

Antonio's curiosity was piqued. He sat down next to his brother and listened in rapt attention.

"We must make a good show of it. We'll have live video feed, both here and in Washington. The Americans must see our heroic men risking their lives in order to try and carry out justice for the grieving American president."

"I know just the man. Sanchez. He's with the Federal Police." Antonio was getting excited. He liked to think he was able to keep up with Hernán's scheming.

Hernán kept his eyes shut. "No. Not him. We need our best man, the head of our best unit. Incorruptible. Undefeated." Hernán searched his photographic memory. "Cruzalta. Colonel Israel Cruzalta."

"*Dios mio.* Yes. If anyone can stand up to Castillo, it's him and his gung-ho Marines." President Barraza patted his brother on his flaccid thigh. "We'll drag those Castillo assholes to the police station in chains if we have to. Their father, too. Excellent suggestion." He checked his Rolex. "I'm late for an important meeting."

Hernán kept his brother's schedule. The important meeting was actually a round of golf with his mistress.

"Make the arrangements and coordinate with the Americans."

"As you say, Mr. President."

Antonio dashed out of the office.

Hernán sighed and poured himself another drink. He despaired at his brother's lack of imagination. He thought about explaining the overall plan he had in mind, but his older sibling would just get confused. Hernán's vision was too complicated, too violent, and too subtle for the actor to comprehend, let alone execute. It was better that Antonio remain a handsome figurehead while Hernán pulled the strings behind the scenes.

At least for now.

Hernán heard his mother's small, pitying voice in his head again, an echo from his childhood.

You can't fight fate, pobrecito.

"To hell with that," Hernán said to nobody as he drained his glass.

12

Near the Snake River, Wyoming

Pearce hadn't built his worldwide company in less than a decade by micromanaging. By temperament and training, he was an analyst, always looking for the big picture. When he decided to strike out on his own, he saw a world of opportunities thanks to advances in drone technologies. Drones themselves weren't actually new technology. Nikola Tesla earned the world's first patent for wireless remote-controlled vehicles in 1898 and demonstrated the remote-control wireless powerboat in Madison Square Garden that same year.

Pearce's other gift was people. He knew how to hire the right ones to seize those new opportunities.

Drones were changing not only modern warfare but nearly every other aspect of civilian life as well. In the end, drones were just delivery systems. Energy, medicine, agriculture, and transportation were just a few of the areas being transformed by the advent of autonomous, independent, inexpensive, and reliable vehicles.

Under normal circumstances, Pearce's unseen investing partner could've expected an excellent return on the cash used to launch the company. But Pearce's civilian operations had already delivered exceptional returns and promised many, many more for years to come and he was happy to allow others to lead those divisions.

But Pearce Systems security operations were far more lucrative at the moment—and far more dangerous as well, so he took responsibility for the day-to-day operations of that division. As president of the company, it was his responsibility to ensure that both sides of his house were in order because, in fact, they supported each other, directly and indirectly. He did this by regularly contacting his division heads, just to let them know he was still engaged with them and as passionate as they were about their respective projects. It was an exciting time to be alive, for sure.

More often than not, though, Pearce felt as if he were riding on the back of a galloping two-headed tiger. There was no telling where all of this might end up—Skynet was just a writer's nightmare, but was it really so far from the truth anymore? On the other hand, the promise of a technological nirvana seemed just as plausible. Pearce wasn't sure which of the two mouths would eventually swallow him, but he knew exactly which orifice of the beast he'd eventually be vacating when it was all said and done.

Pearce shook his head. It was late. His mind was wandering. He grabbed a beer from the fridge and dropped into his favorite chair in the cabin and tapped on his smartphone. Time to check in.

Dungeness, Kent, United Kingdom

August Mann stood at the top of the old soaring lighthouse, more than forty meters in the air. Due west was the decommissioned Dungeness A nuclear reactor facility. Due south was the English Channel.

The view of the surrounding beaches was fantastic, but it was the stout wind frothing the Channel waters far below that had caught his attention. Perfect conditions for kite surfing. His phone rang. It was Pearce. He picked up immediately.

"Troy. *Wie geht's?*"

"I'm fine, August. How are you?"

"I was just thinking about you! San Onofre," he barked into the phone. The wind gusting through the open window whipped the German's hair.

Ironically, San Onofre also featured a nuclear reactor by the sea, but August was referring to the kite-surfing competition where they first met several years ago.

"Did you bring your board?" Pearce asked.

"*Natürlich!* Bring yours, we'll have good fun."

"Don't tempt me. How are those beautiful daughters of yours?"

August had married three years ago. His wife bore him twin girls a week after the wedding. "Growing fast. I can't wait to get them out on the water here. Thank you for asking."

"So, how's it going over there? Any problems?"

"No. Everything is on schedule. We began defueling operations three days ago. The drones have functioned perfectly, as expected," August said.

Dungeness A was just one of ten Magnox nuclear reactors that were decommissioned in the United Kingdom and scheduled for eventual demolition. Pearce Systems had won one of the first contracts utilizing tracked drones with manipulator arms and laser cutters to reduce waste materials into smaller pieces without risking human contamination. Mann headed up the nuclear decommissioning project for Pearce Systems. He had been a combat engineer in Germany's Bundeswehr and had helped develop his nation's first tracked drones for mine clearing and antipersonnel work. After one tour in Kosovo and another in Iraq, he quit the army to chase the wind. Instead, he found Pearce.

"No casualties on our end?" Pearce asked.

"None, of course. But we deployed one of our rescue bots when a Swedish contractor collapsed inside of the reactor core building. We pulled him out with no problems."

"Radiation?" Pearce asked.

"No. Mild heart attack. He is recuperating in hospital. But again, no risk to personnel in the rescue."

"Outstanding," Pearce offered. "Keep up the good work."

"Come out soon. The wind is fantastic here!"

Mann shut his phone and grinned. The Dungeness operation was running even more smoothly than he'd hoped. He knew his friend was pleased. August headed for the circular staircase. Time to get home to his family.

Once again, Pearce had proven prophetic, Mann thought, as his feet thudded on the steel stairs. The old nuclear reactors like Dungeness were gold mines. They took decades to fully decommission and deconstruct, and safety—for the workers and the environment—was the primary concern, not money. Over four hundred civilian reactors around the world were currently at or beyond their thirty-year design life and scheduled for decommissioning. After the tragedy at Fukushima in 2011, those schedules were being accelerated. Even Chancellor Angela Merkel, herself a Ph.D. in physics, had been affected by the Japanese catastrophe and she completely reversed her own energy policy, choosing instead to phase out all of Germany's nuclear reactors by 2022, despite the fact they currently supplied a quarter of her nation's electrical supply.

But Mann knew that this wasn't just about money for Pearce, or himself for that matter. This was good environmental work that needed to be done and they were both proud to be part of it. Pearce Systems was leaving an important legacy for future generations. The fact that he and Troy would get rich doing it was just an added benefit.

August emerged from the great black lighthouse tower. He held up a hand to guard his blinking eyes against the sand stinging his face. Maybe he would bring his girls out to the beach for a picnic this weekend if the wind died down. But if it didn't, he'd gladly bring his board instead.

Near the Snake River, Wyoming

Pearce finished his beer and picked up his phone to dial again. August was seven hours ahead of Pearce. His next call was four hours behind him on the other side of the world from the lanky German.

Port Allen, Hanapepe Bay, Kaua'i, Hawaii

Dr. Kenji Yamada was barefoot. The converted wharf workshop wasn't technically a "clean room," but it could've been. Sensitive electronic controls, motherboards, and other equipment were susceptible to damage from dust and particulate matter, but Kenji was building *working* vehicles and didn't mind a little real-world challenge. He used his bare feet as contamination sensors, constantly monitoring the state of floor cleanliness, or so he told his graduate students. Truth be told, he just liked being barefoot. His feet were doing a lot of sensing today because everybody was scrambling to load up the last of the equipment on the modified 350 Outrage excursion boat bobbing in the water outside.

The fifty-three-year-old researcher wore his thick silver hair in a braid and sported a downy silver beard that contrasted nicely with his sun-drenched skin. He'd traded in his lab coat for a pair of board shorts decades earlier. His excuse was that he'd found it easier to do lab work in board shorts than it was to surf in a lab coat. His passions were whale research and surfing, in that order, with adventurous women, premium beer, and fresh sushi next on the list, also in order.

The humpback whales had arrived last December in Hawaii to calve and now the pods had just begun leaving for the three-thousand-mile return trip to the Gulf of Alaska. Thanks to Pearce Systems' funding, Yamada had spent the last three years developing an autonomous unmanned underwater vehicle (UUV) designed to swim along with the humpbacks without disturbing them. Yamada had spent the last twenty-five years recording the migratory habits, social relationships, and communication patterns of the giant mammals, but no one had been able to travel with them for an extended period of time, owing in part to the extreme distances and water conditions. Some humpback pods were known to travel up to sixteen thousand miles in their annual migratory loops.

Yamada was on the verge of a revolution in whale research, thanks to

Pearce Systems' support. By translating his hard-won migration data into an artificial intelligence program, he hoped to be able to insert into a whale pod a torpedo-shaped UUV equipped with radar, cameras, extension arms, and other devices needed to monitor the humpbacks in the wild. In order to accomplish this feat, the UUV had to be stealthy, self-powering, able to receive and send data signals to the control base, and perform a dozen other monitoring functions, all without disturbing the whales or disrupting their migratory patterns. Yamada also didn't want his UUV to invoke the fearsome wrath of an angry thirty-five-ton adult, which could crush the UUV and scatter its priceless components on the bottom of the ocean floor with one mighty swipe of its massive fluke.

Yamada's UUV was still under development, but it was far enough along that he wanted to try a short run with one of the pods. The UUV was already in position, but the AI program was still buggy. The best he could hope for was a remote-control test run of a couple hundred miles by following the underwater drone in a surface vessel like the 350 Outrage.

Yamada pointed at a stack of yellow storm-proof camera cases and told one of his grad students, "Don't forget the Pelicans, please." He felt his smartphone vibrate in his shorts pocket. It was Pearce's ring tone.

"Troy! Howzit, brah?" Yamada asked. Born in Japan in 1960, he had migrated like his beloved humpbacks to Hawaii with his family when he was a teenager and had gone completely native. He was fluent in three human languages—Japanese, English, and pidgin—and he was an avid collector of whale songs.

"I was going to ask you the same thing, Kenji. Ready to launch today?" Pearce was aware of the AI bugs but wasn't concerned. He knew Yamada and his team were close to solving them.

"On our way out the door. Wish us luck."

"One more thing. I've scheduled the BP demo for September. I'll need you and your team out in Galveston by August fifteenth at the latest. Will that be a problem?"

"Ah, brah. Serious?" Yamada whined. "Texas? How about Cali?" Ya-mada had earned his doctorate at the Scripps Institution of Oceanography at UC San Diego.

"Sorry, 'brah.' Gotta go where the customers are. You'll be back before December."

Yamada cringed. "Meh. Humpbacks are my customers."

"I'm after greenbacks. The Brits have 'em in spades. That UUV you're building is perfectly designed to run automated repair and maintenance routes on ocean-floor pipelines all over the world. We sign this BP contract, you'll have more money for your whales than you'll know what to do with."

"And the rest of our deal?" Yamada asked. The hippie scientist agreed to join Pearce Systems and allow Pearce to fund his whale research operations so long as his UUV was never deployed for military purposes. Pearce was happy to comply. Like he told Yamada when he first met him, he really liked whales, too. *Especially if you cook them just right.* Fortunately for Pearce, Kenji had a sense of humor—and a busted bank account.

"Still the deal. Scout's honor."

"K, brah. See you in Texas. We talk logistics later. Gotta run."

"Good luck, Kenji. I'm excited for you. Keep me posted."

13

Highway 24, Sierra Madre Occidental, Mexico

The small convoy of Renault Sherpa 2s climbed the winding snake of asphalt known as Highway 24. It curved its way through the rugged, pine-covered mountains of eastern Sinaloa, not far from the bordering state of Durango. The road wasn't heavily traveled. The only traffic was the occasional pickup or eighteen-wheeler hauling farm goods down the mountain from one of the *ranchitas* farther up.

Sixteen Infantería de Marina, among Mexico's fiercest and most loyal soldiers in the drug war, were packed into the French-manufactured Humvee-style vehicles, each carrying a roof-mounted Heckler & Koch HK21 7.62mm machine gun. Oscar Obregón was in the lead command vehicle, standing inside the open-air weapon station. His helmet was equipped with a video camera providing a live "first-person shooter" broadcast. He was a freshly minted *subteniente*, the equivalent of a second lieutenant in American rank. Like all good young officers, he was determined to outperform on his first assignment with the unit.

A Hughes OH-6 Cayuse light observation helicopter provided overhead visual security. A video camera mounted on the helicopter provided an additional live feed of the events. It was piloted by another Marine lieutenant and the battalion commander, Colonel Israel Cruzalta, the most highly decorated man in the service. His unit had been responsible for more drug busts and weapons seizures, and had engaged in more fire-fights, than any other military or police unit in all of Mexico. He had inherited a deep, broad chest and a cleft chin from his German grandfather, along with his height and bald head, which, combined with his dark eyes and complexion, gave him a fearsome, commanding presence.

The convoy was racing toward one of Castillo's hideouts, thanks to a tip received by the Mexican Federal Police. A *Marina* forward observation team had been put on the ground two days earlier, and they had confirmed the presence of Ulises and Aquiles Castillo as recently as thirty minutes ago. The forward observation post also kept a live camera feed on the compound. They had identified the presence of two additional adult males, each armed with AK-47 assault rifles, who were alternating duty in twelve-hour shifts. Their long-range camera had also caught sight of two attractive young women in the compound, usually in bikinis and lounging near the outdoor pool. As the observation team reported, the buxom young women were definitely unarmed, but they were packing some serious heat.

In short, security at the compound was extremely light and no match for the two squads of highly trained combat infantry racing toward them.

All three live feeds were being fed simultaneously to monitors in command centers located at both Los Pinos and the White House.

The Situation Room, the White House

As soon as she was notified the convoy was en route, President Myers ordered her secretary to cancel all of her afternoon appointments because of "illness." She didn't want to set the town talking again with the news of yet another emergency meeting at the White House.

Madrigal, Early, Jeffers, and Vice President Greyhill were the only other people in the room with her watching the live feed on three separate monitors.

"They call that a resort compound? I see a shooting range, an obstacle course, and an outbuilding that looks like a barracks to me. Are they sure there's no one else up on that hill?" Madrigal asked.

"They'd better be sure. Otherwise, they're going to need a whole lot more firepower," Early said.

Obregón's helmet camera bounced and jostled as the stiff suspension of the Sherpa 2 rattled over the uneven mountain road. His head was on a swivel, and the camera swept in broad circles frequently on the lookout for trouble.

Occasionally Obregón's camera ducked down into the personnel compartment where three young Marines—a corporal and two privates—were riding in bone-jarring silence.

"I'm getting motion sickness watching that guy's helmet cam," Jeffers said.

"How much longer, Mike?" Myers asked.

Early checked his watch. "Ten minutes, maybe fifteen."

"Why couldn't the Castillos have just come in?" Myers said.

No one answered. They all knew the question was rhetorical.

Cruzalta's OH-6 Cayuse

The helicopter rotors hammered against the cloudless blue sky, spun by a Rolls-Royce turboshaft engine roaring overhead.

Los Pinos had decided to run the op during the day because of the terrain. It was closer to an arrest than an assault. If it had been an assault, the soldiers would have gone in at night. The Marines' night-vision capabilities gave them a significant advantage over most opponents, though syndicate soldiers had been known to deploy the same technology on occasion.

Colonel Cruzalta scanned the road ahead with his field glasses. A wicked hairpin turn following a switchback was about five hundred meters ahead. A steep mountain with loose rocks walled one side of the road;

the other side was nothing but air and a thousand-meter drop into the gorge below.

"Obregón. Tell your driver to slow down. There's a nasty curve up ahead."

"Yes, Colonel," echoed in Cruzalta's headset, along with the Sherpa's four-cylinder diesel engine whining in the background.

Like all true warriors, Cruzalta was anxious. Only armchair generals and fat-assed politicians thumped their chests and laughed at danger because they never really had to face any. Without fear, courage was impossible. Fear kept a man alive while courage kept him in the fight.

Cruzalta's orders were to escort the Castillos back to Culiacán, by force if necessary, where an assistant attorney general was waiting to ask questions in the air-conditioned comfort of a federal building. If the twins requested it, Cruzalta was ordered to escort the Castillos back to their resort compound. It was possible that the Castillos would forcibly resist the attempt to bring them in for questioning, but the appearance of elite *Marinas* should cause them to think twice. However, it had been determined by the president's office that a minimum of force was preferable in order to avoid any unnecessary provocation. Cruzalta prayed that the Castillo boys were wiser than their youth suggested.

Several hundred meters ahead, an ancient tractor-trailer rig belched clouds of oily smoke from its vertical exhaust pipes. *The driver is doing a bad job of downshifting,* Cruzalta thought to himself. The trailers were fully enclosed but ventilated. Cruzalta guessed the truck must be hauling cattle down the hill to the slaughterhouses in Culiacán.

Obregón's Sherpa 2

Loaded out in his combat gear, including a Kevlar vest, Obregón sweated fiercely, but he could sense a slight cooling in the air temperature as they gained altitude.

He glanced up and over at his two o'clock, watching Cruzalta's heli-copter on station, keeping an eye on things. He was glad the old man was up there watching out for them. Cruzalta's reputation was second to none in the *Marinas*. He had always led his battalion into battle from the front and he had the wounds to prove it.

Obregón ducked his head back into the crew compartment. The three young soldiers sat grim and determined beneath their camouflaged hel-mets, rifles locked between their knees.

"You girls ready to dance?" Obregón shouted over the noise.

"Sir, yes, sir!" they shouted back in unison, smiles creasing their fierce, young faces.

"Good. Won't be long now."

The Situation Room, the White House

Greyhill frowned. "Okay, now I'm starting to get carsick."

Early grinned. "Trust me, it's worse for them, especially the guys in the back."

"Boys," Myers whispered. "They're just young boys."

Cruzalta's OH-6 Cayuse

Cruzalta watched Obregón's lead vehicle enter the southern end of the mile-long tunnel that cut through the mountain. The other Sherpas were close behind. The drivers were tired and distracted after a three-hour ride in the twisting mountains.

"Keep your vehicles spread out," Cruzalta ordered through his mic, but Obregón didn't respond. They had lost voice communication inside the tunnel.

The cattle truck entered the northern end and disappeared.

The Situation Room, the White House

Obregón's video monitor cut to black.

"What's going on?" Myers asked.

"They're inside the mountain. The video will be back up as soon as they're on the other side," Early assured her.

Myers glanced at the live feed of the compound. The Castillo brothers were outside now in the pool playing a game of volleyball in the shallow end with the two young women, who were now completely topless.

"Better enjoy it while it lasts, assholes," Early said.

Obregón's Sherpa 2

Obregón was glad to be in the cool of the wide two-lane tunnel. The sun had been grinding him down for the last three hours. His eyes were still adjusting to the dark. He glanced up at the tunnel ceiling. There were lights up there, but they weren't turned on. *Civilians,* he muttered to himself, as he cracked open his canteen and took another sip of water.

Obregón glanced backward at the other Sherpas spread out behind him, each about two seconds apart. That was cutting it pretty close, and in a combat situation he would push them back and keep them spread much farther apart. He could barely see the anxious face of the young private driving the vehicle behind him, clutching the steering wheel with an iron grip. The private's frowning eyes finally caught Obregón's and Obregón flashed him a thumbs-up. It took a couple of seconds, but the young driver finally managed a wide, nervous grin.

Obregón turned around. He glanced up ahead. A pair of cockeyed headlights from an oncoming diesel tractor rattled in the dark up ahead. He could just make out the shadows of the trailers it was hauling behind it.

Cruzalta's OH-6 Cayuse

"Come around," Cruzalta ordered his pilot. The helicopter had flown in an elliptical pattern all day, racing ahead of the slower-moving convoy, then circling around and catching up with them, keeping an eye on threats in front of and behind his men. The OH-6 had gotten far ahead again and now the pilot circled back on his commander's order. The nose of the helicopter turned just in time to give Cruzalta a God's-eye view of the tunnel.

The Situation Room, the White House

Myers was fixed on the helicopter video monitor. Flames suddenly jetted out of both ends of the mountain tunnel.

"Oh my God!" Myers shouted.

Fire continued to boil out of both ends as the helicopter camera plunged toward the tunnel. Cruzalta's voice shouted over the speakers, screaming for the pilot to land.

Cruzalta's OH-6 Cayuse

"OBREGÓN! OBREGÓN! COME IN!" Cruzalta shouted as the helicopter rocketed down toward the highway below. Just as the helicopter's skids hit the hot asphalt, a long-horned bull shrouded in flames charged out of the tunnel entrance. Even above the rotor wash, Cruzalta could hear its agonizing screams as it thundered past the cockpit and hurled itself blindly over the side of the mountain into the gorge below.

The Situation Room, the White House ·

Myers's eyes darted over to the other monitor. The laughing Castillo boys were still batting the volleyball around with their girlfriends in the pool, oblivious to the carnage in the hills below them.

"Jesus, what a goat fuck," Greyhill blurted. He turned to Myers. "Good thing you weren't directly involved in this, Margaret. It would've been your Bay of Pigs."

The Situation Room, Los Pinos

President Barraza sat in stunned silence, staring at the monitors. He finally managed to speak, his voice cracking with emotion. "This is a disaster, Hernán. Those poor kids."

Hernán Barraza turned toward his brother. "We sent the best we have. The Americans will realize that, won't they?" His voice was etched with pained sincerity. He even managed to wet his eyes a little. Hernán had practiced both for hours last night in front of a mirror. Antonio wasn't the only actor in the family.

The president bolted to his feet. "If that Myers bitch thinks we're going to do this again, she's crazy. If that isn't good enough for her, then fuck her. Do you understand me?"

Hernán Barraza nodded thoughtfully. "Yes. I understand perfectly."

14

Camp David, Maryland

President Myers admired the tall pines through the large picture window. She loved the presidential retreat nestled in the low wooded hills of Catoctin Mountain Park. It reminded her of her mountain home in Colorado. The main building where she stood was, in fact, a lodge, just one of many reasons she felt more comfortable here than in the White House.

She needed another meeting with her inner circle. The problem now was secrecy. There had already been too many scheduled meetings with the same people not to draw outside attention, and the Washington rumor mill was in full grind. Myers wasn't ignorant of the political forces on both sides of the aisle arrayed against her. Just being kept out of these meetings was causing something of a scandal among senior congressional leadership, especially in her own party, Senator Diele the most vocal among them. Myers had discovered early on that Washington, D.C., was just like high school, only with money—other people's money, technically. Jealousy, cliques, and rivalries were the stock-in-trade for the preening, precious egos that populated the Hill.

"Sorry to drag you out in the woods away from your families on a Saturday, but we needed to talk about yesterday's fiasco," Myers began.

"It's our job, Madame President. No need to apologize," Jeffers said.

Lancet flashed a sympathetic smile. "I used to have a pastor who said, 'There's no rest for the wicked, and the righteous don't need any.' So we're good to go."

"Thank you. Let's get to it so we can get you all back home at a reasonable hour. Mike, what exactly happened down there?"

"Near as we can tell, somebody must have dropped a dime on the operation and the Castillos set a trap."

"What about operational security?"

"There are many honest cops and some truly terrific people fighting the good fight down there, including Colonel Cruzalta and his Marines," Lancet said.

"You're sure about Cruzalta?" Myers asked. "We all know there is a tremendous amount of corruption in the police and even military ranks."

"The people I really trust say that Cruzalta is the best there is," Lancet said. "Loyal, smart, and incorruptible. He understands what the drug trade is doing to his nation. But you're right. There is a lot of corruption in Mexico. 'Plata o plomo,' they call it. Silver or lead. It's the cartel's way of saying either you accept the bribe or the bullet, but either way, you're going to cooperate with us. And of course, once someone does cooperate, they're compromised forever. So no matter how secure they think an operation is, there's always a good chance someone—a clerk, a secretary, a disgruntled traffic cop—is going to call it in when they see the trucks roll out of the gate."

"The explosion was horrific," Myers said, her face clouding with emotion.

Lancet nodded. "Castillo employs some of the world's finest chemists in his labs. Some of them are concocting pesticides and herbicides for his legit businesses, but others are cooking meth. Any of his labs can put together a batch of napalm. Near as we can tell, the poor bastard driving the truck didn't know he was hauling more than cattle."

"So, Mike, give me some options," Myers said.

"President Barraza has shown that there's a limit to what he's able to do, at least tactically. And given the political reality today, he's probably hit the limit on what he's willing to do."

"Faye?"

"As we discussed the other day, legally we've hit a wall. We still can't technically prove that the Castillos are guilty of the El Paso massacre, at least not by American legal standards—"

"Setting those boys on fire looked like a confession of guilt to me," Myers interrupted. "If nothing else, they're guilty of murdering those Marines."

"Again, not provable, but I don't disagree with you. That makes it a Mexican problem, not ours. The El Paso massacre is a criminal matter, with both domestic and international dimensions. American and international criminal law is quite specific about what we may and may not do. We also have extensive treaty obligations with Mexico, as well as Memoranda of Cooperation and Memoranda of Understanding with them in regard to criminal matters. In short, we have no legal standing to pursue this case any further as a legal matter without Mexican cooperation, and we've seen what their cooperation has gotten us."

"Can we set up some sort of a sting? A trap? Lure the Castillos out of Mexico and back up here?" Myers asked.

Lancet shrugged. "Maybe. Maybe not. Either way, we'd have to spend a great deal of money and time to set up a scheme that would be convincing enough and tempting enough to lure them out of Mexico. That means getting a lot more people involved, and that has its dangers, too. The syndicate isn't without resources on our side of the border, either, except over here, they use more *sexo* than *plomo* to get cooperation. Corruption isn't as bad here as it is down there, but the problem is getting bigger up here, for sure."

"So I'm asking you both again. What are our options? How do we get justice for the families who lost loved ones in El Paso?"

Lancet shrugged. "You've ruled out American troops on the ground. The Mexicans have ruled out further military action on their end. And the law prevents you from carrying out any law enforcement function without the express permission of Mexico, which they aren't going to give, at least not right now. Maybe in a few years if and/or when you get the new immigration and trade agreements rammed through Congress. Maybe that will give you some leverage."

"Mike? You agree with Faye's assessment?"

Early shrugged. "You've pretty much eliminated all of the reasonable options, that's for sure."

"Then I want the unreasonable ones. Do you have any?"

Early rubbed the stubble on his unshaven chin. "It just so happens I know a guy."

New York City, New York
September 13, 2004

"You think Early knows?" Annie asked. She was spooning into Pearce, his arms wrapped around her naked torso. They were lying beneath high-thread-count sheets in a penthouse suite overlooking Manhattan.

"About us? If he hasn't figured it out, he isn't much of an intelligence analyst," Pearce said. "Of course, he isn't a professional spook like we'uns."

"What do you think he'd say if he knew?" she asked. She rolled over and kissed Pearce on the nose.

"He'd say, 'Why not me?'"

"Besides that, goof." She rolled back over off the bed, padding toward the floor-to-ceiling window.

"He'd say, 'Pearce, you're one lucky sumbitch. Don't screw this up.'"

"Lucky? Why? Don't you get laid very often?" Annie teased.

"Lately, I've been doing okay, I guess." Pearce stretched and yawned. "But what I think he was referring to was the emotional component. I'm usually not very good at that sort of thing." Pearce rolled out of bed, too, grabbing the top sheet. He stood behind Annie and wrapped both of them in the sheet, pulling her close to him. They gazed out over the amazing Manhattan skyline beneath their feet.

"Oh. So this is emotional for you, is it?" she whispered.

"Yeah."

"You're such a girl."

"Some girls," he said with a playful smile. "But I wasn't looking for it."

"Me neither," she said.

"But I'm glad we found it. Found each other."

"Me, too."

Pearce kissed the back of her head, relieved.

"So what should we do about this?" she asked.

"I dunno. Go steady? By the way, you never told me how you can afford this place."

"My dad owns it." She slipped out beneath his embrace and headed for the kitchen.

"Why didn't you tell me your dad was rich?" Pearce followed her into the kitchen. The tile was cold on his bare feet.

"I'm a spy, remember? I'm supposed to keep secrets, not give them away."

"Since when do trust-fund babies go to war?" Pearce meant it as a joke, but it came off as flippant.

"Rich people love their country too, asshole."

"Sorry. Didn't mean it like that. It's just . . . unusual, that's all."

"Coffee?" That was easier for her to say than *you're forgiven*.

"Sounds great. And eggs, bacon, and toast while you're at it. So you're loaded and you can cook, too?"

"And I bang it like a porn star, in case you hadn't noticed. But I was thinking more like room service," she said. "Right now I'm just grabbing some water. Want some?" She yanked open the big Viking refrigerator door.

Pearce admired the view. She was buck naked, bent at the waist, reaching into the refrigerator for a bottled water, her breasts swaying with the effort. She was utterly comfortable in her own marvelous skin, even the patches of it laced with small shrapnel scars.

"Yeah, I want some," Pearce said. He was getting hard.

"I meant water."

"That, too. I'm a little dehydrated, if you catch my drift."

A bottle of water sailed toward his head. He caught it at the last second.

"Drink up. You're gonna need it later," she promised as she cracked open her bottle. He did the same. They both took a long pull, just like they were back in the field.

"So, seriously. What do we do about this?" she asked again.

"'This'? You mean 'us.' I like 'us.' Don't you?"

"Is this enough?" she asked.

"For now."

"And later"? She finished her water and crushed the bottle. Tossed it into the empty sink.

"What do you want me to say, Annie?"

"It's what I don't want you to say."

"What don't you want me to say?"

"Don't say you'd give it all up for me."

"I would."

"You don't listen very well, do you?"

"But it's true."

"We can't just stop doing what we're doing and play house."

"Why not?" Suddenly he wasn't hard anymore. Not even close.

Annie padded back toward the bedroom. Pearce right behind her. She reached for her pair of jeans on the floor and pulled them on. No panties. Commando.

Pearce reached for his underwear. "Why not? That's what grown-up people do, you know."

She buttoned up her fly and stared at him. Her breasts bunched beneath her crossed arms.

Pearce's heart melted. Again. *Could she be any more beautiful?*

"Look, I don't mean to go all Bogart on you here, but there's something a helluva lot more important than us going on in the world right now. More important than what you and I want, no matter how badly we want it." She grabbed her T-shirt and pulled it on. No bra.

Thank you, Jesus.

"So you *do* want it?" Pearce asked, distracted.

"I'm crazy about you, numbnuts. But I signed up with the Agency, not eHarmony. I'm supposed to be killing guys, not marrying them."

She approached him, wrapped her arms around his neck. "You're the best man I know, Troy, and that's saying a lot because I know a lot of really great guys, Early included. But this isn't our time. At least not right now."

"There aren't many people who have what we have."

"And even fewer people who can do what we do. That means we have a responsibility. Maybe we get to have what we want later."

"When's that?"

"When the war's over, I guess."

Pearce gazed into her sparkling blue eyes. "And when's that going to happen?"

She leaned her head against his chest and held on tight, listening to his heartbeat. It wasn't much of an answer, but it was all she had.

15

Coeur d'Alene, Idaho

It was one-thirty in the morning but the place was packed with locals. It was a sea of pierced noses, sleeve tattoos, and black T-shirts—and that was just the women. A girl in the corner with unwashed hair in her eyes played Alanis Morissette on a rosewood mandolin. Behind her, moose heads, snowshoes, and salmon trophies were nailed on the rough timbered walls.

Early fell into the booth at the back of the crowded hipster café, away from the picture windows. Pearce was already there. He was wearing a red and white Stanford University T-shirt, blue jeans, and a pair of Ropers. A ranch coat lay on the bench seat next to him, and a small iron pot of herbal tea steeped on the table.

"You do realize I'm on East Coast time, right?" Early wore his fatigue like a five o'clock shadow. His cross-country adventure had started late and it had only gotten much later. He'd flown into Fairchild AFB from Washington, D.C., on a DoD Gulfstream C-37A, then borrowed an unmarked Air Police sedan to make the hour's drive from the air base to the coffeehouse. "Couldn't we have done this tomorrow?"

Pearce grinned. "How the heck have you been, Mikey?"

A waitress with a buzz cut who was wearing skinny black jeans and neck tats sauntered over to the table. Her long, thin fingers held a notepad and a badly chewed pencil.

"Whatchyawant, amigo?" she asked Early.

Early's eyes drifted to her chest and the small, firm breasts underneath her tank top. Pink letters flashed the restaurant name: GLORY BOX.

"What's good here, sister?"

Her listless black eyes wandered around the room.

"Everything."

"What do *you* like?"

"Veggie empanada's good."

Early admired her tongue stud. "Got any meat to go with that?"

"Beef. Chicken. It's all organic and range-fed."

"I suspected as much. Toss some chicken in the empanada. And some coffee would be great."

"What kind? We've got fifteen different blends in the pots."

"Black. Hot. You pick the rest, okay?" Early smiled at her. "I'm a real good tipper."

Her eyes drifted back to his. The corner of her mouth tugged just a little. Almost a smile.

"'Kay." Her eyes lingered on him for a moment. Early wasn't hard to look at. She wandered off.

"When did you go hippie?" Early asked, glancing around the room.

Pearce poured his first cup of tea.

"Food's good here. The tea's better. Got to eat right, you know. You look like shit, by the way."

"I missed you, too. It's been, what, eight years?" Early asked.

Pearce shrugged, a bad memory suddenly on his shoulder. "Something like that. How's Kate? Still in remission?"

"Yeah, thank God. Thanks for asking."

"You married up. Everybody knows that except her." Pearce smiled. "But she did all right, I guess."

"I'm a lucky bastard, no doubt about it."

"And you climbed the ladder. Congratulations." Pearce raised his cup in salute.

"It's a job." Early looked around the dark room. "Maybe if it doesn't work out, you can put a word in for me. I could dig working in a place like this." The beefy former special forces operator glanced around the room. "I wonder if they have a health plan."

"What brings you to this neck of the woods?" Pearce asked.

"You, amigo." Early smiled.

"Well, here I am." Pearce took a sip of tea. "That about do it for you?"

"We need your services."

"Who is 'we'?" Pearce asked.

"'We' is me and the number one boss lady."

"Seems to me the boss lady has a lot of employees to carry her water. You don't need me."

"For this job, we do. No one else can hack it." Early turned serious.

"Off the books, I take it."

"Yup."

Pearce thought about it for a moment. Took another sip of tea. "No, thanks."

Early frowned. "It's damn good money. I thought you were in business."

"I am. Doesn't mean I take every job. Don't have to. That's why they call it 'free' enterprise."

"It's for a good cause, Troy. You remember those, don't you?"

"I used to believe in Santy Claus, too. Good causes get people killed, just like the bad ones." Pearce leaned in a little closer. "You remember that, don't you?"

Early's foul mood turned even darker. He did remember. It's why he'd left the service a few years after Troy did.

"Yeah. But this time it's different," Early said.

"That's what they always say, until it's not."

"No, seriously. Myers is different." Early meant it. "You know Kate's loaded. I could be reef diving in Fiji right now if I wanted."

Pearce smiled. "You were always such a Boy Scout, Mikey. You think this president is different because she's in the other party? Don't be naive."

"No, I'm not talking about that. She's in there for the right reasons, doing the right things. Or at least trying to."

"Really? Then why hire me? Sounds like she's trying to cover her ass on something."

"No. She's straight up. Trust me."

The waitress sauntered back over with Early's plate and a cup of coffee. She set them down on the table. "Chicken empanada and sides."

"Looks good," Early said.

"Is good," she insisted.

"What kind of joe did you bring me?"

"Tanzanian peaberry." She turned to Pearce. Her face softened. "More tea?"

"In a while. Thanks."

"I'll check back in a few." She drifted to another table.

Early watched her for a moment. Caught her stealing a glance back at Pearce. Early stuck his fork into the empanada. "She's sweet on you."

Pearce shrugged. "She had a little boyfriend trouble a while back. I made it go away. That's all."

"And you call me a Boy Scout." Early shook his head with a smile as he took another bite.

"You know how you can tell when a politician is lying?" Pearce asked. "When their lips are moving."

"Man, this is really good." Empanada churned in his mouth like tube socks in a laundromat dryer. "You want some?"

"No, but thanks."

Early took a sip of coffee. Examined the cup. "This is unbelievable. Maybe she's sweet on me, too."

"She probably heard you were a good tipper."

Early pulled a cell phone out of his shirt pocket and set it in front of Pearce.

"I've already got a phone. But thanks."

"Not with that number on it. Pick it up and call her."

"Who?"

"Who do you think?"

Pearce frowned. "She's on East Coast time, you know."

"She's at work. Call her. Tell her she's a liar and I'll go away. We never met. I won't bother you again, and neither will she." Early stabbed his fork into a chunk of roasted rosemary potato glistening with olive oil.

Pearce picked up the phone. Leaned back in the booth. Thought about it for a few seconds, then punched the call button. It rang twice.

"Hello, Mr. Pearce," Myers answered.

Pearce shot a curious glance at Early. *Is this a joke?*

Early grinned. *No, it's not.*

"Mike asked me to call you," Pearce said.

"That means you turned down his offer. I'm sorry to hear that. He's a big fan of yours."

"Mikey's always been a cheerleader for lost causes. Including yours, I'm afraid."

"He told you about the situation?"

"I turned him down before we got that far."

"I actually prefer doing business face-to-face. If it's at all possible, I'd like to meet with you later today and put all of my cards on the table. You can fly back with Mike."

"It's going to be a very short meeting, ma'am, and I don't think you're going to like it."

"If you can spare the time, I'd be grateful." Myers clicked off.

Pearce stared at the phone in his hand for a long time. Old habits die hard. *How do you say no to the president?*

"She's a pistol, ain't she?" Early smiled.

Pearce slid out of the booth as Early took another bite of food.

"What's the verdict, chief?" Early asked.

Pearce grabbed his ranch coat and stood up.

"I've got a boat needs refinishing this afternoon. So if we're going to do this, let's go."

Pearce pulled on his coat.

Early dropped his fork and leaped up.

"Give me your wallet," Pearce demanded.

"What for?"

Pearce motioned impatiently with his hand.

Early handed Pearce his wallet. Pearce fished out a hundred-dollar bill and tossed it on the table.

"What are you doing?" Early asked.

"She's got a kid. And you were never a good tipper."

Pearce tossed Early's wallet back at him, turned, and marched toward the door. ·

The White House, Washington, D.C.

It was just after seven in the morning when Early and Pearce arrived at the private VIP entrance to the West Wing.

Early and Pearce checked their weapons with the duty officer behind the security desk, a striking Haitian-American woman with luminous green eyes.

Early placed the palm of his right hand on the security scanner.

"What? No smile today?" Early asked.

"Sorry, Mr. Early. Everybody's jittery. Someone called in another bomb threat an hour ago. That's the third this week."

"Just another crank. Won't amount to anything," Early assured her.

"Hope you're right."

A few moments later, Early's personnel page pulled up on the security monitor. It included his latest headshot, a short bio, his job title and security status. The guard nodded him through to the unmarked door behind her.

"Thanks, Simone. Take it easy." Early strode through the checkpoint.

Pearce didn't budge.

"You coming?" Early asked.

"You need to wave me through."

"He can't. We have a strict security protocol," Simone said.

"This isn't a good idea," Pearce said to Early.

Another security agent stood close by. A big slab of meat in a crew cut wearing a name tag that read HANK. He shifted his weight, his thick body visibly tensing.

"The president's waiting," Early said.

"Sir, you have to place your hand on the scanner," Hank said. His cold, gray eyes weren't asking.

Pearce looked him up and down with a smirk, then turned back to Simone. "Don't say I didn't warn you." He stepped over to the glass and put his hand on the scanner.

Simone flashed a dazzling smile. "Thank you, sir. I promise this will only take a second."

Pearce left his hand on the scanner but glanced over his shoulder at Hank, who was still eyeing him.

Simone frowned. "I'm sorry, sir. Something's wrong. Mr. Early's file pulled up again. Would you mind removing your hand for a second?"

"Sure thing." Pearce smiled.

Simone tapped a few keys to relaunch the program. When it pulled back up, she said, "Please put your hand back on the scanner."

Pearce put his hand back on the glass screen.

Vice President Greyhill's file pulled up.

"I don't understand," Simone whispered to herself. "You're not the vice president."

"Maybe I'm wearing a disguise," Pearce offered.

"What's the matter?" Hank asked Simone.

"A glitch. Let me try something." Simone turned to Pearce. "I'm sorry, but this will take a few moments."

"We're already late, Simone," Early said.

"The president will have to wait a little longer, sir," Hank said. He glared at Pearce. "You need to step back."

Pearce smirked. "I'm fine right here."

Hank took a step toward Pearce.

"Oh, Jesus," Early whispered. He knew Pearce wouldn't back down. But Simone saved the day.

"Ah. The system's back up. Please, sir. Once more, if you don't mind."

"Not at all." Pearce put his hand on the glass for the third time.

Simone frowned. "Your name isn't Elvis Presley, is it?"

"Afraid not," Pearce said.

Alarms rang on Simone's computer. The monitor snapped to black.

"*Qu'est-ce qui se passe?*" Simone hissed. She tapped keys furiously.

"Your system just crashed," Pearce said.

Early's eyes screamed a question at Pearce. *What have you done?*

Pearce shrugged.

"Told you it wasn't a good idea."

Hank grabbed Pearce by the shoulder.

Big mistake.

16

The President's Dining Room, West Wing, the White House

"Sure you don't want anything to eat, Mr. Pearce?" Myers asked. She was just sitting down to a couple of poached eggs and a cup of black coffee.

"No, thank you. We ate on the plane," Pearce said. He sipped his green tea.

"MREs," Early grumbled. He was working on his second cup of coffee already.

"Mike tells me you're quite a fisherman. You ever fish salmon?"

"Only every chance I get."

"I had the hardest time learning to tie the Jock Scott. My husband had the patience of Job."

"They say that the hardest flies to tie are your first one and your last one," Pearce said.

She took a bite of egg.

"That was quite a little show you put on downstairs. I see why Mike puts such faith in you."

"One of the reasons I get hired is that I don't leave any footprints behind."

"You mean, besides the one you left on Hank's face?" Early grinned.

"From what Mikey tells me, it's probably best for all concerned that I was never here to begin with."

"Technically, you broke the law when you tampered with our security system, but I'm the one who called this meeting, so this one's on me, Mr. Pearce."

Pearce took another sip of tea.

"That's where you say something civilized like 'Thank you, Madame President,'" Early said.

Pearce ignored him. Early was still fuming over the embarrassment Pearce had caused him at the security desk.

Myers leaned back in her chair. "I understand you're reluctant to accept the assignment I have for you, even though you don't know what it is."

"Let's just say I have trust issues," Pearce said. He glanced around the room. It was well appointed with period-style furniture. His eyes fixed on a large oil painting of Lincoln and his war cabinet. "It's the decisions people like you make in rooms like this that cause most of the suffering in the world."

"I have trust issues, too," Myers said. "But I still think you're just the man I'm looking for."

"How do you know that? Mike's an old buddy, but even he hasn't kept up with me for the last few years. And as you've seen, nobody else has, either."

"I usually make up my mind about a person in thirty seconds, and I seldom change it." Myers smiled over the edge of her coffee cup.

"Let me see if I can change it, then." Pearce pulled out his smartphone and tapped on the photo gallery icon. He slid the phone over to Myers. She glanced at the first photo. Her face darkened.

"Royce Simmons. The man who killed my husband."

"DUI. Three priors. Driving with a suspended license the day he plowed into your husband's Lexus. Increasing the DUI penalties in Colorado was what got you into politics in the first place," Pearce noted.

"That's old news, Mr. Pearce. What's that got to do with us?"

"Slide it to the next photo."

Myers stiffened for a moment. She wasn't used to being told what to do, but she complied.

Pearce saw her eyes light up for a moment, then dim again. "Mr. Simmons in a morgue. Broke his neck in a fall, I read."

"Mike, you mind giving us a second?" Pearce asked.

"Sure. I need to call the hospital and check up on Hank anyway. I'll send him your love." Early turned to the president. "Call me when you need me, ma'am." Early closed the door behind him.

"I take it there's another picture you want to show me?" Myers asked.

Pearce nodded.

She flicked the touch screen. A man's face.

"Cliff Calhoun," she said.

"Tell me about him."

Myers set the phone down and glared at Pearce. "What do you want me to tell you that you don't obviously already know? When I learned Simmons was due for early release, I hired Cliff to follow him. And I gave Cliff the order to kill Simmons if he caught him driving drunk again."

"How soon before Calhoun caught him drinking?"

"The first night he was released. He was in a bar, celebrating. Cliff said he knocked back a half dozen whiskey shots and as many beers in less than an hour. Got up, stumbled out to a borrowed car. No license, of course. Bastard was going to drive home. Sidewalks were slick with ice. Cliff broke his neck. Made it look like Simmons slipped and fell. Nobody cried for the son of a bitch, not even his own mother. I hope your intel told you that, too. As far as I'm concerned, it was a public service. If Simmons hadn't gotten drunk again, he'd be alive today, or at least, he wouldn't have been killed by me."

Pearce thought about her answer. He could put her in jail for twenty-five to life with that confession. The only problem was, Pearce hated drunk drivers, too.

"Did I pass your test, Mr. Pearce? Can we quit playing games now?"

"Still not interested."

"Why? Because I hired a man to kill a drunk before he could kill somebody else's husband and father? I've never talked about it because I didn't want to go to jail. Calhoun's been dead for years, so I don't even know how you could have possibly found out. But if you're asking me to apologize, I won't."

"I'm not asking you to. I'm a businessman, not a therapist. I don't do personal vendettas. It doesn't fit the company mission statement." Pearce stood to leave. "You need to find somebody else."

"Sit down," she said.

Pearce ignored her.

"Please."

Pearce hesitated, his hand on the doorknob.

Baghdad, Iraq
August 21, 2005

"Dick holsters. All of 'em."

Annie stood in front of Troy's steel desk reading the airstrike request denial again. She gripped the paper so hard her hands trembled.

It was only the two of them in the spartan operations office that morning. Troy sat and listened to Annie rant, but he was focused on the ring in his pocket. He'd been carrying it for a week, waiting for just the right moment to ask her. Somehow that moment never seemed to arrive, today included.

IEDs had been cutting down American soldiers and Iraqi policemen for months now, and slaughtering innocent civilians, too. Instead of chasing the bombers, Annie decided it was smarter to find the source of the remote-controlled bombs.

Ba'athists and Iraqi insurgents—many of them former Revolutionary Guards—had enough technical know-how to set off crude timed charges. But the Iranians had been supplying IEDs with sophisticated timers and remote-control detonators, many of which, ironically, were manufactured in the United States and smuggled via Singapore into Iran. The Quds

Force operators were also particularly adept at fashioning shaped-charge IEDs, the kind of munitions that could even punch holes through the thick steel hull of the mighty Abrams main battle tank.

Annie worked her sources hard for weeks even as she turned new ones, chasing leads on the IED suppliers. She favored the "aggressive" interrogation of captured insurgents and had been reprimanded twice for the physical harm she'd caused to those in her severe custody. She once even sifted bare-handed through the shredded remains of a dead insurgent after he accidentally detonated a device he was trying to set. But it was a piece of hard intel shared by a friend in Israel's Mossad that finally pinpointed Baneh, Iran, as the target.

Annie's request for a satellite redeploy over the city gave her superiors the visual confirmation they needed to order an airstrike. But the request for an airstrike was denied from higher up the chain of command. President Bush's political opposition had drawn a line in the sand at the Iraq-Iran border. The Republicans were afraid they wouldn't get the war they wanted so badly if they asked for a declaration of war; the Democrats were too afraid to oppose a war that had gained such widespread popularity among the public. A compromise was reached. The undeclared Iraq war could continue indefinitely, but Iran was strictly off-limits. Reelection was the driving reality of Washington politics.

The reality in Iraq, however, was that dozens of people were getting injured or killed by Iranian-built IEDs every day, and the severity and frequency of the attacks were increasing.

In Annie's mind, the gutless politicians back home were just as guilty of the carnage as the Iraqi insurgents.

"They're all dick holsters," Annie grunted again. She crushed the paper into a hard little ball and threw it across the room.

"You've got to let it go, Annie," Troy said.

"I can't. You know that."

"What else can we do?"

"We could go in ourselves."

"We'd never get approval."

"Who's asking for permission?"

"No support? On a mission like this? Good chance of getting killed that way."

"Maybe. But more of our people will get killed if we don't. Guaranteed."

"I don't want you to go."

"Is that your head or your dick talking?"

"You mean my head or my heart?"

"Yeah, that, too."

"Both," Pearce said.

"Sorry. Pick one."

"Okay. Heart."

Annie dropped in Pearce's lap. She pulled a handful of hair behind her ear. That was her tell. Pearce braced himself.

Annie's bright eyes bore into his.

"Sorry, mister. Wrong answer. We didn't come over here to go steady. We came here to win a war. Right?"

Pearce took a deep breath. Old ground.

"Right."

She smiled. "Good boy." She affirmed his answer by patting his broad chest with her hands. Felt something in one of his shirt pockets. It was the ring, of course. But this wasn't the time.

"What's that?" she asked.

"Nothing."

She started to say something but held her tongue.

Pearce thought about asking her what she was going to say, but he knew she wouldn't answer. Her mind had already turned to the mission.

Annie slipped off his lap and grabbed her cell phone. "I'll handle logistics," she told Pearce as she dialed. "You handle Mike."

The President's Dining Room, West Wing, the White House

Pearce took his hand off the doorknob, turned around, and took his seat.

"Unfortunately, it took the death of my son to wake me up to what's been going on down in Mexico. The horrific violence. The sheer volume of drugs like methamphetamine and brown tar heroin flooding into our country, killing our children. I was too damn busy making a pile of money in the IT industry, or running a state government, to pay attention to any of it."

"We had to deal with the heroin trade in the Sand Box," Pearce said. "It was a primary revenue source for the bad guys. Some of our guys got caught up into it, too."

Myers took another sip of coffee. Pearce drank his tea.

"Mike briefed you on the ambush of the *Marinas*?" Myers asked.

"Yeah. Somebody obviously leaked. They find out who?"

"Not yet. Probably doesn't matter. If they find the guy—or gal—there'll just be another one next time. I'm afraid the Castillos were sending us a message, and they set those poor young Marines on fire to make sure we got it. They want us to know that the Mexican government can't fight this war, let alone win it."

"And neither can you, at least not with American troops. Otherwise, you've broken one of your campaign promises, right?"

"It wasn't just an empty campaign promise to win votes. Too much blood and too much treasure have already been spent fighting the War on Terror for more than a decade now. If we invade Mexico, we're probably in for another ten years of bloody warfare. I'm not saying it wouldn't be worth it. I'm not even saying we couldn't win it. But the American people don't have the will to start another war right now, let alone to make the necessary sacrifices to see it through."

"So what's your plan? Where do I fit in?"

"I can't fight and win the drug war. But I've got to send my own message. I can't control what Castillo does in Mexico, but I've got to keep him from crossing the border at will and killing American citizens with impunity."

"Hire more Border Patrol agents. Call up the National Guard. Seal the border."

"Can't. At least not now. The budget freeze cuts across every department of government, Border Patrol included. And troops on the border are considered racist, fascist, and xenophobic by the rabid left and increasingly so by the middling center. Frankly, I don't give a rat's ass what they think, but the political reality is that the moderates in Congress won't authorize troops on the border or slash other welfare programs to beef up the Border Patrol. More important, a great deal of trade takes place across that border. We gum it up too much, and we hurt the economies of both countries."

"That doesn't leave many options," Pearce observed. "Maybe it's best to let this dog lie."

"I was raised with the belief that action is morality. It's quoted so often it's a cliché now, but Burke's aphorism is still true. All it takes for evil to thrive is for good men to do nothing."

Pearce shook his head. "The only problem with that kind of thinking is that every zealot with a suicide vest thinks he's the good guy fighting evil, even when the bus he blows up is full of innocent civilians."

"I'm not talking about ideology or politics. I'm no moral crusader. I'm talking about putting down a rabid dog before it bites somebody else. My job is to save American lives. I think that's something you understand quite well."

Once again, Pearce had to process for a moment. "So what do you want to do?"

"I believe in Occam's razor. In this case, the simplest solution is the best one. I want to send Castillo a clear message. Blood for blood. I'm convinced he killed my son, so I'm going to kill one of his sons. Tit-for-tat."

"A telegram would be cheaper."

"I'm willing to pay the price," Myers said.

"Why only one son if they're both killers?"

"So Castillo won't retaliate. He gets to keep one son alive if he keeps a cool head. The dead son will be a daily reminder to him to keep his war on his side of the border."

"But what if he does retaliate? You take out his other son? Then he retaliates again. Then what do you do?"

"You were CIA. You must have read about the Phoenix Program?" She was referring to the CIA program that assassinated key Vietcong leaders during the Vietnam War.

"We studied it. A lot of mistakes were made."

"But according to William Colby, the North Vietnamese said that the Phoenix Program was the most effective thing we ever did during the entire war."

"Of course he'd say that. It was his program."

"You think he lied about it?"

"I have no way of knowing. It was before my time."

Pearce had mixed feelings about that war. His father had served in it and eventually died from it. "What I do know is that the Phoenix Program killed nearly thirty thousand Vietnamese."

"I only want to kill one Mexican."

"And that's where my company comes in."

"Yes. But it must be kept secret."

"Who else knows about this, besides you, me, and Early?"

"Sandy Jeffers, my chief of staff, and the attorney general."

"What does she say about all of this?"

"You don't strike me as someone overly concerned with matters of the law."

"I have people to worry about."

"Without getting into the specifics, you're operating under my authority as commander in chief, the same way President Obama dispatched SEAL Team snipers to take out the Somali pirates."

"Our situation is a little different. We're private contractors."

"Then just think of it as a private contract for taking out the garbage."

"And if this thing goes south?"

"Doubting yourself, Mr. Pearce?"

"Not at all. But humor me."

"Then I'll have your back. Mike will vouch for me."

"He already did. I just wanted to hear it from you."

"Is that why you're recording our conversation?" Myers asked. It was an educated guess.

"Trust, but verify. In case I'm not around," Pearce said. "Speaking of trust, why isn't Greyhill in the loop?"

"I take it you don't follow politics very closely. We had a shotgun wedding. Only the shotgun was pointed at me."

"Is the operation covert or clandestine?" Pearce chose his words carefully. "Covert" actions fell under Title 50 of the U.S. Code, "clandestine" under Title 10. What Pearce was really asking was: are you notifying the armed services committees or the intelligence committees about this action?

"Neither. Or both. It's irrelevant. This is a tactical operation. Congress doesn't have the right to micromanage national security."

"In other words, you want to keep this secret because your political opponents would make a lot of hay over this, even if it does go right."

"I need to keep this secret because if I publicly shame Castillo, he'd be forced to retaliate."

Myers locked eyes with Pearce. All her cards were on the table.

"Are you in or out?" she asked.

Pearce had an instructor at the Farm. He was one of the original cold warriors with the missing fingernails to prove it. The old man had drilled the *Hagakure* into their heads like sixteen-penny nails into wet lumber. Even now he could hear the spymaster's raspy voice in his head.

The warrior makes all of his decisions within the span of seven breaths.

Pearce took just two.

Old habits die hard.

"Better call Mike back in," Pearce said.

Myers pressed the intercom. "Please send Mr. Early back in."

Early came in, a fresh cup of coffee in his hand. "You want me to throw this bum out?" he asked with a smile.

Pearce pushed out the chair next to him with his foot. Early fell into it. Pearce turned to Myers.

"No JAG lawyers looking over my shoulder. No bean counters asking for receipts. No squawking when I hand you guys the bill—and it's gonna be a doozy. I do this my way, with my team, no questions. Are we clear on that?"

Myers and Early both nodded. "Agreed," Myers added.

"I'm also going to need access to DEA intelligence and NSA databases, at least the ones my firm hasn't already hacked. Without their knowledge, of course."

"Mike will handle all of that," Myers said.

"One more thing. I'm going to need you to flip the switch on DAS down there."

"DAS?" Early asked.

"Domain Awareness System," Myers said. "The domestic version is up and running in New York City. You know, like that TV show, *Person of Interest*. Links all of the CCTV cameras, criminal databases, public records, and just about every other surveillance or intelligence database to a central processing hub for total information awareness."

Both men's faces posed the same question to her. *How do you know about DAS?*

Myers grinned. "My company subcontracted some of the DAS software package on an NSA contract a few years back. The NSA uses a more robust suite of assets for covert surveillance in noncompliant cities. Deep web stuff." She was referring to the fact that NSA was tapped into every major telecom, search engine, and ISP around the world, by either tacit agreement or covert operation, often through backdoor software and compromised system components. Essentially, there wasn't a private or public database in the world that NSA couldn't break into, especially in Latin America. "But isn't deploying DAS a little bit of overkill, Mr. Pearce?"

"Pulling the trigger is always the easy part. Target acquisition is the name of the game. I can't shoot 'em if I can't see 'em. The more data we have, the better. We want to crack open as many of the Mexican intel databases as we can, but phone records, driver's licenses, and car registrations will go a long way, too."

"So long as we can do that without alerting the Mexican government. I want to keep this as limited as possible. One kill, one message. End this thing, or at least contain it," Myers said.

"Suits me fine. One kill, one job, and we're done. I doubt you'll be able to stop at one and I don't have any intention of standing under the tree after we swat the hornets' nest."

"Understood, Mr. Pearce. One job and you're done," Myers agreed.

"If you can spare him, I'd like Mike to liaison for us."

"He's all yours, Mr. Pearce." Myers stood up, extended Pearce her hand. He took it. She had a firm grip.

"I'm just glad we never met," she smiled.

17

Pearce Systems Research Facility, Dearborn, Michigan

Pearce stood with Udi Stern next to an oversize treadmill. The former Israeli paratrooper was three inches shorter than Pearce, but broader in the chest.

"Go ahead, Udi. Try." Dr. Rao smiled.

Udi smiled nervously at her. "I don't want to break it," he said, in heavily accented English.

"You won't," she said.

Udi stepped closer to the Petman 3, a third-generation Boston Dynamics humanoid robot that was on loan to Pearce Systems. It was jogging at exactly five miles per hour on the treadmill. Its legs pumped effortlessly, and the combat boots it wore pounded on the oversize treadmill's rubber pad in a faultless heel-and-toe strike.

Dr. Rao's team had recently perfected the software that enabled it to run for the first time, and she had renamed the robot "Usain Bolts" after the famous Jamaican runner. But the experimental drone was still a headless mechanical monster with a skinless aluminum-titanium frame, the stuff of science-fiction nightmares. On its chest it wore a black case that housed the video sensor package.

Udi lifted his own steel-toed boot and lightly kicked the Petman 3, but the robot barely budged. It was still connected to a thick power cable hanging down from overhead, but the cable was providing no physical support.

"She said to try and knock it over, not ask it for a date," Pearce said.

Udi's dark eyes narrowed. He threw a hard side kick into the robot's hip. Usain Bolts was shoved hard to the left, but it never broke stride, and quickly returned to center.

"Try using your hands," Dr. Rao suggested. "Give it a good shove."

Udi spit in both hands, lowered himself, then lunged at the upper torso, careful to not catch himself in the rapidly pumping arms. He whacked it good. The robot's upper torso twisted violently away from Udi. Its right arm windmilled high while its left arm swung low to help it keep balance. The twisting torso also twisted the hips, and the legs followed the hips. Just as it looked like it was about to crash, the robot did a quick shuffling step, turned on the balls of its feet without losing stride, and righted itself again. Within moments, it was jogging once again in the center of the broad treadmill.

Pearce laughed. "I knew I should've brought your wife instead."

"Can you imagine a platoon of these parachuting out of the sky, then racing through the enemy's streets? The psychological impact alone would be devastating." Dr. Rao's eyes gleamed with awe at the future soldier she was helping to create.

"This place always makes me depressed," Udi lamented.

"Not to worry. It will be at least five more years before you're obsolete." She giggled, patting Udi on his thick shoulder.

Pearce shook his head, incredulous. "Thanks for the demo. We'd better push on to the main event."

Inside the brightly lit conference room at the lab, Dr. Rao engaged a large video monitor on the center table with a tablet device in her hand. Pearce and Udi stood next to her. The other operators Pearce had selected for the

Castillo mission were already doing advance work in Mexico or prepping the computer and communications networks.

Rao opened the hinged lid of a small aluminum case that was also on the table.

She reached into the case and lifted something out with a pair of tweezers and set it on the pad. "Watch the monitor, please."

She tapped the tablet in her hand and a live image of Udi's clasped, hairy hands popped onto the screen. When Udi realized those were his hands, he moved them, suddenly self-conscious.

"Hey! A mini spy camera. Nice," Udi said.

"Oh, no. Much more than that," Rao said. "Watch."

Rao engaged the tablet again, and the image on the monitor turned toward the ceiling tiles, then rocketed for one of them. The camera looked like it was going to crash into the ceiling, but instead, it stopped abruptly. The image on the monitor turned upside down, and now Rao, Pearce, and Udi were on the monitor far below. Within a second, however, the image righted itself and enlarged to full frame on the monitor.

"Now let's have some fun." Rao punched another button, and the lights shut off. The room was pitch-black, but a new infrared image appeared on the video monitor. Blue wire-mesh overlays—facial recognition software—instantly engaged, scanning all three faces. In less than a second, the blue lines flashed red.

"Apparently none of us is Aquiles Castillo," Dr. Rao said. "If one of us had been, the appropriate facial image would have flashed green."

"Impressive," Pearce said.

Rao pressed another virtual button on her tablet. The lights snapped back on and the monitor displayed a swift, uneven flight back toward the black box. The onboard camera hovered just an inch above it for a moment. Five more miniature mosquito drones were parked in the box. Rao tapped one last button and the camera eye landed on the black foam padding inside the box, the last image displayed before the monitor shut off.

Udi and Pearce exchanged a glance.

"Amazing. But they look very fragile," Udi said.

"Open your hand, please," Rao said. She picked up one of the mosquito drones between her elegant fingers and dropped it into Udi's broad open palm.

"I can hardly feel it," Udi said. He raised and lowered his open hand like a measuring scale. "In fact, I really can't feel it at all." Udi brought his hand close to his face.

"It looks exactly like a little mosquito. Incredible."

Rao picked up another one and handed it to Pearce. He examined it closely as well.

"They're surprisingly durable. And they're so light, our targets won't notice they're on them until it's too late," Rao said.

"What's the battery life?" Udi asked.

"Two hours maximum. But they can tap into a light fixture, a lightbulb, even the static electricity on human skin, and recharge."

"How does facial recognition work with identical twins? They share the same DNA," Pearce asked.

"Identical twins aren't truly identical. That's a misnomer. Even their fingerprints aren't the same. It's like your own face. The left side of your face is always slightly different from the right side, even though it's all the same DNA," Rao said.

"How many are we deploying?" Pearce asked.

"Six mosquito drones. Three lethals for Aquiles. They have a blue mark on the belly. The other three carry nonlethal identity chips for tracking Ulises. All six are already charged and preprogrammed with the correct facial target recognition."

"Why six bugs? Why not just two?" Udi asked as he examined his bug more closely. It really did look like a tiny aluminum mosquito with tissue-thin wings.

"Redundancy. Maybe the bad guys own a fly swatter. Who knows what you may encounter. Besides, we're not paying for them." Rao smiled. "Any other questions?"

"Range? Limitations?" Pearce asked.

"In a windless environment, a two-hour charge will get you a half mile maximum, flying straight. Any kind of wind resistance drops that considerably, as does maneuvering around objects. Windspeed above five miles per hour will be extremely problematic, even prohibitive. These drones are really designed for close indoor operations. They operate independently, day or night." She held up the tablet. "Use this to activate them or make programming changes, but otherwise, you don't need it for flight controls unless you want to. Their Achilles' heel, obviously, is that you have to have some sort of a delivery system that can deposit them safely within the operating environment."

"I've got a delivery system in mind." Pearce pointed at Udi. "Him."

Cabo San Lucas, Mexico

Two days later, two gorgeous women in bikinis rocketed across the deep blue water of the Gulf of California in a sparkling white ski boat. It was a perfect day in paradise beneath a brilliant, cloudless sky. The occasional gull swooped overhead.

Stella Kang drove the boat, towing Tamar Stern on a single high-performance water ski. The inboard engine whined like a jet turbine. The boat ran so fast that Tamar threw a ten-foot-tall rooster tail behind her.

Their circuit took them directly past a number of luxury yachts anchored in a three-mile-long line of privilege in the waters off of Cabo, including the Castillo boat, which was parked at the farthest end, some distance away from the others.

The first time around, the girls drew quite a bit of attention to themselves. Stella was a stunning Korean-American woman. Her thick black hair whipped behind her like a battle flag. Tamar was half Ashkenazi and half Ethiopian, with piercing green eyes and short-cropped hair. The two women were attractive enough to draw attention to themselves, but nobody in Cabo had ever seen anyone fly as fast as Tamar did on her ski.

On the second pass, all hands were on deck on the yachts. The men whooped and hollered, raised their glasses and bottles, whistled and cheered. A few boats even blew their big horns as the two laughing women rocketed past. The two skiers waved and smiled at their admirers. Even the party girls on the big yachts cheered, in awe of the show that Stella and Tamar were putting on.

A half mile away, Udi and Pearce kept discreet watch from a fishing boat they'd rented. They pretended to be sport fishing mako sharks, which were running hot this time of year, but their eyes were fixed on the surveillance gear they'd rigged to keep tabs on both the Castillos and the two women on their team. A couple of big rods and reels were rammed into their holders in the back of the boat, and thick steel shark lines trailed in the water behind them. Pearce sat strapped in the fighting chair holding another rod, the butt end jammed into the gimbal between his feet. Udi was in the cabin, the boat cruising slowly on autopilot. Pearce chummed the water behind the slow-moving boat every now and then, mostly to keep a half dozen gulls circling overhead.

"Your wife can really ski, Udi."

"Base jumping, parasailing. She does it all. Well, except cook."

"Next pass, Udi."

"Roger that."

Stella brought the ski boat around for another run. The big inboard engine whined even louder as she pushed the needle on the tach into the red zone. Tamar leaned deep into the curves she was cutting in broad swathes through the ocean. They pushed past the Castillo yacht and out into the blue water, getting ready for another turn.

Suddenly, the ski boat's inboard motor sputtered, then cut out, and the high-pitched whine disappeared. The silence was startling.

The ski boat's bow had ridden high like a haughty stallion when the engine roared; now it sagged into the water, spent. Tamar had tossed the rope aside as soon as the engine died. She glided to a graceful halt until she gently sank into the water near the ski boat. Voices echoed on the water, some cheering, some booing. The Castillo boat was nearest, but it was at least a quarter mile away. A gull wheeled in the sunlight above it.

Tamar grabbed hold of her ski and paddled to the back of the ski boat where Stella helped her up onto the skier's platform. Stella took the ski and stowed it as Tamar climbed all the way in. They flashed a lot of skin in the process.

More cheering erupted from the Castillo yacht.

The two gorgeous women stood in front of the engine compartment, feigning confusion.

Udi watched the Castillo boat. Nobody was racing out to rescue the damsels. "What's taking them so long?"

"Maybe chivalry is dead. You ready?"

"Yeah." Udi had slid into the cabin and was working a joystick. A video display was in front of him.

"There," Pearce said, without pointing.

A small rubber launch with an outdoor motor pushed off from the near side of the Castillo yacht and buzzed toward the two stranded women. Pearce lifted a pair of civilian-grade field glasses.

"Two of them. Mexicans."

"You were expecting Italians?" Udi asked.

"You're up, wisenheimer."

Pearce watched the motor launch approach the stranded ski boat. They tossed a line over and Stella caught it and secured it to one of the davits. Pearce could hear the men in his earpiece ask in Spanish what was wrong. Stella pretended to not speak any Spanish, though she was more fluent than Pearce was. The two Mexicans were just deckhands from the Castillo boat, not the Castillos themselves, thankfully. No telling what stunt the twins would have tried to pull on two vulnerable women in a

boat on open water this far from shore. The Castillos still weren't scheduled to arrive on their yacht until tomorrow night.

Pearce swung his binoculars over to the Castillo yacht. An M40A5
bolt-action sniper rifle with a Leupold Mark 4 scope was tucked under a
piece of canvas by his feet just in case things went south. There was even
more powerful ordnance stored in the cabin if things went *really* south.
He watched the gull circling high overhead.

Inside the cabin of their fishing boat, Udi was working the joystick
controlling the SmartBird drone, a perfect example of biomimicry. It was
designed and patterned to fly like a gull, including the long, rhythmic
beats of its wings that appeared perfectly organic, so much so that it often
found itself in the company of other gulls. Pearce had purchased the
second-generation drone—smaller, faster, and even more anatomically
correct than the original—from the German manufacturer Festo a few
months earlier, but this was the first chance he'd had to deploy it in an
operation.

The SmartBird drone featured an onboard camera, of course, and the
Castillo yacht was fixed squarely in the center of Udi's video screen. Udi
maneuvered the drone in a leisurely circle, careful to keep the gull between the sun and the yacht. If anyone decided to watch the mechanical
bird, the blinding sun would keep the surveillance brief.

Pearce watched the two Mexican deckhands lift the inboard motor
cover and inspect the ski boat's dead engine. The girls giggled and
shrugged, feigning stupidity. "Academy Awards all around, ladies," Pearce
chuckled.

Stella slipped a hand behind her back and flipped Pearce the bird.

Udi gently dropped the gull drone down to thirty feet above the yacht
and released the pod containing the mosquito drones. They activated
upon release. A separate wide-screen monitor flashed all six camera images from the six minuscule machines as they made their way onto the
eighty-foot-long roof of the Castillo vessel. They were programmed for
evasion and quickly scuttled for cover under vent hoods and rails, spread-

ing out as far as possible to avoid detection. Two cameras went black when two mosquitoes—one lethal, one not—were blown into the water by a random gust of wind.

"Done," Udi called out. He pressed another button on a separate remote-control unit. "Boat's ready to go."

Pearce whispered a command to Stella. "We're done here. Fire it up."

Stella heard the command in her earpiece. She immediately stepped over to the starter button and pushed it.

The ski boat's engine roared to life, echoing like a gunshot across the water. The two Mexicans nearly jumped out of their skins. Before they could react any further, or worse, become suspicious, the two girls clapped and shouted like cheerleaders, then playfully shooed the men off of their ski boat and back onto their motor launch. As soon as Stella untied the rope on the davit, the motor launch sped away, the men all smiles and waves as Stella and Tamar smiled and waved back. Pearce finally lowered his glasses when he saw Stella and Tamar rocket away, back toward shore.

Udi stepped out of the cabin. "So far, so good, eh?"

The fishing reel in the gimbal screamed with a big strike. The quivering line bent the big rod nearly in half.

"Look at that! Too bad we're heading back in," Udi said.

Pearce leaped back into his fighting chair and strapped himself in.

"We've got plenty of time," Pearce grunted as he began reeling up the steel line. "Grab yourself a beer and keep the boat steady."

Udi shook his head, laughing. "Sure thing. You're the boss."

"Yup. And rank hath its privileges."

Castillo Yacht, Cabo San Lucas

Thirty-six hours later, the crew heard the girl scream.

The hot little blonde from Baylor University in Waco, Texas, had been studying Spanish for a year in Mexico on her daddy's dime.

Though a gifted language student, she was at a loss for words at the moment, moaning like a porn star with Aquiles on top of her, thrusting like a bull. Her eyes were tightly shut in anticipation of her own ferocious climax when she heard Aquiles howl. She felt something warm and wet splash onto her face, and her eyes snapped open.

Aquiles's face was twisted in a silent scream. Blood cascaded from his mouth and nose. She watched the last flicker of light leave his panicked eyes just as he collapsed, trapping her beneath his heavy corpse in a puddle of sticky hot blood.

And that's how the crew found her, half crazed and keening.

JUNE

18

Isla Paraíso, Mexico

César Castillo sat with a glass of Cuban rum in one hand, his third so far. His grieving, red-rimmed eyes stared at nothing in particular.

Ulises sat next to him, pensive. He wasn't drinking, though. He suffered the loss that only a twin can feel, a psychic ache, like a throbbing phantom limb. A thought woke him out of his stupor.

"It's genetic, isn't it?" Ulises asked. "A genetic defect?"

His father shrugged. "How should I know? I'm not a doctor." He slurred a little.

"I should get an MRI. They can find aneurysms with an MRI, I think."

"Go ahead. But you might find out you have a ticking time bomb in here." César poked his son's forehead. "Knowing that could drive you crazy."

"Maybe there's a treatment. Pills or something."

A knock on the door.

"Come," César ordered.

Ali entered the room. He carried a large manila envelope, unmarked.

"What do you want, Arab?" César asked. He didn't invite Ali to sit down.

"He's Persian, Father. Not Arab."

"He's not my son. He's not my blood. What do I care what he is?"

"I am your loyal servant, Señor Castillo, prepared to sacrifice myself in your service."

"Will your death bring me back my boy, Arab?"

"No, but he will greet you in heaven with kisses when he sees you have avenged his murder."

"What are you talking about, Ali? Aquiles died from an aneurysm," Ulises asked.

"Don't you think it strange that a man in Aquiles's supreme physical condition would die from something like that? He was young. You have no family history of such things. He didn't use meth or cocaine. So how can it be possible?"

"The coroner said that it is not unheard of for a young person like him to die of an aneurysm," Ulises said.

"It is not unheard of for someone to be struck by a meteor, either. But it is extremely unlikely," Ali said.

"What's your point?" César barked.

"Myers's son is killed. The *Marinas* launch an assault to capture your sons. The assault fails. Two weeks later, your son dies. Not by a bullet, not by a bomb. But he dies in a very bloody and violent way."

"Poison?" Ulises asked.

"None was detected in the autopsy," Ali said. "Though perhaps the toxin was bioengineered to escape the blood panels. The CIA is constantly developing such weapons. But I do not believe it was poison."

"The Americans?" César's face flushed with rage. "You said the Americans would never link my sons to the El Paso massacre!"

Ali sensed the crazed drunk would lunge at him at any moment. He could easily reach for the pistol in his holster and kill the older man along with his idiot son, but then his mission would fail. He needed the Castillos to live a while longer, even if it meant his own death.

"I was wrong, *jefe*. Forgive me," Ali said. He lowered his eyes as an act of contrition, fully expecting to be killed.

César's fists clenched and he began to rise, but Ulises stopped him.

"It's not his fault, Father. Aquiles and I ran the operation. Ali had nothing to do with it. We still need him, especially if the Americans are after us now."

César glowered at Ali for another moment, then his face resumed its normal color. He finally sat back down and nodded at Ali, the closest he could get to an apology. "Why are you sure it's the Americans?"

Ali opened the envelope. Removed a red lanyard with a plastic badge attached. Handed it to César.

"This arrived today."

"Who sent it?" César demanded.

"No return address or name. No note," Ali said. "But there can be no question."

César glanced at the plastic badge. It was labeled FRIDA KAHLO ARTS ACADEMY, and had the name and face of Ryan Martinez. A bullet hole puckered the badge, and dried blood smeared the photo.

"An eye for an eye, *jefe*," Ali said.

"Why not kill him?" César asked, pointing at Ulises.

"Myers is offering you a deal. A son for a son. She thinks you are stupid enough to take it," Ali said.

César's face darkened with thought. "One dead son is enough, isn't it?"

"One dead son is too many, *jefe*." Ali sighed. "And it might be a deal worth taking, if that's all there was to it . . ."

"What else is there, Arab?"

Ali pointed at Ulises. "She has twisted your son into a collar around your neck. By leaving him alive, she keeps you chained to a post, like a dog, snarling and snapping, but hurting no one. Anyone can walk by. And if the dog charges?" Ali yanked violently on his own shirt collar. "The dog gets pulled down."

Ulises's face reddened. A vein bulged in his forehead.

Ali's words had landed perfectly. He fought the urge to smile. By sending her son's identity badge to César, Myers had given Ali the perfect tool to leverage the drug lord into action.

Ulises leaped to his feet. "We'll kill some more *yanqui* bastards. Ali, let's put together a strike team. We'll hit San Diego, maybe L.A.—"

"With what? Bombs? Rockets? Machine guns? Don't be stupid. The Americans have more of those than there are stars in the sky," César snapped.

"But you can't let the Americans get away with killing Aquiles," Ulises said.

"Your son is right. The other cartels will see your inaction as a sign of weakness. It puts you and your son in even greater danger." Ali was worried now. He needed César to retaliate against the Americans immediately.

"And so what do you propose?" César asked.

Ali smiled. "You do not know the Americans like I do. They are cowards. They hide behind their machines and their body armor. If they take a few casualties, they quit and go home. You have nothing to fear by striking out at them, and much to fear from your enemies if you do not."

César crossed to the bar and refilled his glass, lost in thought. Ulises and Ali followed him with their eyes as he returned, but he didn't sit down.

"I agree with you, Ali. We must strike back, but in a way that the Americans can't respond to." César took a sip of rum. "How?"

The men racked their brains in silence for a few moments.

"By attacking them with a weapon they don't have," Ulises finally said.

"Asymmetrical warfare. Excellent," Ali said.

"Does such a weapon exist?" César asked.

"Yes, in abundance," Ulises said. He explained his idea. It was simple, doable, and lethal.

César liked it, but wasn't certain. "What do you think, Ali? You're the expert."

Ali hesitated. He wanted a more direct course of action, but he didn't dare offend the younger Castillo. Besides, it would definitely work and it might finally provoke the Americans into an all-out assault.

"It is a brilliant suggestion, *jefe.*"

Ulises beamed with pride. So did his father.

So far, so good, Ali thought.

"But I suggest one additional course of action we should take first. It will likely yield nothing, but it costs nothing, and perhaps it will be a diversion for the Americans while Ulises executes his plan."

"What needs to be done?" César asked.

Los Pinos, Mexico D.F.

Hernán Barraza paced the floor of his private office, a cell phone glued to his ear. César Castillo was on the other line. It was past midnight. The line was secure because it was Castillo's own private cell network.

"What do you expect the president to do? Invade the United States?" Hernán sweated. Castillo had never called him directly before. It was a complete breach of their security arrangement, and now he was making insane demands.

"The gringos killed my son on Mexican soil and the Mexican government has no interest in this matter?" Castillo roared on the other end of the line.

"Forgive me for saying so, but as an attorney, I don't believe you have enough proof that the Americans killed your son."

"I've explained to you the proof! But that's not the point, is it? Tell me, Barraza, what if you did have your lawyer's proof? Would your brother the president have the *huevos* to do anything about it?"

Hernán paused. There was no good answer. An attack on the United States was out of the question. Surely Castillo understood that. But doing nothing was out of the question as well. Hernán understood that perfectly. In his gut, he believed the Americans probably were behind it. "Do you have any suggestions, César?"

"Yes." Castillo detailed what he wanted the president to do for him. But Castillo didn't explain what his own course of action would be or that his Iranian security chief had concocted the scheme.

"Very well. Consider it done," Hernán said.

"When?"

"Starting tomorrow. You have my word." Hernán clicked off the phone, then opened the cell-phone case, extracting the SIM card and shredding it in his high-security shredder. He didn't want that psychopath calling him directly ever again.

He then crossed over to his desk and picked up a landline. He called his brother.

"At this hour?" the president asked. "Can't it wait?"

"I just had a call from our friend, the Farmer."

"What did he want?"

Hernán described Castillo's request.

"That's all?" the president asked. "I'll do it tomorrow."

"There is one more thing. We need the Federal Police and other drug enforcement agencies to back off of him for a while. He needs 'room to maneuver.' His words, not mine."

"Is that a good idea?"

"Yes. I have a feeling that Castillo's reach is about to exceed his grasp." Hernán grinned. "Our friend could stand a dose of humility."

The Oval Office, the White House

Dr. Strasburg was on the couch, perched in his usual spot. He held a cup and saucer in his slightly trembling hands, a symptom of the Parkinson's that he had recently developed. The cup was brimming with freshly brewed coffee, despite doctor's orders. They had been discussing Russia's recent diplomatic offensive in the Caucasus when Myers received the urgent message that a call was coming through. He nodded reassuringly at her to take it.

President Myers took her seat behind the famous desk. She picked up her phone. "Put him through, Maggie."

The receiver clicked as the call was rerouted. Myers pressed another button and put the call on speakerphone so that Strasburg could hear it as well. A familiar voice came on the line.

"Madame President. Thank you for taking my call." It was President Barraza on the other end. His tone was icy.

"I understand it is a matter of some urgency, Mr. President. By the way, Dr. Karl Strasburg is in the room with me. I hope that's not a problem."

"No. In fact, I prefer it. Dr. Strasburg is a wise man. I hope he will give us both good counsel."

"How may I be of assistance to you today?" Myers asked.

"It has come to my attention that the United States has engaged in covert military action against one of our sovereign citizens while in Mexican territorial waters. Is this true?"

Myers blanched. *How could Barraza possibly know about Pearce and his operation?*

"To whom are you referring, Mr. President?" Myers stalled for time.

"Aquiles Castillo, of course. He died of a massive hemorrhage in the brain."

"I'm sorry. Who?"

"One of the sons of César Castillo. I'm sure you're familiar with *his* name," Barraza sniffed.

"A parent's worst nightmare. I understand his grief."

"We believe that some form of covert action was taken by your government against him that caused the brain hemorrhage."

Myers glanced at Strasburg.

"That's quite an accusation, Mr. President. It seems a little far-fetched, if you don't mind my saying so," Myers said.

"Dr. Strasburg?"

"Yes, Mr. President?"

"Please remind President Myers of America's long history of 'far-fetched' covert operations. For example, the CIA's attempt to assassinate Castro with exploding poisonous cigars."

Strasburg set his coffee down. "We're all well aware of those attempts, Mr. President, along with Mr. Castro's long record of torturing and killing his political opponents. We also know that the CIA is currently prohibited by law from assassinating governmental leaders. The fact that Fidel Castro is alive and well suggests that the CIA's capabilities in that area were never terribly effective anyway, wouldn't you agree?"

"Madame President, let me ask you directly. Did you authorize a covert mission to kill Aquiles Castillo?"

"No. And I resent the fact that you would even consider me capable of such action."

"Then perhaps the CIA has a rogue operative, or there are other elements at work in your government that you are not aware of. Since you are not able to take responsibility for this crime, then I must. I am informing you that Mexico will take whatever action is necessary to prevent further incursions over our border and to protect Mexican national sovereignty. In addition to mobilizing additional troops, I am placing our military and police units on the border on high alert, and I am authorizing them to fire on any unauthorized persons found on Mexican territory or in territorial waters or airspace. Is that perfectly clear, Madame President?"

"Frankly, I'm stunned. I don't know what to say."

"Mr. President, I respectfully suggest that a summit be arranged immediately so that these matters can be discussed further," Strasburg said. "May we instruct Ambassador Romero to contact your Foreign Office and begin to make arrangements?"

There was silence on the line for a moment. "You may instruct him to do so, but I have no interest in anything less than a frank and substantive discussion of the matter."

"I would expect nothing less from either party," Myers said. "We'll see to the arrangements."

"Until the summit concludes, the new heightened security measures will remain in place. Good day to you both." Barraza hung up.

Myers stared at Strasburg. "What was that all about?"

"He's afraid."

"Of whom? Us?"

"More likely Castillo. He must have contacted Barraza."

"So they are in collusion," Myers said.

"Not necessarily. Castillo is a citizen of Mexico. It is not unreasonable for him to seek out his government's assistance regarding the death of his son."

"How many Mexican citizens can dial 911 and get President Barraza on the line?" Myers asked.

"Not many, I'll grant you. But who else could Castillo call to get protection from us?"

"That's a good sign. If Castillo's calling President Barraza for help, that means he thinks he has no way of retaliating against us, right?"

Strasburg shrugged. "That is my sincere hope, Madame President."

19

Dallas, Texas

Parkland Memorial was the hospital they rushed JFK to when he was shot and it's the hospital where they pronounced him dead. As Dallas County's public hospital, it processed over 140,000 cases through its emergency room every year—many of them indigents—making the Parkland ER one of the busiest in the nation. They handled gunshots, stab wounds, car wrecks, and heart attacks on a daily basis, but the last two weeks had been a real horror show.

The ambulance cut its sirens as it swung into the Parkland ER parking lot, screeching to a halt beneath a portico already jammed with three other trucks desperately unloading their dying patients.

The driver bolted out of his door and dashed for the rear. The EMT inside the vehicle threw the back doors open and leaped out. They grabbed the stretcher on a fast three-count and lifted it out, lowering it to the ground on the spring-loaded undercarriage. The girl on the stretcher, "Hispanic, teenage, female, no name," convulsed beneath the restraining straps like a demoniac, her tiny fists clenched against the agony raging in her skull.

A weeping older couple stumbled outside through the sliding glass doors, numb to the world when the EMTs shouted, "Coming through!" as they raced the stretcher through the doors. The ambulance driver's hip crashed into the elderly man, nearly knocking him over.

Inside the doors, a triage nurse ran over to them. "Bay three." She pointed.

"How long?" the EMT asked. "She's already coded twice."

"She's number four right now," the nurse said. She glanced down at the sweat-drenched girl, mewling like a scalded cat. "I'm sorry."

The girl on the stretcher coughed, then a geyser of vomit burst out of her cracked lips. Her contracting stomach muscles simultaneously forced an involuntary bowel movement that filled her filthy jeans with blistering diarrhea.

The driver swung the girl's head to the side and put two blue-gloved fingers into her mouth to scoop out any obstruction to her airway. But her breathing had turned into short, spasmodic gasps that sucked back the vomit into her lungs, choking her.

"She's coding again!"

The nurse ran for the portable defibrillator on the wall station, grabbed it, and dashed back to the gurney.

Too late.

She was gone.

The White House, Washington, D.C.

The DEA's Roy Jackson continued relating the bad news.

"Los Angeles, Chicago, and New York, of course, but even Omaha, Salt Lake City, Eugene, and Buffalo have seen significant spikes in the numbers of deaths—all due to overdoses of meth. The ERs and neighborhood clinics have been inundated. It has put a real strain on already scarce resources in the impoverished areas. And God only knows how many new addicts there are now."

"And all free?" Myers asked.

"It's the oldest trick in the book. Every dealer knows to give a free bump to a prospective client. They get a taste for it, then they get hooked," Madrigal said. The DEA chief had been an effective undercover agent in her early years with the agency.

"The only difference is, the free bump has turned into a full ride. Two full weeks and still counting, from what our CIs are telling us. This little stunt that Castillo has pulled must have cost him tens of millions of dollars, not counting his loss of profits," Jackson added.

"And once Castillo started handing out meth like Pez candies, the other dealers outside of the Castillo network had to do the same. You know, a price war. Only the price was zero. At that price point it's all about getting new clients or keeping current ones. I hate the son of a bitch for doing it, but you have to admire the sheer genius of it," Madrigal said.

Myers picked up the evidence bag again. Fingered its contents through the plastic. A campaign button from last year. She read it. MYERS. FOR A BRIGHTER FUTURE. She turned to Jackson, grimacing. "Every bag?"

"The ones Castillo passed out. Probably knockoffs of the original. His message is as subtle as a heart attack," Jackson said.

"Well, that's what I get for trying to send my own message to a psychopath." Myers tossed the bag back onto the table.

"He can't give free meth away forever. He'll eventually go bankrupt, or his network will turn against him. The only thing more addictive than meth is money," Jackson said.

"I want options for shutting down Castillo's whole network over here. Maybe all the other networks, too."

Madrigal sighed. *What did Myers think the law enforcement community had been trying to do for the last thirty years?* "More agents in the field," Madrigal offered. She already knew the answer.

"Tell Congress to cut some fat somewhere else and you can get them. But I wouldn't hold your breath," Myers said.

Jeffers laughed. "Good thing the vice president didn't hear you say that." Greyhill had been dispatched to a base-closing ceremony in Virginia yesterday.

"Finish the border fence. Now," Early said.

"Again, Congress. No money, no will. They've been promising to finish it for years."

"Why not just strengthen the Mexican military and police forces?" Jeffers asked. "Let them do the heavy lifting."

Donovan took that one. "It's a damn mess down there. Just recently, three Mexican army generals were arrested for drug trafficking, including the second in command at their Defense Ministry, and corrupt Federal Police murdered two of our CIA agents." Donovan shook his head. "Back in '97, the head of the INCD—their version of the DEA—was arrested for working with a couple of the cartels."

"Are you suggesting that every Mexican official is corrupt?" Jeffers asked.

"Not at all. The problem is, you can never be sure which one is—or soon will be. And it's not just Mexico. Back during the Clinton years, we tried to clean up the corruption in Guatemala. Over the years, they've had several generals and former intelligence chiefs arrested for drug trafficking. So somebody got the bright idea to build our own incorruptible version of a Guatemalan DEA—an outfit called DOAN. We spent millions on it. We handpicked the recruits, paid them good salaries, armed them, trained them—the whole nine yards. Wasn't long before we caught those guys torturing and killing the competition in order to get a leg up on their own drug trafficking operations. That's why we just shipped two hundred of our own U.S. Marines down to Guatemala to do the fighting. The bottom line is that when we arm and train anybody south of the border for antidrug operations, there's a good chance they'll eventually use that training against us. Unless you change the culture of corruption, the institutions will continue to become corrupted."

Myers frowned. "As I recall, that was a line I used in my campaign against *Washington* politics."

Donovan nodded back. "I know. I was there when you delivered it at the convention."

"What if we just stay out of the mess altogether? Let the cartels keep fighting it out among themselves down there. Eventually they'll bleed themselves to death, won't they?" Early asked.

"Perhaps, but they may well bring down the entire Mexican government in the process," Strasburg said. He'd been carefully listening to the whole conversation.

"How?" Early asked.

"The primary function of the state is to provide for common security. Cartel violence, once it escalates beyond a critical point, will cause individuals to abandon the state and resort to their own private means to find their own security. Anarchy will be the result."

"Civil war and mass migration wouldn't be far behind," Donovan speculated.

"Our primary interest in Mexico is stability. The ongoing drug wars within Mexico are destroying any hope of maintaining that stability, and the United States cannot afford to share two thousand miles of border with a failed state. Beyond the fact that Mexico is a significant trading partner, a failed Mexico would become a haven for our worst enemies, much the same way as Afghanistan, Pakistan, and Yemen have harbored al-Qaeda."

Strasburg took a sip of water. "At the risk of seeming too pedantic, I would remind those present of the history of the Peloponnesian War. Athens and Sparta were the two dominant powers in Greece, with all other lesser city-states allied with one or the other. This is analogous to the present-day situation in Mexico. The two most powerful cartels are the Castillo Syndicate and the Bravo Alliance. All of the lesser cartels have aligned themselves with one of these two organizations. Is that an accurate analysis, Mr. Jackson?"

Jackson nodded. "Quite accurate, and an appropriate analogy."

"As I recall, the end result of the Peloponnesian War was utter economic devastation and the end to the Golden Age of Greece," Myers added.

"That is correct," Strasburg said. "And exactly the scenario we're looking at if present trends continue."

"Almost all of the violence associated with the drug war, particularly the slaughter in Mexico, but to a lesser extent, also in this country, is an attempt to gain monopolistic control of the drug trade, including manufacturing in Mexico and distribution in the U.S. Bribes and corruption are part of the same pattern," Madrigal added.

"Then the best thing we can do is to pick sides, it seems to me," Myers concluded. "Pick one side and end the war. At least that would stop the violence and bring some form of stability."

The room went silent, processing the implications of that statement.

"Objections?"

"How would you accomplish that?" Donovan asked.

Myers and Early shared a look. They kept their secret weapon— Pearce—to themselves.

"Decapitate the Castillo cartel." Myers spat it out like the answer to an algebra problem. No emotion. Just fact.

"That's quite an escalation, if you don't mind my saying," Donovan said.

"It's what we did to take out the al-Qaeda leadership. It's even how we battled the Mafia in this country. If you take out the Castillo leadership, you don't have a Castillo organization," Myers countered.

"With the added bonus that the Bravos will know we took out Castillo, will know we put them in power, and will know that we can take them out, too, if they cross us," Early said.

"Just for argument's sake, under what authority would you carry this out?" Donovan asked.

"According to the Constitution, the presidency possesses sole and supreme authority to wage war against all enemies, foreign and domestic," Myers said.

"But Castillo is a criminal, not a terrorist," Donovan countered.

"What's the difference between a criminal and a terrorist? Legally?" Jeffers asked.

"All terrorists are criminals in the eyes of the law, but not all criminals are terrorists," Lancet answered. "And criminals have rights that terrorists don't."

"So what is a terrorist?" Early asked.

"That's another interesting question. International law has no set definition of terrorism, which makes sense, considering the fact that one man's terrorist is another man's freedom fighter. The U.S. Criminal Code, on the other hand, sets out a number of acts that fall under the rubric of either international or domestic terrorism, including acts that are 'dangerous to human life that are a violation of the criminal laws of the United States' and that appear to be intended 'to affect the conduct of a government by mass destruction.'"

"The 'free meth' attack perfectly fits that description in my mind," Myers said. "Who decides if 'free meth' is an act of terrorism or if these men really are terrorists?"

"You," Lancet said.

"That's convenient," Jeffers said.

Lancet continued. "You can thank the previous administration for that. The Holder DOJ issued a white paper that said, in effect, it's lawful for the United States to conduct a lethal operation outside of the United States so long as 'an informed, high-level government official' of the U.S. government has determined that the targeted individual poses an imminent threat of violent attack against the United States. 'Imminent,' of course, being broadly redefined to mean 'not necessarily in the near future,' believe it or not."

"But wasn't that white paper referring specifically to the targeted killings of American citizens abroad who were members of al-Qaeda?" Donovan asked.

"Yes, but the principle would apply even more so to foreign nationals, in my opinion, at least according to the Constitution."

"So the bottom line is, if I determine that the Castillo organization is a terrorist organization and poses an imminent threat to the health and safety of this country, I have the constitutional authority to act against them?" Myers asked.

Lancet nodded. "In terms of constitutionality, I would say yes. Congress, on the other hand, would almost definitely disagree."

"The vice president as well, I'm sure," Jeffers added.

"You're referring to the War Powers Resolution," Myers said.

"Yes, and by extension, the Authorization to Use Military Force that was passed in 2001 in response to 9/11. Congress authorized the president to deploy U.S. military forces to kill or capture members of al-Qaeda and related organizations responsible for the attack. The drone attacks and targeted killings of terrorists since then have all fallen under the AUMF. Congress hasn't given you such authorization yet for operations against the drug cartels."

"Because I haven't asked for it. Should I?"

"You could," Jeffers said. "But then they wouldn't give it to you, at least not without steep concessions. The hawks would want all of their spending increases restored, and the progressives would want their piece of the fiscal pie, too, so say good-bye to your budget freeze and the balanced budget amendment."

"So I have to fight Congress before I can fight Castillo? No, thank you," Myers said. "Besides, many legal scholars question the constitutionality of the WPR. No president from Nixon through Obama has ever agreed that the WPR has binding authority over the office. Isn't that correct, Dr. Strasburg?"

"That is correct, Madame President," Strasburg said with a smile. "Yourself included, apparently."

Jeffers nodded. "No president has ever agreed that the WPR is legally binding, but for the most part, they've all adhered to the WPR out of political expediency because Congress is the place where the defense checks get written."

"Which actually leads to another broad area of law to consider," Lancet said. "It's a question of scale. The constitutional debates surrounding the War Powers Resolution notwithstanding, the president has the unchallenged right to deploy limited force in specific situations. The point of War Powers was to keep us out of large-scale foreign wars without congressional approval, not to keep us out of all military engagements."

"So, just to be clear, if I issue an executive order declaring Castillo and his organization an imminent terrorist threat, I have at least some legal ground to stand on?" Myers asked.

"In my opinion, yes, so long as the attack complies with the four fundamental law-of-war principles."

"Which are?"

"Necessity, distinction, proportionality, and humanity—avoiding unnecessary civilian deaths. Feasibility of capture and undue risk to U.S. personnel should also be taken into consideration. That's why targeted drone strikes have been so popular. They tend to meet all of those law-of-war principles."

Myers and Early exchanged another glance. Still not the time to talk about Pearce.

"Would the ACLU agree with your analysis?" Jeffers asked.

Lancet barked out a laugh. "Hell, no! There are as many opponents to drone strikes as there are supporters, and they are on both sides of the aisle. But opinions change, don't they? Harold Koh was one of the Bush administration's harshest critics, particularly in regard to waterboarding, which he viewed as an act of torture and a violation of human rights. But when he became the legal advisor for President Obama's State Department, he suddenly became an ardent proponent of targeted killings and drone strikes."

"So splashing a little water on my face is bad, but blowing me up with a Hellfire missile is okay?" Early asked.

"Where you stand depends on where you sit, right?" Lancet said. "You know, there's actually one interesting argument about drones. Because they are unmanned weapons systems, no actual U.S. personnel are sent into combat. Some folks think that means drones aren't technically 'armed forces' and therefore War Powers doesn't apply anyway."

Donovan leaned forward on his elbows. "Aren't we missing something here? We're talking about an attack on Mexican citizens on Mexican soil. Isn't that an act of war?"

Strasburg cleared his throat. "The Mexican government might take umbrage at the assault, but I doubt they'd consider it an act of war. If they did, they would have to respond in kind." The old diplomat allowed himself a smile. "There isn't much chance of that, is there? Consider the Pakistanis. SEAL Team Six sent troops into Pakistan without either their knowledge or permission and killed Bin Laden, primarily because we couldn't trust the Pakistanis to not betray the operation or warn Bin Laden in advance. The Pakistani government was deeply offended by the Bin Laden raid and our relationship with them is still badly strained. But in the final analysis, what are they going to do about it?"

"I would think the Mexican government would be grateful to us for the elimination of the most powerful drug cartel inside their nation," Myers said.

"You'd think," Madrigal said.

"Faye, would you be kind enough to draft the executive order I've suggested?"

Lancet nodded. "Of course. I'll coordinate with Sandy. What about your Office of Legal Counsel?" She was referring to the department within the DOJ that represents the president's legal interests. That person was always an assistant attorney general.

"I need as few cooks in the kitchen as possible, at least for now. I'd consider it a favor if you could draft the documents in question personally."

"I'll also prepare a brief on the legal issues we've discussed, as well as a thorough review of all the other pertinent issues. No telling when it might come in handy."

"Like during an impeachment hearing?" Jeffers chuckled.

Myers added, "Please be sure to write it up as a national security measure. That way it can remain secret and exempt from any FOIA requests, should they arise."

"You know they will, eventually," Jeffers said.

"Good, then. I think that concludes our business for today."

That was Myers's signal that the meeting was adjourned. The other cabinet members began filing out.

"Mike, do you mind staying behind for a few minutes?"

"Not at all."

When they were finally alone, Myers said, "I need you to call Pearce."

"I don't think that's an option. He told us one job, one mission only," Early reminded her. "Besides, you don't need him. You already have the security apparatus in place and the Predators to do it with."

"You mean the Committee?" Myers was referring to the national security team responsible for helping draw up the kill list that President Obama used to personally pick the human targets for Predator strikes. She shuddered. Over a hundred people teleconferencing on a weekly basis, debating the merits of each case, like lawyers cross-examining silent defendants and then answering for them. If the answers came out wrong, the defendants were executed, courtesy of a Hellfire missile.

Myers had inherited the system from the previous administration, but after one tortuous session debating the biographies of suspected terrorists, she ceded her role on the Committee to the secretary of defense. She didn't have any qualms about selecting targets and taking them out. She just hated micromanaging, so, unlike her predecessor, she left the final selection of al-Qaeda targets to the al-Qaeda experts.

"No, Mike. Too many people involved. Too many turf battles. Too many uncoordinated bureaucratic systems trying to mesh together—army, navy, air force, CIA—each with their own SOPs. I still need this thing to be kept under wraps and I can only do that if it's done quickly, with surgical precision."

"You really do need Pearce, then."

"I do. So go get him for me."

20

Snake River, Wyoming

Pearce was up to his waist in the slow-moving river, dead drifting with a dry Yellow Sally for spotted brown salmon, when Early moseyed up behind him on shore.

"You're like a bad penny," Pearce said. He didn't bother to turn around. "Can't you see I'm busy?"

"You didn't pick up your damn phone. Twenty times you didn't pick up." Early watched Pearce make another cast. "You got an extra rig I can borrow?"

"Reception's bad around here. And, no, I don't. Not for amateurs like you, anyway."

Early glanced around. There were a few other anglers around, all within earshot. He stepped closer to the riverbank. He lowered his voice. "We need to talk."

"Can't hear you," Pearce said.

Early glanced around again. He didn't want to draw attention to himself. He waded a few feet into the water. He was wearing hiking boots, not waders.

"I'm serious, Troy. It's important."

Pearce sighed and reeled in his line. "Fine."

Without looking at Early, Pearce marched onto the shore toward his pickup truck parked a quarter mile back.

Early raced after him, his boots squishing with water. "If these boots get ruined, I'm sending you the bill."

"You do that," Pearce called over his shoulder, hiding his grin.

The two men stood over a stump. Early had a beer in his hand. Pearce cradled an ax in his two hands and was stripped to the waist. An ice chest squatted in the shade near his grandfather's cabin.

"So, are you ready to talk?" Early asked.

"Sure, if you're ready to hear a one-word answer." Pearce swung the ax, easily splitting the log on the stump. He tossed the two pieces aside and grabbed another log.

"We had some bad news."

"Yeah, I know. 'Free meth.'"

Whap! Another log split in half.

"How'd you know?" Early asked.

Pearce threw him a cutting glance.

"Of course. You still have access to the DEA mainframes."

"Uh-huh."

"As a common courtesy, you shouldn't be doing that."

"I figure I'm doing the DEA a favor. Might help motivate them to do a better job with their network security."

"Myers has another job for you," Early said. He decided he might as well get the first blow in.

"I told her and I told you, one job, one mission, that's it."

Pearce lifted the ax high over his head. His deltoids bunched. Whap! Pearce cleared the pieces away. "It was pretty damn obvious that this thing wouldn't stay contained. I don't want any part of it."

"You don't even know what the job is."

"Decapitation. Has to be."

Early flinched. He should have known Pearce had already figured things out.

"At least she's bright enough not to continue with the tit-for-tat bullshit. We both know where that winds up," Early countered. He was referring to the Vietnam War, an endless escalation up a staircase of increasing casualties. Americans never won that kind of conflict. "She made a strong case for it. And I think she's right. If I didn't, I wouldn't be here. You know that."

"Yeah. I hear she gives good speech." Pearce pulled a beer out of the ice chest and cracked it open. His torso glistened with sweat.

Early bristled. "A little respect for the boss, okay?"

"That's your problem right there, Mikey. She's not my boss. She's supposed to be a public servant, not God Almighty. I'm the taxpayer. She works for me, not the other way around."

"I checked your tax records, Troy. You haven't paid any taxes in five years. You just better damn well hope the IRS doesn't go all Occupy on your one percent ass."

Pearce shrugged. "What can I say? I've got a good accountant." He pointed at the ax with his beer bottle. "Why don't you make yourself useful?" He took a swig.

"Funny, I was going to say the same thing to you," Early said. He tossed his empty bottle into a bag and stripped off his shirt. There were a few pounds of behind-the-desk flab around his gut, but he was still in fighting shape. He snatched up the ax.

"I'm surprised you know which end to hold," Pearce chuckled.

Early placed a log on the stump, spit in his hands, and grabbed the ax handle. "I don't see what the problem is. You're still in the business of hurting people and breaking things, aren't you? I mean with your toys?" Early raised the ax high over his head and smashed it down, but he misjudged the distance and hit the log with the ax handle. A stinger jolted through both of his arms.

"Son of a—" Early dropped the ax and shook out the tingling sensation from his arms.

"Don't break my ax," Pearce said. "And, yes, I use 'toys' because I want my people to stay safe. Haven't lost a man yet." He hesitated, then added darkly, "Or a woman."

Early turned to him. "Is that what this is all about?"

"What?"

"Annie."

Pearced daggered Early with his eyes. "Don't even think about going there."

Baneh, Iran
August 24, 2005

A fertilizer warehouse squatted in the western district of the city, a converted American army Quonset hut from the '50s. Electric light glowed beneath the wooden side doors and from behind the shuttered windows. There were no other lights on in the area. There was a quarter moon that night, but no street lamps. At least none that worked. The small regional capital of seventy thousand people was just across the border from Iraq.

Troy, Mike, and Annie had worked their way to the warehouse by foot after traveling overland from Iraq in a battered 1979 Toyota Land Cruiser, a common vehicle in these parts. They dressed like civilian day laborers but wore soft Kevlar vests beneath their cotton shirts. Annie wore a keffiyeh to hide her face and hair.

Annie peeked through a gap in the warehouse window shutter while Troy and Mike stood guard. She counted seven stolen 155mm artillery shells, huge and lethal, lined up along the far wall. One of the American-made shells was lying on a table like a surgical patient surrounded by three Quds Force technicians. They were connecting wires to detonators and a remote control.

The only locals on the street were a couple of wild dogs feeding on a bag of garbage lying in the gutter, too famished to pay attention to strangers.

Annie flashed hand signals. Mike gently tried the handle on a side door. He signaled with a nod that it was unlocked. Troy pulled out two flash bangs, and Annie slid her short-stock MP5 9mm submachine gun into firing position. She knew it was better to not fire her weapon if at all possible. Just one of those 155mm shells was powerful enough to flatten the entire block.

Troy nodded to Mike, who cracked the door open just enough for Troy to toss in the two flash bangs. Mike shut the door. The charges cracked sharply on the concrete floor in the large open room—perfect for flash bangs. Nowhere to hide when they went off.

Troy dashed in first in a low crouch, a suppressed 9mm Glock in his hand. Mike followed in right behind him, pistol drawn, while Annie stayed put, scanning the perimeter behind them. She watched the dogs skitter away, frightened by the flash bangs. When she was certain it was all clear, she made her way inside the building.

Annie turned the corner into the doorway just in time to see Mike and Troy popping caps into the heads of two unconscious men slumped on the floor. The three bomb makers were the actual targets; they were far more lethal than the ordnance in the room.

"Clock's ticking," Annie said. Her voice distorted by a slight electronic buzz in the microphone.

"I'm killing as fast as I can," Troy said as he put a slug into the temple of the last technician. They all agreed it would have been better to bring at least one back for interrogation, but there was no way they could pull off an extraction with such limited resources.

"Wish there'd been ten more of 'em," Mike said.

Annie pointed at the detonators, r/c units, timers, and motherboards on the table. "Grab those. Evidence."

"Roger that," Mike replied. He opened up his rucksack and started loading them in.

Troy scooted over to the far wall where the artillery shells were lined up. He slapped a wad of C4 onto three of them, then ran wires to a digital timer and set it. By blowing the ordnance, it would appear as if the Iranian technicians had accidentally killed themselves.

"Three minutes," he said.

Annie stepped back over to the door and sighted her weapon in the direction they'd come in from. Early scooped up the last detonators and remote-control units.

"Damn it!" Annie shouted.

Troy whipped around just in time to see a hand grenade bounce onto the concrete floor. It was halfway between her and Mike. Troy was still on the other side of the room.

Like in every bad war movie Troy had ever seen, time slowed to a near crawl. It was the adrenaline kicking in, heightening his senses.

Annie glanced up at him. Her bright eyes locked with his for an eternity.

For a second.

She smiled.

And then she whispered, "It was a ring."

The ring that was still in Troy's pocket.

Before Troy could react, Annie took three slow bounding steps toward the grenade.

Troy shouted for her to stop. Bullets shattered the door and spanged on the sheet-metal wall curving above his head.

Annie leaped onto the hand grenade. A muffled thump. Her body bounced a few inches into the air.

Troy's senses recovered. The shit was hitting the fan in real time now.

He raced over to Annie. A Quds soldier stepped into the doorway, an AK-47 sloped in Mike's direction. Troy raised his pistol and shot the man in the throat, just below his scraggly beard. The AK-47 clattered to the floor. The fighter crumpled to his knees, grasping at his neck, choking on his own blood.

Troy grabbed Annie's corpse by the collar, pulling her behind him toward the rear door. The toes of her Reeboks dragged through her own blood on the floor.

Mike shouldered his loaded rucksack and followed Troy. Troy didn't even try the exit door; he just smashed a size-fourteen foot against the wood and the door broke off of its frame. He dragged Annie's limp body outside just around the corner, scanning for trouble. He whispered, "Clear," and Mike bolted out into the street as Troy lifted Annie onto his back in a fireman's carry and followed him. They ducked into the shadows of an alley two blocks away and turned a corner just as the C4 ripped. The artillery shells roared. The earth shivered beneath their feet as the sky lit up like a sunrise. Neither man stopped to look back. Both shared the same desperate thought as they raced down the alleyway.

Time to get Annie home.

Snake River, Wyoming

"Annie was a soldier and a good one. She knew what she was getting into when she signed on. We all did. She had a job to do, and she did it."

"Shut your piehole, Mikey."

"She paid the price. It could've been us. *Should* have been us. I get that, believe me. I think about it every damn day."

Pearce got in Early's face.

"She laid it all down all right, but for what? So that a shit-faced senator can dodge an awkward question at a cocktail party? You know those pukes. The Ivy Leaguers call all the shots for guys like us, but less than one half of one percent of them ever swear the oath themselves. We're the ones who do the bleeding and the dying out in the boonies while they're doing reach-arounds in the clubhouse sauna. To hell with them. I'll take their money, but I won't bleed for them anymore, and I won't let my people die for them, either."

"That's why we need you. We don't want anyone to get hurt, not on our side, at least. Take the job. Besides, it'll make you filthy rich, I promise."

"I already am filthy rich. And the nice thing about being rich is that you don't have to do anything you don't want to do. And by the way, nobody ever got killed for saying no."

Pearce grabbed another beer. "You need to get out of this thing, Mikey. It's going to go south in a hurry. She's going to march your ass straight into a shooting war and a lot of people are going to die on both sides."

"That's exactly why I can't leave. I've got to do what I can. I don't want another American soldier to die in a war we don't have to fight. Besides, I swore an oath to protect and defend the nation. So did you."

"I didn't break my oath. They did."

"Bullshit. You walked away. I can't make politicians or bureaucrats or the ring knockers do the right thing, but I sure as hell can stand up like a man and do my job. Myers is right. The nation is under assault. You want to keep us out of a shooting war? So does she. The only difference is, you're the only one who can prevent one by doing what you do best. Now. Before it's too late."

"It's not that simple," Pearce said.

"Sure it is. You're hiding behind a bad memory. You loved her. She died. I get it. But ask yourself this. What would Annie do if she were you?"

Early tossed the ax aside, grabbed up his shirt, and yanked it on.

"Where are you going, muffin top?" Pearce asked.

"Plane to catch." Early stormed toward his government car.

"Hold on," Pearce called out.

Early whipped around. "What?"

Pearce opened his mouth to speak, but nothing came out. He still had Annie's voice in his head. Knew exactly what she'd say to him.

Still had her ring, too.

"Say again?" Early asked.

Pearce snapped out of his fog.

"Wait up. I'll grab my stuff."

21

CIA Headquarters, Langley, Virginia
November 28, 2005

Pearce stood as cold and lifeless as the Vermont marble wall in the lobby. The ceremony was over. Everyone else had left. Even Early. The newest star had been carved into the Memorial Wall.

Annie's.

No name, of course. None of them had names. But even in the black leather book sealed under glass attached to the wall there was only a gold star by her number. Her name would be kept secret forever. Killed on a mission she shouldn't have been on. Killed in a country she wasn't supposed to be in. Killed because some political fucks were playing their political fuck games instead of fighting the real goddamn war.

So Annie stepped up. Hell, they all did. But Annie was the one who laid it all down. Now she was a nameless star. One among many. There'd be more.

Pearce's vacant eyes scanned the inscription in gold block letters again.

IN HONOR OF THOSE MEMBERS OF THE CENTRAL INTELLIGENCE AGENCY WHO GAVE THEIR LIVES IN THE SERVICE OF THEIR COUNTRY.

That was Annie all right.

Pearce had resigned a month ago. The deputy DCI had personally asked him to take a sabbatical, think it over. He was too important to the war effort to quit. Needed him to lead a team into Syria right away. The best we have.

The country needs you.

Pearce turned him down. Mumbled something about how he loved his country, hated politics. Should've said "politicians," too. Maybe he did.

The deputy said he understood. Had the decency to include Pearce in Annie's memorial. Early was there. So were her parents.

Annie was a spook to the end. Kept her secrets. Hadn't told her folks about Pearce so he hadn't been invited to her funeral. It was just as well. He'd stood beside too many graves already.

Pearce left. Stepped out into the cold Virginia sunshine and didn't look back.

Coronado, California

Pearce lived in a high-rise condo on the beach, not a hand grenade's throw from the famed Naval Amphibious Base, home to the West Coast Navy SEALs, among other commands. There was nothing like watching a Pacific sunset from his penthouse balcony, but he also enjoyed rooting for the soaking wet BUD/S trainees pounding the sand in front of his building, hauling a three-hundred-pound Zodiac over their shaved heads into the freezing surf.

The CIA's Secret Activities Division (SAD) recruited heavily from among the SEAL teams for its paramilitary Special Operations Group (SOG), to which Pearce had belonged. *And not the other way around,* he'd remind his squid friends with a nudge. In the special forces community, SOG was considered the elite of the elite. Pearce had been one of the few SOG members recruited directly from civilian life straight out of grad school. Still, some of his best friends from his SOG days had been former frogmen and he felt a deep kinship with anybody wearing the fearsome SEAL trident.

Pearce wasn't on his balcony tonight. Instead, he was in his media room on a video conference call with his team. Early was still in Washington with Jackson, while the rest of Pearce's team was already in position around their various targets in Mexico.

Early had developed the target list with Jackson's help. The DEA had kept close tabs on the Castillo organization's leadership for years.

"When you said decapitation, you weren't fooling around. This is almost genetic cleansing," Early told Jackson as he reviewed the list. Nearly every name on the list was related to César Castillo.

"Castillo's a bad seed. We're just weeding out the garden," Jackson said. "Castillo puts a lot of faith in blood relations. He doesn't trust outsiders much. He's the one who's condemned his family to be blotted out, not us."

With the list of targets in hand, DAS had gone to work two weeks earlier, sifting through terabytes of information sucked out of public and restricted databases. People are creatures of habit, and DAS exploited that human frailty to the maximum. DAS established travel patterns, identified the most frequented locations, and tagged the regularly used vehicles of the fourteen targets through data provided by Mexican city, traffic, and surveillance cameras; local and national air-traffic-control flight data; and even cell tower usage.

Pearce decided to divide his team into five operational groups. Three groups were responsible for four targets each, and those targets were sorted by geographic proximity. The three lieutenants directly under César Castillo were his three brothers—Napoleon, Alejandro, and Julio—and each of them had three lieutenants within their suborganizations. Napoleon's organization was based in Chihuahua, Alejandro's in Nogales, and Julio's in Tijuana.

The fourth operational group was tasked with monitoring Ulises Castillo while he sojourned in Venezuela. He was the thirteenth target. They did not have permission to engage that target unless he crossed into international waters or returned to Mexican territory. In Pearce's opinion,

Myers was being too cautious, but she didn't want to provoke the new Venezuelan president unnecessarily. He was already a staunch opponent of American interests in the region and was looking for any excuse to escalate tensions.

The last operational group would be headed up by Pearce. His target was the big dog himself: César Castillo. He had special plans for the crime lord.

All five teams had already done their preliminary scouting and intel work, and had designed their assault plans. Now they were just waiting for the signal to jump.

Pearce also decided to deploy several high-altitude UAVs equipped with data-link payloads for his drone command-and-control operations rather than rent or hijack satellite bandwidth. The data-link drones not only gave him over-the-horizon capabilities, they also provided a greater measure of operational safety. One of the reasons why so many air force drones had crashed over the years was because of the signal delay between control station, satellite orbit, and drone location that sometimes lasted as long as four seconds. A fatal flaw when trying to fly and fire a precision instrument. He also wanted to create as small a digital footprint as possible in order to keep the entire mission off the record.

The most difficult task that Pearce's operation faced had been to find a relatively narrow window in which to carry out the entire operation. Once the first bodies dropped, the others would likely hear about it quickly and quail. With every target located and identified, it was vital that they all be taken down within twenty-four hours of one another, if not sooner. That window of opportunity had just been identified twenty minutes ago.

"Everybody has been briefed on their mission parameters, Mike, and they're in position. We're good to go," Pearce said.

"Then light it up," Early said. "And good hunting."

22

Barranca del Cobre, Mexico

The ancient hacienda clung to the side of the steep cliff like a barnacle on the hull of a stranded ship. Originally built by a Swiss copper magnate in 1883, the stone-and-wood mansion was built to maximize the spectacular views afforded by Copper Canyon, which was actually a complex of twenty canyons carved out of the high rock by six broad rivers. This made Copper Canyon seven times larger than its more famous cousin in the north, the Grand Canyon. It was the perfect place to hide.

The hacienda was now occupied by Napoleon Castillo, César's older brother. He'd wanted to escape the sweltering summer heat of the lavish Mid-century Modern home he'd built in the desert outside of Chihuahua. Even with the home's two luxury pools and Trane air-conditioning system, it was too unbearable to live there this time of year. So he had made the annual trek up north to his "eagle's nest" on the side of the mountain.

Normally at this time of day, the short and stocky man, who shared the same anatomical shape as his infamous younger brother, would have been standing outside on the veranda smoking an excellent cigar. Had Napoleon been outside, he might have accidentally caught the glint of sunlight on a wing high above the canyon floor. It's doubtful, however, that he would have accurately identified it as a Heron, an Israeli-manufactured, medium-altitude, long-endurance drone similar in capabilities to the more famous U.S.-manufactured Predator. The Heron contained a standard video optical surveillance package, but it had also been equipped with forward-looking infrared radar and ELINT (electronic intelligence) packages. But Pearce Systems had modified the surveillance drone, weaponizing it with two hard points on the wings for missile racks.

The Heron gave Stella Kang both eyes and ears on the ground and in the house. Phone intercepts of Castillo's brother and his physician indicated that Napoleon was sick in bed. Advance surveillance had already identified several people inside the hacienda, including Napoleon's young American-born wife, Suzanna, and his three American "anchor babies," his preteen daughters Luisa, Carlita, and Victoria. Earlier, Stella had counted only two guards on the estate, but right now one was at the pharmacy and the other was in town, drinking.

Stella's explicit orders from Pearce were to limit the strike to Napoleon only. With the drug lord hunkered down beneath his bedsheets with a fever, a missile strike was out of the question. Stella's partner, Johnny Paloma, was a former LAPD SWAT team leader. He had parked himself behind a McMillan Tac-50 sniper rifle, but now that wasn't an option, either. Time also wasn't Stella's friend. The other strike teams were already in motion and she desperately wanted to be the first team with a kill.

Stella fell on her backup plan and redeployed Johnny. Minutes later, he was ripping around the curving single-lane mountain road on a Yamaha YZ450F bike. When he reached the hacienda, he slowed down enough to reach into his backpack and toss the ten-pound surveillance drone onto the pavement, then he gunned the engine and raced away.

The iRobot 110 FirstLook drone was about the size and shape of an old encyclopedia, and was outfitted with tracks instead of wheels, along with cameras on both ends. It didn't matter which way it landed when you tossed it because it could roll in both directions, and it had rotator arms that could right it without much difficulty if it flipped onto its back.

Stella was two miles away at her laptop control station. She was a very patient and stealthy operator, but the Heron overhead showed her the coast was clear. The drone scurried toward an open gate in the back and paused while Stella checked for an entry point. She found it. One of the sliding glass doors had been left open.

Once inside the house, the robot rolled along almost silently on the pink terrazzo tiles that covered all of the floors. It even climbed the stair-case with relative ease. One of the cleaning staff, Rosa, saw it scrambling silently down the hallway. She laughed to herself, assuming it was some new toy that belonged to one of the girls. She didn't watch it long enough to observe it duck into the master suite and take up position in Napo-leon's private bathroom.

Napoleon Castillo didn't notice the drone when he came stumbling in. The iRobot was parked just behind the toilet when he pulled down his pajama trousers and lowered his flabby, sweating buttocks onto the cool porcelain seat. He was so preoccupied lighting a cigarette that he barely noticed the tracked drone when it rolled out from behind the toilet and parked itself between his feet.

Castillo didn't hear the explosion.

His brain barely perceived the blinding flash, and that for only an in-stant. He was dead before the slower-moving sound waves could strike his eardrum and stimulate the aural nerve. In fact, his entire brain case, in-cluding the aural nerve, had been splattered like an overripe melon against the bathroom wall tiles, which were also a lustrous pink terrazzo.

But far down the hallway in another room, Rosa heard the explosion. To her, it sounded more like a thump. She shrugged and figured if there was a mess to clean up, Mr. Castillo would call her soon enough.

"Target down," Stella reported to Pearce.

"Proceed to your exfiltration route, Stella. Tell your team they won the case of beer. You were first on the board."

"Thank you, sir. Will do. We're moving and grooving."

"Roger that."

Nogales, Mexico

ICE had discovered several smuggling tunnels leading from Mexico to the United States over the past few years by employing sophisticated ground-penetrating radar. The earlier tunnels they had uncovered were relatively shallow and crudely dug by unemployed local miners who carved small niches into the rock every hundred yards or so. The niches were crowded with plastic saints, melted candles, and strips of paper with prayers for protection for both the miners and the travelers, mostly smuggled migrants.

The more recent tunnels were somewhat deeper and more sophisticated by an order of magnitude, displaying a level of engineering prowess beyond the reach of day laborers. Sheer walls, wooden floors, and a lighting system were standard. It was unclear to ICE who had designed or built the tunnels, but they were definitely paid for by the Castillo Syndicate for running drugs and people under the heavily secured surface above. They were probably four to five times as expensive to construct as well.

What the ICE teams hadn't figured out yet was that at least half of the shallow tunnels were meant to be found in order to absorb ICE's scarce investigative resources, while the deeper tunnels continued sluicing major profits back to the syndicate. These latter tunnels were highly sophisticated cement structures, designed and built by a Chinese engineering firm specializing in military construction projects for the People's Liberation Army. One even contained a small rail-car system.

The most important smuggling tunnel in the network was also linked to an underground meth lab, as well as to sleeping quarters and offices for Alejandro Castillo and his lieutenants. Pearce and his team had found it almost by accident. Ian had intercepted a U.S. Army Corps of Engineers geological survey recently conducted in the area that speculated about the existence of a new smuggling tunnel network. The report hadn't made its way up the chain of command yet, let alone into the interagency data stream.

August Mann was in charge of this operation. He based his plan to take out the tunnel complex on a similar job he'd carried out in Ukraine last year before taking on the Dungeness project. He even flew in the same group of subcontractors he'd used to pull it off. Twenty-four hours earlier, his intel team had flown a miniature 3-D mapping camera drone through the underground maze that had generated a perfect image of the tunnel complex. Two hours ago, the same drone cameras had located and identified the tunnel occupants, all of whom carried weapons. That made all of them fair game.

August stationed an insertion team at the tunnel exit on the American side, and an insertion team at the tunnel entrance on the Mexican side. The American exit was located inside of a Castillo-owned tire warehouse; the Mexican entrance was located inside of a blue stucco Assemblies of God church, also owned by the Castillo organization. Both ends of the tunnel were lightly guarded by a few armed men stationed aboveground.

When the six tunnel occupants had bedded down for the night, August signaled both teams to take out the tunnel guards. August didn't want the robots to have all of the fun. He let his human team members drop the tunnel guards with suppressed rifle fire.

After cutting all of the power down in the hole, each insertion team lowered two Talon SWORDS tracked robots into their respective entrances. The large suitcase-portable tracked vehicles were loaded out with similar packages. In addition to video optics, two of the tracks were mounted with 6mm grenade launchers and 5.56mm semiauto rifles; the other two tracks were outfitted with breaching devices and smoke delivery systems.

One of both types of drone was dropped in each entrance, along with signal relay boosters to ensure continuous video feeds and radio-control operation of the Talons from the surface.

August watched the green, ghostly night-vision images of the chaos wrought by the robots with scientific detachment. Groggy, blinded in the dark, and choking on smoke, the defenders shot wildly at the mechanical sounds they heard in the lightless void, but within minutes, the first five targets had been gunned down or shredded with grenade fragments.

The lone survivor, Alejandro Castillo, had miraculously escaped into an office space and bolted the heavy wooden door. It took August another ten minutes to breach it. The Talon SWORDS had been used extensively in bomb disposal and bunker-breaching missions during the Iraq and Afghanistan conflicts. A simple wooden door was no match. The SWORDS blew off its hinges, revealing Alejandro cowering in the dark. Thirty rounds of steel-jacketed ammo broke his torso open like a crab hammer.

"*Sehr gut,* August," Pearce whispered in the German's earpiece.

"*Danke.*" August switched channels and barked orders to his team. They had to pull those units out and evacuate the area before the *federales* showed up, which Mann estimated would be in fifteen minutes.

They left behind a timed demolition charge that collapsed the entire tunnel structure minutes after they egressed. Forty-five minutes after the operation had begun, August, his men, and his robots were all safely back on American territory.

23

Tijuana, Mexico

A black Cadillac Escalade rocketed down the parking garage ramp, skid plates throwing sparks as it banged over a speed bump.

"There!" Julio Castillo screamed as he pointed at the exit turn.

The driver threw himself into the sharp left-hand turn, slamming his chest against the shoulder belt with the centrifugal pull. The big SUV tires shrieked on the slick concrete floors of the empty parking garage, still under construction.

A hundred feet behind them, a Schiebel S-100 helicopter fitted with the GTMax artificial intelligence "learn as you fly" autopiloting package and a six-barreled 7.62mm Minigun raced after them. The three-foot-tall German-manufactured helicopter had already chased them off the highway into the parking structure. Julio couldn't believe the helicopter would follow them into such a cramped space. They'd dodged scissor lifts and stacked pallets on every level up, and still it followed. The top of the ramp was blocked, so they had to whip around and head back down. The helicopter had just fired its first short burst and missed, blowing chunks of concrete out of the wall in front of the SUV on the last turn.

Julio glanced back to see that the unmanned helicopter had missed the last turn and was racing past their position. His face was drenched in sweat, but not from the sweltering heat outside.

The driver turned hard again. Julio banged his head against the thick bulletproof glass but he hardly noticed.

"Can't you drive any faster?" Julio screamed.

The driver said nothing but mashed the gas pedal harder. The Escalade roared down the sloping straightaway.

"Where the fuck is it now?" Julio screamed, his head on a swivel. His three lieutenants in back peered through the windows, their big pistols drawn as if they were prepared to shoot the drone down.

The Escalade bucked savagely as it crashed over another speed bump. But the big SUV was flying too fast now. The driver stomped on the brake as he whipped into the next turn. The forward momentum threw all of them against the seat belts, then the sharp left turn crashed their bodies hard into the right-side doors as the Escalade drifted toward the far wall.

BANG! The side panels crumpled and sparked as the SUV scraped against the concrete wall, but the driver soon righted the vehicle and mashed the throttle again. The exit was just a hundred meters ahead, a big black square framed in the harsh sodium lights of the parking garage.

Julio roared with delight. He pounded the driver's shoulders with both of his beefy hands. "You son of a bitch! You did it!" The men in the back laughed, too, until the helicopter dropped into the center of the exit.

"Gun it!" Julio screamed. He knew the copter would pull away before it got rammed. The driver crushed the gas pedal to the floor.

The Minigun flashed. Three hundred armor-piercing incendiary rounds poured through the windshield like liquid lead. The Escalade exploded in a ball of fire.

The helicopter rose at the last second to avoid the fiery wreck as it tumbled end over end out of the exit, finally coming to a halt in the middle of the busy street. Oncoming traffic slammed squealing brakes. Bumpers crashed, glass broke, horns honked.

The burning hulk of the Escalade continued to roar with flames, superheating the already sweltering night air as the pilotless Schiebel slipped away, its stealthy AI navigation program guiding it back to base.

Isla Paraíso, Mexico

Pearce studied his monitor. Ten thousand feet above, one of his surveillance drones drew lazy circles around the small island. César Castillo was nowhere in sight, but Pearce had seen him enter his palatial home earlier that evening. So far, so good.

On the western side of the island, two Castillo guards stretched on loungers by the pool. They were painted like slim gray ghosts in Pearce's thermal-imaging camera. The tips of their cigarettes flared to white-hot pinpoints when they inhaled. The other two guards patrolling the far side of the home were more diligent. Their skin glowed a whiter shade of gray because they were hotter from trudging steadily in the humid night air.

Pearce turned to the other two monitors at his station on the boat. They also featured thermal-imaging cameras, but targeting reticles were centered on the screens as well. These were the cameras mounted on two Spartan Scouts, small unmanned surface vehicles (USVs) stationed on either side of the island. The first Spartan monitor was barely catching the tops of the heads of the two lounging guards on the western side, but the other Spartan Scout reticle easily targeted the first of the two guards patrolling the eastern perimeter.

Pearce engaged the automatic targeting program for the eastern Spartan's weapons system, which was fitted with a suppressed M110 semiauto sniper rifle firing 7.62mm slugs. The western boat was configured exactly the same way. Both vessels were rubber pontoon platforms, like Zodiacs, with reinforced polymer decking for the gun systems. Tonight's sea was choppy, but the guns were mounted on a computerized stabilizer to neutralize the motion.

The eastern Spartan scoped on the rear guard first and dropped him effortlessly. The dead man's rifle clattered on the ground, alerting his partner, who whipped around to face his fallen comrade. A second later he was tossed backward like a rag doll by a slug that caught him high in the chest.

Suppressed weapons aren't silenced weapons; their sound is only dampened. When the guards by the pool heard the two dull shots on the far side of the estate, they leaped to their feet and scrambled into defensive positions, facing the eastern side.

Pearce engaged the western boat. The guards stood taller now and their fully exposed bodies glowed eerily on the video screen. Their heads lit up like flares as adrenaline and exertion raised their body temperature, the additional heat venting out of the tops of their scalps.

The reticle squared on the first man's glowing head just a moment before a bright-white blotch of fluid flowered on the other side of his skull. His corpse dropped silently on the monitor.

The other guard threw down his weapon and dashed in the opposite direction, heading for the western slope leading down to the water.

The Spartan's automatic rifle tracked him as he slipped and twisted down the steep incline.

Pop.

Blood exploded in white petals on the slope behind him. The reticle tracked the limp corpse as it tumbled down the hill.

It almost didn't seem fair to Pearce, despite the fact they were cartel scumbags. Even the best human snipers he'd ever worked with missed their shots sometimes. But not the machines. They never missed.

Human snipers were bounded by human frailty; the weapons systems they used were always superior to the operator using them. Hitting a target was a relatively simple algorithm with known variables: distance, friction, target speed, wind speed, projectile weight. New onboard computational systems and "smart" guided bullets were even solving those equations for human snipers. The profession was quickly becoming a "point and shoot" proposition. But human snipers contended with other variables, too: stinging sweat, the need to breathe, beating hearts, nagging doubts, sick kids back home, lack of sleep, fears. Most missed shots were caused by one or more of these all-too-human frailties.

Pearce disengaged both Spartan weapons systems as a safety precaution, then powered up his own small boat and motored toward the quay, where he tied up his craft next to Castillo's yacht.

Pearce scrambled up the winding path. There was a quarter moon out tonight and he didn't need his night-vision goggles. His pack was heavy and he sweated fiercely. When he reached the house, he ducked inside, carefully scanning for guards he might not have accounted for, but there were none. It was strange that there had only been four men protecting the head of the entire organization.

Was Castillo that confident of his defenses?

Pearce was certain that Castillo was locked away in his panic room bunker twenty feet below the estate. His security protocol would have called for him to immediately escape into the bunker if shots were ever fired.

Pearce proceeded to Castillo's lavish office with its 360-degree view of the gulf and opened up the hidden panel showing the live video feed of Castillo in his panic room bunker. The drug lord carried his favorite gun in one hand, a chromed .50 caliber Desert Eagle encrusted with rubies and diamonds. In his other hand he had a phone connected to a landline that led to a satellite dish on top of the house. Old-fashioned copper wiring was the only way to get a cell signal down in that hole.

Pearce pressed a button on the video console so he could listen in on the conversation. But whoever was on the other end never picked up. Pearce thought that was strange. Either the person on the other end of the line had been asleep on the job or else they weren't following the security protocol.

Pearce watched Castillo rant like a demon, then finally give up. The raging drug lord slammed the phone receiver so hard against the wall it broke in his hands.

Pearce checked his watch. He estimated he still had fifteen minutes before he would have to evacuate. Plenty of time.

The problem with hiring one of the world's premier architectural firms was that they designed everything on high-end CAD systems, then stored the digital blueprints on mainframes for reference on current and future projects. That was Castillo's fatal mistake. Ian had pulled up Castillo's palace blueprints in no time. It was the bunker on the property that convinced Pearce that Castillo would choose this location for his final stand.

Pearce located Castillo's small safe and opened it easily with a computerized lock pick. He pulled out all of the contents and stuffed them into a dry bag. What really caught Pearce's attention was a sandwich baggie full of SD cards, the kind used in video cameras. He couldn't wait to find out what was on them.

Pearce dashed through the house to the kitchen area. According to the blueprints, the bunker's air ducts were hidden behind the tiled walls of the villa, but an access door was located beneath the kitchen sink for duct inspections and repair. Pearce pulled on a gas mask, opened the access door, and snaked a long, thin plastic tube down into it, then he connected a small gas bottle from his utility belt to the line. After he emptied the bottle's contents, he tossed the bottle aside and shut the access door.

After stripping off his mask, he jogged back to the bunker video monitor. Castillo paced furiously, a crazed, caged animal. Pearce held up his smartphone and recorded the monitor images. Castillo's legs soon turned wobbly and he tripped, then stumbled, and finally fell to the floor, his eyes rolling into the back of his head. His arms and legs jerked wildly as his jaw clacked open and shut like a rapidly blinking eye. Seconds later, he was dead.

Satisfied, Pearce exited his phone's camera function and pocketed it.

The last item on Pearce's agenda was in the heavy rucksack he'd hauled up the hill. It contained a specially designed two-stage demolition device. He armed it and set the timer, then jogged back down to his boat.

When his boat and the two Spartans had sped out a couple of miles, he cut the engines and turned around just in time to watch the top of the island erupt with a deafening roar. A mushroom cloud of fire boiled up into the night sky, fueled by a canister of white phosphorus. It almost looked like a volcanic explosion. It lit the ocean surface for twenty miles in all directions. Pearce assumed that NORAD was going crazy right about now.

A gentle ocean breeze brushed against Pearce's face. The phosphorus smelled a little like garlic. He fired up his engines and headed home.

24

Maiquetía, Venzuela

Sandwiched between the steeply rising mountains looming behind it and the vast Caribbean sea on its doorstep, the city of Maiquetía featured a deepwater port, an unlimited coastline, and the Simón Bolívar International Airport. There was also a secured compound that protected a safe house. Ulises Castillo had been its only guest for the last week. The last surviving Castillo was under the special protection of General Agostino Ribas, the defense minister of Venezuela.

Udi and Tamar were bored to tears. They had been floating off the coast of Maiquetía on a sixty-three-foot yacht for three days. Myers had forbidden Pearce to take out Ulises on Venezuelan soil so Udi and Tamar were reduced to babysitting.

The first day the Israelis arrived was the most exciting. They went onshore and planted spider drones equipped with microphones and pinhead-size cameras for data collection on Ulises, but they had been confined to the yacht at sea ever since. The boat was also equipped with long-range laser voice detection and video surveillance systems. They even had an RQ-11 Raven, a miniature unmanned aerial vehicle (UAV) that could be launched by hand at a moment's notice. But that was their only drone. They were too far away from friendly airstrips for ground-launched operations.

When General Ribas suddenly arrived at the safe house with an armed escort, Udi and Tamar scrambled into action. Ribas entered Ulises's living quarters alone, leaving his two personal bodyguards outside the door.

Udi and Tamar tuned in to the conversation that was being recorded on video.

Ribas puffed thoughtfully on a fat cigar, clouding the small living room with blue smoke. The two men sat opposite each other on worn leather couches, separated by a glass coffee table.

"Your father and I have been friends for a long time. That is why he entrusted you to my care." Ribas leaned forward and pointed his cigar at Ulises. "You know, I held you in my arms once when you were a small baby."

"You and *Papa* ran Colombian cocaine together back in the '80s," Ulises said.

"Whores, too. We made good money."

"Still do, from what he says." Ulises smiled.

Ribas roared with laughter. "Just like your old man!" Ribas took a long, thoughtful drag on his cigar before stabbing out the butt in the ashtray on the table. "Look, I have some bad news."

Ulises frowned. "My father?"

"Yes."

"How?" Ulises demanded.

"It does not matter. I am truly sorry."

"The Americans?"

"Yes, of course. Who else could it be? They are animals." Ribas observed the ruthless young Castillo carefully.

Ulises stared at his enormous hands, emotionless. "It was inevitable, I suppose," Ulises said. "The Americans are too powerful."

"You are welcome to remain here, of course," Ribas offered.

Ulises glanced back up, smiling. "I can't kill Americans sitting here."

Ribas laughed again. "Your father would be proud."

"How soon can you get me back to Mexico?"

"How soon can you be ready?"

Ulises stood. "I'm ready now."

Ribas stood as well. "I already have a helicopter waiting for you at the airport."

"Helicopter?" Ulises knew that Mexico was too far away for a helicopter unless it had air-refueling capabilities.

"I have made arrangements for you with one of our agents in Aruba. He is making arrangements to smuggle you from there to Veracruz. We must be extremely cautious, *hijo*, if we hope to get you home alive."

Udi called Pearce with the news, hoping that the kill order would take effect when the helicopter crossed into international waters. Every other team had killed their respective targets. He and Tamar wanted their shot, too.

"Wait until they are at least one hundred kilometers out" was all Pearce said.

"You got it, boss!" Udi beamed.

Thanks to Dr. Rao and the mosquito drones, the GPS implant in Ulises's body still functioned perfectly, drawing energy from the static electricity he generated. Ulises traveled by car to Ribas's private heliport at Simón Bolívar International. Moments later, a big ugly Russian Mi-35 Hind E helicopter landed. The airport was near the water, so Udi and Tamar repositioned their yacht a quarter mile off the coast, out of the flight path of commercial aircraft. Fortunately, there weren't any Venezuelan Coast Guard patrol boats in the area so they could keep their surveillance gear up and running.

Tamar's camera recorded seven Venezuelan commandos in combat fatigues exiting the helicopter. The unit commander was a sergeant according to his insignia. He saluted Ulises, then shook his hand with a curt smile.

Ulises turned and bear-hugged Ribas, then he boarded the chopper after the commandos had loaded back in. The door slammed shut, and the rotors cycled up. The big Hind lifted off the tarmac and swung lazily toward the ocean. Ribas stood below, waving good-bye until the chopper cleared land.

Udi stood on the aft deck of the yacht and watched the helicopter roar overhead through a pair of mil-spec binoculars while Tamar kept the video camera locked on it from inside the cabin. They obviously didn't have the opportunity to place any surveillance equipment on board the military helicopter on such short notice, so they couldn't hear or see what was going on inside.

"We shouldn't follow them immediately," Udi suggested. "No point in getting too close and alerting them. We have plenty of range."

"I agree. But you'll have to drive the boat."

"Why?" Udi asked.

Tamar grinned. "Because it's my turn to shoot the Stinger." She kept the camera focused on the massive helo as it sped north out to sea. Udi started the engine and turned the yacht in the same direction as the helicopter, which had climbed to a thousand feet. A moment later, the Hind froze in space.

"Tamar—"

"I'm getting it, love," she shouted from inside. Pearce needed everything recorded to video.

Tamar watched the helicopter door slide open on the video monitor. "What are they doing?"

A couple of seconds later, Ulises's body tumbled out, falling like a bag of wet cement. Tamar followed his unmistakable corpse all the way down with the camera until it splashed. Udi focused his binoculars at the spot where Ulises's body had hit. No movement in the water.

Udi glanced back up at the helicopter. It rotated 180 degrees on a dime, then roared away back toward the airport. Tamar followed it with

her camera as it flew over the airport and then climbed over the mountains behind the city on a direct course for Caracas.

"Why?" Tamar asked.

"Why not? With his father dead, he became a liability."

"And the idiot walked right into it."

"That's why Ribas had the armed escort. Just in case he came to his
senses."

Tamar radioed in to Pearce as Udi throttled up and sped toward the
splashdown. He knew Pearce would want a DNA sample just to be sure.

JULY

25

"What do you mean Castillo's dead?"

"Castillo, his son Ulises, his three brothers. All of them." Hernán sliced his throat with his thumb.

"The Americans?"

"Who else?"

Antonio fell back into his ornately carved presidential chair, despondent. "If it weren't for César Castillo, I wouldn't be president."

The Barrazas had cut to the front of the political line with cartel muscle and money. Hernán had engineered it all. He knew that many political dynasties had been midwifed by crime syndicates. The Triads in communist China, even the Kennedys and the mob. And God only knew if the rumors about Putin and the Russian mafia were true.

Hernán shuffled over to the credenza and poured himself a whiskey. He held up the bottle and glass to his brother, a silent offer of a drink. But Antonio waved him off. Hernán shrugged and tossed back the glass, then poured himself another.

"You needed Castillo to win the office. You don't need him to keep it," Hernán said. "Now that he's gone, there will be a 'peace dividend' for you and Mexico." He tossed back his second.

"Maybe it was the Bravos who finally took him out," Antonio said. "Maybe we've been backing the wrong horse the whole time."

Hernán poured himself a third glass, then another for his brother. He picked them up and carried them to the president's desk.

"Americans? Bravos? It doesn't matter who took Castillo out. The Bravos are in control now, either way. And you are still the president of Mexico. Sounds like a natural alliance to me." He handed his brother the whiskey glass, then clinked his glass against his brother's.

"Here's to the end of the War on Drugs, and to the new peace for Mexico. *Salut.*"

"*Salut,*" Antonio said, halfheartedly. They both drank.

Antonio leaned forward. "Why do you think there will be a peace now? Won't the Bravos come after us?"

"Why should they, if we leave them alone? Accommodations can be made, just like we had with the Castillo Syndicate."

"With the Americans still breathing down our necks? We can't suddenly stop enforcing all of our drug agreements with them."

"We can put pressure on the little guys on the margins who aren't falling in line with Bravo yet. Break up a few of their shipments. The Americans won't know the difference, but Bravo will appreciate it. He won't mess with us if we don't mess with him. Still . . ." Hernán frowned with concern.

"What?"

"You might want to give Bravo something more. A token of friendship. An offering."

"Like what?"

"Cruzalta and his *Marinas* have been harassing the Bravos for a long time. Pull all of their operations off of the east coast away from Bravo territory and let them go chase Chinese smugglers along Baja. And sack Cruzalta. He needs to retire anyway. That should make Bravo happy."

"How do you know all of these things?" Antonio was genuinely curious.

"It's my job to know them. I've already set up a phone call with Victor

Bravo to see if we can work out some sort of an equitable arrangement. With your permission, of course."

"Yes, of course. As you think best." He drained his glass. "How about another round?"

Hernán nodded and picked up his brother's glass to fetch a refill, adding, "And I have one more idea."

Chichén Itzá, Mexico

Ali trudged up the steps of the Temple of Warriors. There seemed to be no end to the climb beneath the searing sky. He had read that the more famous Pyramid of Kukulkan had 365 steps cut out of the stone, one for each day of the year. But he had no idea how many steps this one had and he'd lost count. In the gross humidity of the day, it felt like it was taking a whole year to make the climb to the top. With each step he uttered silent prayers of protection to Allah against the foreign *djinn* he was certain inhabited this pagan shrine.

Ali was surrounded by a casual but nevertheless armed escort of Bravo's most loyal *sicarios*, all of them former military men—defectors, mostly, from Mexican, Guatemalan, and Salvadoran units—who had swarmed to Victor Bravo's organization a dozen years ago at the prospect of untold wealth. And they were loyal, Ali noted. In fact, more than loyal. *Devoted* to the man was more like it. Like religious disciples. Greed may have first drawn them to him, but Bravo's revolutionary charisma was what kept them bound to him. Bravo valued them highly, but they lacked actual combat experience against Western armies. The kind Ali had in spades.

Victor Bravo was a few steps above Ali, cresting the top of the temple mount first. None of the tourists or guards had to be told to stay clear of this group of terrifying men, not even the dim-witted gringos fresh off of the cruise-liner buses swarming the compound below. As a precaution, Bravo closed the temple to tourists that day.

When Ali and Bravo's men reached the top, the escort fanned out in a loose semicircle. The actual temple on top of the pyramid stood behind them. The black shade beneath its stone roof looked cool and inviting, but Ali shuddered. He imagined himself as a captured warrior standing in this very spot five hundred years ago, staring into that same temple mouth, soon to be led to slaughter on the reclining Chac-Mool idol looming in the dark like a demon from hell.

"Do you know why I brought you up here?" Victor asked. He was staring out over the compound through a pair of mirrored aviator sunglasses. Today he wore his typical uniform: black shirt, black jeans, black cowboy boots with silver tips, and a giant silver belt buckle, topped off with a blazingly white straw cowboy hat, fresh out of the box.

All in all, though, he was modestly dressed for a man of his position. Most *narcotraficantes* wasted money on the trappings of wealth—expensive clothes, jewelry, palatial homes. Not Bravo. Most of his wealth went to his people. He'd built and maintained dozens of private schools, orphanages, and health clinics all over Mexico.

Bravo had once confided to Ali that he had modeled his organization along Hezbollah lines: a military faction to fight his enemies and a humanitarian faction to win the hearts of his people, whom he genuinely cared for. It was one of the many reasons Ali had secretly allied with Bravo even when he was supposedly working for Castillo.

"No, Señor Bravo. Why have you brought me here?"

Victor wiped his long, dripping face with a handkerchief. He was mostly *indio*, shorter and darker than the Mexicans up north, with no facial hair. Ali wasn't sure how old Bravo was. Forties? Fifties? Sixties? No wrinkles in his mahogany-colored flesh or silver strands of hair betrayed his age. He wore his thick black hair long and tucked behind his ears. His melodic Spanish accent was definitely Yucatecan.

"This is the place of my people. Warriors, scientists, poets. We formed a great empire on this continent. We studied the stars, conquered our enemies, contemplated zero."

Ali understood his pride. He was the son of a great world empire, too, but one far more vast and advanced than anything the Mayans had accomplished, and a thousand years older than the one that had mysteriously vanished from the jungle surrounding them. Iran now stood on the doorstep of greatness again, thanks to its nuclear program. Only the Great Satan stood in their way.

"This place is, indeed, the seventh wonder of the world."

"You are truly a religious man, Ali?"

"I am an imperfect servant of the Most High, yes."

"Then you understand me when I say that God has given me a mission and I will fulfill it. You have a mission, too, and you have already fulfilled it by helping me get rid of Castillo and his brood of thieves."

"I am a humble soldier and I obey my orders, nothing more, *jefe*. The master does not thank the slave for doing his work." Ali had said the same thing to César, of course.

"You may be a lot of things, but you are no slave. You set up Castillo's idiot sons on the El Paso hit and you engineered his family's slaughter by the Americans. You're either a magician or a genius, but either way, you've handed me Mexico on a sliver platter."

Bravo snapped his fingers and one of his guards approached with a backpack. "Most of the surviving Castillo captains have already started calling me *jefe*," Bravo said.

"Do you trust them?" Ali asked.

"I trust their fear."

"And Barraza?"

Bravo chuckled. "I spoke with his brother last night. Are you sure you aren't a white wizard?"

Ali shook his head. "No, *jefe*. I am neither a jaguar nor a prophet. Only humble flesh and blood, like you." Ali had provided all of the ELINT security for Bravo's organization, including his encrypted cell phones. However, Ali's technicians had put backdoors on all of Bravo's equipment, so Ali was privy to all of Bravo's communications. He had listened to the conversation with Hernán just an hour ago.

Bravo reached into the backpack and pulled out a black lacquered wooden box, then opened it. There was a pistol inside, nestled in crushed blue velvet. A .45 caliber 1911 Colt semiauto. It was solid gold with a mother-of-pearl handle. He pulled it out.

Ali's eyes narrowed. Maybe today he was going to be a sacrifice after all. He calculated strike points on Bravo first, then on the nearest body-guard. If he could secure the guard's weapon—

Bravo turned the pistol in his hand and held the butt out toward Ali. He smiled. "Take it. It's yours."

Ali frowned. *Was this a trick?*

He picked up the gun. It was much heavier than an ordinary one made of steel. He clicked the magazine release. The magazine was gold-plated, too. He nicked the top bullet with his thumbnail. The bullets were solid gold, too.

"It belonged to Saddam Hussein. I won't tell you how I acquired it, or how much it cost, because it is far less valuable to me than our friendship." Bravo had taken the credit for the destruction of the Castillo Syndicate, and his reputation in the international underworld as an omnipotent force in Mexico had been sealed thanks to the Iranian's scheme.

Ali gazed at the weapon in wonder. His uncles had died as young men in the catastrophic war with Iraq thirty years ago. His whole family cheered the day the filthy Sunni dictator was hanged by his own people, and they laughed with pride when they read that he had cursed his Iraqi executioners by calling them "Persians."

And now I hold the bastard's golden gun in my hands. Ali was genuinely touched.

"I am honored and humbled by this lavish gift, Señor Bravo."

"It is offered with my gratitude for the work you have done."

"But there is still much more to be done. Your newest recruits are being trained even as we speak."

"How are they doing?"

"Very well. I have my best men preparing them. I'll be returning to the camp soon to oversee the last three weeks of their training."

"Excellent. Some of Castillo's Maras up north are still holding out. I need the new men to put them down like the crazed dogs they are. A final assault and we will consolidate our position in Mexico. Our men, your guns."

"A match made in heaven, as the Americans like to say," Ali said. "And what about Castillo's distribution network in the United States? We should take them out as soon as possible."

Bravo draped an arm around Ali's shoulder. "That is the other thing I wanted to talk to you about. This Castillo thing . . ."

"What about it?"

"His whole family wiped out. And for what? Because he killed the wrong kids. Really, just one wrong kid if we're going to be honest about it."

"What's your point, *jefe*?"

"Do you have a wife? Kids?"

"Yes. Two wives and seven sons." Ali didn't think his three daughters were worth mentioning.

Bravo laughed. "Seven sons? That's good. So you understand. I don't want anything to happen to my children. Or to me." Bravo steered him toward the temple.

"You are afraid of Myers? A woman?" Ali was incredulous. "We led her around by the nose. Why worry about a worthless one like that?"

"It's not her I'm worried about. It's her guns. Her planes without pilots. You've heard the rumors."

Ali stopped and smiled. "You do not have to be afraid of such things, my friend. I have fought the Americans and their Predator drones before. Do you know why Americans fight with their robots? It is because they are afraid to fight and die like men. That is why they would not send their soldiers in to deal with Castillo."

Ali was amazed at how much fear these Mexicans had of the effeminate Americans. First he had to bolster Castillo's courage, and now Bravo's.

Bravo shook his head. "You have a short memory, amigo. Remember the Gulf War? Remember the videos? 'Shock and awe.' The Americans destroyed Saddam's army in a few weeks. You fought the Iraqis for almost eight years and couldn't beat them. How many men did you lose?"

"A million martyrs, counting wounded."

"You see? And Hussein had only primitive Soviet equipment for you to fight against. You can't defeat the Americans, Ali. Nobody can. Their technology is too good."

"The Taliban have a saying. 'The Americans have the watches, we have the time.' It has been over eleven years since the Americans invaded Afghanistan. The infidels have their aircraft carriers and supersonic fighters, while the poor Taliban fighters have only their rifles and their guts. The Americans are quitting Afghanistan just like the Russians did, and the Taliban remain. The Great Satan has the will to kill, but not to fight."

"But the Americans defeated Hussein. He had thousands of tanks and hundreds of thousands of soldiers."

"They only defeated Saddam because he was stupid. He left his tanks and his men in the desert for weeks and let the Americans bomb them continuously. Many strategic and tactical mistakes were made by that Ba'athist fool, and the Americans exploited those mistakes to the fullest. Do you not see? The Americans could never have fought an all-out war with Iraq for eight years, but we did. Do not let Myers's actions convince you she is strong when, in fact, she is acting from a position of weakness. She uses drones because she is afraid to fight another real war with soldiers. That should tell you everything you need to know about the Americans."

The ambient air temperature dropped as they entered the cool of the temple.

"Much better in here, isn't it?" Victor asked. He pulled off his sunglasses. So did Ali.

"Yes." Ali's eyes adjusted to the dark. He saw the reclining stone image of the Chac-Mool lounging in the shadows. The idol's lifeless eyes chilled him to the bone.

"What happened to the Mayans, Ali? Do you know?"

"No."

Victor rubbed his hairless chin. "Nobody knows for certain. The best guess is that the ancient Mayans did it to themselves. Perhaps they grew too fast? Or reached too far? Maybe they fought one enemy too many. It doesn't really matter. What matters is that they are gone."

"And that is the real reason why you brought me out here."

Victor laughed. "That obvious, eh? Well, you are right. With Castillo out of the picture, everything changes. Before, we fought turf wars with him over production in this country and distribution in the north. Spilled a lot of blood to defend territory or to expand. We had to fight for both ends of the transaction. But not now. We will soon control one hundred percent of the production, so we will double our profits. Maybe more, since we will now control supply and the demand up there is infinite. I guess you could say that the Americans have the noses and we have the coke."

"That's good news, is it not?"

"Yes, it is. I need you to wipe out the Maras in Tijuana and Juárez, but I can't let you cross into the States right now. I can't afford to piss the Americans off. Do you understand?" It wasn't really a question.

Ali began to worry. He had his own plans for the Bravo men he was training that Victor was not aware of.

"What are you proposing?" Ali asked.

"Myers has satisfied herself with the syndicate's blood. I don't want to give her an excuse to kill me and my sons, too, like that idiot Castillo did."

"Are you not worried that you will lose control of the distribution in the States?"

"Not as worried as I am about those Predators hunting me down. There will be time for that later."

Ali saw the determination in Bravo's searching eyes. The unassuming drug lord had little education yet he was smart enough and ruthless enough to build the second most powerful drug cartel in Latin America that, thanks to Myers, was now the most powerful. But Victor Bravo was still possessed by the habitual fear and wariness of a poor rural farmer so he was unable to fully appreciate the strategic opportunity that Ali had just handed to him. Ali knew there was no arguing with him or with the armed loyalists that surrounded him.

"I bow to your wisdom, *jefe*. I'm leaving for the training camp tonight. When the cycle is finished, I will take the men north and weed out the Maras as you have commanded. When that mission is accomplished, we will return to the training camp and wait for your instructions."

"Excellent." Bravo patted Ali on the back and nodded toward the pistol still in Ali's hands. "I hope you enjoy your new toy."

Ali flashed the golden weapon in his left hand. "With just one of these golden bullets, I can buy another wife." He extended his free hand. They shook. Bravo held on.

"Just be careful where you point that gun, *hermano*. It may be made of gold like a whore's necklace, but it is still dangerous."

Ali smiled, nodded. "I understand, *jefe*."

Ali carefully set the pistol back in its velvet-lined case and shut the lid, wondering how much damage a golden bullet would do to a high sloping forehead like Bravo's.

26

Jackson secured permission from Early to bring Sergio Navarro into the loop. The young analyst had been the one to find the Facebook video that had cracked the Castillo case open, and he wanted to reward him with something far more valuable than just a commendation in his service jacket. Jackson knew that Navarro had a thriving Internet business on the side, providing his own proprietary search engine optimization (SEO) service for online vendors. The DEA could never hope to match the money that Navarro could earn in the private sector, but it could offer him something that a fat paycheck never could: the pride that comes with hunting down the bad guys. By bringing Navarro into the inner circle, Jackson was hoping to convince the brilliant young technician to stay in public service.

After César Castillo's death, all of the SD cards found in the drug lord's safe had been downloaded and transcribed. Unfortunately for Navarro, he was the one who had done the downloading and transcribing. It was practically a snuff film marathon: torture, beheadings, gang rapes, people set on fire, and, on rare occasions, a simple gunshot to the head of Castillo's enemies by Castillo himself with his favorite jewel-encrusted silver pistol. Navarro felt filthy after watching each of the tapes and numb after finishing the last transcription.

Ironically, the very first video he watched was Pearce's crudely shot phone video of Castillo's death by nerve agent. Navarro hated it. It was medieval to execute a human being like that. But after watching the snuff tapes, Navarro became angry. He wished that Castillo had suffered more than he had. In fact, he watched Castillo's death one last time to cleanse his psychic palate before he wrote up his executive summary.

The single most important piece of intelligence Navarro gleaned from the viewing came from the footage of the *Marinas*, burned alive in the tunnel with napalm. It had been shot by two men speaking Farsi.

Coronado, California

Pearce drummed his fingers on his desk, thinking.

César Castillo was dead and that was all that mattered to Early—and by extension, to his boss—but Pearce hated loose ends. His CIA career began in the Clandestine Service Trainee Program where he was trained to be a Core Collector, i.e., a disciplined intelligence case officer. He'd been taught to run down every clue, every source, every suspicion. On Pearce's first day at the Farm, the instructor had passed out a sharp, flat-sided object to each student in the classroom. It was a nail, the kind used to shoe horses. Pearce had only seen them before in books.

"For want of a nail, the shoe was lost," the instructor had said, and she recited the entire proverb in her thick New Jersey accent. "But maybe that's too literal for you postmodern, chaos-theory types. So I'll put it to you another way. You want to keep the tornado from blowing your house down? Then you better go find the friggin' butterfly and tear its wings off before it starts flappin'."

Pearce not only couldn't find the butterfly, he didn't even know what the butterfly was.

The Feds still hadn't figured out who had posted the original El Paso video to Facebook that implicated the Castillo twins. Pearce couldn't stop thinking about the mystery. The working theory that it was a teenage kid at the wrong place at the right time wasn't making much sense to Pearce anymore. An amateur wouldn't be able to hide from Fed hackers this long.

Just as troubling for Pearce was Castillo's last phone call. Who was it made to? Obviously someone connected to the bunker line, which suggested that it was someone connected to Castillo's security. That probably meant one of the four security guards Pearce had just killed. That would make the most sense. But why was the line scrambled? That seemed like overkill. Maybe an enthusiastic salesman had convinced the paranoid drug lord to add an extra layer of security to the only line of communication out of the bunker in the event of an emergency—after all, he would have been under assault, by definition, so secure communications would make sense. So why didn't the other end pick up?

If the person on the other end had just had their brains blown out—like one of the four bodyguards whom Pearce had taken down—that would be a pretty good reason. And that probably was the actual reason.

But then again, Castillo's phone was connected to a satellite uplink. Maybe he was reaching out to someone off the island. Someone with enough power or resources to rescue him. Who would that be? A corrupt general? A cop? A politician? And why didn't that person pick up?

Could it have been an Iranian? Pearce had read Navarro's report. Native Farsi speakers had shot the massacre video—whatever that meant. The Iranian security agencies weren't operating in Latin America as far as he knew, though Hezbollah had made recent inroads. Mercs? Maybe, but highly unlikely. If anything, hired guns would have been on the island with Castillo, not offshore in strategic reserve.

Pearce's options were limited. Ian was a brilliant IT analyst but even he had his limitations, and the Feds hadn't solved the puzzle, either. There was one last hope. Pearce attached a couple of files to a secure e-mail expressing his concerns to Udi and Tamar and fired it off. They still had contacts in Mossad and the Israelis had the best hackers in the world.

Moscow, Russian Federation

President Titov was the one on the mat in a judo *gi* tossing his two-hundred-pound opponent around like a sack of potatoes, but Britnev was the one sweating. All he wanted right now was a cigarette, but the health-crazed president had forbidden smoking in the Kremlin. It would have been easier to smuggle in a missile launcher than a pack of Marlboros into the basement gym.

Britnev had conceived of the audacious plan that was now under way, and he was the point man in the field, so he was in the best position to observe things firsthand. It was only natural that he would be recalled to Moscow for a face-to-face meeting to discuss the latest developments with his boss, a famous micromanager and former KGB colonel.

"You're certain about this?" Titov asked, his hands firmly gripping his opponent's sleeve and collar. Titov was battling a thirty-year-old major in the Presidential Regiment of the FSB, the equivalent of the Russian secret service.

"I'm no metaphysician, Mr. President, but I'm as certain as one can be under the circumstances. In my opinion, the American invasion of Mexico can't be too far off now."

"Then we should move forward," Titov said.

"There is still much to discuss," Britnev said. He was a few years younger than Titov, but he didn't feel like it as he watched his president manhandle the much-younger bull-necked security agent.

Titov grunted another *kiai* as he lifted the former Olympic judo champion up onto his hip, then flung him onto the mat in a lightning-quick throw. The major lay stunned on the mat for half a breath, but whether this was theatrics or not, Britnev wasn't sure. Beating Titov in a judo match would be a career killer for the young agent, but Titov was truly in excellent shape. In either case, the major's hesitation was just long enough for Titov to crash down on him and put him into a choking headlock. The Olympian pounded Titov's back three times in submission and Titov released him. They both stood to their feet, faced each other, and bowed, ending the match. Titov laughed gregariously as he patted the major on his muscled back. "Maybe next time, Gregory."

"Yes, sir. But I doubt it." The major smiled sheepishly and strode away. He had the easy, loping gait of a world-class athlete. It seemed to Britnev that the younger man didn't wear his humiliation well.

Titov picked up a folded towel from a bench and patted his sweating face with it as he approached Britnev, who noticed a slight limp in Titov's stride.

"Let's get some steam, Konstantin. I just had new eucalyptus panels installed. We'll have a chance to talk further about this Mexico situation."

Britnev forced a smile. "Thank you, Mr. President. I could use a good steam." Inwardly, he sighed. It was going to be a long time before he got that cigarette.

27

Mexico City, Mexico

It was five in the morning when Hernán's chauffeur pulled out past the tall, bougainvillea-covered walls of his palatial estate in Lomas de Chapultepec, but it was a long drive across town to Tláhuac, one of the most impoverished barrios of Mexico City, a semirural enclave of muddy streets and urban sprawl on the far eastern side of the nation's capital.

Hernán's armored Land Rover sped along past Carlos Slim's mansion just down the street from his own home, but the multibillionaire had a much larger estate, befitting his unimaginable wealth. No one missed the irony that the world's richest human being lived so close to millions of people living in squalor within the same city limits. In fact, Hernán had used that line in his brother's last campaign speech. Today was a chance to put a down payment on that veiled promise of structural reform. He just hoped that Antonio would arrive on time. Mexico's working poor, despite the racist stereotypes of the *yanquis*, were the hardest-working people on the planet who, according to the Organization of Economic Cooperation and Development, logged more hours per day in paid and unpaid labor than any other OECD citizen. As a point of personal pride, Hernán didn't want his brother to show any disrespect to the people he was appearing to help today, but Antonio wasn't known for being either prompt or an early riser.

Tláhuac, Mexico City

Hernán wasn't easily impressed, but the fact that so many television and newspaper people were here in Tláhuac at this hour of the day so far from their downtown offices meant that Antonio's press relations department had gone the extra mile. He could only imagine what bribes and/or threats were levied to generate this kind of media turnout. Catered breakfast in the press-only tent certainly didn't hurt. No matter what country he had ever traveled to, Hernán found that nobody was more susceptible to the lure of free food than the media.

The locals had turned out in big numbers, too, in their freshly scrubbed cotton shirts and simple print dresses. It was a fabulous and enthusiastic crowd. Lucha Libre wrestling stars were in attendance, along with clowns, balloons, mariachi bands, and bags of candy for the kids. Today it was meant to feel more like a national holiday than a press conference. It was a time for celebration and his rock-star brother did what he did best, all smiles and polished delivery as he cut the ribbon on the new health clinic and school for the neighborhood.

The TV cameras and radio microphones had picked up all the good sound bites, including the one key question Hernán had planted with Octavia Lopez, the super-sexy news anchor of the most watched evening broadcast. Lopez was desperate to change her image from a busty former beauty queen to a serious journalist, and Hernán knew the planted question would please her immensely. He hoped so. Because tonight after the broadcast, in exchange for the favor, she was supposed to please *him* immensely at the little love nest he had set up near her apartment.

"Is it true, Mr. President, that this clinic was funded in part by Victor Bravo and his drug money?" Lopez asked.

Antonio scowled, as if she'd posed an unexpected "gotcha" question rather than a carefully pitched softball. He was, after all, a trained actor. Hernán had prepped him with a carefully crafted response.

"There is an old saying. 'The enemy of my enemy is my friend.' People

think they know who Victor Bravo is. I don't. Not socially. Not politically. The state police tell me he's never been convicted of any drug
crimes; in fact, he's never even been arrested or accused of any crimes at
all. But that's modern-day journalism for you, isn't it? But here is what I
do know: the enemy of Mexico is her poverty. And if Victor Bravo or any
other person is willing to help my administration fight that battle, then
he is a friend of Mexico's, which means he is a friend of mine."

On that last note, the mariachis erupted on cue with a patriotic tune
and the people cheered as the president made his way through an adoring
crowd toward his limousine. Antonio had delivered the riposte perfectly,
as befit his previous profession. Hernán's words in his brother's mouth
would be repeated a thousand times on radio and television over the
course of the twenty-four-hour news cycle.

Surely that would be enough of a first kiss to let Victor Bravo know
that the Barraza wedding bed was warm and friendly enough. All Bravo
had to do was jump in and everybody would have a good time.

Peto, Mexico

Ali had set up the Bravo training camp deep in the heart of the Yucatán
jungle a few miles outside the small town two years earlier, before he'd
begun his security work under Castillo. Infiltrating not one but two
Mexican drug cartels had been the most nerve-racking experience of Ali's
short but violent life, but it was worth it. Quds Force plans in Latin
America hinged on the success of his mission, and the last phase of the
mission was about to begin.

Ali had brought four trusted Quds commandos to carry out the primary training duties while he was earning Castillo's trust and setting the
trap to lure the Americans into battle. The training camp had already
trained three previous cycles of Bravo recruits from around the country.

On the current training cycle, the recruits were locals, mostly poor
young *campesinos* looking for something more than the chance to dig in

the dirt for yams or corn on their own miserable little plots of land or, worse, breaking their backs for a few measly pesos a day on the big *fincas* of the international conglomerates getting fat on NAFTA-fueled contracts. A few could read, a few could write, but mostly they were Ali's "little chestnuts"—small, brown, and hard, like the ones his grandfather grew in the Zagros Mountains. Ali genuinely liked them for their easy smiles and endless capacity for suffering. Because of his religious scruples, Ali refused to allow female recruits to integrate with the men, though several women had served Victor Bravo's organization honorably and ruthlessly over the years.

Ali wished he had an imam with him. *This could be a field ripe for harvest for Allah.* The mission of the Quds Force was to export the revolution worldwide, and imams were essential to that mission. But Victor had his own strange, syncretistic faith and would have opposed Ali if he'd shown up on his doorstep with Muslim missionaries. But Ali was patient. He knew there would be opportunities for the spread of Islam soon enough.

For religious instruction at the training camp, Victor had recruited an aging American Jesuit priest who drummed pagan liberation theology into their illiterate skulls. Father Bob exchanged his liturgical services for an endless supply of filtered cigarettes and the occasional bag of premium weed. When Ali's Quds Force commandos arrived to begin their training duties, Father Bob began preaching against "religious fundamentalism," but within a week, he disappeared. Ali reported to Victor that the old priest had returned to New York to tend to an ailing relative. The truth was the American's throat had been opened by a razor-sharp commando knife and the old infidel's bones were rotting in the bottom of a nearby swamp.

Besides their intensive physical training, the new recruits spent the first few weeks in weapons training, learning not only how to fire the weapons, but also how to break down and reassemble their AK-47s, which the Mexicans called "goat horns" because of the shape of the magazine.

The jungle echoed constantly with the roar of automatic-rifle fire, but no one in the area seemed to notice or care. Local law enforcement had been paid to look—or, technically, listen—the other way, and nobody was being shot. In fact, Victor's presence had saved the local police from the other cartels that used to prey on them.

Once the trainers were convinced the *campesinos* wouldn't accidentally shoot themselves, they introduced them to the basic principles of land navigation, small-unit tactics, and maneuvers. By the time Ali arrived, they had become an effective guerrilla unit.

Ali easily assumed command of the training unit. In his absence, Ali's name had been invoked frequently by the trainers with a mixture of awe and terror, and they regaled the impressionable young men with tales of Ali's heroic exploits against the Western armies in the Middle East. Ali also had a natural command presence, and the fearsome Quds Force soldiers carried out each of his orders with an instant precision that also greatly impressed the peasant recruits.

Under his command, Ali marched the boys twice a day, once in the morning and once in the evening, and frequently tested their combat skills. Ali also used this time to repeatedly drill into his recruits the mission they were assigned.

"Where are you going?" Ali sang in a marching cadence.

"We're going up north!" the Mexicans shouted back.

"They put up a fight?"

"We burn 'em all down!" they called out in breathless unison.

"Where are you going?"

"We're going up north!"

"I can't hear you!"

"WE'RE GOING UP NORTH!"

Mile after mile, chant after chant, they marched and marched and marched.

One afternoon, Ali marched the Mexicans deeper into the jungle for some real fun: RPGs—rocket-propelled grenades.

"Only the top four recruits will have the honor of carrying one of these into battle," Ali said, holding up one of the launchers. The Iranians manufactured their own RPGs, but they opted to smuggle in Vietnamese copies in the unlikely event any of the weapons were seized.

The Iranians strapped the wood-and-steel launchers to their backs along with the packs that held the long-stemmed charges. The big green bulbous warheads poked out of the top of the packs like misshapen bowling pins. The Iranians purposely marched in front of the Mexican recruits as a reminder of who was in charge, but also to keep the RPGs front and center in the peasants' minds. The recruits laughed and nudged one another like schoolboys, lusting after the wicked-looking devices as if they were young women.

When they reached the prepared firing range, the Mexicans gathered around Ali as he cradled one of the weapons in his arms. The panting recruits broke out their canteens and drank as he spoke.

"You men are doing very well. I am very proud of you. So proud that I am going to let you in on a little secret. You are not just being trained to root out Castillo men up on the border. Any gangster with a pistol could do that. No, you have been selected for a very important mission by Victor Bravo himself. A mission *all the way* up north." They listened earnestly, but their eyes were all locked on the launcher in Ali's hands. He patted it. "But more of that later."

Ali pulled out one of the big HEAT rounds and loaded it.

"Stand clear!"

The Iranians pushed the men aside, away from the coming rocket blast. Ali kneeled and lined up one of the large twisted ficus trees in his iron sights.

WHOOSH! Ali loosed the first rocket-propelled grenade. The armor-piercing round slammed into the tree, shattering the trunk and breaking the mighty tree in half. The top came crashing down to the jungle floor.

The Mexicans howled with delight.

"This is how David slays the giant, brothers. Who wants to go first?"

28

Tel Aviv, Israel

Nine days earlier, Pearce had asked Udi and Tamar to find the answers to two questions. The first was, who was Castillo calling from his bunker the night he died? The second was, who originally uploaded the massacre video and where did they upload it from?

Thanks to the Farsi clue Pearce passed on, Israeli intelligence had acquired the answers to both. As former Mossad agents, Udi and Tamar weren't easily surprised, but the answers to the two questions knocked them back on their heels. What had Pearce gotten them into?

Udi picked up his phone and called Pearce. Unfortunately, it was 3:37 a.m. in Wyoming.

"This better be good," Pearce grumbled, still half asleep.

"Castillo was calling Hernán Barraza."

Pearce rubbed his tired face, processing. He sat up. "And he didn't pick up. Why?"

"Maybe Barraza was scared? Surprised?" Udi said.

"Or cutting himself off from Castillo," Tamar chimed in.

"My guess is the latter," Pearce said. "But it doesn't really matter. The big news is that this proves a direct link between Castillo and Hernán. Maybe even the president himself."

Pearce headed for his kitchen, the cell phone still stuck in his ear. It was time to make coffee and get to work. "So how are you doing on the

Facebook thing? I would've thought that would be the easier of the two nuts to crack."

"I know. Crazy, eh? But whoever put that video up really knew his business. My friend says he'll keep at it."

"Any connection between the video upload and the Iranians?" Pearce asked.

"No. It was a dead end," Udi said. "If we find out anything else, I'll call."

"Thanks, Udi. And thank your 'friend' for me. Shalom."

"Shalom." Udi hung up the phone.

Tamar scowled at Udi. "I hate that you lied to him."

"Me? You were on the call, too."

"You know what I mean," Tamar said.

Udi sighed. "I hate it, too. But we owe more to Israel than to Troy."

"That doesn't make it right. He's our friend."

"I know. But we have our orders."

"We don't have 'orders.' We no longer belong to Mossad, remember?"

Pearce had recruited Udi and Tamar to his company on the condition that they leave Mossad and all other Israeli government employment. They had agreed to his terms because they wanted to work with him. But when Mossad hackers had chased Pearce's lead straight into a Quds Force mainframe, they asked Tamar and Udi for help. Mossad was terribly shorthanded in Latin America, and the Sterns knew Mexico well. The former agents couldn't say no to the request or to the possibility of breaking up a Quds Force cell in Mexico.

"This is the last time we're going to lie to Troy, I promise," Udi said.

Tamar shook her head. "You mean until after this mission?"

Peto, Mexico

It had been a good training cycle. His officers had performed a miracle, transforming young, illiterate peasants into combat-ready soldiers. When the *campesinos* had first arrived in camp six months earlier, few of them even owned a pair of shoes, let alone handled a weapon. Now they could fire a rifle and march in order, more or less, and they had learned to obey orders without question. More important, they shared the pride and camaraderie of all men-at-arms who sweat and bleed and suffer together.

They will be doing plenty more bleeding and suffering soon enough, Ali reminded himself. He was training these sheep for slaughter.

With his grueling regimen, Ali had forged them into a unit completely devoted to him. He'd proven to them that he could outshoot, outmarch, and outfight any man in the unit. His men wore their blistered feet and black eyes as evidence. But he also knew how to reward them, particularly on the last night of training camp.

Though it was against his Islamic convictions, Ali allowed the recruits to partake of a particularly potent kilo of genetically modified marijuana. He also issued his men brand-new black fatigues.

They were all sitting together in a circle. One of Ali's Quds Force trainers, Walid Zohar, a tough young Azeri sergeant, taught the Mexicans an old Iranian army song about love and loss, and the Mexicans in turn taught the Iranians a song about the hardship of the peasant's life. The drug-fueled emotions ran high as the sun began to set. Ali signaled a technician to set up the video camera. When it was up and running, Ali barked his orders.

"Get your weapons now!"

Stunned—and stoned—the boys looked at one another and laughed. The dope had made them forget that they were supposed to be real soldiers now.

Ali fired his pistol into the air. *BOOM!*

That got their attention.

"Your weapons! Now!"

The Mexicans scrambled for their AK-47s stacked neatly near the tents, but they crashed and stumbled into one another, cursing and laughing, until all of them had picked up a rifle.

"Line up here!" Ali commanded, pointing to an imaginary line.

Sobering up quickly, the boys formed a line. The four stars of the group lined up in the center, each carrying an RPG and a grenade pack slung on their backs.

"Port, arms!"

The Mexicans slowly but accurately raised their guns diagonally across their bodies. Their bloodshot eyes narrowed with concentration.

Ali began the familiar cadence of the marching chants.

"Where are you going, Bravos?"

"We're going up north!"

"They put up a fight?"

"We burn 'em all down!"

"I can't hear you!"

"WE BURN 'EM ALL DOWN!"

Ali turned to another one of his officers, who picked up a rucksack and approached the Mexicans, passing out black balaclavas.

"Put those on. They make you look like warriors!"

The Mexicans pulled them on despite the stifling heat. They stole glances at one another and tried not to laugh. They thought they really looked badass now.

"Port, arms!"

The guns snapped to position faster than the first time.

Ali ran through the marching chants again and again. The video camera caught every shout, louder and angrier each time, as Ali drove them on.

Suddenly, Ali switched his cadence and began chanting in a low voice. "Bra-vos, Bra-VOS, BRA-VOS!"

The recruits mimicked him exactly until they were finally roaring out the name "BRA-VOS!" then they broke out in a spontaneous cheer. One of the Mexicans, completely caught up in the moment, racked a round in his weapon and opened fire. Seconds later, all twenty-four AKs roared into the air, blasting rounds until the mags emptied.

Everything was caught on camera even better than Ali could have hoped for. Lucky for the recruits. Had these been real Quds Force soldiers in the field, Ali would have pulled out his pistol and shot the first man in the face for breaking fire discipline. What he should do now is run them all for miles until they puked their guts out and dropped.

Instead, Ali marched them back to town for showers, beer, *barbacoa*, and whores. Their skills were minimal but sufficient for the task at hand. He had forged them into a unit loyal to him; a weapon that he could wield in his war in the north, against Victor Bravo's wishes. But he couldn't use them yet. Ali still needed a trigger. One that his computer-warfare specialist in Ramazan would soon help provide.

Mexico City, Mexico

They had taken every possible precaution.

Udi and Tamar arrived at the Benito Juárez International Airport in Mexico City under Canadian passports after a three-hour Aeromexico connecting flight from Havana. But the wearisome journey had begun in Tel Aviv twenty-six hours earlier. Flying Lufthansa to Frankfurt then Air France to London and Aeroflot from London to Havana had kept them off of the American fly lists, which was important, if for no other reason than Pearce had access to all of the DHS databases. They were under strict orders to keep Troy out of the loop. This was a Mossad operation only.

Udi drove the rental car while Tamar called ahead to their contact on a secured cell and arranged for the meet-up later that afternoon at their small, secluded hotel on Sierra Madre, a quiet, tree-lined suburban street not far from the Israeli embassy. That gave them six hours to shower, sleep, and fight off jet lag before Levi Wolf arrived with the guns.

What brought them back to Mexico had caught Mossad by surprise. After penetrating a dozen firewalls and chasing hijacked servers around the globe, they broke into the Quds Force mainframe in Ramazan, Iran, and made off with a file without being detected. When they finally cracked the file, Mossad discovered an agent code name and the location in Mexico City where the video had been uploaded from.

"Maybe we should have told Pearce after all," Udi said. He knew how much Pearce hated the Quds Force and how he would have wanted to be in on the kill.

"Against orders, love. You wanted to tell him? You shouldn't have asked for Menachem's help," Tamar said. Menachem was their direct superior in Mossad. "We were using his guys for the Facebook upload question and they found it, so now he wants those Quds scalps on his wall for himself."

They showered together but they were both too tired to fool around. They weren't scheduled to meet with Levi Wolf for another six hours. Tamar set her watch and Udi called down to the front desk for a wake-up call as a backup. They practically passed out. They'd need every brain cell activated for the snatch-and-grab operation.

29

The White House, Washington, D.C.

It was Roy Jackson's first visit to the Oval Office. He was in awe of the room but tried not to show it as he summarized his latest intelligence briefing for Myers and Strasburg.

"Our analysts confirm that the bulk of the Castillo organization has already been absorbed into the Bravo organization. In our opinion, the Barraza administration will soon make an alliance with the Bravos, if they haven't already done so," Jackson concluded. "Initial reports are that drug-related violence is already in steep decline."

"Congratulations, Madame President. Your decapitation strategy is an apparent success," Strasburg said.

"Then why don't I feel like celebrating?" Myers asked.

"Because you've helped create an unholy alliance. Churchill felt the same way about his partnership with Stalin during the war, but it was necessary in order to defeat Hitler. What matters is that you have achieved your objectives if Mr. Jackson's report continues to hold true."

Myers's face soured. "It's a nasty business, Karl. I don't know how you've put up with it for so long."

"It's sausage making," Strasburg said. "Blood sausage."

"I just hope this really is the end," Myers said.

Strasburg nodded, but said nothing. Hope wasn't a word in his lexicon.

Mexico City, Mexico

Levi Wolf brought more than guns to the hotel that night. He'd recruited two of the embassy security staff for the operation as well. One was already at the location to keep an eye on things.

The stolen Quds file looked legit. Udi had forwarded it to Wolf before they arrived, and Wolf had staked out the location. There was only one Iranian who regularly occupied a warehouse in the barrio known as Tepito, famous for its boxers, crime, and poverty but especially for its *tianguis*—the open-air markets that sold everything from counterfeit Chinese software to seedless watermelons to black-market weapons, if you knew where to look.

Wolf was certain that the five of them could take down the lone Iranian. His man on the scene said he was there now. If the Iranian kept to his schedule, he'd be there for another two hours. Wolf reported that the Iranian looked more like a businessman than a soldier and appeared lightly armed, if at all. No one else had entered or left the warehouse in the last twenty-four hours.

After Wolf briefed Udi on the general layout, he turned the operation over to him. Udi had kicked down more doors than anyone else on the team and there was no time to lose. The idea was simple enough. Grab the Iranian alive and haul him back to the embassy for questioning. The trick was not getting killed doing it.

Tepito reminded Udi of the bazaars he'd been through all over the Middle East, Africa, and the Balkans. Places like Tepito formed a thin, permeable barrier that allowed commerce and crime to commingle without infecting the larger society as a whole. Tepito was a city on the edge of everything civilized. The kind of place where men and women racing through the streets with guns printing beneath their civilian shirts weren't paid much attention to, much less bothered, especially at night.

Drenched in sweat, Udi and the team made their way to one of the back streets behind the markets to a row of crumbling warehouses. The men carried only pistols. Running through the streets with automatic rifles would draw unwanted attention, from either the police or the gangs that controlled this area. For overwatch duty, they gave Tamar the largest weapon in their arsenal, a 9mm Mini-Uzi machine pistol, just in case reinforcements did show up.

Udi couldn't access Pearce's drones without him knowing or use any of the other whizbang gadgets he often deployed. This operation would have to be old-school all the way. Udi even opted for hand signals rather than comms, just in case the Iranians were scanning for them.

Tamar climbed a shaky steel ladder and took her position on the roof across the street from the target warehouse. The Iranian's big rolling steel door was shuttered tight with a rusted lock that looked like it had never been opened. A small entrance door fronted the main street, and a rear door opened to an alleyway. One of the security men was posted to the back alley exit, while Udi, Wolf, and the other security man approached the front.

After Tamar gave the all-clear sign, Udi and his men slipped quietly through the unlocked front door into the dim warehouse. There was an office with a large covered window and a closed door on a second-story landing. The Iranian's shadow wandered back and forth across the drawn shade, hand to his head, as if he were on a phone call.

Udi led the way up the short flight of rickety stairs and paused at the closed door. An AM radio played scratchy Middle Eastern pop tunes on the other side.

When the shadow faced away from the door, he gently tried the handle. It appeared unlocked.

Udi believed in leading from the front. He signaled his men, then pushed his way inside, pistol drawn.

Tamar bit her lip. Wolf's assurances that the Iranian was an easy target didn't calm her fears. She'd learned the hard way that nothing was ever easy in this business, but she knew that her husband was a pro. The team had broken in thirty seconds ago, but it seemed like a lifetime to her because she couldn't see or hear what was going on inside.

Then gunfire. Like hammers banging on sheet metal.

Tamar guessed fifty shots, mostly pistols, but at least one automatic rifle firing three-round bursts. As quickly as it had started, the shooting stopped, but Tamar was already sliding down the ladder fireman-style. She dropped the last four feet to the concrete and raced across the street, bursting through the entrance door just in time to see a man at the rear exit turn and open fire at her.

The door frame shattered by her face and she flinched as a jagged splinter tore into her cheek. She dropped to one knee and fired back, but the man had already fled. Something caught her eye. She glanced up at the office. Wolf's leg had caught between the stairs. The rest of his swinging torso hung upside down off of the staircase, facing her, arms reaching for the floor, like a man forever falling, chest clawed open, face masked in seeping blood.

Tamar dashed for the rear exit, ducked low in the frame, and turned the corner, leading with her weapon.

No one in the alley. Alive.

Just the wide-eyed corpse of one of the security men, his jaw shot away, belly split open to the fetid air.

Tamar turned back and raced up the rickety stairs two at a time and dashed into the office, fearing the worst.

She found it.

Her Nikes splashed in blood. The other security man was dead on the floor, shredded by large-caliber slugs in close quarters.

But Udi was gone.

Coronado, California

It was still dark outside. Pearce could hear the waves crashing on the beach below, hissing as they raced away.

He had just put the water on to boil for his first cup of tea when his phone rang. He read the caller ID. Picked up.

"Tamar?"

Sobbing on the other end. Finally, "Troy . . ."

She filled in the details. *Couldn't find Udi. Couldn't call the cops. Tried everything. No one else to turn to.* "I'm sorry—"

"Forget that. Are you at the embassy?"

"No."

"Are you secure?"

"Yes."

"Stay put. I'll call you back."

"Udi . . ."

"I know." Pearce clicked off. Speed-dialed Early. "Need a favor."

Early knew that tone of voice. "Name it."

Pearce named it.

Early laughed. "Is that all?"

"Since you're asking." Pearce named two more. Called Ian, then Judy. Texted Tamar when and where to meet him.

Prayed he wasn't too late.

30

On board the Pearce Systems HondaJet

Thirty minutes later, Judy banked the HondaJet away from San Diego onto a southeastern course for Mexico City. Pearce tapped on the iPad he was using to zero in on his missing friend.

"So, how did you find Udi?"

"Uniquely coded carbon nanotube transponder implants. Ian's jacked into an air force recon satellite and tracked the signature." Pearce zipped open a small tactical pack. "I've implanted all of my people with them for situations like this."

"That's cool." Then it hit her. "Wait, you just said 'my people.'"

"Yes. You have them, too."

"I never gave you permission—"

"Here." Pearce held out a Glock 19 pistol.

Her face soured. She touched her stomach. Felt queasy, violated. "How?"

Pearce pressed the weapon closer to her. "You're gonna need this."

Judy pushed it away. "You know I don't do guns," Judy said.

"We're not exactly going to Bible study."

"Don't do those, either."

Pearce thought about pressing the issue but let it drop. Judy had lost her faith years ago, but not her moral sensibilities. Her only religion now was flying.

He shoved the 9mm pistol back in the bag. "I don't make any apologies for protecting my people."

"We're gonna have to talk when this is all over."

"ETA?"

"Ten-thirteen, local."

Pearce glanced at the instrument panel. Judy's Polaroid was missing. He hoped that wasn't a sign of things to come.

Benito Juárez International Airport, Mexico City

Judy taxied to a stop inside a private hangar just as Tamar rolled up in a beater Chevy Impala with rusted Durango plates and a scorpion sticker plastered across the rear window.

"Perfect," Pearce said. He'd trained his people to steal old cars. No GPS or OnStar systems to track them.

Judy piled into the backseat, wiping the greasy fast-food wrappers and crushed beer cans onto the filthy carpet with a sweep of her arm. Pearce tossed a mil-spec first-aid kit and a duffel bag loaded with rifles and ammo next to her. Within minutes they were on Avenue 602 heading east out of town, Tamar behind the wheel. Pearce was glued to the tablet while Judy watched Mexico City slide past through the grimy windshield. The car had no air-conditioning. It was going to be a long, hot ride.

Forty minutes outside of Mexico City, Tamar turned onto a rutted dirt track leading back into farm country. Against her instincts, she had to slow down as the rocks thudded sharply against the car's undercarriage. No telling what damage they were doing. They had to roll their windows up against the clouds of dust they were throwing up.

All three of them wore ear mics, linked to one another. Pearce had other channels open, including Ian's.

"In a hundred meters, pull off to the right," Pearce said. "Let's get a visual." The air force satellite Ian had access to was only a signals intelligence unit. It couldn't provide video surveillance.

Tamar pulled over and killed the engine. A small berm gave them some cover from the small farm thirty meters off of the road. Udi's signal had been flashing from there since Ian had found it earlier that morning.

They unloaded quietly and scoped out the ramshackle farm. The house was barely more than a shack. In the front, a couple of goats chewed on grass and a half dozen chickens wandered around a tractor that hadn't moved since the Carter administration. Off the near side of the house, five huge sows shouldered against one another in a muddy pen, grunting as they fed greedily from a trough, fat stinging flies buzzing in their flicking ears. Otherwise, no other sounds or movement.

"There." Pearce pointed at a dirt bike dropped in the grass.

Three yards from the bike, a body.

Tamar gasped.

"Not Udi. Too young. Let's move."

Pearce carried a short-stock M-4 carbine. Tamar gripped her Mini-Uzi. Judy hauled the medical kit.

The three of them crouch-walked past the motorcycle. Key still in the ignition. Smell of gas. They reached the body. A teenage boy, fourteen, maybe fifteen. Single gunshot to the side of his head. "He tumbled off the back and the bike kept rolling," Pearce whispered in his mic.

Judy felt for a pulse. Knew there wouldn't be one. "Dead awhile." She shooed the flies off of the boy's head wound.

"Wait here," Pearce said to Judy. He nodded at Tamar, gave her a hand signal. Tamar sped around back, keeping low to the ground, as Pearce approached the front door.

"Another body back here," Tamar whispered. "Probably the boy's mother. Throat cut."

"Bastards," Ian hissed in Pearce's ear.

Pearce reached the porch. The door was shut, but a front window was open.

"In position," Tamar said.

"Hold," Pearce replied. He pulled a four-inch-long Black Hornet Nano helicopter drone from his pocket and activated the flight software on his iPhone. The half-ounce surveillance drone featured a small camera. No telling what or who might be waiting inside. Pearce powered up the unit and tossed it through the window. Forty seconds later, the Norwegian-built drone had circumnavigated the two-room shack. No trip wires, no bad guys.

"All clear," Pearce said. "But stay frosty. Go."

Pearce and Tamar burst into the two-room shack at the same time. They cleared the shack.

Cigarette butts on the plywood floor, ashtrays overflowing on the card table. Dirty dishes in the filthy washtub. Christ on the bedroom wall staring down at the unmade bed tangled with bloody sheets.

Pearce pocketed the Hornet.

"Clear."

"Clear."

Tamar's eyes posed the obvious question.

Pearce checked his tablet. The transponder signal still flashed. It was only accurate to ten meters. "Better check outside," he said.

He stepped off of the porch into the blinding sun, heading for the far side of the house. Clothes already sticky with sweat. Tamar took the opposite tack and headed for the animals. Judy was still crouched low by the boy, shooing flies. She'd covered his lifeless face with a square of gauze from the medical kit.

Pearce checked the side of the shack. A rabbit cage with three fat rabbits and a rusty rake leaning against the wall. Farther back, an outhouse. Flies. Stink.

A bad kind of stink.

Pistol up, Pearce opened the door. A corpse. Pants down around his ankles. Bled out. Pearce didn't have to raise the slumped head.

Must be the dad, he told himself.

Tamar screamed.

Pearce bolted toward her. She stood near the pig trough, clutching her horrified face in her hands.

It was Udi.

Pearce recognized the mop of hair and the thick hands, but not much else. The pigs had gutted him. Had devoured his face.

Tamar howled, crazed with rage. Her Uzi split the air, slugs slapping the huge pig bellies. The swine screamed as if possessed, charging and slipping through the mud and gore, dropping one by one, as 9mm rounds sliced through their spinal cords and brain stems.

Tamar stopped firing, pirouetted, arms flailing. The Uzi sailed through the air as she spilled into the grass, her shoulder painted red.

A shot rang out. The bullet *zoop*ed like an angry bee past Pearce's ear. He dropped to one knee, trying to see where it came from.

Judy ran full throttle toward Tamar, despite Troy screaming in her ear, "Down, down, down!" until she dropped by her friend's side with the med kit. She began unzipping it when a geyser of dirt leaped up between them.

"Let's go!" Pearce shouted as he grabbed Tamar's shirt collar and dragged her toward the tractor, Judy close behind.

Pearce lay Tamar behind the shelter of the big rear steel wheel where Judy could safely work on her. Pearce crouched behind the small front wheel. Another rifle crack. A round spanged against the tractor.

"Status!" Ian shouted.

Judy tore open the med kit and ripped open bandages.

"Tamar's hit. Judy and I are under cover."

"I'm calling in support—"

"Stand down, Ian. I need that guy alive."

"But Troy—"

"That's an order." Pearce tapped his earpiece, cutting Ian off. He pulled his Glock from his holster and handed it to Judy. "Take this." And he added, "Just in case."

Another bullet hit the tractor. The steel fender rang like a church bell.

Judy shook her head as she applied pressure bandages to Tamar's shoulder wound. "Forget it. Just go!"

Pearce glanced through the tractor. Two hundred yards away, sunlight winked off of a scope. A man stood in the bed of a pickup truck using the roof as a rifle bench. Too close for comfort, especially with a scope.

Judy was right.

Just go.

Pearce dashed back toward the motorcycle in the grass. He'd seen the key in the ignition. He prayed there was still enough gas in the tank. Dirt puffed next to his foot. Pearce pumped the kick-starter twice and the engine roared to life. He gunned the throttle hard, popping the clutch and shifting gears as fast as he could. The bike tore up dirt clods behind him as he raced toward the berm. He took the hill at an angle and jumped it easily, crashing both tires into the dirt road just a few feet behind the pickup, fishtailing ahead of him, racing away. The man in the back of the battered gray Dodge crashed to the steel deck, dropping his rifle in the bed. Otherwise he could've shot Pearce dead without even aiming.

The truck picked up speed, throwing dirt and rocks behind it. Pearce could feel the grit blasting against his face; his Oakleys saved his eyes. He kept the throttle full-on with his right hand while he slid the M-4 sling around with his left. He raised the carbine up and fired three three-round bursts, trying not to hit anyone.

Slugs sparked on the tailgate, then shattered the rear glass. The truck didn't slow down—in fact, it kept gaining speed, but the man in back ducked down. The bike Pearce was on was only 125cc, too small to keep up with a big V-8 truck engine running full bore. He fired again, twice, aiming for the tires. He missed. Fifteen rounds left.

The shooter in the back of the truck sat back up, aiming his gun. Pearce ducked low as he swerved the bike side to side. The big semiauto rifle thundered.

Pearce felt the heavy rounds blow past his head even with the wind and the dust whipping his face. He raised his gun again, firing at the tires.

The left rear truck tire blew. It must have been a retread. The tire unwound like a strip of tubular dough and wrapped itself around the rear axle. The truck bucked and swerved as the driver lost control. The big Dodge plowed into a ditch on the side of the road and flipped over.

Pearce dropped his carbine to downshift. He was still a hundred yards back and didn't want to come racing up to a hail of bullets. The rifle cracked again. Pearce ducked off the side of the road and dropped the bike, finding cover behind a rock. A bullet shaved a fleck of stone just above Pearce's head. He shifted to one side of the rock and opened fire, emptying his mag.

WHOOSH!

The truck erupted in a cloud of fire and steel. Shrapnel whistled past. The pressure wave rocked the trees overhead.

"I SAID I NEEDED THEM ALIVE!" Pearce screamed.

"Wasn't us, boss. Still haven't armed the missiles," Stella said. She had been on overwatch with an extended-range Reaper drone temporarily "borrowed" from an air force maintenance hangar. A $14 million favor, courtesy of Mike Early. Pearce wasn't stupid enough to think he could handle the mission without a Hellfire angel on his shoulder.

Pearce tapped his earpiece as he raced toward the burning hulk. "Ian. Are we alone out here?"

"All clear."

"Must have been a suicide bomb," Pearce said. "Damn it."

Pearce stopped. Stood as close to the flames as he could stand. No survivors. "Judy, how's Tamar?"

"The bullet passed clean through the shoulder, but she's in shock. I've stopped the blood flow and got her on a plasma drip. She's stable for the moment, but she needs help now."

"Ian, call in a medevac."

"Already on the way," Ian said. He'd notified a private air-ambulance service out of Veracruz on standby. "ETA two minutes."

"Can she talk?" Pearce asked Judy, running back to the bike.

"She's out." But knowing Pearce, added, "I know she'd tell you this wasn't your fault."

He almost believed her.

Washington, D.C.

Britnev sat in one of the computer carrels at the Georgetown public library. He hated computers, at least for this kind of effort. He'd been trained in the early '80s in the traditional methods of tradecraft—dead drops, brush passes, and one-time pads. Britnev believed that using any kind of electronic communications was the clandestine equivalent of walking around with his fly open. But in this case, it couldn't be helped. His contact in Mexico refused to communicate with anyone but him and this was the best arrangement they could make.

After covering the PC's webcam with a sticky note—he always assumed a computer's webcam was hacked—Britnev logged in under his fake identity and pulled up a coded e-mail in his Dropbox account left there by his Mexican contact, Ali Abdi.

Britnev memorized the jumble of numbers and symbols in the e-mail message—they would have looked like gibberish to anyone passing by—then deleted both the e-mail and the Dropbox account.

He took a short but sweaty walk to a nearby Starbucks and ordered a venti black iced tea with lemon, no sugar, and took a seat in the back, away from the windows. Britnev pulled out a pen and deciphered the code in his head, scratching each letter onto a napkin. Ali had already informed him last week about the Castillo decapitation strike. What Ali hadn't been able to find out was who was behind it.

Until now.

Britnev was a little queasy. The intel had come from the Israeli Ali had tortured and killed in Mexico. He knew what terrible things Ali had done to get it, but he pushed the butchery from his mind and finished the transcription. The first letters on the napkin spelled a name.

Troy Pearce.

Britnev transcribed the rest. A request from Ali for intel on Pearce and Pearce Systems. Britnev took a sip of tea, crumpled the napkin, and pocketed it.

Ali had found his trigger and handed it to Britnev. Now it was up to him to pull it.

31

Texas City, Texas

The *Estrella de la Virgen* was a privately owned twenty-five-thousand-ton Mexican oil tanker ported out of Veracruz but sailing under a Panamanian flag and captained by an American, Gil Norquist.

The *Estrella* had arrived at the Millennium Oil refinery on the Texas Gulf Coast loaded with a shipment of gasoline from PEMEX, the state-owned petroleum company of Mexico. Millennium was experiencing a shortage of summer-blend gasoline for its distributors and had made the emergency purchase after a recent spike in market price. It was a pretty standard run and the *Estrella* had made the exact same trip several times earlier in the year, though not always to the Millennium facility. BP, Marathon, Valero, and several other refineries were located in the Houston port area as well.

When Captain Norquist confirmed that his Grand Cayman bank account had received a deposit of $50,000, he gladly turned a blind eye to the twenty-eight unregistered civilian passengers and the unmarked crates of cargo they had hauled on board his ship. He assumed it was another drug and guns shipment; he'd had this arrangement with the Bravo organization for years. The *Estrella* had special passenger and storage compartments fitted out for just such transactions. The passengers always stayed clear of the crew on the short voyage, and the crew knew not to venture down to where the mysterious passengers were located. His ship was never inspected on the Mexican side because Bravo owned the Veracruz port authority. Clearing customs on the American side wasn't much more difficult. It was just a matter of timing the unloading with the shifts of the customs officers who were on the Bravo payroll. Security on both sides had been something of a joke for years now.

A brilliant orange sunset greeted the *Estrella* as she docked in Texas. Once her lines were secured and the marine loading arms attached to the *Estrella*'s cargo manifolds, the unloading procedures began. The marine surveyor was already on board gathering samples from the cargo tanks to test for purity.

The captain stepped into the cargo control room along with his first officer and radioed in to the loadmaster person in charge (LPIC) on-shore. The order of tanks to be emptied, their flow rates, and the destination tanks on the tank farm were all agreed to and soon the gasoline began to flow.

During the gulf crossing, the Bravo soldiers and their Quds Force officers remained well hidden belowdecks. They used their time to change out of civilian clothes into their combat gear. The officers also had the men break down, clean, and reassemble their weapons to keep their anxious young minds occupied.

After an hour, Captain Norquist checked his watch and decided it was time to go. The eager redheaded mistress he kept in Houston would be waiting for him in her cherry red Mercedes SL convertible down in the port parking lot. They would go out for a couple of thick rib eyes at Charley's Steakhouse, and then he would spend the evening with her at her downtown condo, messing the sheets up for the better part of the night. They'd grab breakfast at their favorite diner first thing in the morning and then she'd drive him back just in time to cast off and set sail back to Veracruz. They were both creatures of pleasure and routine, and it had been a mutually satisfying arrangement for the past five years.

He turned over the control-room responsibilities and the overnight watch to his extremely competent Filipino first mate and headed for his small private cabin. At forty-eight years of age, Norquist still cut a dashing figure, like an old Hollywood leading man, with just a hint of silver in his thick blond hair. He didn't bother changing into his civvies because his mistress said she loved him dressed like a sailor in his crisp white captain's uniform.

Norquist stepped into his bathroom and ran the water in his small steel sink. His mouth watered; he could already taste the succulent slab of beef he'd soon be tucking into at Charley's. He leaned over and splashed his face with cold water, then rose up just in time to feel a hand slap his forehead and yank his head back, exposing an enormous Adam's apple. Norquist didn't even feel the razor-sharp blade slice open his throat, but he heard the tremendous gush of air escaping out of his lungs through the gaping wound, and his dimming eyes caught sight of the arterial spray spattering against the mirror. The last thing his unconscious mind registered was the sound of his own body thudding against the steel deck.

The Quds Force commandos and their Bravo recruits were clad in black from head to foot, their faces hidden beneath balaclava masks despite the suffocating humid night air. They burst into the port control room and slaughtered the port technicians with suppressed semiautomatic pistols, then remotely opened the valves on the massive port storage tanks, emptying thousands of gallons of gasoline and oil, flooding the storage yard. They had already slapped magnetic demolition packs to several of the tanks and set the timed detonators to blow with just enough time for them to make their escape.

Hamid Nezhat led the team out of the main gate, careful to run in full view of the security cameras high up on the lampposts illuminating the parking lot. The Quds commandos all lugged the antiquated AK-47s and RPG-7s even though they had trained on superior German and Israeli equipment back in Iran, but it was necessary for the show.

Nezhat spotted a red Mercedes convertible shot to hell in a reserved parking space. The long, busty torso of a woman had tumbled out of it, her corpse half trapped inside the car while her upper body twisted out and her bright red hair splayed like a fan on the hot asphalt. Wide, green, lifeless eyes stared unblinkingly at a hazy night sky. *A pity and a waste,* Nezhat thought to himself. What he could do to a woman like that.

Two big Chevy panel trucks were parked haphazardly near the Mercedes and Walid Zohar, Ali's Azeri sergeant, stood in front of the first one. He was dressed the same way as the rest of the team and also had his head covered.

"No problems, brother?" Nezhat asked in Spanish as his men loaded into the two vans.

"One guard at the gate, neutralized. Roads are clear."

"Good." He checked his watch. "Seven minutes to clear out." He slapped Walid on the shoulder and the two men crawled into the big van, Walid taking the driver's side. Nezhat was pleased. Phase one of the plan had been a complete success. Phase two would be even more spectacular, he thought, but also far more difficult to execute. He glanced back over at the Mercedes. He prayed that one of the virgins waiting for him in heaven was a big-breasted redhead like that one.

32

The White House, Washington, D.C.

Myers stood up from behind her desk and checked her watch. It was nearly 10 p.m. "The meeting begins in two minutes."

"Then you should go. We can discuss this matter later," Strasburg said, remaining seated. His arthritic knees were particularly troublesome lately.

"You spoke about timing, Doctor. I'd say this tragedy starts the ball rolling on our plan, wouldn't you?"

"Perhaps." Strasburg polished his glasses with the silk pocket square from his elegant Savile Row suit. "But it's not without its risks."

"It's a simple risk-versus-reward calculation. The reward is clearly greater than the fallout if we fail," Myers said. "We can't just keep swatting bugs, especially now that they're swatting back. It's time to drain the swamp."

"Your critics will accuse you of 'nation building,' an activity you promised never to engage in."

"I have no interest in nation building. What I want is a free and democratic Mexico, governed by and for Mexicans. Tell me a better way to accomplish that goal than what I'm proposing and I'll take it."

Strasburg shrugged with a smile, defeated. "I can't."

"Would you be willing to contact Cruzalta? Make the inquiry on my behalf?"

"I think it would be more persuasive if it came from you, Madame President."

"Perhaps you're right. Well, it's time for me to go. Will you be joining me?"

"I'd rather be waterboarded. With your permission, I'd prefer to make a few phone calls from here."

"Of course. Make yourself at home."

Dr. Strasburg had been in the Oval Office faithfully serving presidents of both parties for over forty years. *Maybe I'm the one who should be asking his permission to use the phone,* Myers thought to herself as she headed for the Situation Room.

Time to find out if the world really had come to an end.

The Situation Room, the White House

Organized chaos.

The room was packed despite the late hour. *Too many people,* Myers thought to herself. *Who are they? What are they even doing here?* A dozen department, agency, and committee heads sat around the table in a carefully choreographed pecking order. Congress was on summer recess, but the bigwigs had hung around or flown back in just for this meeting. Seated behind their bosses in a row of smaller chairs were the senior staff members of each high potentate, and standing off to the sides and behind the senior staff were the young junior staff and assistants. The room burbled with a hundred whispered conversations and urgently tapping keyboards.

Some of these people were a strange breed of adrenaline junkie who just wanted to be in on the action. Others were simply afraid to *not* be in the room, for reasons of ego and perception. All of them wanted to be near the seat of power.

Crisis was the time when the presidency became paramount in importance, primarily because a singular voice and singular mind were more effective in the short, intensive time frame of a national emergency. Congress usually dithered at times like these, seldom mustering more than nonbinding resolutions and patriotic proclamations. There was nothing decisive about 535 men and women organized into committees designed to ensure their incumbencies in perpetuity. *Who in her right mind would turn to a madhouse of caterwauling whores like the U.S. Congress when real decisions had to be made?*

"Bill, let's bring this meeting to order now, please."

Donovan gaveled the room to order like a circuit court judge. Voices hushed. Lights were lowered. A big digital screen flashed satellite images of what was being called the Houston catastrophe. Huge gouts of fire raged in the night above a dozen large circular tanks in the overhead shot. A burning tanker ship—the *Estrella de la Virgen*—was half sunk next to the dock.

"As you can see here, it appears that an attack on the Millennium Oil storage depot in Texas City, Texas, occurred some three hours ago. Firefighting units from seven municipalities, along with Houston Port Authority firefighters, firefighting tugs, and oil-fighting specialists, have all converged. Police, army, and National Guard units have been activated and deployed for security and evacuation."

"Has anywhere else been hit?" Myers asked.

"Not that we're aware of. We've alerted every storage facility and refinery in the nation and additional security personnel have been deployed."

"Where are the attackers now? Any captured or killed?" Early asked.

FBI Director Jackie West answered. "They've gone to ground. No bodies, no clues. We have a massive search under way."

"Who's responsible?" Senator Diele demanded.

Donovan nodded to his assistant running the laptop. Port security-camera video flashed on the big media screen. Two dozen armed men wearing black combat fatigues and black hoods running, shooting rifles, or planting bombs were displayed in a wide variety of camera angles. The video was alternately black and white, night vision, wide angle, or close-up, depending upon the make, model, age, and location of the security camera.

Donovan narrated. "You can see the assailants. Military dress, no insignia, AK-47 assault rifles, and RPG-7 rocket-propelled grenades. A few carry sidearms. My guess is that they're all male. But with their faces and bodies covered and no audio available from any of these cameras, we're unable to determine the nationality or affiliation of these terrorists."

Director West discreetly answered her vibrating smartphone. She frowned.

"Bill, I'm sorry to interrupt. Can you pull up the al-Jazeera website on your laptop?"

Donovan's assistant nodded and tapped a few keys. Moments later, the live English-language broadcast appeared. It was the jungle video showing the Bravos in their masks and uniforms and brandishing their weapons and repeatedly shouting, "Burn them all down!"

The attractive Lebanese-American news anchor read her teleprompter. "To repeat, members of the Bravo Alliance have posted this video to our website claiming responsibility for the attack on the Houston oil refinery early this morning, local time. They claim it was in retaliation for the attempted murder of the Bravo family by Israeli assassins hired by the American CIA. They also condemn the illegal mass assassinations of the Castillo crime syndicate carried out by the administration of President Margaret Myers earlier in the year."

"Shut it off, please," Myers asked.

"What was that about Israelis and assassins?" Diele asked.

"It's bullshit," Early said.

Jeffers turned to the treasury secretary. "On a different subject, what's this attack going to do to the stock market when it opens tomorrow?"

The treasury secretary read from her smartphone. "Dow futures are already down five hundred points, and oil is spiking to over $120 per barrel on the open spot market."

It was the oil price that worried Myers most. The fragile economy, still limping along at 1.5 percent annual GDP growth, was barely above stall speed and could easily tumble into a tailspin if those prices didn't come back down quickly. The cost of just about everything—especially food, transportation, and utilities—all depended upon the price of oil. More important, consumer spending accounted for 70 percent of the nation's economic activity, and high fuel costs robbed the average consumer of what little discretionary income was available.

"That oil price will sound like music in the ears of OPEC. Russia, too," the energy secretary added. The Oklahoma native was intimately familiar with petroleum economics. Her entire family was in the oil business, as was her husband's.

She isn't going to do too badly in this crisis, either, Myers thought.

"What we need is a decisive military response." All eyes turned toward Senator Diele.

"Are you proposing an invasion of Mexico, Senator?" Early asked. "We could dust off Plan Green," he said with an easy smile.

Plan Green was a plan to invade Mexico that was drafted by the American secretary of war in 1919 and had been recently republished. Surprisingly, it hit the *New York Times* best-seller list for nonfiction almost overnight.

"We do have current contingency plans for a Mexico invasion. Canada, too, for that matter," General Winchell said. Senator Diele's friend was dead serious.

"It wouldn't necessarily have to be a full-scale invasion. But our lack of serious action sends a very powerful signal that we are weak. President Myers, with all due respect, your failure to provide a more violent and timely response to the El Paso massacre is partly to blame here," Diele said.

The room erupted in debate.

"You're out of line, Gary. Back it *way* up," Senator Velázquez growled. The normally affable Texan had family in Houston.

"I apologize, Madame President, if I've offended you, but I hope you see my point. This attack was an outrage. Another Pearl Harbor or 9/11. It demands a swift and violent response."

"An invasion of any size isn't justified by this singular act, horrible as it is, but I'll take your suggestion under advisement."

Myers turned to the secretary of state. "What do the Mexicans have to say about all of this?"

"President Barraza's office has expressed his outrage and concern, as well as his support, but then again, so has Trinidad and Tobago, so I don't know what it's worth. I'll be curious to see what the Mexican government's response will be following this al-Jazeera report, but my guess is that they'll just offer more of the same."

"Is there any chance at all the Mexican government is behind this?" Greyhill demanded. He was skyping from an air force base in Greenland and clearly agitated.

"To what purpose?" Strasburg said, incredulous.

"Dr. Strasburg's right. There's no indication of official Mexican involvement," Donovan added.

"They better damn well be kicking down doors and taking names trying to get at these guys," Diele insisted. "If we're not going to kick some ass, somebody has to."

"Right now we have an economic crisis on our hands. I have complete confidence in the Department of Homeland Security to find and arrest the bastards who did this," Myers said.

Donovan sat a little taller in his chair. "Thank you, Madame President. We'll catch them before they strike again."

Myers addressed the rest of the room. "So for the moment, let's focus on our options for tackling the economic issues. Suggestions?"

She sat silent as a sphinx as she listened to the options. Some were conventional, some out of the box. All of them had carry costs. None of them was a perfect solution. Factions began to form. Arguments broke out.

After an hour had passed, Myers held up the palm of her hand. The room silenced.

"Thank you all. I've made up my mind."

"Would you care to share it with us?" Diele asked.

She stood, and gathered up her papers.

"I'll be holding a little press conference tomorrow morning, Senator. Tune in, if you can. I think you might get a kick out of it."

33

Gulf of Mexico, near the Texas coast

The stock market opened on Monday morning and immediately plunged over 650 points before the secretary of the treasury ordered trading suspended on the New York Stock Exchange "for reasons of national security," an order the NYSE directors complied with happily and immediately. Unfortunately, the secretary had no such authority over the Asian markets, which had plunged precipitously the night before, and the European markets had jumped off of the same fiscal cliff as the rest of the world before trading was suspended there, too.

The price of oil was holding steady at $127 a barrel this morning, after a steep 30 percent increase in just twenty-four hours. The only reason the spot price was holding, according to Myers's advisors, was that if the economies of the world really were going to crash—as it seemed they probably would at any moment—then the demand for oil would plummet, and the price would drop. It appeared as if the oil speculators were giving her some breathing room, albeit temporarily. The financial markets waited eagerly to see what she would do with the respite.

Myers flew to Houston on *Air Force One*, which was crammed with the Washington press corps. They all then loaded into a fleet of Bell Ranger helicopters and choppered out to one of Chevron's biggest oil rigs in the Gulf of Mexico.

Myers began her early morning press conference on the blustery deck of the big rig, flanked by the CEOs of Chevron, Shell, ConocoPhillips, ExxonMobil, Baker Hughes, and Halliburton, along with the rig's oil-begrimed crew of roughnecks, roustabouts, and derrickhands, some of whom were sitting high in the superstructure. Against Jeffers's recommendation, Myers excluded all members of Congress, wanting to keep the event as apolitical as possible.

Myers wore blue jeans and steel-toed workboots along with a denim shirt and a white hard hat that sported an American flag on the front. The sounds of a working rig—turbines, drills, hammers, chains, and ocean wind—filled the air. A crisp morning sun rose just above her shoulder. It was an image of hardworking Americans beginning a brand-new day.

"My fellow Americans. First of all, let me express my deepest condolences to the families of the three firefighters who lost their lives last night battling the oil fires down in the Houston area. Because of their brave sacrifice, along with the heroic efforts of all of our first responders, National Guardsmen, and military units, the fires have been finally contained. Our nation is grateful to all of you for your courage and skill, and I want to thank each of you personally for what you have accomplished. I have been told that the fires will be completely extinguished by noon tomorrow, local time.

"Second, let me assure you, my fellow citizens, that we're monitoring events very closely at home and around the world. The catastrophe in Houston has caused crude oil prices to spike, which in turn threatens to throw our economy—along with the rest of the world's—back into a recession, or worse. This morning I am signing an executive order that puts a temporary freeze on all environmental regulations related to oil exploration, drilling, production, and refining, as well as removing all restrictions on drilling on federally protected lands. I am clearing the path for the construction of new oil and gas refineries as well. It's time for 'Drill, baby, drill!'"

The rig crew roared with approval. Grinning CEOs clapped and hollered.

"This same executive order applies to the American natural gas and coal industries as well. I am also opening the strategic petroleum reserve and clearing the way for the Keystone Pipeline construction to begin immediately. In short, I am declaring America's energy independence today. Before the end of my first term, America will no longer be an energy importer, which means we will stop funding global terrorism at our gas pumps. By 2020, I intend for the United States to be the world's largest and most profitable energy exporter, creating tens of thousands of new high-skill, high-paying, high-tech energy jobs this year and every year that will refuel and replenish the next American century."

Another round of raucous applause and cheers rang out.

"Third, I want to assure the American people that national security is of the utmost importance to my administration. The horrific violence inflicted upon the Mexican people as a result of the drug wars has now crossed our borders and as many of you know, that violence has touched my own family in the recent past. Thousands of federal, state, and local law enforcement officials are on the hunt for these narcoterrorists at this very moment, and I promise you, they *will* be brought to justice. Thank you, and God bless each of you here today, and all over this great nation, who make the energy industry possible, and God bless the United States of America!"

The steel platform thundered with cheers and shouts of "USA! USA! USA!" as Myers smiled and waved at the adoring rig crew.

Within eleven minutes of Myers's press conference, the Dow Jones futures had reversed their steeply downward trend. Trading was resumed.

By the time Myers landed back in Houston an hour later, the Dow had climbed back into positive territory, and when her plane touched down at Andrews Joint Air Force Base at 1:14 p.m. EST, she was greeted with the unbelievable news that the spot price of oil had simmered back down to just $102 a barrel.

Because oil prices had responded so favorably to her new energy policy, the Dow actually began screaming upward and reached a new market

high for the year. Investors were betting heavily that a new American re-
naissance had just been launched and that an era of prosperity and job
growth appeared to be just around the corner. Foreign markets followed
suit.

Jeffers read the economic headlines out loud, straight off of the Internet feeds as *Air Force One* was taxiing to a stop. So far, it was all great
news, especially on the employment front. Tens of thousands of jobs in
the energy sector, along with ancillary occupations like transportation
and machine building, were projected to be filled in the months to come.

But Jeffers stumbled across a couple of critics, too. The "usual suspects" whined about the imminent destruction of the environment and
the hastened onset of global warming as a result of Myers's new energy
policy.

. "What's wrong with these people? You just saved the global economy,
and you're bringing new jobs to America," Jeffers said.

"If my critics saw me walking over the Potomac, they would say it was
because I couldn't swim," Myers joked. "You need to stop reading those
'nattering nabobs of negativism.' They'll only give you indigestion."

Jeffers threw a thumb at the passenger compartment where the press
corps was seated, his face reddening.

"But half of those dick wipes are sitting back there sucking down mi-
mosas and cheese blintzes on our dime. Effing ingrates. I ought to kick
them out onto the tarmac right now."

"I'll hold the door open for you, if that would help."

Jeffers ran his fingers through his thick silver hair. "This job's going to
kill me, I swear."

"I can probably find you an easier one roughnecking on an oil rig. I
met a few guys today I can introduce you to."

"Ha-ha, Madame President. Speaking of critics, Diele wants a meeting
with you. Today, if at all possible." Jeffers checked her calendar. "You're
free at two this afternoon, if you can stomach the idea."

"What do you think he wants?"

Jeffers grinned. "Your job."

"Speaking of which, where's the vice president?"

"Probably sitting in your chair with his feet up on the Lincoln desk. You want to talk to him?"

"Not if I can avoid it."

34

The White House, Washington, D.C.

Diele arrived at the Oval Office ten minutes late, his petty reminder to the president of his seniority in elected office. Myers had invited Dr. Strasburg and Mike Early to join them, along with the vice president.

The Senate Armed Services Committee chairman was clearly agitated that he wasn't getting a private meeting with the president as he'd requested. Everybody took their seats on the sofas and chairs in front of Myers's desk.

"To what do I owe the pleasure, Senator Diele?"

"First of all, congratulations on that oil rig speech. Great optics. I just wish you would've invited a few of your friends on the Hill to accompany you."

By "friends," Diele meant himself, of course. Screw everyone else. There were several big energy companies based out of his state and they stood to profit handsomely from Myers's "Drill, baby, drill!" policy. So did Diele.

"Then let's put together some comprehensive energy legislation and pass it, and I'll give you all the optics you want, Gary, along with all of the credit, if that's what it takes."

"You misjudge me, Madame President. All I want is what's best for the American people, which leads to the reason why I've asked for this meeting."

Diele took a sip of coffee. Myers had taken the liberty to order it with heavy cream and three sugars, the way she knew Diele liked it. So did the White House steward. He'd been schlepping coffees for the rancid old legislator for years.

"And what have I done—or failed to do—that leads you to think the American national interest isn't being served?"

"I believe I made my position clear the other day. We need a strong, forceful military response to the Houston attack, not a 'law enforcement' exercise. Have you seen the papers? Every op-ed page around the country is calling for some sort of military strike."

"Gary's right, Margaret. The nation is scared. A swift, surgical strike into Mexico and you'll get a 'rally-round-the-flag' bump in the polls." Greyhill had seen plenty of presidents use military action to bolster public approval when the opinion polls flagged.

"I've thought about it a lot, Gary. The Houston attack underscores the reality that the drug lords represent a strategic threat to the United States. My responsibility as president is to defend our borders against such attacks."

Diele smiled. "We're in agreement on that point, I assure you."

"I've initiated a plan to seal the U.S.-Mexico border. The Department of Homeland Security is coordinating with the relevant federal law enforcement agencies, state governments, and the Pentagon to ensure that no undocumented person may enter the country, and no illegal drugs or weapons, either."

"You're aiming at the wrong target," Greyhill insisted. "It isn't the dishwashers and the pool cleaners who are threatening our way of life—"

"And I'm calling for the full enforcement of the immigration laws we currently have on the books, including fines, penalties, and jail time for those employers who are employing illegal aliens."

She leaned forward in her chair.

"This isn't just a terrorism issue, it's a public-safety issue. Tens of thousands of illegal aliens fill our jails and prisons. Many of them are members of criminal gangs like the Bravos. One GAO report stated that illegal aliens committed over seven hundred thousand crimes in just one year, over eighty thousand of which were for violent offenses like murder, robbery, assault, and sex crimes. It's estimated that between 1,800 and 2,500 Americans are killed by illegals every year, and too many of those who die are law enforcement officers. Many illegal immigrant criminals are repeat offenders and, worse, have been deported on multiple occasions. This will not continue during my administration."

"But you can't close the border. A billion dollars a day crosses over on twelve thousand trucks and railcars." Diele's voice rose a couple of octaves when he got excited. Many of his big donors relied on cheap illegal labor to run their enterprises at a profit. This new policy wouldn't sit well with them at all.

"A lot of the problems we're facing—human smuggling, drugs, guns— are coming in through those NAFTA trucks," Early said.

Greyhill shook his head. "You're biting the hand that feeds you. American industry needs the raw materials and manufactured goods that those trucks carry. The National Association of Manufacturers is going to jump down your throat on this one."

Myers took a sip of coffee.

"I'm more worried about the American worker than the NAM. We've got to turn off the spigot of cheap, undocumented workers that flood our labor market decade after decade. It depresses wages while draining away expensive, taxpayer-funded public services for lawful citizens. If Congress wants to change the immigration laws, fine, but until they do, it's my constitutional responsibility to vigorously enforce the laws that Congress has already put on the books."

"You know you're going to be painted as a racist xenophobe, don't you?" Diele asked. "Punishing poor Hispanic migrant workers who are just trying to feed their families so that you can protect the oil companies—"

"I don't care what other people think. I know my own motives. Do you doubt me on this?"

"Not at all. I'm just trying to protect you. After all, we're in the same party." Diele turned to Strasburg. "What is your opinion on these matters, Doctor?"

"I believe, Senator, that your analysis is fundamentally correct but incomplete. By shutting down the border, more pressure is put on the Barraza administration than ours. The Mexican economy is far more fragile and far more export-dependent than our own."

"That should put a fire under their tails to get at Bravo and his thugs, pronto," Early added. "Let them do the dirty work of kicking down doors and midnight raids."

"That is what you asked for, isn't it?" Myers asked. "Put pressure on the Mexican government to act?"

"I see," Diele said, setting down his coffee. He smiled thinly at Myers. "It appears that this was less of a meeting of minds than a school lesson for yours truly. Be it far from me to try to dissuade you from your plans. After all, *you* are the president."

Myers fought the urge to laugh. Diele was a frustrated presidential candidate from years past, and Greyhill's number one supporter last year. Was he merely lamenting the fact she was the person occupying the office? Or just reminding himself that he wasn't? *Probably both,* she told herself.

Diele made a point of checking his watch, then stood. "Looks like I'm late for my next meeting. Thank you for your time, Madame President." His smile faded. "Mr. Vice President. Gentlemen." He turned on his well-polished heels and left.

"That didn't go well," Greyhill said.

"Why would you say that?" Myers asked.

"He's a dangerous man. Not one to be trifled with."

"What do you want me to do? Invade Mexico so that Diele's feelings won't be hurt?"

"There is some value to listening to the opinions of others. Especially ones with decades of experience in these matters."

Myers wasn't sure if Greyhill was referring to Diele or himself.

"I do listen, Robert. Carefully. And what I hear is a frustrated old man more worried about his reputation than his country." Myers hoped Greyhill caught her double meaning.

He did.

35

Near the Snake River, Wyoming

It was late. Pearce was skyping with Tamar on a secure line. She was propped up in her hospital bed with her arm bound in a sling.

"I wanted you to know how it happened. Menachem just briefed me," Tamar said.

"You should rest," Pearce insisted.

"Mossad really had broken into the Quds Force mainframe all right, but Quds had planted a sentinel program at the portal. When we broke in, the Quds program was alerted, and the sentinel program followed our signal all the way back to our mainframe. The Iranians knew which file had been stolen and the contents of those files."

"And they used that intel to set up the ambush," Pearce concluded. "What was the name of the Iranian you and Udi were chasing?"

"Ali Abdi. Udi said you knew him?"

"Quds Force commander. A real shit bird. We ran into his outfit in Iraq a few times. Big on IEDs and ambushes. Last I heard he was in Syria."

"Now he's in Mexico. Or was. We have no idea what his current location is." Tamar laid her head back, exhausted.

"I'll find him, and I'll kill him. You have my word on that."

"I know. I just wish I could be there to help you when you do it."

The President's Private Quarters, the White House

It was after midnight when Myers received a call on her private number. She had passed out, exhausted from the frenetic pace of the last twenty-four hours. But she was a light sleeper and the phone woke her easily. It was Jeffers.

"It's Pearce, on Skype. You want me to patch him through?"

"He wouldn't call at this hour if it wasn't important. Give me two minutes."

Myers rose with a yawn and stretched and headed for the bathroom. She saw herself in the mirror and suddenly became self-conscious about the way she looked, but she wasn't sure why. It was just Pearce, after all. She splashed cold water on her face and brushed out her hair just the same. Looked pretty darn good for having just rolled out of bed, even without makeup, which she hardly needed to use anyway.

After pulling on a pair of form-fitting track pants, a sports bra, and a Red Hot Chili Peppers concert T-shirt, she dashed back to her desk in her bedroom suite and fell into the chair, then woke up her laptop computer. It was already opened to Skype. She logged on.

Pearce was already online, his grim face weathered and rough like the rustic cabin wall behind him. Early had briefed Myers on the failed rescue attempt and Udi's tragic death.

"Hello, Troy. What can I do for you?"

"I know who took out Udi and his team." Pearce told her everything he knew about Ali Abdi, but that wasn't much, and how Ali's trail had gone cold, despite Ian's best efforts. The Israelis didn't have any luck, either. "This is getting to be a bad habit, but I need another favor."

"That's what friends are for. What do you need?"

"I need you to redeploy some assets for me. CIA and NSA, for starters."

"All of our intelligence assets are pointed at the Bravo terrorists right now. As soon as that's resolved—"

"Ali was working with Castillo. Now that he's out of the picture, maybe Ali's partnered with Bravo. Find Ali and you'll find the Bravos, I'm sure of it."

"I was thinking the other way around. Once we find the Bravos, maybe we'll find your killer. So help us find them."

"The Bravos aren't my problem. I need to stay focused on hunting Ali."

"You once told me that personal vendettas weren't in your mission statement," Myers reminded him.

"The mission statement got changed."

"I need you to see the big picture here, Troy. If the Iranians are somehow involved in Mexico, it means we're in a whole new strategic situation. I need your help."

"To do what? Take out the Bravos? Then who comes after that? You can't keep escalating this war tit-for-tat. It's a losing game."

"I have no intention of playing that kind of game. I'm going to overturn the whole damn board."

"What do you mean?"

"I'm going to change the government of Mexico."

Pearce shook his head in disbelief. "You've got a pair on you, ma'am, if you don't mind my saying. You don't mess around, do you?"

"Not when it comes to the security of the United States."

"Or anything else, I bet."

She smiled, barely. "No, not really."

She leaned in closer to the screen. "I can't do this without your help."

"I don't see how you can pull it off."

She gave Pearce the big-picture summary. He asked probing questions. Myers was impressed with the depth and breadth of Pearce's grasp of Mexican politics and the geopolitical landscape.

"So, what's the verdict?" Myers asked. "You think this will work?"

"On paper, sure. In reality? I'd say it's a definite maybe at best. Who else is backing you on this?"

"My cabinet, mostly."

"Is Greyhill still out of the loop?" Pearce asked.

"Yes."

"What about congressional support?"

"We've put out a few feelers, but we can't afford to tip our hand just yet. It's better to hand Congress a fait accompli. If I open it up to debate, nothing will get done and the opportunity we have right now will be lost. But I'm still missing the most important piece of the puzzle."

"What's that?" Pearce asked.

"You. I still need your services to pull off the strike piece."

"You're in charge of the world's largest killing machine. Use it."

"Nothing's changed on our end," Myers said. "I still can't put boots on the ground."

"I can't help you, either. My operations aren't big enough to carry out the unmanned part of the mission. You need more assets."

"Like the Pentagon?"

"For what you want to accomplish in the time frame you're talking about? No. Check that. Make that *hell, no*. Not the way things are currently organized."

"What do you mean?" Myers asked.

"Once you open the Pentagon door, you're begging for trouble. First of all, you have army, navy, Marine, and air force units that all operate various drone and robotics systems. Many of those systems aren't compatible and they certainly don't all coordinate or communicate with one another, with the limited exception of the JCE, and that's just the army and the air force and *that's* just for UAVs. And then you have all of the command and control problems that come with the jurisdictional bullshit. But that's just the beginning of your woes. Once you activate the U.S. military, they're going to draw on other national intelligence assets like the NSA and all of the DoD resources. Once you've done that, you've triggered congressional oversight and micromanagement. There are over one hundred congressional committees that have jurisdiction on homeland security alone. Add in subcommittees on intelligence, defense, Latin America—you're just warming up the big brass tubas for a gigantic Hungarian cluster dance."

Myers laughed.

Pearce had never heard her laugh before. He was charmed.

"I'm not much of a dancer, Hungarian or otherwise, so what would you propose?"

"Like many other areas of modern life, you should imitate the Germans. Go find your best war fighter and form a separate operational structure under him. Call it 'Robotics Command' or 'Drone Command.' Let him pick and choose the best weapons systems and the best operators wherever you find them. If they're military, pull them out of their respective service hierarchies, at least temporarily, the way NASA does for their astronaut cadre. Keep everything lean and nimble. This can't be about medals or pulling rank or promotions. It's about getting the job done fast and efficiently."

"How about you? You'd be perfect for the job."

"No, thanks. Desks and paperwork make me itch."

"Then whom?"

"Have Early contact Dr. T. J. Ashley. She's the current assistant director of National Intelligence for Acquisition, Technology, and Facilities. She's former navy with combat experience and has the technical chops for the job."

"How do you know her?" Myers asked.

"In 2007, Early was going to run an op in the Persian Gulf near Iranian waters and he'd requested one of the new UAV support teams for an intel assist, but the local commander turned him down."

"But Dr. Ashley stepped in?" Myers asked.

"It was a good thing she did. Her drone disabled an Iranian patrol boat and saved the lives of Early and his team, but it nearly earned her a court-martial. She told Early she didn't care because she thought she had done the Lord's work. That makes her good people in Early's book."

"Mine, too," Myers said.

"Early pulled a few strings and got her off the hook. In fact, he even got her promoted. But she resigned her commission right after that and took a research position with the University of Texas. That's when I tried to hire her into my firm, but she turned me down. She's a dyed-in-the-wool patriot and wanted to get back into government service."

"Sounds like she's the one," Myers said.

"She won't say no to Early."

"Okay."

"One more thing. Please tell me that Jackson didn't turn off DAS."

"You'd have to speak with him about that."

"He needs to get Stellar Wind rolling, too, if it isn't already. And we can't keep pointing both of them in just one direction, if you catch my drift."

"Stellar Wind?" She wasn't expecting that. The libertarian in her struggled with the idea of using warrantless antiterror search technology on her fellow citizens, even the rotten ones.

"Dillinger said he robbed banks because that's where the money was. A lot of the bad guys you'll be hunting are running around up here."

"You're right. Still . . ."

"Something else bothering you?" Pearce asked.

"It's 'Big Brother' technology. I just hate the idea of the government knowing everything there is to know about everybody."

"You'll hate not knowing where your targets are even more."

"I'll tell Mike I'm authorizing Stellar Wind. Thanks again for your help. Your country owes you a great debt."

"Yeah, it does. Early still hasn't cut me a check for the last job. So, how about that favor?"

Myers was caught between a rock and a hard place. She wanted to help her friend, but the nation came first. "How about a compromise? I can't redeploy any of our intelligence assets away from our search, but I can give your people full access to everything we generate in the data stream. Will that work for now?"

"I'll take what I can get. Thanks."

"But it'll cost you," Myers said.

"Why am I not surprised?"

"I need you to talk to somebody for me."

Myers posted Cruzalta's name and address to Pearce.

Pearce read it. "In person, I take it?"

"I've found that face-to-face is always more effective."

"I'm not so sure about that."

She smiled coyly. "It worked on you, didn't it?"

Pearce remembered his first meeting with Myers with a grin. "Apparently."

She turned serious. "Just be sure you realize that without him, we can't move forward."

Pearce's grin faded. "Yes, I believe I do."

"Good. Because we're totally FUBAR if you drop the ball on this."

36

Boca de Tomatlán, Mexico

Just a quarter mile north of the sleepy little bay village was an open-air bar called El Pirata Libre. It perched on a collection of steps on a cliff overlooking the Pacific Ocean, its various palm-frond roofs jutting up at sharp angles. The place felt more Polynesian than Mexican despite the stone floors and round tiled tables. It was a favorite haunt of Canadian snowbirds and retired Americans who crowded the place every sunset to say good-bye to the great golden disc as it plunged into the sea. Cruzalta liked it because the booze was cheap and strong, and the endless tracks of Jimmy Buffett music were loud enough to drown out the mindless conversations taking place all around him. A perfect place for a middle-aged man to hide in plain sight.

Cruzalta wore the same gaudy tropical shirt, cargo shorts, and flip-flops that every other *güero* in the bar was wearing. It was the natural camouflage for the terrain. The only difference was that Cruzalta wasn't cramming a beer-barrel gut beneath his Tommy Bahama shirt and his calves were sculpted like diamonds from his daily five-mile run.

Cruzalta stood at the far rail on the lowest level of the bar nearest the ocean, drink in hand, staring out at the purpling sky, the setting sun half submerged on the far horizon.

"Colonel Cruzalta, a word, please," whispered in his ear.

Cruzalta's first instinct was to reach for the pistol in his concealed holster, but the voice in his ear was distinctly American and he felt neither the point of a blade nor the blunt edge of a pistol barrel in his back.

"Why not?" Cruzalta said.

Cruzalta turned around. He didn't recognize the fortysomething-year-old man standing in front of him, but he had the poise of a fighter in repose, completely relaxed and yet able to strike at the blink of an eye. There was a fierce, welcoming intelligence behind the man's clear blue eyes as well.

"You must be Pearce," Cruzalta said. "You travel fast. I wasn't expecting you until tomorrow."

"My pilot has a lead foot," Pearce said. He was referring to Judy Hopper, of course. She'd flown Pearce down in the company HondaJet and was getting the plane refueled at that very moment. "What's good to drink here?"

Cruzalta held up his whiskey glass. "Anything without an umbrella. Follow me."

Cruzalta slipped into the gray-haired crowd, brushing past the wide asses and veiny legs peeking out of too-short shorts. They made their way to the bar at the top level and ordered a couple of Johnnie Walker Blacks.

"Cheers," Cruzalta said as he clinked glasses with Pearce. They both tossed back their drinks.

"Another round," Cruzalta barked in Spanish to the barkeep. Two more were set up. Two more tossed down.

"You're the man who took out our friend Castillo, aren't you?" Cruzalta asked.

"Me and my team."

"Impressive. You did more in one day against Castillo than I was able to do in twenty years. I just wish you'd done it earlier." Cruzalta picked up a third whiskey and knocked it back. Pearce didn't touch his.

"You tired of feeling sorry for yourself, Colonel?"

Cruzalta's face hardened. "How would you feel if it was your soldiers who were burned to death?"

"For what it's worth, I think you ran the operation as well as could have been expected, given your orders."

"I did what I was told to do. That was my error. A good commander takes initiative. I should have disobeyed my orders. Taken more precautions."

"Soldiers are supposed to obey orders. Your reward was to be treated dishonorably. But then again, what else should one expect from a dishonorable man like Barraza?"

Cruzalta cursed. "Politicians. They're all the same, no?"

"I used to think they were. But I've recently learned that a few are capable of doing the right thing for the right reasons."

The Marine snorted. "Like your Myers? She's just another gringa with a gun pointed at our heads."

"No, she's not. In fact, that's why I'm here. She wants me to ask you a question."

Cruzalta blinked his bloodshot eyes. "Ask me a question? What question?"

"Is there somewhere else we can talk?"

"My brother's place, up on the hill."

"Does he have a satellite dish?"

Cruzalta pulled a couple of cold Tecates out of the fridge.

Pearce was on his cell phone as he flipped through several satellite television channels until he found an unused station.

Cruzalta set Pearce's beer on the table and fell onto the couch. He popped open his bottle and took a swig.

Pearce thanked whoever was on the other end of the call and clicked off. He picked up his beer and opened it.

"So your president wanted you to come down here to show me movies, Señor Pearce?"

"Not exactly. Cheers." He took a sip.

The TV channel acquired a signal. An empty chair appeared on-screen. A portrait of Winston Churchill hung on a wall behind the chair. A moment later, Myers stepped into the frame and sat down.

Cruzalta instinctively stood up.

"Colonel Cruzalta. Thank you so much for meeting with me. Please, have a seat."

Cruzalta glanced at Pearce, confused.

Pearce grinned. "We're pretty casual north of the border. Relax."

Cruzalta sat down. He realized he still had the beer in his hand and set it down on the table.

"Colonel, let me speak directly. We need your help. We have reason to believe that the Iranians have partnered with one or more of the drug cartels and that this alliance poses a strategic threat to both the United States and Mexico."

Cruzalta shook his head. "There have always been such rumors. Where is the evidence?"

Pearce clicked a button on a remote. A new image appeared. It had the point of view of a hidden handheld video camera. It was tracking Cruzalta's doomed convoy heading for the tunnel on the way to pick up the Castillo boys. As the vehicles raced down the highway, the image came in and out of focus as the automatic focus feature engaged.

The blood drained out of Cruzalta's face.

The camera swung up into the air to catch Cruzalta's helicopter. One of the camera operators chattered in Farsi.

Pearce translated. "He just said, 'Keep the camera on the convoy. It's coming to the tunnel.'"

"An Iranian?" Cruzalta asked.

Pearce nodded.

The camera swung back down shakily just in time to catch the convoy dash into the tunnel. The Iranian voice whispered loudly.

Pearce translated again. "He's saying, 'Wait for it . . . wait for it . . .'"

BOOM! An explosion in the tunnel. Napalm-fueled fire jetted out of the tunnel entrance.

The two Iranian camera operators roared with laughter. No translation was needed.

"Turn it off," Cruzalta demanded. Pearce did.

Myers reappeared. "I'm sorry to have upset you, Colonel. But you asked for evidence. We now suspect that the Iranians may be working with the Bravos."

"Why? What would the Iranians get from an alliance with Victor Bravo?"

"The Iranians have weapons and training. The Bravos have smuggling routes and safe houses throughout North America."

"Perhaps the Iranians were always working with the Bravos," Cruzalta suggested.

"Why would you say that?" Pearce asked.

"Bravo and Castillo have been trying to wipe each other out for years—a true 'Mexican standoff.' Neither could prevail. And yet, one did—arguably the weaker one. How?"

"We took out the Castillos," Myers said.

"Yes, of course. But why?"

"Because of the cross-border violence," Myers said. "Including my own son."

"But what changed? Why would the Castillos attack El Paso?"

"Stupidity? Accident? Misjudgment?" Myers offered.

"Perhaps. But look at the result. Now the Bravos and the Iranians are in control. The attack could have been made by accident or stupidity—"

"Or by design," Pearce concluded.

"That seems more reasonable to me," Cruzalta said.

"If true, that means the Iranians have been playing a very sophisticated game," Myers said. "And playing me like a banjo."

"We must inform my government immediately," Cruzalta said.

"Unfortunately, there's more to our story," Myers said.

Pearce pulled out a digital recorder and played an intercepted call between Victor Bravo and Hernán Barraza in which Bravo assures Hernán that he had nothing to do with the Houston attack and Hernán, in turn, assures Victor that *their alliance is still intact.*

"How did you get this?" Cruzalta asked, incredulous.

"Once the Bravos were identified in the Houston attack, we turned our attention to Victor Bravo. Exactly how we intercepted the call I'm not at liberty to discuss," Myers said.

Cruzalta shook his head in disbelief. "This means the Bravos will be able to create the first true narcostate in the Western Hemisphere in cooperation with the Barrazas."

Pearce took another sip of beer. "And the Iranians would have a government friendly to their cause and a base of operations that gives them a two-thousand-mile contiguous border with the Great Satan. What the Soviets could only dream of with communist Cuba, the Iranians would actually have with Hernán Barraza's Narco-Mexico."

"Are the Barrazas working with the Iranians as well? Or just Bravo?"

"All we know for sure is that Hernán and Victor Bravo have been talking. It would be smart for Bravo to keep his relationship with the Iranians hidden from the Barrazas. Otherwise, it might appear to be a threat to them, especially if we found out about it," Pearce said.

"And now we have," Myers said.

Cruzalta stood back up and began pacing, trying to process the massive data dump.

"Why have you told me all of these things? I'm a retired soldier. There's nothing I can do."

Myers smiled. "I have told you all of these things because I know that you are a patriot and love your country as much as I love mine. You have fought bravely against your nation's enemies, and your reputation is beyond reproach." Myers let that sink in for a moment then added, "That's why I want you to be the next president of Mexico."

Cruzalta laughed.

"And how would you accomplish that? An invasion? A CIA coup? No, thank you. The last thing Latin America needs is another government installed by the U.S. security services."

"It's not possible to change a country from the outside. Mexico itself must change. It needs new leadership that will create a real democracy."

"Do you think this is your original idea? There are many of us in Mexico who have dreamed of such a thing. But the ruling parties have a stranglehold on power."

"And that power has been based on the *narcotraficantes* for the last twenty years. If I help you eliminate them, then legitimate power can rule again. Under your leadership."

"No. I am not the man. But I know the one who is. And a dozen governors who would back him if they knew that a Bravo *sicario* wouldn't blow their heads off the next day."

"The fact that you don't want to be president makes you the perfect candidate, Colonel Cruzalta," Myers lamented. "But you know yourself better than anyone else does. And we need your guidance on this matter. I have no desire to do any nation building or remake Mexico in our image. I just want a free, prosperous, and democratic Mexico that no longer poses a strategic threat to my country."

"Then you would find many willing hands to help you, I assure you," Cruzalta said.

"We've already begun preparation for an operation to eliminate the Bravos. How long before you can contact your candidate and work out some sort of a schedule?" Pearce asked.

Cruzalta shook his head, incredulous. "You are presuming I am agreeing with this madness. As attractive as it sounds, I hope you will both understand that I have a hard time believing any of it is true. Americans always do what is best for Americans. *¡Pobre México! ¡Tan lejos de Dios y tan cerca de los Estados Unidos!'*"

"I cannot undo the past. Our countries have a shared history and not all of it is good. But together we can create a new future. But I also understand that trust must be earned, so let me propose this: we have located the Castillo killers responsible for the deaths of your men in the tunnel. They are currently residing in California. You are free to choose a team of your best men and take them down."

"Arrest them? Or kill them?"

"Whichever you prefer. Mr. Pearce?"

Pearce pulled a paper out of his pocket and handed it to Cruzalta.

Myers continued. "That is my executive order declaring the Castillo killers listed as enemy combatants and terrorists. I have the legal authority to name them as such. They are on American soil. I am now deputizing you to carry out the order to eliminate them as a threat. Mr. Pearce is a witness."

Cruzalta stared at the paper. He couldn't believe his eyes. "If I were to release this to the newspapers, it would destroy your presidency."

"Yes, it would. My fate is in your hands. But so is the fate of Mexico. So here is my proposal. Coordinate your efforts with Mr. Pearce. Any equipment you might need, transportation, whatever it takes, he will make available to you. After you have had your vengeance, then decide if my offer is real. If you think it is, we can move ahead with our plans."

"And if I still refuse?"

"I would understand completely. If I were in your shoes, I would be skeptical, too. I will do everything in my power to see Mexico become the prosperous and democratic nation I think it could be. But make no mistake. I will protect my country at whatever cost, with or without Mexico's help."

Cruzalta folded the paper and put it in his pocket. He looked at Pearce. "When can we leave?"

AUGUST

37

The White House, Washington, D.C.

Another meeting. Myers felt better about this one, though. At least it was a smaller circle of trusted advisors.

FBI Director Jackie West reported the bad news first: still no leads on the Bravo commandos who blew up the oil storage facility and sunk the *Estrella* in its moorings.

"Bill, is there any chance the Bravos made it back across the border to Mexico?" Myers asked.

The secretary of homeland security hesitated. "Since we don't know where they are, then technically we can't be certain. But my best guess is that they're holed up somewhere in the U.S., waiting to strike again."

Myers sighed with frustration. After her meeting with Diele, she backed off of her idea to seal the borders. He was the worst kind of politician, but that didn't mean he was stupid. The country was still euphoric after the "Drill, baby, drill!" speech and the surging stock markets. Her favorability rating peaked to its highest level ever. Jeffers had counseled her to hold off on the border decision because it would kick up a storm that would rob her of the momentum she now enjoyed, and she was going to need every ounce of political capital she had to weather the coming weeks. She had agreed, reluctantly. Now she was beginning to regret that decision.

"Any chance that *more* Bravos have crossed over to our side?" Myers asked.

"Again, no telling. They shouldn't have been able to the first time. But with the heightened alert, I'm confident we're probably okay," Donovan said.

"Probably okay? That's hardly reassuring."

"I told you I'd always shoot straight with you. I never promised I'd always hit the target."

"Fair enough," Myers said. She turned to the rest of the group. "I'm rethinking the border closing. Thoughts?"

"My father taught me that you can break a man's fingers one at a time," Strasburg said, holding up a splayed hand and then clenching it. "Unless he first makes a fist and beats you to death with it."

"Meaning?" Jeffers asked.

"It's always better to present all of your controversial ideas at one time. It makes them much harder to unpack. If President Myers dribbles them out one at a time, they can each get broken, and the cumulative effect is devastating."

Strasburg turned to Myers. "You're about to make an address to the nation. That will give you an opportunity to show your enemies your fist. I suggest keeping the border question tucked safely away until then."

Myers nodded in agreement, but her thoughts had turned somewhere else.

Yucca Valley, California

The high-desert altitude kept the nights cool, even during the summer months, and a good dusting of snow was common every now and again during the winters. Not like Palm Springs down on the valley floor where the humidity wrapped around your lungs like a hot, wet blanket this time of year, even after sundown.

Yucca Valley's claim to fame—true or not, it didn't really matter to the locals—was that an old Rat Pack love nest was located there, a Mid-century Modern that squatted on the very top of a hill on the edge of town. The helipad for the helicopter that flew in the girls and the dope was still visible from one of the main drags through the sleepy little desert town.

Old motor lodges, coin laundromats, and a dozen used-car lots littered the sides of Twentynine Palms Highway, which snaked north from I-10 out of L.A. up the steep mountain passes to the high desert. Yucca Valley was the perfect location for an enterprising drug operation, feeding the insatiable maw of Southern California addictions to the south or running shipments through the nearby Marine base, which, unfortunately, had a few bad apples willing to deal locally and transport globally.

Whereas the resort of Palm Springs featured multimillion-dollar estates, manicured private golf courses, world-class restaurants, and frequent visits by Hollywood celebrities, its uglier, deformed, and acne-scarred sister city up in the high desert had a slightly more modest appeal. It wasn't the Pizza Hut, the Walmart, or even the Starbucks that had tempted so many to make this a permanent home. In fact, these civilizing institutions nearly killed the place.

The reason why most people found purchase in the stony ground was because of its desolate isolation. Joshua Tree National Park was nearby, but the land around it was equally beautiful, cruel, and unforgivingly dry. The area had long been home to survivalists, painters, ex-con bikers, dishonorably discharged vets, child-support deadbeats, religious fanatics, and other reclusives. There were even miners still working a few active claims up in the hills.

Pearce and Early alerted the county sheriff about a possible national security exercise occurring that night, but only at the last minute—a courtesy call, nothing else. Gunfire wasn't entirely uncommon around here; the Twentynine Palms Marine Corps Base was just twenty miles up the road.

Castillo's men had relocated to Yucca Valley to take over a meth lab situated in an abandoned silver mine up in the hills above the town. A pair of surveillance drones had been tracking the three of them for the past thirty-six hours. They normally lived in a big five-bedroom rancher with a saltwater pool closer to town, but tonight they were in the meth lab cooking up a new batch.

Sergio Navarro had actually located a schematic of the operation from an old U.S. Bureau of Mines microfiche that had only recently been digitally scanned and archived. The good news was that there was only one way to access the mine, a single point of entry and exit. Perfect for a napalm attack or even a mass burial beneath the rock and dust. But Cruzalta opted for neither. He and his handpicked team wanted bloody vengeance, up close and personal.

Cruzalta had invited Pearce to come with him on the mission, but only as an observer. Pearce accepted. He wanted to study Cruzalta's tactics and small-unit operations firsthand. He knew there was always more to learn in the world's most dangerous game, and Cruzalta was one of the best players around.

The *Marinas* utilized a German EMT Aladin drone for scouting, a battery-powered plane of similar design to the American RQ-11 Raven that was about the size of a large model airplane and flown with a remote control. The infrared camera indicated that no guards had been posted, but three scrawny coyotes were lingering within thirty feet of the mine entrance.

A *Marina* sniper took out the three coyotes with his suppressed rifle. They barely yipped as the slugs ripped through their emaciated bodies, shredding their internal organs in an instant. Cruzalta generally liked animals more than people, but he couldn't take a chance on the feral canines barking once his men approached.

When the point man reached the mine entrance, he checked for trip wires and laser alarms. There weren't any. He advanced twenty feet into the mine, taking position behind a large ancient Dumpster on skids. He whispered in his mic, *"Claro,"* and the rest of the squad followed him in.

A corporal set a modified Boston Dynamics RHex rough-terrain robot on the ground and guided the six-legged metal brick into the shaft. Fluorescent lights shone in the distance. Air-venting systems hummed, vacuum pumps rattled, and men occasionally shouted in Spanish above the industrial din. It was a good thing the shaft was noisy. The RHex's six metallic legs—shaped in half circles and coated with rubber—thrummed like a washer with an unbalanced load. It made too much noise for Pearce's liking, but the RHex was a reliable, battle-tested drone that could climb up, over, or through creeks, logs, sand, rocks, stairs, drainpipes, and just about anything else you threw at it—in both directions, upside down, or right side up.

The nearly two-foot-long scouting bot chugged along one of the rough-cut walls. Cruzalta and Pearce watched the operator's face. With fore and aft cameras displaying both infrared and normal vision modes, it was easy enough to navigate the tunnel and locate a secure position from which to observe the occupants. The corporal signaled his target count with the world's oldest "digital" display—holding up a finger or thumb each time he identified one of the Castillo men or another criminal associate in one of the rooms. They knew there were three Castillo men and seven associates and, judging by the lighting, three rooms in use. Cruzalta needed to know how the men in the rooms were distributed.

The little boxy robot scrunched its way over a pile of tailings on the way to the last lit room. The loose rock on the pile gave way and the bot tumbled down to the floor. Its thirty-pound metal body clanged sharply against a stone.

The voices in the third room suddenly stopped.

Pearce instinctively clutched his weapon tighter.

A shadow emerged out of the far room, a human form backlit by the lab's fluorescent lamp. The gas mask on his head and his bulky chemical suit gave him an odd, otherworldly silhouette.

Cruzalta glanced over at his corporal.

The corporal signaled *associate*. He looked back down at his laptop.

The hapless investigator had just picked up the RHex and held it close to his face in the dark, studying its camera eyes.

On the corporal's IR screen, the man's face was a white glowing mask, heavily distorted by the lens in such close proximity.

The lab worker shouted over his shoulder to someone in the back room. His chemical suit squeaked as he turned.

"Hey! Look what I—"

Thwump-thwump. A silenced 9mm round tore out his larynx before he could finish the sentence and a second round severed his brain stem. His lifeless hands dropped the robot.

Cruzalta whispered commands in his throat mic before the meth cooker's corpse hit the dirt. His men rushed forward, MP5s in front of their helmeted faces, silent as cats, tossing flash bangs against the walls that caromed into the rooms. Pearce and Cruzalta followed right behind. The targets screamed as the concussive explosions burst their eardrums and their retinas seared in the blinding light.

The *Marinas* dashed in. Pearce stood back. He heard six muffled pops—silenced pistols dispatching the remaining workers—and watched three men dressed in chemical suits being frog-walked out into the main shaft, black bags over their heads, howling muffled curses through mouths stuffed with cotton rags and duct-taped shut.

Cruzalta signaled Pearce into the first room. It was definitely a meth lab. Pearce wasn't an expert but it looked to him like they were just about to begin a cook. Container barrels had been opened and plastic jugs full of clear liquids were stacked in rows on a tarnished steel table. Three corpses with their brains blown out lay crumpled against the far wall, red gore spattered on their bright yellow chemical suits.

"Two more rooms, two more labs. What do you want me to do with the bodies?" Cruzalta asked.

Pearce shrugged. "Leave them to rot. A lesson to anybody who wanders in here."

Cruzalta nodded. "Food for the rats." He then pointed at the barrel

and jugs. "What about the chemical precursors? Those are very dangerous materials."

"I'll call Early. We'll get a DEA hazmat team to pull them out."

Cruzalta grinned at Pearce. "Aren't you curious what I'm going to do
with those three *pendejos*?"

"Not as curious as they are, I'm sure."

A sergeant appeared out of the dark. He asked Cruzalta a question in
Spanish. Cruzalta nodded.

The sergeant lifted a razor-sharp tomahawk, the kind the U.S. military first issued in Vietnam. He crossed over to one of the corpses, stepped
on the lifeless forearm, and raised the ax high. The blade *tinked* on the
rocky soil as it cleanly severed the man's hand at the wrist. The sergeant
snapped open a clear gallon-size evidence bag out of a pocket and tossed
the hand in. He proceeded to the other body.

Pearce frowned a question at Cruzalta.

"That's how we collect fingerprints in my unit," Cruzalta said with
a grin.

Two hours later, Myers got the call from Pearce.

"Cruzalta is a true believer now. He sends his thanks and is awaiting
your instructions."

"Once again, I'm in your debt. Good luck, and good hunting."

38

The White House, Washington, D.C.

Myers was grateful for Pearce's phone call but it was anticlimactic. Myers hadn't been waiting idly for Cruzalta's approval. She'd always suspected he'd throw in with her. She knew in her bones that a patriot like Cruzalta would do whatever it took to save his nation from its enemies. As soon as Myers and Pearce had broken their Skype connection four days ago, Myers began ramping up so that when Cruzalta did formally agree to join forces they'd already be running in full stride.

The overall plan was simple enough, at least in theory. The drug cartels had held Mexican society in a stranglehold for decades, corrupting the political system with either cash or violence. By wiping out the Bravo organization, Cruzalta and his compatriots would be able to push aside the Barraza regime and help assemble a new national government. It would be a dangerous and lengthy venture for sure, but it was the first and perhaps only chance Mexico would have to form a new and fair democratic government, free from the tyranny of narcopolitics.

To assist Cruzalta and his allies in the formation of a new Mexican government, Myers directed Attorney General Lancet to provide a secure means by which the hundreds of Mexican politicians, military men, and law enforcement officers who were living in official and unofficial exile in the United States could be safely vetted, contacted, and recruited for voluntary service in the Mexican project.

Myers also promised Cruzalta that the United States and Mexico would soon draft new trade, border, and security treaties subject to approval by both national legislatures. More than anything, the new treaties represented Myers's sincere attempt to assuage any Mexican fears that the U.S. was somehow imposing a new kind of hegemony over Mexico rather than trying to form a genuine political and economic partnership.

That was the big picture. Myers knew there would be many smaller steps that had to be taken to begin this incredibly arduous journey. But given the scope of the undertaking and the breakneck timing, she couldn't afford a linear approach. She had to attack several fronts all at once, putting her most trusted staff to work on each one independently. If all the pieces didn't fall into place on time, the entire plan would fail.

After speaking with Pearce on Skype, Myers made three phone calls. The first was to Jackson, authorizing him to begin assembling a most-wanted list. The next morning, Jackson contacted the DEA, FBI, and DHS for recommendations. Twenty-four hours later, fifty names had been selected: twenty-five in Mexico, twenty-five in the United States. The trick now was to both find and track them all. Jackson focused DAS, RIOT, and Mind's Eye operations on the task, particularly for the Mexican list. The American list would be easier to find and track, thanks to the NSA, which had warrantlessly recorded, sorted, and stored every e-mail, phone call, tweet, and Facebook post of every American for the last few years as part of the counterterrorism efforts of the federal government, often in contravention to FISA restrictions. The "big data" analytics that had been originally pioneered by American corporations like Google and IBM to predict consumer behavior were now being perfected and deployed by the federal government to secure the nation against future terrorist attacks. In fact, dozens of private companies were wittingly or unwittingly participating in the NSA's global data-mining efforts.

An hour after Pearce called with the good news about Cruzalta, Jackson reported that all fifty targets had been identified and were being tracked. He couldn't guarantee how long that would last, so time was of the essence.

Myers's second phone call on the night of July 29 was to Attorney General Lancet. She was tasked with creating the legal framework for Drone Command. Lancet built organizational firewalls around Drone Command so that it would report directly to the president, completely insulating it from both the DNI and DoD command structures. Though a legal fiction, it was made an extension of JSOC, which operated with near impunity from congressional oversight and could invoke either Title 10 or Title 50 protections as needed.

Myers's last phone call had been to Early. He immediately contacted T. J. Ashley with the Drone Command offer and she accepted it on the spot because it sounded "interesting," knowing full well she would be shaping the future of U.S. drone warfare for the next decade—and maybe even changing the face of warfare itself.

Yes. Interesting.

Early brought her in to meet Myers six hours later. Ashley wasn't the least bit intimidated by her first visit to the White House or her first meeting with the commander in chief. Myers immediately liked the self-possessed younger woman. So did Jeffers, yawning over a cup of coffee. Just over five feet tall, with short-cropped dirty blond hair and hazel eyes, the trim, athletic engineer was a firm handshake and all business.

"What do you think you're going to need to begin operations in seven days?" Myers wanted to know.

"Depends on the targets," Ashley said. "When will I have those?"

"Soon, including locations. Give me your best estimate."

"More hours in the day and a boatload of money should do the trick," Ashley said.

"Money I can find. More hours I can't."

"Then I'll take the money and sleep less. Do you want to review the organizational plan I've put together?" Ashley opened a leather satchel and handed Myers an inch-thick document.

"How could you have possibly drawn up an organizational plan already?" Myers asked.

"I wrote it a year ago as a kind of thought experiment. It seemed to me that this was the natural direction our defense establishment would be taking in the near future. I just didn't realize when I wrote it how near the future actually was."

Myers mentioned Pearce's suggestions for Drone Command organization. Ashley had already incorporated them. She and Pearce had discussed the essential concepts a few years ago when he was trying to recruit her into Pearce Systems.

Early grinned like a hyena. "Can Pearce pick 'em or what?"

Jeffers nodded. "He sure can."

Myers dropped the organizational plan on her desk. "I don't need to read this. You just be ready to jump when I give the go signal. The rest I'll leave up to you."

"Yes, ma'am." Ashley couldn't believe her good fortune.

"Mike will be your liaison with the attorney general. See her next. Any other details, run them past Sandy."

"Anytime, day or night," Jeffers said.

"Thank you, sir. I'll take you up on that." Ashley checked her watch. "Better get to work." She glanced at Early and he nodded, grabbing his cell phone as they both exited the office.

"So far, so good, don't you think?" Myers asked her chief of staff.

"Just one question," Jeffers said, pouring himself another cup of coffee. "Have you thought about how you're going to start building a coalition in Congress for this thing?"

"You played sports in college, didn't you?"

"If you call intramural tennis a sport."

"What do you know about old-school, smash-mouth football?" Myers asked.

"You know I suck at metaphors, especially at this time of day."

"Give it a shot," Myers said.

"I take it you mean a ground game with lots of mud?" Jeffers asked.

"No. More like a Hail Mary."

Drone Command Headquarters, Fort Meade, Maryland

Having the most-wanted kill-list names and locations was one thing, but human targets had a nasty habit of moving around, especially if they ever got wind that they were on something like a kill list. With any luck, Drone Command would be able to take them all out in one fell swoop, but that was highly unlikely. Ashley needed to keep them under constant surveillance. For that she'd need to deploy the "persistent stare" technology of ARGUS-IS married to MQ-9 Reaper drones. The Autonomous Real-time Ground Ubiquitous Surveillance Imaging System provided live wide-area video images by employing a 1.8-gigapixel digital camera, itself a construct of 368 5-megapixel smartphone-camera CCD sensors. At high altitudes, the ARGUS-IS could track all of the movement within an entire city simultaneously, resolving objects as small as license plates. By storing almost three days of video imagery, analysts could replay suspicious movements and establish potentially threatening patterns of behavior.

ARGUS-IS was an ideal surveillance platform for battlefield commanders, but civil libertarians in the United States claimed that such "persistent stare" capabilities were the equivalent of warrantless searches of private individuals. Ashley deployed ARGUS-IS over her U.S. targets anyway because Lancet had drafted an executive order exonerating Drone Command from any such legal liabilities should the issue arise.

With the proven ARGUS-IS system in place, Ashley decided to experiment with two other systems. She paired the new Stalker drones that, in theory, could stay aloft forever by means of an electric battery that was recharged by either a ground-based or air-based laser, to the new Hitachi camera facial-recognition systems, capable of scanning 36 million biometric faces per second—equal to the entire population of Canada. A perfect combination for finding their target needles in human haystacks.

Ashley even managed to borrow one of NASA's repurposed RQ-4 Global Hawks. With a range of over eight thousand miles and an integrated sensor suite of infrared, optical, and radar systems, the Global Hawk could provide reliable high-altitude surveillance capacity if needed.

All the data collected by these various systems would be bounced off of satellites and then pumped into a specially designated terminal at the Utah Data Center, the NSA's massive, multibillion-dollar data collection, storage, and processing facility near Bluffdale.

Ashley's strike plans also fell into place rapidly. Radar-jamming UAVs would provide electronic cover in Mexican airspace if needed. She was confident that Drone Command would be ready to launch by the time Myers gave her the command to strike. Once the first attack was launched, Ashley and her team had just sixty days to complete the mission in the unlikely event that War Powers would be invoked by Congress and funding withdrawn for operations. Her personal goal was to complete the mission in twenty.

39

Washington, D.C.

On the morning of August 11, the White House communications director made a surprise announcement to the networks, notifying C-SPAN and the other news media outlets that President Myers was going to make a major policy address that evening at the unusual hour of 11 p.m. EST.

When asked what the announcement was, or why it was being held at such a late hour, the director replied, "No comment," because she did not, in fact, have any idea what the speech was all about, which was highly unusual, and even more startling was the lack of a written transcript of the speech, which was typically provided several hours before any presidential broadcast so that both pundits and producers could prepare. Speculation was rampant.

Myers had been famously frustrated by the petty politics of state government as a governor, but that was high school locker room stuff compared to what one female senator termed "the jail shower free-for-all cocksmanship" that was Washington, D.C. Perhaps Myers was tired of the whole mess and craved the simplicity of just being the CEO of her own privately held firm, or so the speculation ran.

"Distracted" was the word most frequently used to describe her of late, but the frequency of use was due primarily to the fact that journalists were among the least original thinkers on the planet. The pseudopsychologists suggested that the death of her son had taken a deeper psychic

toll on her than she or anyone else had imagined and that she was entering into a kind of post-traumatic stress syndrome. They further speculated that the stress of the office hadn't given her the time to grieve, but
they were unaware of the fact that Myers had refused to allow her grief to
be televised for political gain.

Vice President Greyhill was on a trade mission in Toronto when he
was asked by the Canadian media about the president's announcement,
and he also issued a "no comment." That was because he, too, lacked any
insight, and his own attempts to secure a private meeting or even a phone
call with Myers were politely rebuffed by Jeffers. Greyhill wondered if the
oil rig catastrophe had finally overwhelmed Myers and her staff. He'd
long felt that the office was far above her limited capabilities and had
raised that very issue in the primaries. She was an ingénue when it came
to international politics, and practically a rube off the turnip truck when
it came to the Beltway.

Greyhill had inherited both his father's patrician good looks and his
Senate seat, but it was his late mother's Calvinist conviction that he was
predestined for greatness that drove him. Why was he standing in a hotel
room in Toronto instead of in the White House?

He should have won the primary. Greyhill was the first one to label
Myers "the Ice Queen" for the pain and suffering her budget freeze proposal
would cause. *Had caused,* he reminded himself. But his handlers—the
same tired old cadre of overpaid political hacks perennially hired by the
GOP establishment—had told him to remain "above the fray" and trust
their messaging. Meanwhile, Myers's upstart campaign ran a series of
brilliant TV ads that showed her sitting around a kitchen table with a
single mom, or a widow, or a young family and letting them talk about
how they had to balance their checkbooks at the end of every month no
matter how tough times got. "Why can't Congress do the same?" each of
them asked at the end. *Why hadn't his team thought of that?*

Greyhill had run against the Democrats in the primary while Myers
ran against Congress. Ironically, Greyhill counted many liberal Demo-

crat congressmen as his closest friends and colleagues, but he loathed Myers, never more so than now.

For the last several weeks Greyhill had been completely cut out of Myers's inner circle and banished to the hinterland of international PR junkets, dignitaries' funerals, and military base closings to get him away from her. He knew it was because she was hiding something from him. But what?

The banishment had sucked all of the juice out of him. He felt as dry and angry as old kindling. The secrecy of tonight's speech fueled an irrational rage in him. Greyhill was determined to find a way to run Myers out of office before her term was up.

Senator Diele was forced to wait like the ordinary mortals to find out what Myers had in mind. He feigned a lack of interest to friends and colleagues during the day of the announcement, but when 10:59 p.m. rolled around, his keister was firmly planted on the leather sofa in his luxury suite at the Watergate Hotel, eyes fixed to his big-screen television.

Diele had been desperate to sway her to his way of thinking. He was a formidable ally and an unrelenting opponent. Like all congressmen, his reelection prospects hinged on what he could bring back home to his state, and like a dutiful milkman, he had been delivering the goods for over thirty years.

As any freshman political science major knew, the only way that every congressman could bring home the bacon was to be sure there were enough pigs at the trough to be slaughtered. Every Washington politician—liberal or conservative, urban or rural, Egyptian-American female or eighth-generation WASP—had the same goal: get reelected by giving their constituents whatever they wanted. Period. The cruel genius of the crushing national debt was that it was, in reality, the largest election campaign slush fund the world had ever seen. All of that borrowed money had one singular purpose: to keep incumbents in office. Every politician paid lip service to the crippling effect the escalating debt would have on the future generations who would be the ones forced to pay it all back. But the brutal fact was that most incumbent politicians couldn't care less about future generations because future generations couldn't vote.

Congressional constituents were nearly as corrupt as their representatives. All of the voter hand-wringing about the deficit faded once they were confronted with the possibility that their own fat subsidy checks, cushy government jobs, generous federal contracts, or arcane university research grants could all go away if the deficit was reduced by a single penny. Spend less and somebody got less, and that made voters mad, and mad voters scared the hell out of politicians.

Diele was happy to navigate those tricky waters for Myers, but for a price, of course. His state was disproportionately more dependent upon government spending—particularly defense spending—than other states. If she had been willing to preserve his piece of the rice bowl rather than demanding that everyone sacrifice equally, he would have gone to the mattresses for her. But she was a stone-cold bitch and she could rot in hell as far as he was concerned.

Diele took another sip of his Scotch. He kept the talking news heads on mute. They were just rambling about what the speech might be about. Or more precisely, the airheads were reading aloud from the teleprompter the opinions of the real news writers who were expressing what they thought the president might be speaking about but who were too ugly to appear on camera themselves.

The news anchor then ran a clip of Myers at the oil rig platform. Diele had to admit, she was a good-looking woman, even in a hard hat.

40

Washington, D.C.

At precisely 11 p.m. EST, President Myers appeared on Diele's television screen. She wore an elegant but understated blue business suit. An American flag was draped prominently behind her as she sat at her desk in the Oval Office. A bust of Teddy Roosevelt was also conspicuously displayed off to one side.

"Good evening, my fellow Americans. I'm addressing you tonight because of a number of recent developments that, taken together, pose a significant security threat to our nation. Beginning with the cross-border assault in El Paso and extending all the way to the Houston oil fire, it has become increasingly clear that the United States faces a new strategic threat. The question is, what exactly is the nature of that threat and how should we deal with it?

"As most of you realize, our country is still wrestling with the economic and physical effects of fighting the War on Terror for more than a decade. There are any number of arguments for or against that war, but no one can doubt the bravery and sacrifice of our men and women on the frontlines of the battlefield, many of whom paid the ultimate price to help secure our nation against another catastrophic attack by Islamist extremists. Thousands of our soldiers have died and tens of thousands have been wounded, physically and mentally, by a seemingly endless war that has cost our nation two trillion dollars to prosecute so far, and perhaps another two to four trillion as we care for the brave men and women who have suffered for their service.

"I was elected, in part, to honor that sacrifice in blood and treasure, and to maintain constant vigilance against any future attacks by our enemies, but the American people have also made it clear that the era of sending American soldiers into battle in faraway lands is over. While we will always honor our treaty commitments with our allies, we are no longer willing to shoulder the primary defense burden for those who are capable of defending themselves.

"My administration is committed to what has been termed the Powell Doctrine, the tenets of which are well known. Is a vital national security interest threatened? Do we have a clear, attainable objective? Have the risks and costs been fully and frankly analyzed? Have all other nonviolent policy means been fully exhausted? Is there a plausible exit strategy to avoid endless entanglement? Have the consequences of our action been fully considered?"

Myers's face softened.

"Please forgive me for what must sound like another long-winded political speech. But it's terribly important that I share with you my thoughts tonight and that we speak honestly with each other. It's the failure to speak boldly and clearly about the challenges that face us that has brought our nation to the brink of economic and social disaster. With your help, and with the help of the courageous congressmen and senators from both parties who have joined with us, we've finally managed to begin to put our fiscal house in order. The budget freeze that's been put in place is projected to slow the growth of federal spending and eventually balance the federal budget within ten years. It will require constant vigilance and iron-willed discipline to maintain the freeze, but no more vigilance or discipline than many of you have been forced to exercise as a result of the devastating job losses and wage reductions of the last decade.

"Every single mother trying to balance her checkbook, every small-business owner trying to stay in business, and every freshman college student working a part-time job to pay for school knows that you can't spend more than you take in without courting financial catastrophe. The fact that a generation of politicians has ignored this self-evident truth is one of the reasons our nation is in trouble. On that front, at least, we have made significant progress."

Diele took another sip of Scotch. *What was she getting at?* He found himself literally sitting on the edge of his seat. The force of her voice, her earnest demeanor, the firm but calming cadence of her speech had riveted him. He wondered if she was having the same effect on everyone else.

Myers continued.

"But the single mother also knows that, while she must balance the checkbook, her children must still remain safe. And the truth of the matter is that America is not safe. We haven't been for a long while. That truth was brought home to me in the worst possible way several weeks ago when my son and over a dozen of his students were brutally murdered by a Mexican drug cartel hit squad. I was overwhelmed by the sympathy, prayers, and many other kindnesses you bestowed upon me and my family during our time of grief. But that tragedy instilled in me a resolve to address an issue that we have been all too willing to ignore, let alone combat. The great irony is that while we have been willing to fight battles in distant fields like Afghanistan and Iraq, we've been losing a terrible war here at home in cities like Los Angeles, Chicago, and Dallas.

"It was President Nixon who first declared the War on Drugs over forty years ago. That was also at a time when we were winding down from a decade-long war on the Asian continent. For forty years, American law enforcement personnel at the national, state, and local levels have fought valiantly against drug dealers despite limited resources and imposed legal restraints. Billions have been spent. But the sad truth is that hundreds of thousands of Americans have either died or have been incapacitated mentally or physically over the decades as a result of our failed attempt to win the War on Drugs.

"But it doesn't stop there. Even as I speak, over half a million people are incarcerated for drugs and drug-related offenses, including violent crimes and property crimes. Incarceration, in turn, imposes its own burdens and costs on inmates and their families, as well as an enormous cost to the society as a whole. Over half a million Americans will visit an emergency room this year as a result of drug abuse, costing billions to taxpayers and insurers. And more Americans will die this year as a result of drug overdoses than they will from car wrecks. That's about the same number of soldiers who were killed in three years of combat during the Korean War.

"Simply put, illegal drugs are destroying too many of our citizens, our families, our neighborhoods, our communities. Illegal drug use crowds our prisons, floods our health care system, cripples our schools, and robs the futures of millions of people. We lose tens of billions of dollars each year in tax dollars and personal income that should otherwise have been spent on our families and our communities for schools and housing and retirement.

"And in the spirit of full disclosure, let's admit our complicity in the horrific violence that has torn apart our neighbors to the south. Over fifty thousand Mexican citizens have been killed in the last several years as a result of the Mexican government's attempt to battle the drug cartels on our behalf. Today, Mexico earns more American cash from illegal drug sales in our nation than from legitimate exports to our country. Mexican cartels produce the preponderance of hard drugs that are the primary sources of that revenue, and the great sums of money they generate have been the catalyst for the bloody turf wars that have also been the cause of many innocent Mexicans' deaths. Mexican society has suffered greatly because of our addictions and we bear some of the responsibility for that suffering.

"To be perfectly clear, I believe it's time to end the so-called War on Drugs."

Diele couldn't believe what he was hearing. *Did she really just say that?* He quickly rewound the DVR.

Yeah, she did.

Myers continued.

"Wars can be ended by quitting the battlefield—or by defeating the enemy. The reason why we're losing the War on Drugs is because we have never really fought it like a real war. We must change course.

"While the future of the Middle East remains quite uncertain, what is positively clear is that we have not suffered another attack on U.S. soil like the one we suffered on 9/11 because of the sacrifices we have made and continue to make waging *real war* on our enemies in the War on Terror. In that sense, we've won that war—and continue to win it—and will always guard against Islamic terrorists who would destroy our nation.

"But there is another kind of terror. It takes more lives, causes more destruction, costs more money. We haven't won the War on Drugs because we haven't fought it like a real war. That has been our failure. We have two choices. Quit the war or really fight it. I choose to fight. Tonight, I am asking Congress to join with me to fight a real War on Drugs. It must be fought with the same intensity and clarity as any other war and in compliance with the Powell Doctrine I discussed earlier. Here is what I propose.

"First, is a vital national security interest threatened? The answer is yes. The extraordinary human and financial costs have just been explained. But let's not miss the obvious, either. The recent attack on the Houston oil facility was conducted by members of the Bravo drug organization.

The drug lords have long waged a war of terror on their victims—fear is one of their chief weapons. Burnings, beheadings, torture, kidnap, rape—these have all been used by the Mexican narcoterrorists against Mexican citizens. Increasingly, they're being used against American citizens on American soil as well. As the commander in chief, I am responsible for the protection of American lives and property, and I intend to carry out my responsibility in full. It is my considered judgment that the narcoterrorists pose a national security threat. This is not a war on the government of Mexico or the people of Mexico. It is a war against the narcoterrorists, wherever they may be found.

"Second, do we have a clear, attainable objective? Yes, we do. Every patriotic American felt a justifiable sense of pride and accomplishment when SEAL Team Six put a bullet in the skull of Osama bin Laden, the man most directly responsible for the death of three thousand Americans on 9/11. We have destroyed al-Qaeda's capacity to attack us at home because we have killed the leaders of that organization.

"I propose the same strategy that was employed by both the Bush and Obama administrations in regard to terrorists, which also enjoyed wide congressional approval. My administration has drawn up a most-wanted list of the fifty most powerful and violent drug lords and drug dealers in both Mexico and the United States. Eliminating the key leadership will cripple the production and distribution networks in Mexico and the United States, and serve as a warning to those seeking to succeed them.

"My policy is simple. You deal, you die—or you go away forever. For Americans, the choice is equally clear. Either you are for the narcoterrorists or you are against them. There is no middle ground."

Diele fumed at the television screen. "You mean, either I support your militarized drug policy or I'm an enemy of the state? A narcoterrorist? Bullshit!"

Myers continued.

"I understand it's not possible to completely eliminate the sale or use of illegal drugs but that is not our goal. Our goal is to curtail them significantly. History has shown that this approach is difficult, but effective. There is no drug dealing when the dealers are dead. Dealers are no longer considered criminals in my administration. My administration considers them to be enemy combatants and terrorists.

"Let me raise a few more salient points. Everything I've discussed tonight will be posted on my website, and I'm asking Congress to meet in an emergency session as soon as possible so that these new policies can be put into law. Until then, however, I will be using executive orders in the exact same way my two immediate predecessors, Barack Obama and George Bush, used them to prosecute the War on Terror.

"My first executive order is to declare the fifty members of the most-wanted list as terrorists and enemy combatants. That gives them the same legal status as Osama bin Laden, who killed three thousand Americans a decade ago. The fifty drug terrorists on the most-wanted list and their evil empires are responsible for ten times as many American deaths *each year* in our country as Osama bin Laden murdered on that terrible day.

"My second executive order is that no American service members will be put on Mexican soil. This would be a clear violation of existing bilateral and international treaties. However, just as we've used drones in Yemen to kill American-born terrorists, we will use them wherever we find the drug terrorists we've targeted. Because I am not deploying American troops on foreign soil, the War Powers Resolution does not apply. If Congress attempts to cut off funding of this operation in the future, I urge voters to contact any representative who is aiding and abetting the drug dealers that are killing our children and express their concern.

"My third executive order provides for an immediate review of federal prisons. Any prisoner who is guilty of only nonviolent drug-related crimes will have their case reviewed and, if possible, they will be not only released but also pardoned, and their records expunged if they are not arrested again for any other reason and they remain drug-free for three years. This will result in enormous cost savings for the federal government. I urge states to follow my example.

"My fourth executive order concerns the addiction problem itself. Through the cost-saving measures of the pardon program, my administration will make medical resources available free of charge to any indigent drug addict or hard-core drug user who genuinely seeks a cure through a program of strict and guided supervision.

"My fifth executive order is to end all federal regulations against the private use and possession of medically supervised marijuana for individuals over the age of twenty-five. This clears the way for states to decide for themselves what policies they want to enact in regard to private marijuana use. As a former governor and strict constitutionalist, I believe the federal government has exceeded its authority in regard to the states. States are the great laboratories of democracy, not federal bureaucracies. As an aside, as president, it is not appropriate for me to decide this issue, but if I were still a governor, I would have actively opposed the legalization of marijuana in any form in my home state of Colorado.

"My final executive order is in regard to our borders. Our long-term goal is to create a border that is open enough to allow for the free movement of capital, labor, and goods, but secure enough to prevent unwanted persons or materials from crossing. One of the primary ways to accomplish this balancing act is to keep track of who crosses our borders. I have authorized the Immigration and Customs Enforcement Agency to begin immediate implementation of retinal, fingerprint, and DNA documentation for any person entering our country, and those records are to be maintained for future reference. Known criminals, undocumented workers, and former deportees will be denied entrance into our country. I am also activating National Guard units to enforce the current laws on the books already passed by Congress to secure our borders. I invite Congress to change the current laws if they deem them too restrictive or punitive.

"In conclusion, one of the most important tenets of the Powell Doctrine is that actions such as I have taken tonight should be supported by the American people. If you support this new War on Drugs, then I urge you to contact your elected representatives and tell them that you support our efforts to make our nation more secure and more prosperous.

"I know that some, or perhaps all, of what I have proposed this evening will not be popular, but I did not become president in order to be liked. I became president in order to do what is right for the American people. I came into politics because there is a conflict between good and evil in the world, and I believe that, in the end, good will triumph if we fight for it. Only the brave are free.

"May God bless you all, and God bless the United States of America. Good night."

The camera lights shut off and Myers stood up from behind her desk, motioning to Jeffers to follow her to her private study.

"So that's what a Hail Mary looks like," Jeffers said, beaming.

"That was just the throw. Let's wait and see where it lands."

41

Toronto, Canada

Fifteen minutes after President Myers's broadcast had concluded, Vice President Greyhill picked up his cell phone and dialed an unlisted number.

Senator Diele picked up after the first ring.

"Gary, we need to talk," was all the VP said.

Washington, D.C.

Senator Diele stood at his picture window admiring the lights of the city. He was on his cell phone, grinning. Alliances were quickly forming. Myers had finally gone too far.

"Yes, Mr. Vice President. I suppose we do."

San Pedro Garza García, Mexico

Target 03 lived in a quiet, tree-lined suburban city just southeast of the Universidad de Monterrey, one of Mexico's finest institutions of higher education. Separated from the great sprawling metropolis of Monterrey a few miles to the east by the Rio Santa Catarina, it was a safe and tranquil place to raise his family away from the terror and carnage of the cartel turf wars.

Until tonight.

Target 03 had been visually acquired three hours prior. The drone operator was waiting for everyone in the sprawling house to settle down for the night. Infrared sensors onboard the MQ-9 Reaper verified his location and, more important, the location of the rest of the family. Drone Command orders were to minimize collateral damage if at all possible.

As soon as his wife and four children were bedded down, Target 03 stepped outside by the pool. The sharp flare on his image indicated he was lighting up a cigarette. He then dialed his cell phone. The call to his mistress was recorded for a voice confirmation.

The drone operator checked the time again. 10:59:57 p.m. EST. The president's speech would begin in three seconds. She watched the seconds tick off, then armed the Reaper's two laser-guided 70mm Lockheed Martin DAGR rockets, which were much smaller versions of the more famous Hellfire missiles and were intended to minimize collateral damage. The operator was given authority to fire at will.

She did.

The operator's screen erupted in a halo of white-hot flame. When the halo dimmed, she recorded the result.

A smoldering crater.

Smashed concrete and tile.

Chunks of warm meat that glowed white with heat in the cold rectangle of the pool.

"Mission completed," she added.

Twelve extended-range (ER) MQ-9 Reaper drones had been deployed that night, fanning out all across Mexico from private airfields just across the border. Mounting two extra fuel tanks on hard points originally designed for weapons, the modified Reapers had nearly double the range of their predecessors, allowing them to strike deep into Mexico. Most fired rockets, others were specially fitted with rotary weapons for low-altitude strikes. Both kinds of weapons systems proved equally effective, achieving similar results to the Target 03 mission, most within a few hours of one another.

A speeding convoy of three armored Chevy Suburbans racing for Nuevo Laredo was strafed with armor-piercing rounds. Targets 09, 11, and 13 were shredded in the assault along with a dozen unidentified armed associates.

In Guadalajara, a 70mm DAGR rocket smashed through the plate-glass window of Target 04's twenty-fifth-floor penthouse suite. She and the two men she slept with were turned to smoking chum by the white-hot fléchettes of molten glass from the initial strike. Had they survived the first blast, the explosive round would have finished the job.

Incendiary slugs ignited the gas tank of a seventy-foot bay cruiser anchored a half mile off of the coast of Veracruz, burning Target 25 to death, along with his heavily armed crew.

Target 08 drowned, trapped inside his vessel when it sank to the bottom of Lake Chapala, strafed by radar-controlled gunfire.

Targets 05 (Campeche) and 20 (Durango) were believed critically wounded by separate Reaper strikes, but confirmation of death was still pending.

Squads of commandos handpicked by Cruzalta took out six more targets with old-school wet work (blades, garrotes, semiauto pistols) while off-duty *Marina* snipers transformed the brain pans of three other targets into puffs of pink mist.

But not everything went according to plan that night. Target 01— Victor Bravo—was located at a fortified compound in rural Chiapas. Two extended-range Reapers were dispatched for the high-value target; rockets were loosed. Bravo escaped, miraculously, when the first rocket misfired and veered off course, alerting him to the attack. Three unidentifieds were killed.

A total of nineteen of the twenty-five primary Mexican targets had been eliminated. The rest were on the run.

The attacks in the U.S. were equally successful. Seventeen of twenty-five primary targets were taken out with no civilian collateral damage, including Bravo's top lieutenants in Washington State, Texas, and Louisiana. In the end, there was surprisingly little protest over the use of drones themselves against American citizens. The public understood that it ultimately made no difference if the American targets were killed with bullets fired from manned or unmanned vehicles. Bad guys were bad guys and dead was dead.

Pearce had selected a strike team for ground operations to take out targets not accessible by remote control. But he held his own people in reserve for a snatch-and-grab of Ali Abdi in the event they ever located him. Privately, Pearce was concerned that Ali had somehow slipped the net and made it back to Iran.

By any measure, the initial decapitation strike had been a brilliant success—better than they could have hoped. What it led to next, however, nobody could have foreseen.

San Diego, California

Pearce was stuck in traffic. Again. It fouled his already lousy mood.

"Still no leads on Ali?" Pearce grumbled. His tech wizard Ian was on the other end.

"The problem is too many leads. I can't process the data flow fast enough." The million-square-foot Utah Data Center was gushing a torrent of data—billions of bytes per hour—and all Ian had, comparatively, was a sippy cup to catch it with.

"Thanks. Call when you have something." Pearce signed off.

The San Diego–Coronado Bridge was jammed in both directions and so was Harbor Drive. Unless he wanted to abandon his car in the middle of the road and walk over the bridge, he'd just have to sit here and enjoy the view. California dreamin'.

There were worse views in the world. God knows, he'd seen them. Had even caused some of them. But his frustration was at an all-time

high. He knew that almost any code could be cracked given enough computing power and time. Ian had the computing power—backed by the
limitless resources of the federal government. Unfortunately, it was Pearce
who had the time on his hands, and waiting for a breakthrough was killing him. Ali Abdi must have been one hell of an operator. He certainly
knew the first rule of the game.

They can't hurt you if they can't find you.

Pearce's one consolation was the electronic billboard flashing up ahead.
A slideshow of most-wanted listers, their faces, names, and stats rolling
past, each slide ending with the promise of a $100,000 reward "for infor-
mation leading to the arrest of . . ." He'd seen them all over Southern
California. They'd been posted all over the country as well. There weren't
many names left. Right now, Pearce hoped that one of those asshats
would get captured or turn themselves in and spill the beans on Ali Abdi.
That was as likely as this traffic jam clearing up anytime soon.

42

Myers's startling national address triggered several responses with astonishing rapidity. Of course, the radio talk-show pundits were gibbering about it within minutes after it had aired, and while the majority of those shows had conservative hosts and audiences, even they had mixed reactions, at least initially. Of course, few people actually saw or heard the live presidential telecast because it had aired so late.

The chattering classes went into overdrive the next day on television and radio; satellite, cable, and network stations were inundated with nothing but the Myers announcement. The Christian Right was particularly incensed at the thought of "legalized marijuana," though technically, Myers hadn't legalized it. In fact, it had been a rather cynical ploy on her part. Every governor she had ever worked with had demanded greater state autonomy from the federal government so she was only giving them exactly what they wanted. Besides, only Colorado and Washington had legalized recreational marijuana in 2012; every other state—including liberal California—still considered it an illegal drug outside of medicinal usage.

The few liberal talk shows that were still on the air teed off on just about every other issue she raised, but the idea of targeted killings was the hammer that rang the most alarm bells for them. Those self-same moralists didn't raise an eyebrow when President Obama had taken credit for personally selecting human beings as targets for drone strikes—including the killings of four American citizens who had been neither tried nor convicted of any crime—nor had they complained when President Clinton had thrown cruise missiles around the Horn of Africa like a wobbly drunk playing a game of darts at the King's Head pub back in the '90s.

Cries of another Nixonian "imperial presidency" were leveled by liberal critics for Myers's excessive use of executive orders to bypass Congress, conveniently ignoring the over one hundred EOs issued by President Obama. They also didn't seem to mind President Obama's use of dozens of unelected and unapproved "czars" who issued thousands of new regulations that carried the force of law.

Conservative pundits who applauded Myers's use of executive orders to carry out her actions, however, were screaming tyranny when President Obama had used them previously. And where were they when President Bush had issued 291 executive orders during his two terms of office? But then again, Bush was a slacker compared to Bill Clinton's record issue of 363 executive orders. If Myers was guilty of an "imperial presidency," it was because she stood on the shoulders of the elected emperors from both parties who preceded her.

But that was just the beginning of the debate. Hours and hours of heated exchanges about sovereignty, globalism, executive powers, free trade, the causes of drug abuse, the failings of the criminal justice system, and just about every other aspect of modern American life were discussed ad nauseam. It was a national town hall, but most of the speakers seemed to suffer from political Tourette's syndrome.

Within days, thousands of protestors had taken to the streets in larger urban areas. The Occupy Wall Street crowd had long since lost its original focus, but the president's announcements gave them renewed purpose. They reemerged in their disorganized glory, a collection of unhygienic malcontents, bored trust-fund kids, unemployed anthropology majors, and D-list Hollywood airheads camping out on courthouse lawns and civic-center plazas on both coasts, smoking dope and swapping STDs in bouts of equally unorganized, angry, and pointless sexual encounters.

The only problem was that the OWS types often protested against themselves. The antiglobalists and legalized-dope advocates wound up in screaming matches with the borderless-world advocates and Ivy League romantics. The anarchists protested everybody and everything, merely on principle.

But the OWS rabble was only a tiny fraction of the turnout. The Tides Foundation, the SEIU, the reorganized and rebranded ACORN radicals, and a half dozen other left-wing groups had quickly mobilized their standing armies of professional "volunteers" in "spontaneous" rallies. Hispanic protestors were conspicuously absent from these initial events.

But the radical left's response nevertheless prompted the various Tea Party, Posse Comitatus, and Minute Man factions to rally around their respective historic flags (national, state, and Confederate), mostly in suburban and rural areas, far away from the maddening urban crowds. All in all, it was as ugly and beautiful a spectacle of free speech and free assembly democracy as anyone could have hoped for in the morally hazardous climes of the twenty-first century.

American public opinion among educated people was strongly uncertain on the whole affair. Myers enjoyed incredible pluralities of public support for specific aspects of her announcements, but there was no clear majority that favored *all* of her actions. Two fault lines fractured public opinion: the need for security versus the protection of civil liberties. Most valued both, but not equally, especially when they were in conflict.

Even the most-wanted list couldn't drive the needle all the way over in her direction, despite the fact it was posted on the FBI's Most Wanted web page, the White House web page, and dozens of law enforcement pages, along with millions of private Facebook, Twitter, Tumblr, Pinterest, and other social-media sites, not to mention the tens of millions of private e-mails blasting around the Internet daily. If anything should have won her overwhelming public approval, the most-wanted list should have done it, Jeffers had reasoned. The most-wanted list was a roll call of sociopaths who were deeply connected to the drug trade but also guilty of violent crimes far exceeding their involvement with drugs. And yet, a considerable plurality of Americans on both sides of the political spectrum were still troubled by the use of lethal force against American citizens without benefit of trial, whether or not drones were used, even if the threat was imminent and catastrophic.

At the top of the Mexican list were Victor Bravo and his top ten lieutenants, some of whom were Castillo bosses who now swore loyalty to the Bravos. The top of the American list included Bravo's top ten lieutenants operating on U.S. soil. But dealers from other organizations, including Chinese Triads, Salvadoran gangs, Jamaican posses, and white power bikers, were also on the list. Fifteen of the targets were women charged with some of the most heinous crimes imaginable. None of the targets was under the age of twenty-one, as per Myers's direction.

The one thing the targeted drug dealers all shared in common was that they were evil personified. In addition to drug dealing, each of them was guilty of at least one or more violent crimes, including murder, torture, rape, arson, armed robbery, or kidnapping. Victims were often innocent; too often they were law enforcement officers in Mexico or the United States, or even military personnel. Hispanics clearly dominated both sides of the list (on the Mexican side it was almost entirely Hispanic), but a number of Anglos, African Americans, and even a few Asians on the American side ensured that the list couldn't be construed as anti-Latino, though that charge would be repeated over and over in the days and weeks to come.

The Mexican government's official response was predictable: outrage. Mexican politicians raged on radio and television.

"A violation of international legal norms."

"A betrayal of decades of mutual cooperation and trust."

"A matter to be taken to the International Court of Justice."

And so forth.

———

Mexican newspaper editorials were somewhat less restrained.

"Another *yanqui* stab in the back."

"Naked hegemony!"

"A strange, cruel attempt to repeal NAFTA."

"The end of history."

But not every Mexican newspaper looked unfavorably upon what was being termed the "Myers Doctrine." Stranger still, the Mexican public was mostly in favor of it. *Anything to break the back of the* narcotraficantes *that had tormented them for so long.*

President Barraza ordered the Mexican armed forces to the border "to prevent American terrorist and criminal elements from entering *our* country" and declared Mexican airspace "inviolable," with solemn pledges to shoot down any American drones that dared cross into it. He also summoned Ambassador Romero to Los Pinos for an excoriating lecture on the megalomaniacal and dictatorial posturing of "that woman" before dismissing him unceremoniously from both his office and the nation.

Privately, however, President Barraza craved retaliation. Would it be possible to acquire drones of their own for operations within the United States? Was the Mexican military capable of engaging American troops along the border—snipers, short incursions, harassments? He raised these possibilities with his capo, Hernán, who counseled restraint.

"Let's see how this plays out, Antonio. Nothing may yet come of it. We have options we can exercise later if we need to."

"What options?"

"Trust me, brother. It's better if you don't know what they are." Problem was, Hernán didn't know either. He was just hoping Victor Bravo had something up his sleeve.

San Diego, California

Ali Abdi's response to the whole situation was borderline despair.

What else must I do to provoke the effeminate Americans to invade these idol-worshipping Catholics?

If the Americans didn't invade Mexico, then Ali's plan with the Russians would be in jeopardy.

More important, his larger plan that even the Russians weren't aware of would fail completely.

He had no choice.

Ali had hoped to hold the Bravo men and his own Quds Force soldiers in reserve, especially now that they were well hidden on American soil. His original intention was to use them in partisan-style actions, harassing American supply lines when the U.S. military finally invaded Mexico.

But the invasion never happened.

Ali would have to unleash his forces now if there was any hope of provoking a full-on American military assault into Mexico, and he had just the plan to do it.

43

Capitol Hill, Washington, D.C.

Myers had called for an emergency session of Congress to codify into law what she had already initiated on behalf of American national security and sovereignty through a series of executive orders.

She got only half of what she'd hoped for.

Senator Diele had, indeed, called for an emergency session, but only of the Senate Armed Services Committee, which he chaired. It took several days for the vacationing senators and their staffs to return to the sweltering humidity of Washington, D.C., and for Diele to assemble and summon his witness list.

As both president pro tempore of that august body and as chairman of the committee, Diele had the authority to call his committee into emergency session, as Myers had publicly requested be done. That was a mistake, in Diele's opinion, one of several she had recently made. It was the mistake that would lead to her impeachment if he had anything to do with it.

According to the U.S. Constitution, the vice president was the president of the Senate, but in practical terms this was a largely ceremonial function. Vice President Greyhill, in theory, could have called the Senate into session as well, but Diele and Greyhill had decided in private that it would be best if Greyhill kept his cards close to his vest for now. Diele had already been an outspoken critic of Myers and it might prove useful if Greyhill feigned allegiance to Myers on the off-hand chance she decided to pull him back into her inner circle. More important, once Myers was thrown out of office, the mantle of the presidency would fall upon Greyhill's shoulders. He would lose legitimacy in the eyes of the American people if he was seen as having a hand in Myers's downfall, which would be viewed for the naked power grab it obviously was. No, it was far better for Greyhill to keep his hands off of the whole affair until Diele handed him the office. That's when Greyhill could afford to be demonstrably appreciative of Diele's efforts.

The first day of the committee hearings featured a parade of witnesses selected by Diele. Members of his own party protested; several of them supported at least part of Myers's agenda and wanted to help buttress her position, but Diele would have none of it. Even a few of the principled Democrats, some of whom also supported some of Myers's positions, balked at Diele's heavy-handedness. But Diele assured them that the administration and its supporters would have every opportunity to present their case. Diele wanted to be first out of the box because he knew the American people had very short attention spans and it was best to be the first shiny object in their ADD-riven fields of view.

A predictable collection of academics, civil libertarians, think-tank denizens, and Latino community organizers presented their arguments. Their positions varied from the idea that Myers was, at best, misguided and, at worst, guilty of international criminal and human rights violations. Savvy witnesses who dropped the best lines got the most play in the twenty-four-hour news cycle. Some of these included:

Politicians want a costless war. Generals want a riskless war. Drones satisfy both and the collateral damage will be peace.

Violating Mexican sovereignty in defense of our own is an act of criminal irony.

President Myers has proven that taking humans out of war to reduce the cost of war only makes war more likely.

Drug consumption is an American problem. Killing Mexicans can't be the solution.

If this president is so concerned about the drug war, maybe she should start by investigating the CIA's long career as the biggest drug pusher in Latin America.

One word, ladies and gentlemen: Skynet.

But if there was one aria that Diele's opera sang over and over, it was the War Powers Resolution. By not submitting herself to its requirements—basically, getting permission from Congress to attack other countries—she was destroying democracy and inviting tyranny both in the United States and around the world. She was violating the Constitution that she had sworn to uphold and defend. No one used the actual phrase but "an impeachable offense" hung in the air like a fart in church.

True to his word, Diele did permit administration supporters to testify. Attorney General Lancet was the last to testify, and the only cabinet member to do so. As such, she spoke for the president.

Diele fired the first salvo.

"How does this administration legally justify an attack on another sovereign state without congressional approval, as specified by War Powers, let alone without a formal declaration of war? This is, after all, a war, isn't it?"

"Yes, it is, Mr. Chairman. And the president has asked Congress to commit wholeheartedly to fighting and winning it."

"Then why didn't the president come to us beforehand? If she truly considers it a war and was always planning on seeking our approval, then she knowingly began a war without a declaration of war. Her very actions testify against her as having violated the law."

"A couple of points, Senator. First of all, this administration did not attack the Mexican government or its national institutions so we are not waging war against a sovereign state, any more than President Obama waged a war against Pakistan when he sent SEAL Team Six in to kill Osama bin Laden in Abbottabad."

"So you're suggesting that American drones aren't operating in Mexican sovereign airspace?" Diele fired back.

"Of course they are. But they're targeting individuals within Mexico, not the Mexican military or government, just as American helicopters ferried troops to OBL's compound."

"Osama bin Laden was a sworn enemy of the United States and was recognized as such by the AUMF. President Obama had the legal right to carry out that action. This cuts to the very heart of the matter, Ms. Lancet."

"I agree. The al-Qaeda terrorists have been a threat to the United States, but far more Americans have been killed, directly and indirectly, by the Mexican drug cartels than by al-Qaeda. That makes the drug lords a bigger threat, in our opinion, a threat this Congress has failed to adequately recognize, let alone address."

"Then why didn't President Myers come to us and request an Authorization to Use Military Force in this case?"

"Why should she? AUMF is derivative of WPR and, as we've stated, we don't believe that WPR applies. Which leads to my second point. President Myers believed this nation faced an imminent security threat from the cartels and their affiliates, and deemed immediate action necessary, as is her prerogative as commander in chief. The purpose of WPR is to prevent the United States from entering into another decade-long debacle like Vietnam. But the president has no intention of waging an extended conflict against the narcoterrorists. It's a limited, well-defined action. So once again, the WPR doesn't apply.

"Third, the WPR only requires the president to *report* to Congress the deployment of U.S. forces abroad within forty-eight hours, not request permission to deploy those forces. For the record, no U.S. military personnel have been dispatched to Mexico, only unmanned drone systems, so by definition, the WPR once again does not apply."

"You're splitting hairs on that one," Diele insisted. "American drones are being flown by American personnel, even if they are located in Fort Huachuca, Arizona."

"We're both lawyers, Senator. Splitting hairs is what we do best."

A laugh rolled through the gallery. Diele lightly tapped his gavel.

"But the most important point is this. President Myers did not seek the advice and consent of Congress prior to this action because she believes Congress is increasingly irrelevant to any of the solutions this nation needs, including the present crisis. In fact, Congress is the cause of many of the crises we face."

The gallery exploded with cheers and applause, and a scattering of boos. Some senators threw up their hands in disgust; others applauded. A few grabbed their microphones and began shouting at one another. Diele gaveled the room into silence under penalty of expulsion.

"For the record, Ms. Lancet, you are aware of the doctrine of the separation of powers? The three separate and distinct branches of government? It comes from that pesky little document known as the Constitution of the United States."

"I am indeed, sir. So is the president. Her desire is that the Senate and the House live up to the responsibilities of their respective institutions. Case in point. President Obama launched over three hundred drone strikes against Pakistan in his first term in office—also a sovereign, independent nation like Mexico—and not a single congressional vote was ever taken on any one of those strikes. In fact, since the first known drone strike in 2004, at least forty-seven hundred people have been killed."

"Those drone strikes were conducted under the AUMF," Diele insisted.

"But there was no AUMF for Libya when President Obama committed American drones to combat in Libya—another sovereign nation, by the way—for the purpose of helping to topple the existing government, which, ironically, was an American ally in the fight against al-Qaeda. The Libyan action was not an act of self-defense, no American lives were at risk, no treaty commitments to an ally were invoked. More to the point, no congressional approval was apparently needed, nor was congressional interest aroused in the slightest. By your definition, President Obama invaded a sovereign state and did it without a declaration of war, which, under the separation of powers doctrine, is your assigned constitutional responsibility."

Myers's supporters on the committee applauded, as did a number of people in the gallery. Diele gaveled them quiet. Lancet continued.

"The United States has not declared a war since 1941, but the litany of conflicts we've been in—'wars' by any other name that involve the loss of American lives—is incredible: the Korean War, the Vietnam War, the first and second Gulf wars are just the big ones. There were twice as many covert operations that were no less acts of war, including a dozen coups d'état in Asia and Latin America during the hottest years of the cold war. So the president's question for you, Senator, is why has Congress been so interested in fighting wars over the past seven decades but not in declaring them?"

"The president should be worried about fulfilling the legal responsibilities of her office, not lecturing us on how to conduct our affairs."

"Her legal responsibility is to protect and defend the nation. This nation has suffered grievously for a lack of leadership, particularly from Congress. She hasn't tried to avoid the Constitution, Senator, she's trying to invoke it. You know the numbers as well as anyone: drugs have killed far more Americans than any foreign enemy from any war we've ever fought. And what have you done about it?"

Diele banged his gavel.

"You will show respect to this committee or you will be held in contempt."

"Mr. Chairman, you first came to Washington over thirty years ago.

What was the national debt when you arrived? What was our balance of trade? What was the annual budget deficit? What was the price of the average home? How much did it cost to educate a child? How much was a gallon of gas? Please name for us, for the record, one significant social problem this Congress has not exacerbated, let alone resolved."

Diele banged the gavel again and again as the gallery howled with delight.

"I am going to hold you in contempt, Attorney General Lancet, if you don't control your tongue."

"As every public opinion poll has demonstrated for the last twenty years, sir, the American people already hold Congress in contempt. For the sake of the Republic, and for the legitimacy of this institution, it's time for you to help us fight and win this horrific war being waged against our cities, our culture, our children. Help us—or get out of the damn way."

Lancet grabbed her satchel and stormed past the cheering gallery that stood and clapped for her defiant performance as she marched toward the exit.

Diele banged his gavel in vain, trying to call the hearing back to order. When his colleagues began to rise and quit the room, he banged the gavel again and announced the hearing dismissed until further notice, but the damage had already been done.

The television cameras caught everything, just as Diele had hoped. He just hadn't planned on getting his ass handed to him by a Junior Leaguer like Lancet.

Fortunately for Diele, there was one man who had watched the entire scene with a great deal of interest. Ambassador Britnev had the weapon Diele needed to bring Myers down, and he was sure that the broken old man he saw on his television screen would be desperate enough to use it.

44

Yucatán Peninsula, near Peto, Mexico

Victor Bravo complained that he hadn't had a beer in a week.

He and his men had been hiding from the American satellites swinging overhead in an abandoned mission compound and he couldn't exactly run down to the local *mercado* and restock the refrigerator.

Eleazar Medina took Victor's thirst as a sign from God.

Raised in a devoutly evangelical home in rural Guatemala, Eleazar was one of fourteen children of a lay Foursquare Gospel minister in a remote village in the north. All of the Medina children had been forced to memorize whole books of the Bible, but 2 Samuel was a favorite of Eleazar's because it was the passage of the Old Testament from whence he had gotten his name. "Eleazar, son of Dodo" was one of David's "mighty men of valor," and little Eleazar's skinny brown chest puffed out three sizes larger every time he recited it boastfully to his childhood friends.

But that had been a long time ago, and Eleazar was a different person now, one of Bravo's most trusted lieutenants. He'd done terrible things for Bravo, things for which he'd often prayed for forgiveness, but the guilt always remained. He could never quite get the feeling that the blood on his hands had been washed off even though the blood he'd shed had been, well, necessary, hadn't it?

As soon as Bravo had said he wanted a beer, a familiar verse came back to Eleazar: *Y David dijo con vehemencia: ¡Quién me diera a beber del agua del pozo de Belén que está junto a la puerta!*

Eleazar remembered that the verse was from 2 Samuel 23:15. And didn't his father always say, *God always makes a way of escape?*

There was no question in Eleazar's mind that God was opening a door for true forgiveness for him, if he would just have the courage to step through it. Just like Victor Bravo, King David was hiding in his wilderness stronghold in the midst of his enemies when he longed for a drink from a faraway well. And wasn't Eleazar, son of Dodo, one of the three mighty men who fetched it for him?

"I'll get you some beer, *hermano*. Leave it to me," Eleazar said.

Victor's eyes narrowed.

"No. It's too dangerous. You might get killed."

"I'd rather die trying to steal a cold beer than wait for a hot rocket to fly up my ass," Eleazar answered cheerfully. Everybody in the room laughed, including Victor.

"Okay, then. Get me some beer. We'll keep our asses locked up tight until you get back."

The other men howled with delight and stared at Victor hopefully. He laughed again, reading their minds. "Get enough for them, too!"

Eleazar threw a sloppy salute and scrambled away with a grin plastered across his face. Moments later, he leaped on an ancient moped and gunned the lawn-mower-size engine, scrambling out of the walled compound and onto the dirt path that wound through the jungle back toward Peto. Eleazar hoped his cell phone still carried a charge.

Three hours passed. The heat of the day rose like a tide from hell, wrapping the compound in a shroud of suffocating humidity. The sentry stood underneath the stone portico of the abandoned mission. It kept the sentry out of the sun, but it didn't help him cool off. He wished he was inside the sanctuary where it was cooler. Bravo and the others were enjoying their afternoon siesta, snoring in hammocks slung between the columns.

The sentry checked his canteen. Empty. He'd drained it an hour ago. But if he came off the wall to refill it, he'd be shot for abandoning his post. He'd just have to tough it out a few more hours and then he could get a drink of water and even get some shut-eye, too.

The sentry heard the whine of a truck engine approaching through the trees. He needed to check it out, but he was under strict orders to stay under cover if at all possible, just in case there was overhead surveillance. He stayed underneath the roof line and raised his binoculars. What he saw made him laugh.

That *pendejo* Eleazar.

A big beer delivery truck came lumbering out of the trees, rolling slowly over the deeply rutted dirt road. The logo on the side of the beer truck was a giant Mayan head, drawn in the traditional style, tilted back and chugging down a cold bottle of Sol. A local pop radio station blared inside the cab.

The sentry raced down the wooden ladder and ran across the compound to unlock the front gate. He could already taste the cold beer splashing in the back of his throat.

The truck stopped on the other side of the locked gate. Eleazar grinned inside the air-conditioned cab. He was gesturing *Hurry up!* through the cold windshield that was fogging up against the warm, damp air outside.

The young sentry unbolted the iron gate and swung it open on its rusty hinges. He jumped up on the truck's running board on the driver's side as Eleazar pulled in.

The sentry tapped on the cool glass. Eleazar rolled the window down. The truck's refrigeration unit roared overhead.

"Where did you steal this from, *hermano*?"

"Back in Peto. It was at the Super Willy's across from the *zócalo*. I don't think they'll miss it, do you?" Eleazar beamed with pride.

"If they do, too bad for them!"

Eleazar stopped the truck in the middle of the compound, several feet from the church. He leaned on the horn.

"What are you doing?" the sentry asked.

"Waking those lazy asses up. Time to drink some beer."

"Let them sleep! More beer for us."

"Don't be such a greedy pig. We're socialists now, remember?" Eleazar leaned on the horn again. A few bleary-eyed comrades stumbled out into the bright light. Their faces lit up when they saw the truck.

"Let me in the back," the sentry begged.

"Not yet."

"Give me the key or I'll bust it open."

"Just wait. Trust me." Eleazar finally saw Victor emerge into the shadow of the front portico. He stood there, smiling, clasping his hands together and shaking them like a rattle by his head, the universal sign of approval.

"Fuck you, Eleazar. I want some beer," the sentry said.

"Just wait a minute, will you?"

Victor ambled out into the harsh sunlight, making his way toward the truck.

The sentry dropped down onto the ground and headed for the back of the truck.

The first Bravo out of the church was just a few feet away from the truck now, licking his lips. But Victor was still too far away.

The thirsty sentry swung the back door open. He saw the muzzle flash from the suppressed end of a pistol. The hollow-point slug punched a small hole into his forehead, but the subsequent intracranial shock wave blew out the back of his skull and all of its contents while he was still on his feet. His corpse was knocked to the ground by the first soldier out of the truck.

Eleazar felt more than heard the squad of *Marinas* scramble out of his vehicle. Seconds later, they fanned out around the compound. Eleazar remained locked in the truck as ordered.

An eight-bladed Draganflyer X8 surveillance rotocopter zoomed over the compound. The drone was flown by another squad of *Marinas* that had followed Eleazar's truck from Peto a half mile back.

The *Marinas* had told Eleazar to stay in the truck no matter what, out of concern for his safety, but as he watched Victor Bravo race unnoticed back into the church, Eleazar feared Victor would get to the escape tunnel and seal the entrance before the *Marinas* could reach him.

Eleazar couldn't let the Devil get away. How else could he pay his debt to God?

Eleazar grabbed his pistol out of the glove box, leaped from the cab, and tore after him. An AK-47 opened up. Bullets clawed him from his groin to his belly.

Eleazar clutched his stomach. His hands were full of intestines, pink and wet with blood, like an offering.

Eleazar's wobbly legs gave way. His eyes dimmed.

He felt himself falling into the darkness, afraid that God wouldn't catch him.

45

Victor Bravo was dead.

Hernán drained his third glass of whiskey. He was worried.

Without cartel muscle behind them, the fragile web of Barraza alliances—strung together by fear and corruption—would quickly melt away. And then the mice would come out to play with their machetes, seeking revenge.

Hernán could run. He had a chalet in Switzerland, a flat in Paris, and a fat bankroll stashed in Paraguay. Life could be good.

His other option was to answer the damn phone. The one flashing Victor Bravo's number, even though Victor was dead. Answer it, even if it was a mouse calling him.

"Yes?"

"Señor Barraza, I know you were a friend of Victor's."

"What do you want?"

"He was a friend of mine, too. My name is Ali Abdi. We need to talk."

Ali understood Hernán's situation perfectly. Offered the use of his trained men, fiercely loyal to him. "You know what they're capable of doing."

"Houston?"

"Of course."

Hernán was intrigued. "Your services in exchange for what?"

Ali explained. The terms were acceptable. More than acceptable. Hernán agreed. They worked out a plan.

No need to leave Mexico after all.

Hernán smiled.

Poured himself another whiskey. Time to call in favors from his friends in Caracas and Havana. Start the plan rolling *ahora*.

He drained his glass.

Fuck the mice.

Two days later, one of the big media conglomerates began running a Victor Bravo memorial piece, extolling his virtues as an advocate for the poor, his charitable work among the *campesinos*, and the vast array of clinics, orphanages, and education centers he'd built around the country over the last two decades. The show featured glowing interviews with grateful farmers, Indians, admiring *telenovela* stars, and several staged "man-on-the-street" encounters, and all of it was scored with popular folk music that had been written about him over the years. The media conglomerate—a big supporter of the Barraza campaign during the last election—had already put it together even before the death of Victor Bravo. With orders from Hernán, they released it to any television station or cable satellite programmer that wanted to run it free of charge.

The hugely popular show was picked up immediately by the Spanish-language networks in the United States. Local news shows then ran their own follow-up programming, tying together all of the recent events, including the terrible border-crossing situation affecting so many Hispanics in both countries. Like their English-language counterparts, Telemundo, Univision, and the other majors had distinct political agendas that favored a particular point of view slanting against the Myers administration, which was increasingly vilified on these networks because of the new border regulations. What most Anglos didn't realize was that Spanish-language news shows were the number one rated shows of *any language* in Los Angeles,

Dallas, Phoenix, and Houston. The Victor Bravo mythology—and his death, which was now being characterized as a martyrdom—was spreading like wildfire on both sides of the border.

Bay of Campeche, Mexico

One hundred and seven miles offshore from Veracruz, a PEMEX oil rig, the *Aztec Dream*, was topping off a giant oil tanker with crude pumped directly from the gulf floor. Bill Gordon was the offshore operations engineer (OOE), which made him the senior technical authority on the PEMEX rig. The middle-aged Texan in the burnt orange UT Longhorns ball cap had worked on offshore oil rigs all over the world, including the Persian Gulf, before joining PEMEX.

Bill was finishing up a cigarette in the designated smoking area way up high near the rig office, right next to one of the emergency lifeboats, enjoying a million-dollar ocean view. He flicked the butt off the rail and watched it drift down the two hundred feet or so toward the churning gulf waters below, but he lost sight of it before it hit the waves.

A glint of silver caught his eye and he glanced up. Bill had seen plenty of drones when he worked in the Persian Gulf and easily recognized the one circling overhead. Flying low.

He supported Myers's most-wanted-list policy wholeheartedly, but kept that opinion to himself, since his Mexican counterparts on the rig were mostly against it. When he saw the Reaper, his heart skipped a beat. He was damn proud to be an American, and that little piece of technology roaring around in front of that four-cylinder turbocharged engine up there was yet another proof of American technological dominance.

What he couldn't quite understand was why it was flying around his rig. He scanned the water around him, searching for a renegade Zodiac or maybe some frogmen who might be trying to sabotage the vulnerable platform, but he didn't see anything.

He wondered if the Reaper was on some kind of routine patrol. Whoever was flying it must have been new on the job, though, because the wings kept wobbling and the plane yawed back and forth, as if it were fighting a stiff crosswind. He guessed it was a training mission for a young pilot stuck in a trailer in Nevada somewhere.

The Reaper circled lower and closer until Bill could see the big American flag on the fuselage and the two antitank missiles slung under its wings. It was close enough that he pulled out his smartphone and zoomed in on the drone with the built-in video camera.

WHOOSH! A missile roared off of its rack in a jet of flame and smoke.

"Shit!"

Bill nearly dropped his phone. He watched the missile track until it slammed into the side of the big oil tanker, just above the water line. The thin steel skin of the tanker erupted under the force of a warhead designed to penetrate heavy tank armor. Flaming oil gushed out into the gulf, forming a fiery slick near the ship and the pumping boom that connected it to the rig.

Bill raced for the door of his office to call it in when he heard another WHOOSH! overhead. It sounded so different from the first one, he instinctively knew it hadn't been fired at the tanker.

A massive explosion rocked the oil rig. The missile had smashed into the wellhead assembly, the worst possible location. High-pressure oil and gases from deep within the earth's crust now burst free and caught fire, creating a seventy-foot-tall blowtorch of white-hot flame. Fire quickly spread onto the main deck, fueled by the fine mist of oil clouding the air. New explosions rocked the steel decking under Bill's feet as gas welding canisters and storage tanks exploded like a chain of firecrackers, throwing shards of jagged steel whistling through the air.

Within moments, the lower decks were enveloped in a cauldron of fire. Men roasting alive screamed as they threw themselves over the rails toward the ocean below. Fire crews grabbed hoses and fire extinguishers, and charged toward the advancing flames, but it was too late. The rig's installation manager sounded the alarm. Sirens wailed. The few surviving crew members who weren't trapped or already dead raced for the bright orange lifeboats hanging in their stanchions, Bill among them, but the sea itself was on fire. Chances were that they would be boiled alive inside the boats like lobsters in a pot.

The *Aztec Dream* had become a nightmare of the damned.

One hundred and twenty-five miles away, the Iranian drone technician maneuvered the Reaper back toward a hidden Bravo landing strip, his mission with the hijacked American Reaper a complete success.

46

New York City, New York

Oil prices skyrocketed once again and stock markets roiled around the world on the news of the American drone attack on the Mexican offshore oil rig.

Despite her administration's protests to the contrary, the world firmly believed that Myers had taken out the oil rig in retaliation for the attack on the Houston tank farm weeks before.

Privately, the oil-producing nations thoroughly enjoyed the price spike. Countries like Saudi Arabia had crested their peak oil reserves in recent years; sooner rather than later the tap would run dry. Any boost in revenues, for whatever reason, was seen as a huge benefit.

Publicly, of course, those same oil-producing nations—Venezuela the most vociferous among them—decried the attacks on the PEMEX facility as an attack not just on an oil facility, but on the entire global marketplace, driven as it was by the free flow of petroleum. The Venezuelans claimed that America was just another "fading superpower" that was simply lashing out in a vain, unbridled attempt to crush the emerging Mexican economy. Socialist, Marxist, and racialist explanations were soon forthcoming from the usual sources both inside and outside of the United States.

But it was the UN secretary-general who surprised everybody when he introduced a resolution approving the most recent findings of the self-appointed Global Commission on Drug Policy (GCDP), whose members included the former presidents of Mexico, Colombia, and Chile, along with luminaries from the entertainment and financial industries. Myers's unilateral actions had struck a sensitive nerve with the secretary-general and he'd long sought a means to combat them. The Mexican oil rig attack had finally given him the opportunity. Privately, the Russian delegation encouraged the secretary-general in his efforts.

The essential finding of the GCDP was that the War on Drugs was not only a failure but actually fueled other social crises, including the spread of HIV/AIDS. The GCDP was distinctly "antiwar" in every sense and advocated that all international efforts to curb drug use must focus exclusively on the prevention and treatment of drug abuse. The UN secretary-general called for a vote. He wanted the United Nations to formally affirm the GCDP's finding.

In other words, the UN was voting against the Americans' highly militarized approach to the drug problems their nation faced. What was particularly stinging about the resolution was that the GCDP findings were presented to the General Assembly by two other GCDP commissioners: a former chairman of the U.S. Federal Reserve Board and a former secretary of state, both distinguished Americans. The nonbinding resolution passed with an overwhelming majority. Understandably, the United States protested and, ultimately, abstained from the vote.

The mainstream media picked up the UN story and ran with it, along with interviews with the oil rig survivors, including three Americans. Hospitalized in a medically induced coma, Bill Gordon was so badly burned that both of his arms had to be amputated above the elbows. But it was his video that had identified the Reaper as an American aircraft.

The Mexican government expressed its outrage in no uncertain terms. President Barraza, guided by Hernán's counsel, began a national tour of historic sites, promoting Mexican nationalism and patriotic fervor. He was careful, however, to play up the victim angle, pledging to "resist as far as humanly possible the natural desire for justice and revenge that the Mexican people are calling for," which was actually true after the oil rig attack.

The oil rig attack, coupled with the anti-Myers media blitz, fueled further protests in the United States. Whereas before the protestors had numbered only in the hundreds, the new protestors actually numbered in the tens of thousands. The biggest concentrations were in Los Angeles, Phoenix, Dallas, Chicago, and New York, all cities with significant Hispanic populations.

Worse, the protests coincided with a "Day Without a Mexican" strike. As the day unfolded across the nation, America woke up to a new kind of "brownout." Anglo America discovered that their yards weren't being cut, their pools weren't being cleaned, their cars weren't being washed, and their burgers weren't being flipped.

This strange rapture of cheap service labor wasn't limited to the wealthy, either. Even middle-class families were hit by the startling phenomenon. Whole restaurant chains—from the high-end sit-downs to the lowliest fast-food drive-thrus—suddenly shut their doors. Busboys, valets, checkout girls, fry cooks, sous chefs, and managers hadn't shown up for work, either.

In Texas, freeway construction ground to a halt. In Iowa and Arkansas, the meat-slaughtering plants shut down. Home building and city services (especially garbage, sewer, and landscaping) nearly collapsed in the major urban areas. In the rural areas, farms and food processors that depended on the backbreaking and mind-numbing labor of pickers, handlers, and sorters could no longer function.

The spirit of César Chávez, the long-dead Chicano community and union organizer who first coined the term *Sí, se puede* (Yes, we can) forty years before Barack Obama had used it, had revivified, at least among Hispanics, fueled by the organizational and financial support of the Venezuelan agitprop mastermind behind the strike. Spanish-language radio stations and social-media sites spread the word like wildfire: "Yes, we can send a message. You Anglos killed Victor Bravo, you've tightened up the border, and you're harassing us for documents *you all know we don't have*, and we're not happy about any of this."

The strike threatened to spread and linger through the week, if not longer.

Angry, frustrated, self-righteous middle-class people from both parties, concerned *over the well-being of their Hispanic friends, of course*, complained bitterly.

Myers's public opinion polls plummeted.

Washington, D.C.

Myers met with Early over morning coffee minutes before the Presidential Daily Briefing was about to begin.

"We're sure this wasn't a Drone Command screwup? I'm not looking to chop off heads, I just need to know," Myers asked.

"They think it was a hijack. It's happened before. A few years ago, the Iranians pulled down an RQ-170 Sentinel drone that had been flying over Pakistan. They reconfigured the drone's GPS coordinates, fooling it into thinking it was landing back at base when it was really landing in Iran."

"But this is more sophisticated than just swapping out map coordinates, isn't it?"

"Yeah, it's got Ashley in a real lather. Someone actually took control of the drone—flew it, fired its weapons."

"What has she done about it? Or can this happen again?"

"She says they've put together a new, more sophisticated encryption package on the satellite uplinks. That should solve the problem. The fleet is grounded until you give the okay."

"'Should' solve the problem? I need better than that."

"Your only ironclad guarantee against another hijack would be to keep the drone fleet grounded, drain the fuel tanks, and lock them up in storage."

"That's not acceptable, either."

"There's no such thing as a perfect weapons system. They all have vulnerabilities. You just have to decide if the risk of the vulnerability is worth the mission profile they fulfill."

"What do you think, Mike?"

"I say keep them flying. If it happens again, then ground them again. Otherwise, the bad guys have taken away our biggest asset, and you'll be forced back to conventional warfare options if you want to continue the full-court press."

"Why can't we track the Reaper's GPS now and find it?"

"Its GPS system isn't responding. Probably disengaged."

"You said the Iranians hijacked one of our drones before. Are they the ones behind this?"

"Maybe. But the Iranians aren't the only ones with that kind of technical know-how."

"You mean the Chinese? The Russians?"

"Yeah, or the Indians or the Germans or the French or a hundred private companies right here at home. There's no telling where the *technology* came from. Who's using it is another matter."

"Cui bono?" Myers asked.

"Excuse me, ma'am?"

"It's Latin. It means 'Who benefits?'"

"As in higher oil prices?"

"Yes."

"That's a pretty short list of countries, but it also includes some Americans who stand to profit personally."

"All right. Then who benefits from us getting tangled up in a war with Mexico or even all of Latin America?"

"That's another list. Much longer, by the way."

"And would some of the countries and names on the first list appear on the second list as well? Who benefits doubly from our predicament? That would be our third list."

"That's a very interesting question."

"Yes, isn't it?" She took a sip of coffee. "If Ashley feels good about it, keep the drones flying. I trust her judgment better than my own on this matter."

"Will do. And I'll keep my puzzler turned on. That third list is gonna be a humdinger."

Galveston, Texas

Dr. Yamada punched in Pearce's cell number.

"You okay, Kenji?" Pearce asked.

"I was gonna ask the same about you, brah. Lot goin' down."

"I've got my hands full." Pearce didn't tell him with what. He knew he wouldn't want to hear he was hunting another human being. "How's the beach down there?"

"Bah! Don't call dat a beach. Air humid. Water hot like a bathtub, tar balls in there, too. Three-foot-high pile of seaweed all along the shore, and stinging sand flies. And worse? No waves!"

"You getting settled in okay?"

"Great facility. Everything arrived okay. Putting the puzzle pieces together. We'll be ready to go for your oil-baron buddies next month."

"Thanks, Kenji. Good to know there's one thing I don't have to worry about."

"You keep safe, brah. Me and my whales need you."

47

Hollywood, California

It was another beautiful late-summer evening in Southern California. It had been a warm day, but once the sun went down, a light breeze blew in from the Pacific and the temperature dropped to a pleasant seventy-four degrees.

The cool air was good for the Friday night tourists who packed the sidewalks of Hollywood Boulevard, still mostly dressed in shorts and flip-flops from their daytime adventures. But it wasn't so good for Jacinto and his little *paleta* pushcart, still half full of rum, coconut, and *arroz con leche* ice cream bars that he had a hard time selling to the gringos, who seemed to want only chocolate and vanilla.

Jacinto wanted to finish the night by selling out his cart, a point of personal pride. Most of the other guys just worked their *paletas* until quitting time, but not Jacinto. He didn't quit until he was sold out. Ever.

Except maybe tonight.

The sidewalk was so crowded that he pushed his cart out into the street. There was no parking on the street this time of day, so it was easier to do. The cops wouldn't stop him with all of the crowds around, and it would cause too much of a traffic jam if they did stop to bother him. He jingled his little bell every few feet and flashed a gold-toothed smile. "*Paletas, paletas,*" he'd half sing as he made his way toward the big movie house.

Grauman's Chinese Theatre faced Hollywood Boulevard. Jacinto knew it was probably the most famous movie theater in the world with its Chinese pagoda and all of the hand- and footprints of movie stars out front in the forecourt. Jacinto had been there many times before. He'd even put his hands down on the handprints in the cement to see which hands fit his. He found one once, but he couldn't read the name.

Jacinto had never seen a movie at this theater because he only watched films made in Spanish, and even then, he could only afford to rent movies, not spend ten or fifteen bucks to buy a movie ticket in places like this one. He also knew he'd never be a movie star, or have his handprints or footprints in the cement out front. But that was fine with Jacinto. He had no desire to be famous.

There was a huge crowd in front of Grauman's tonight, larger than usual. It was another big movie premiere. He wasn't sure what the movie was about; he couldn't read the newspaper, but not because it was in English. He could hardly read Spanish, either. He'd dropped out of school in the second grade to work in the fields with his father and never went back. But that was a long time ago.

The movie was some American movie, though. There were lots of American flags all around, and the movie posters showed American soldiers wearing their war paint and holding guns. *Maybe that's why there were so many people here tonight.* Americans liked war movies as much as they liked war, it seemed to Jacinto. Maybe some of these gringos would like some of his ice cream while they waited in line.

Jacinto steered the little pushcart back onto the sidewalk in order to reach the theater. A man dressed like Superman stood in his way, and when Jacinto tried to move around him, a woman dressed like a cat blocked him again. So many of these gringos weren't just strange, they were rude. It was very crowded and hard to push the cart into the forecourt. But he'd promised he'd try, so he was trying.

"Paletas, paletas," he half mumbled, knowing that no one was paying

attention to him. He was just another little brown ice cream cart pusher in a city full of little brown ice cream cart pushers. Still, it would be good if someone bought at least one more ice cream tonight. Maybe that would be a sign.

He nudged his cart and rang his little bell, and people would sometimes frown at him and sometimes cuss at him. He knew they were cussing because their faces turned so ugly, but it didn't bother him because he couldn't understand what they were saying. But sometimes someone would smile nicely at him, and he would smile back, a big toothy grin, flashing his front gold tooth.

Jacinto checked his watch. It was 6:58 p.m. If he could sell just one more coconut bar, that would be the best thing ever, he decided.

"Paletas, paletas. El coco. Muy dulce." But no one wanted to buy a coconut bar from him.

He thought about Victor Bravo. It made him sad. He knew Victor. They were kids together, even friends. What the Americans did to Victor was wrong. Victor was a good man just trying to help the poor people. What did he ever do to the Americans?

When Jacinto's wife got sick a long time ago, he took her to one of Victor's clinics. It was her appendix, and they took it out for free. Very nice people, he remembered. And he remembered how surprised he was when Victor came in to see him and his wife. Mr. Bravo, everyone said. But Jacinto called him Victor, because they were children together, and they were friends. It made Jacinto very happy to see his old friend.

But his friend was killed by the Americans. *God damn them,* he thought.

A man came to Jacinto yesterday. He said he was Victor's friend. That made Jacinto happy. Jacinto told him he was Victor's friend, too.

"Really? That's an amazing coincidence. It's almost like Victor wanted us to meet," the man had said.

Jacinto thought about that. The man was right. It truly was amazing.

The man talked to Jacinto about Victor for a long time, about what a good man he was. Then he asked Jacinto to push his ice cream cart to Grauman's Chinese Theatre tonight.

"Why?" Jacinto asked. He didn't push his cart in that direction very often.

"Because Victor would want you to. Aren't you his friend?"

"Yes, I am."

"Then will you do this thing for Victor? He would want you to."

Jacinto thought about it. "Yes. I will do this thing. For Victor."

So Jacinto did it.

And when the man told Jacinto to push his cart into the crowd as far as he could go, he did. And when he told him to be there at seven o'clock, and not one minute later, he did that, too, didn't he? Jacinto didn't know why he was supposed to be there at seven. But he did it because Victor would want him to do these things.

Because Victor was his friend.

Jacinto checked his watch again. It read 7:03.

The sun exploded. At least that's what it seemed like to Jacinto.

A blinding white light. And noise, like ice picks in his ears.

The explosion shredded Jacinto's little ice cream cart. People were blown over in a big circle all around him, like cornstalks after the harvest.

Jacinto didn't know that Victor's friend had packed his cart with C4 embedded with hundreds of ball bearings that morning. When it exploded, it acted like a daisy cutter, mowing down everyone in its path, including Jacinto, who was cut in half at the waist.

The side of Jacinto's face hurt where it was smashed against one of the cement squares with handprints. He couldn't move, but he watched the blood filling up the handprint next to his face. The hand was much bigger than Jacinto's. He wondered whose hand it was.

48

Washington, D.C.

Early Saturday morning, Bill Donovan briefed President Myers and her cabinet.

"At least a dozen attacks in as many states, with more reports coming in."

"Sounds like they're on the move," Early said.

"Casualties?" Myers asked.

"So far, thirty dead, ten times that many wounded, mostly minor injuries. RPGs, drive-by shootings, grenade attacks. Bombs were detonated at a movie theater in Hollywood, a Walmart in Knoxville, and a rodeo in Oklahoma City."

"And we think it's Bravo people?" Myers asked.

"Printed flyers read *¡VIVA VICTOR!* at several sites; Facebook posts and Twitter feeds say the same thing. Sure looks like these attacks were in retaliation for the death of Victor Bravo."

"You can thank the damn Mexican television and radio stations in this country for that. They're putting blood in the water," one of Donovan's assistant secretaries offered. "We can pull their FCC licenses right now, shut them down until they agree to stop running the Victor Bravo love letters."

"Then they would just run them on the Internet," West countered. The FBI director was clearly frustrated. "They're already there anyway."

"Then we shut those down, too, on the basis that they're fostering terror attacks. The Patriot Act grants us that power."

"I don't think free speech is the enemy here," Myers said. She turned to Donovan. "Question for you, Bill. The Hollywood and Oklahoma City bombings look like suicide attacks. Were they?"

"We've got security camera footage on both. Neither exhibited the classic signs—nervousness, eyes straight ahead, and the other telltale psychological markers. Locals ran fingerprints but no hits in our threat or crime databases. Probably illegals. We'll know more about Knoxville in a couple of hours."

"And we're certain it's the Bravos behind all of this?"

"Fans of Victor Bravo, for sure," Donovan said.

"Or who want us to think they're fans," Early offered.

"What do you mean?" Myers asked.

"The voices on the Cruzalta tape. The Iranians are connected to this somehow."

"If the Iranians were connected with anyone, it was Castillo, not Bravo," Donovan said. "And there were only two voices on the tape. No way an operation this size could be carried out by just two assholes. I still think it's the Bravos."

"I do, too. But weapons, training—the Iranians have contributed something," Early insisted. "The Iranians had uploaded the El Paso footage, too. Their finger's in the pie somewhere."

"What does that get us, Mike?" Myers asked.

"Not much at this point, especially if the Iranians are independent operators."

"You mean like mercenaries?" Myers asked.

"Yeah. But if this is a state-sanctioned op, we need to know. Have the DNI put more NSA assets on the Iranians. Maybe we can pick up some chatter on that end and get a better handle on this thing."

"Good idea, but it's not enough. I want to know who's on the ground right now killing Americans. What's our best guess?"

"The Bravos who blew the tank farm in Houston never reappeared. Those are the best candidates, without question," West said.

"What's their next move?" Myers asked.

"No way of knowing," West said. "The targets have been random and geographically diverse."

"So we're just waiting for the other shoe to drop?" Myers asked.

No one said a word. The answer was obvious.

Grapevine, Texas

Six hours later, the other shoe dropped.

Construction on local highways and interchanges, particularly the 114, the 121, and I-635, had been going on for years, and still had years to go, thanks to the Texas Department of Transportation (TxDOT) and the billions of federal stimulus dollars that the "anti–big government" Texas congressional delegation had siphoned out of Washington coffers for their constituents.

Grapevine residents had grown wearily accustomed to the massive construction vehicles lumbering along on the crowded freeways, usually clogged by lane closures and traffic cones, as whole sections of the interstate were being rerouted to fit the new TxDOT master plan. The big vehicles often had to exit and cross over surface streets where freeway ramps had been closed, so it wasn't unusual to see asphalt tankers, cement mixers, flatbed tractor-trailers, and the like running through the city.

That's the reason no one paid any attention when a big rusty dump truck rattled into the back parking lot of the two-story Grapevine Christian Academy on a Saturday midmorning. In fact, the school had allowed construction vehicles to park there on more than one occasion. The school was just a mile or so from a section of Highway 114 that had been heavily renovated lately. The school parking lot was empty except for a late-model yellow Volkswagen Bug out front.

Tom and Barbara Cole were the high school drama teachers and they were inside preparing for an early afternoon rehearsal, rearranging some of the musical scores from *Godspell* that the kids would be putting on in the fall. The building was brand-new and well insulated from the brutal Texas heat. The heavy insulation also masked the sound of the roaring jumbo jets that flew directly over the school in their flight paths to DFW Airport just two miles away.

Barbara had just finished a particularly bawdy rendition of "Turn Back, O Man" on the big Yamaha piano when she and her husband both heard a giant *whump* coming from out back. It sounded like a big timpani drum was booming out in the parking lot. There were no windows where they were located so they couldn't see what was going on, but it could well have been something connected with all of the construction. They were about to play the tune again when they heard another *whump* and then a third, fourth, fifth, and sixth in quick succession.

"What's going on out there?" Barbara asked.

"Sounds like a pile driver," Tom offered, only half believing it himself.

She stood up from the piano and the two of them crossed to the back wall where there was a big steel exit door. The *whump*ing continued and, in fact, got louder the closer they came to the door.

Tom flung the door open and saw the big rusty dump truck parked just a few feet behind the building, but that's the last thing he saw. A suppressed 9mm machine gun stitched bullets across his chest and into the wall behind him. He crumpled to the ground, blocking the doorway with his corpse.

That gave Barbara enough time to scream, turn, and run back inside, with the sound of the 120mm mortar rounds still *whump*ing in the bed of the big truck behind her, but the man who had killed her husband leaped over his corpse and chased after her. The Bravo opened fire just as she reached the big Yamaha piano. He emptied his magazine in her direction, splintering the black lacquered wood into a thousand pieces and putting two bullets in her spine. The piano strings thudded in ugly half notes as the slugs split them in two.

The killer ran back out the door as the last of the sixteen mortar rounds arced into the air. It had taken the mortar crew just one minute and eleven seconds to loft all sixteen of the finned rockets.

A gray Chrysler 300 screeched to a halt behind the dump truck and all four men of the mortar crew—three Bravos and Walid Zohar, Ali's trusted Azeri sergeant—piled into the vehicle and raced away. They left the Israeli-manufactured Soltam K6 mortar behind because they didn't have any more shells left to fire, and when the Americans found it, they would only be able to trace the serial number back to the Nicaraguan army depot where it had been stolen from two years ago, along with the shells.

Dallas–Fort Worth International Airport, Texas

The first 120mm shell slammed into the tarmac just short of Terminal A right next to a parked American Airlines 737 being loaded with passengers through a movable jet bridge. The explosion instantly killed three bag handlers and shattered the big starboard Snecma/GE turbofan engine.

Mortar shrapnel ignited the fuel truck loading up the 737, which set off another explosion that immediately engulfed the aircraft and the jet bridge. Alarms began wailing.

The passengers in Terminal A dropped to the floor as security personnel scrambled to preplanned defensive positions. Automated TSA warning messages blared on the overheads. "Remain where you are, stay under cover. Remain where you are, stay under cover."

Mortars kept falling. Accuracy wasn't needed, just speed. The targets were thin-skinned commercial aircraft and fragile aluminum-and-glass airline terminals. Round after round slammed down within a quarter-mile radius of the terminal, each strike ripping the air like a thunderclap.

Inside Terminal A, passengers cowered beneath food-court tables or inside the terminal restrooms, alarms still blaring, survivors screaming, moaning, praying in the swirling dust and smoke.

And then the mortars stopped.

Able-bodied survivors finally screwed up the courage to look around. Some tended the injured. Most crossed to the big picture windows—or to what was left of them—shattered glass crunching beneath their feet.

The tarmac was littered with burning aircraft, smashed trucks, and scattered baggage carts, along with shoes, underwear, soda cans, styrofoam cups, golf clubs, and a thousand other artifacts.

And then there was the carnage. Corpses broken, twisted, burning. Limbs scattered like leaves. A few bodies still strapped in their seats, smashed into the tarmac.

It was hard to believe that so much damage could be inflicted in just one minute and eleven seconds.

49

"Yes, I'm watching it now, on Fox," Myers sighed into her phone. Donovan was on the other end. "It looks like Dante's Inferno."

The camera trucks were blockaded from the airport entrances so they could only manage long-distance shots. Black columns of smoke mushroomed into the bright blue Texas sky.

"We're shutting down all outbound flights around the country until we're sure this thing is over with," Donovan said. "We're also putting every surveillance helicopter we can lay our hands on—metro police departments, military units, executive shuttles, even news copters—on a five-mile radius sweep of every major airport in the nation. There haven't been any other reports of similar attacks, but there's no point in taking any chances."

"Damn it. We're still playing catch-up with these bastards. We've got to get ahead of them, right now."

"I'm initiating Plan Orange," Donovan replied. "Unless you're ready to announce a national emergency."

"Not yet. But I'm calling in all of the other National Guard units not already activated, just in case."

"Understood," Donovan said.

"Looks like we'll be putting boots on the ground after all, Bill. I just never thought it would be in my own country."

State of Veracruz, Mexico

Mo Mirza sweated like a pig.

He'd grown up in Westwood near UCLA, his alma mater. Beach weather mostly. Not the smothering heat of a Mexican jungle. But here he had privacy. And his own landing strip.

Mo was twenty-four years old, but looked like he was barely out of his teens. His thin beard was patchy and untrimmed, and his dark short-cropped hair was mottled with blue coloring. With his thick black-framed glasses, red high-top Converse basketball shoes, plaid Tony Hawk skater shorts, and a faded Ramones concert T-shirt, he looked every inch the quintessential American slacker.

He was anything but.

The jungle hangar was little more than a thatched roof on polls, but the natural material was perfect for thwarting optical and infrared surveillance. No walls, but plenty of room for the Reaper's twenty-meter wing span and the big drums of aviation fuel.

The Bravo airfield was primitive by any measure, but sufficient for the task at hand. Four of Ali's Quds men with automatic rifles were a grim comfort, but the airstrip's extreme isolation was their best defense. The locals didn't bother them. This was a Bravo camp and they knew to stay far away, even if Victor was dead.

Mo slapped at another mosquito on his neck and cursed as he ran another diagnostic check on the avionics package. The Chinese unit was a piece of crap, but he couldn't risk using the American one. Either they'd track it or lock him out remotely. Both were bad news. He'd flown the Reaper with a portable ground-control station from a third-party vendor out of New York that played just like a video game, and the Israeli uplinks connected perfectly with Nasir 1, Iran's global navigational satellite. But the Chinese unit sucked balls and made the Reaper hard to fly.

Mo's phone rang.

"Will you be ready?" Ali asked.

"Rechecking everything now. Any luck on the Blue Arrows?"

Ali had a lead on a couple of the Chinese Hellfire knockoffs, designed for use with the CH-4, the Chinese Predator knockoff, also stolen from the U.S. arsenal. When Mo hijacked the Reaper, it only had two missiles left. Now it had none.

"They'll arrive in three days."

"Awesome. Then everything will be ready."

San Diego, California

Pearce's phone rang. It was his tech guru, Ian.

"Tell me you found him," Pearce said.

"Not Ali. His uncle."

"Where?"

Ian chuckled. "You're not going to believe it."

50

Washington, D.C.

Myers stood in the situation room of the DHS, studying the wall-length electronic touch-screen display map of the United States with Bill Donovan.

Previous attacks had been color-coded according to severity. Red markers indicated wounded; black indicated fatalities. Tapping on any of the markers pulled up a text window with all available data, including victim photos, crime scene information, agency in charge at the scene, etc.

The best shot they had to predict the future was to process the fire hose of data that was pouring in from the Utah facility as it daily analyzed petabytes—billions of megabytes—of images and data inputs it was receiving from all of the law enforcement agencies, along with the Domain Awareness Systems, which were linked to the thousands of security cameras guarding most public buildings. The only thing they were sure about so far was that the Bravos had split up their forces and spread their operations over the widest possible area. Soft targets were the norm.

Drone Command had continued to beg, borrow, steal, and lease several more drone systems as well, including the recently decommissioned Blue Devil 2 hybrid airship, which the air force had spent over $200 million to develop but had decided to mothball. The nearly four-hundred-foot-long airship was capable of carrying thousands of pounds of surveillance payloads and keeping them aloft for twelve hours at a time. Ashley had deployed the Blue Devil 2 with a Gorgon Stare wide-area surveillance package over Los Angeles just two days before the Hollywood attack and was eager to find out what evil the Mind's Eye "visual intelligence" software had uncovered. Until they could discern an attack pattern, DHS had ordered a general mobilization of all LEO resources. State, county, and city law enforcement agencies were on high alert; police reserve units were called up; television and radio stations ran public service ads extolling citizens, "If you see something, say something. Don't be afraid to call in anything suspicious."

The unfortunate side effect of the extra security precautions was that the anxiety level of the average citizen shot through the roof; emergency rooms were filling up with as many heart attacks as panic attacks. Valium prescriptions were at an all-time high. Paranoia was increasing, too, and the number of concealed-carry permit applications had overwhelmed the ATF online application system. DHS urged the public to remain both calm and vigilant, but the number of cities declaring martial law rose daily. Racial and ethnic tensions were rising as well. Just like after 9/11, American flags were popping up everywhere, especially on cars. But now, so were Mexican flags, with the same intensity. Ironically, American Hispanics—many of whom had served in the U.S. military or had relatives on active duty—were flying the American flags. Mexican flags were most commonly flown on American university campuses like UC Berkeley by liberal Anglos and foreign-born nationals.

What stung Myers most was the right-wing militia and "prepper" groups harping about impending martial law. She actually shared that concern and had raised it with her attorney general. The 2007 National Defense Authorization Act (signed into law by President Bush) and the 2011 NDAA (signed into law by President Obama) gave Myers ample legal warrant to deploy U.S. armed forces in counterterror work on U.S. soil, in effect, turning them into cops on the beat.

It was getting harder and harder to tell the cops from the troops. More and more police brandished assault rifles and flash bangs, wore tactical vests and helmets, and rolled through town in armored vehicles. Civil libertarians wondered if they were local law enforcement or an occupying army.

For over a hundred years, the Posse Comitatus Act and the Insurrection Act had strictly forbidden the use of federal military forces to perform police functions on American soil out of fear that future presidents would be tempted to use them to achieve their political objectives, suppress political opposition, or overthrow the government entirely. Two hundred years of Latin American history had proven those fears fully warranted.

But the twenty-first century posed global threats and challenges to the nation far beyond the scope and resources of the local city cop on the beat who polished his apple and swung a nightstick as a deterrent to local mischief. It was a slippery slope, to be sure, but a necessary one. Police were taking on more and more military-style operations.

The only alternative to the heightened security measures, as extreme as they appeared to be at the moment, was to do nothing and simply hope the violent chaos spree would just go away. Myers knew it wouldn't, so the extra precautions and higher alerts were initiated. She'd do whatever it would take to guarantee public safety, even if the public didn't like it.

Malibu, California

Pearce and Johnny Paloma sped along the Pacific Coast Highway in Johnny's restored '73 Stingray.

"So this writer guy is in on this mess?" Johnny asked.

Pearce pressed the release button on his Glock, checked to see that the .45 magazine was fully loaded.

"According to Ian, Babak Ghorbani is Ali's uncle on his mother's side. That puts him in it up to his neck until I find out otherwise." Pearce slammed the magazine back into place and racked the slide.

———

Ten minutes later, Pearce and Johnny Paloma approached the high-walled beach house under cover of early morning darkness. The distant surf down below hissed softly in the sand as low tide ebbed away.

A former L.A. cop, Johnny easily disabled the civilian security system, then proceeded to the rear entrance while Pearce picked the front door lock. After Johnny had cleared the back slider lock, Pearce gave the signal and they both made their way in.

The house was silent. Pearce and Johnny met up in the living room. Minimalist modern furnishings. Hand-scraped hardwoods. Hell of a view of the Pacific through a big picture window.

They made their way to the master bedroom.

Two people slept beneath a white silk comforter. Pearce yanked it off, grabbed the middle-aged man by his silk pajama top, pulled him onto the floor, and shoved his Glock in the startled face.

"Please! Please! Don't kill me!" Ghorbani screamed in Farsi.

Johnny snapped the bedroom lights on.

Pearce saw out of the corner of his eye that Johnny had a gun in the face of Ghorbani's bed partner, also on the floor.

"Where's Ali Abdi?" Pearce roared in Farsi.

"Who?" Ghorbani asked in English, blinking heavily. "My glasses, I can't see."

Pearce saw a pair of rimless glasses on the nightstand.

"Try something stupid, please. I'm begging you," Pearce snapped.

The middle-aged man's quavering hand reached up to the nightstand and found the glasses. He pulled them on. He frowned at Pearce in confusion.

"Is this a robbery? Please, take anything."

Pearce jammed the cold muzzle of the gun barrel against the man's deeply lined forehead. Ghorbani's partner whimpered from the other side of the bed.

"I'll ask one more time. Where's Ali Abdi? Your nephew?"

"I don't know."

CRACK! Pearce whipped the steel barrel of the Glock against the side of the man's head, knocking his glasses off. Ghorbani howled in pain and clutched at the wound, balling up into a fetal position on the floor.

Pearce kicked the man's feet apart, then stepped on one of his bare ankles, bearing down with his full weight until the small bones cracked beneath his steel-toed boot.

Ghorbani shrieked with the new jolt of pain, completely forgetting his bleeding head wound, and clutched at his broken ankle. Pearce unsheathed his razor-sharp KA-BAR knife and stuck the tip of the blade into the left nostril of the bearded man's face.

"Last chance. If you don't want to whistle like a tea kettle every time you sneeze from now on, you'd better start talking."

Ghorbani's mouth opened and closed a few times, trying to form words through his panic and pain. The syllables finally caught in his throat, like a cold engine finally turning over on a winter morning.

"I . . . I haven't seen him since I was last in Iran, twenty years ago. He hates me. So does his mother, my sister."

"And why should I believe that?"

"Because it's the truth!"

"Hey, chief, come take a look." Johnny motioned with his pistol at the figure on the floor. Pearce frowned. Crossed over.

The simpering voice cowering by the side of the bed turned out to be a twenty-year-old Iranian boy, pretty and fey in a pink UCLA tank top.

"This your girlfriend, Babak?" Pearce asked.

Ghorbani nodded. "My sister's family are religious fanatics. Ali swore he would kill me if they ever saw my face again."

Pearce believed him. Homosexuals had a short life expectancy in the Islamic Republic of Iran these days.

"Does Ali know you're here?"

"If he did, I'd be dead. Why?"

Pearce holstered his weapon, frustrated. "He might be in the neighborhood. If you do hear anything from him, better call the FBI."

"Yes, of course."

Pearce nodded at Johnny. "Let's go."

Turlock, California

Brian Heppner was sound asleep on his pricey adjustable air mattress. His alarm was set to go off in twenty more minutes at 4 a.m. for the first milking of the day, but he hadn't gotten into bed until after midnight. Worse, he'd loaded up on NyQuil because he had a summer cold that he couldn't shake and the coughing wouldn't let him fall asleep.

A third-generation dairy farmer, Brian had grown up with the remarkable work ethic—and commensurate sleep deprivation—that went along with owning your own herd. Dairy sales had tanked in the last few years. That meant even more hours and less sleep just to stay out of bankruptcy.

Brian kept a twelve-gauge Mossberg 590 pump shotgun loaded with double-aught buckshot next to his bed because thieves had been breaking into isolated farm homes all over the valley for the last few years and budget cutbacks had kept county sheriff patrols to a minimum. He'd practiced grabbing it out of his sleep a hundred times so he wouldn't have to think about it when the time came to use it. His wife hated the gun and joked that he slept so deeply that the thieves could steal the bed out from under him and he'd never even know it.

BAM! The bedroom door busted off of its hinges.

A squad of black-clad men stormed in, UMP9s ready, hollering in Spanish. Brian's wife screamed.

Half awake, Brian lunged for the shotgun.

A machine pistol fired.

Three jacketed rounds ripped into Brian's rib cage.

Two minutes later, the SWAT lieutenant called for an ambulance with Brian's blood-spattered wife still screaming in the background.

Washington, D.C.

Donovan took the call. Another fatal shooting, this time in Turlock, California.

Damn it.

Some poor dairy farmer had been killed because somebody called in and said that they heard screaming and what sounded like machine-gun fire.

Brian Heppner had just been SWATed—a dangerous trick used by extremist crazies to harass political opponents back in 2012. The tactic was ugly and effective. Just call in a gun-related emergency to 911 and the dispatcher would automatically send in the SWAT team. That way you let the cops do your intimidation for you, and your opponents lived in sleepless fear of another break-in for the next six weeks.

The LEO community was on high alert. Every call was taken as seriously as possible. What else could they do but respond?

According to the reports he'd received, Donovan knew it was the Bravos behind all of it. There had been at least fifty-three SWATings across the country in the last hour, all of the emergency calls reporting the same thing. Thank God there had been only two fatalities so far.

So now the bastards were letting us do the terrorizing for them, Donovan thought. It was only 7:18 in the morning, but Donovan uncorked his bottle of Bushmills and took a sip anyway. It was going to be another long damn day and he dreaded calling Myers with this new round of bad news.

When was it going to end?

SEPTEMBER

51

Pearce's tablet flashed. Skype was ringing in.

"Anything?" Pearce asked, knowing the answer.

"Nothing. The poor bastard hasn't even left the house since your visit. Even has his groceries delivered now."

"No calls? No contacts?"

"Zip, zilch, nada," Stella said.

Pearce believed her. She was his best drone pilot, and he'd put her on drone surveillance over Babak Ghorbani's house since the day he and Johnny had paid the writer a visit. Stella had cut her teeth on surveillance missions. After getting arrested for shoplifting in her junior year at USC, Stella was hauled before a judge. Noting she was a major in video-game design, he gave her the old "army or jail" offer. She took the army offer and six months later was flying Israeli-built RQ-7 Shadows over Afghanistan, eventually logging over two hundred combat missions before her hitch was up.

"You want me to stay on him?" she asked.

"Go ahead and shut it down. It's a bust," Pearce said, logging off of Skype.

Washington, D.C.

Jeffers scratched his head, frustrated. "You've got to give them something, Margaret. The midterm elections are just three months away and your congressional supporters are really feeling the heat."

"Give them something? How about a backbone? I can lend them mine, I suppose." Myers was frustrated, to say the least.

The "Day Without a Mexican" strike had stretched into an entire week, and it was just one more hurricane in the storm of chaos that had enveloped the nation. Myers thought it would be helpful if someone in her own party would stand beside her during the current debacle, but she was out of luck. Many had privately assured her that they were in complete support of her policies, even though publicly they were being forced to say something different, or nothing at all. That kind of self-serving duplicity was almost more painful than the outright betrayal that Diele and others had openly displayed. At least Diele was completely honest in his contempt for her and her ideas.

"We're several months away from building an efficient technical solution for border crossing. Why not ease up a little until the technology falls into place? Take a little pressure off, build up a little goodwill?" Jeffers asked.

"That's a great suggestion. Tell me, how many more Bravos do we need to let cross before you think La Raza will invite me to their annual gala?"

"That's not fair, Margaret. Consensus is how democratic governments work." Jeffers was frustrated, too. Myers had no idea of what he had to put up with to keep her shielded from the long knives slashing all around her. The only good news lately was that there hadn't been any more airport attacks.

"Consensus? How about the national interest? Just once, let Congress rally around what's best for the country instead of what's most likely to get them reelected. That's the only kind of 'consensus' I can actually support."

Jeffers took a deep breath to calm down. "Everything's a damn mess right now. Like a slow-motion car wreck."

"The 'mess' we're in is proof we're doing the right thing. The 'mess' we're in is exactly why my predecessors haven't tried to tackle these issues before—too difficult, too complicated, too costly, too hard. But doing the right thing is always harder and more complicated than doing nothing."

"You know, they're calling you *La Bruja Mala* in the Hispanic media because you make good people disappear."

"I've been called worse than a witch before. If they're reduced to calling me names, it means they're out of political arguments."

"Or they've moved beyond them." Jeffers sighed. He knew he couldn't win this battle with her.

"We're only a few weeks into this. Tell our 'supporters' to man up a little. Casualties have been relatively light, and our law enforcement resources are just now fully deployed and focused. With any luck, the worst is over."

Jeffers knew she was right. She'd made a gutsy call, and it took even more guts to stick with it. That's why he threw in his lot with her to begin with—she had a bigger nut sack than any man he knew in politics, himself included. "If luck is what you're counting on, Madame President, you better get on your pointy hat and broom, and conjure some up for yourself. This thing isn't over yet."

Myers chuckled. "I'll do my best. Just make sure you keep your ruby slippers in the closet. I can't afford to have you disappearing on me right now."

"I'm not going anywhere. Diele's out there just waiting for the first chance to drop a great big old farmhouse on your head and I want to be there to pick up the pieces when it hits."

They wouldn't have long to wait.

52

Baku, Azerbaijan

The Azeri Spring the previous year had been mostly a nonviolent revolution that drove out a relatively benign but utterly corrupt government and replaced it with a coalition of parties committed to complete secularization, Western modernization, and integration into both the EU and NATO. The government itself put up virtually no fight at all and dissolved within days without firing a shot. All of the battle casualties had been between forces within the Azeri Spring uprising and the radical Shia elements demanding the implementation of sharia law. Poorly organized and equipped, the Shia radicals were quickly suppressed.

The new president of the Republic of Azerbaijan, a Harvard-educated MBA and former oil industry executive, was the first Azeri woman to serve in that office. Her government had recently signed Memoranda of Understanding with the appropriate European agencies to begin the long process of full economic and military integration with the EU and NATO. The Azerbaijanis needed both if they hoped to escape absorption by either Russia to the north or Iran to the south. New discoveries of vast offshore gas and oil reserves promised Azerbaijan a new century of untold prosperity for the entire nation if the new reserves were managed carefully and honestly. Azerbaijan was the world's oldest known oil producer, transporting oil to neighboring countries 2,500 years before the first American oil well was drilled in Titusville, Pennsylvania, in 1859.

Azerbaijan's future looked as bright as the dawn until the morning that waves of Russian fighter bombers and radar-controlled naval guns unleashed their fury, destroying Azerbaijan's air force jets on the ground, army tanks in their storage sheds, and navy ships in their piers within minutes. Cruise missiles blasted communications facilities, including the nation's only broadcast television station, and decimated several government buildings, including the Ministry of National Security, Parliament, the Government House, and the presidential residence.

Russian paratroopers dropped into the nation's capital seven minutes after the final air assault and Russian tanks and armored personnel carriers streamed across the border moments after the first jets had taken off.

Russian forces also deployed a half dozen unarmed Searcher II surveillance drones, recently purchased from Israel Aerospace Industries. Their own drone program was in a shambles.

By noon, oil-rich Azerbaijan had once again become a Russian possession.

Washington, D.C.

As chairman of the Armed Services Committee, Senator Diele was entitled to the most up-to-date global security information available. He was duly summoned to the White House just before 11:30 a.m. for an emergency briefing, the subject of which had not been disclosed on his unsecured line.

When he arrived at the Cabinet Room, the secretaries of state, commerce, energy, and defense were already present, along with the DNI and select congressional leaders. Diele found his customary seat just as Myers and Early entered the room.

"It's a briefing, General, so please, cut to the chase," Myers said.

"Yes, ma'am." General Winchell, the air force chief of staff and Diele's close ally, was presenting the facts.

Lights darkened and the digital projector flashed satellite imagery that had recorded the Russian invasion. Winchell filled in the details. When he finished, he asked, "Questions?"

"Let's start with the most obvious. Why?" Myers asked.

"They claim they were responding to repeated terrorist incursions on their homeland by Azeri and Shia radicals," Winchell explained. "And cited the Myers Doctrine as precedent for their actions." He said it like a slur rather than a fact.

"Why now?"

"They probably believe we're distracted at the moment," Diele answered. "Which I'd say we are, wouldn't you?"

Myers glared at him, then turned her gaze back to the general. "How does this affect our security?"

"Say good-bye to Azeri NATO membership, for one," Tom Eddleston said.

"And how does that affect us? I mean, directly?" Myers countered.

The secretary of defense laid out Azerbaijan's previously helpful, though not decisive, contribution to the War on Terror, which was winding down anyway. A future NATO military base, to be built by an American contractor, had been in the works, along with defense purchases of American military equipment for the Azeri armed forces.

Myers turned to the commerce secretary. "What about oil?"

"Another price shock, to be expected. Don't know how many more of these the markets will tolerate. Might keep the price of oil inordinately high for some time."

"Good for OPEC, good for the Russians, the Iranians," the energy secretary threw in.

"And good for us," Myers countered. "We sell oil, too, remember? But does this hurt our energy supplies in any way?"

"No. The Azeri oil and gas pipelines service the European markets exclusively. If anyone will have a problem, it's them."

"That makes it a NATO problem, which makes it a strategic problem, which still makes it our problem," Diele said.

All eyes turned to Myers.

"It's a market problem, not a NATO problem. The Russians or the Azerbaijanis or the Inuits for that matter can't sell oil or gas or anything else for more than the Europeans are willing to pay for it. If the Europeans want a cheaper source of energy, they can shop around, or they can find alternatives."

"The European economies are already on life support. This might just pull the plug. They're still our primary trading partners. If Europe goes down, we go down." Diele's eyes were daggers.

"The European economies are on life support because they're highly unionized socialist economies with low birthrates and thirty-hour workweeks. They've spent themselves into oblivion on social programs while we bore the primary costs of their defense for the past six decades. I'll not shed American blood to keep the cost of European vacations down."

The room went silent. Everyone saw the blood flushing Diele's face as he stared thoughtfully at his hands clasped in his lap. He was famously ill-tempered. Eyewitnesses swear he cussed out Bush 41 to his face in a PDB one time, and even threw a punch at Alexander Haig when the retired general was President Ford's chief of staff.

But instead of the expected tirade, Diele surprised everyone.

He simply smiled.

"As you say, Madame President."

Jeffers knew full well what was behind that withered, grinning mask. Diele had just declared war on Myers.

53

I-30 East, Arkansas

Traffic was backed up for miles.

The Arkansas State Police had set up a sobriety checkpoint about halfway between Hope and Arkadelphia, stopping every car in both eastbound lanes for inspections. Of course, they were actually looking for possible terrorists and their weapons.

A federal judge had recently blocked the governor's antiterror stop-and-frisk policy, but no court had ever held against sobriety checkpoints, given the scourge that drunken driving had become, taking thousands of innocent lives every year. The governor, a huge Myers supporter, had suddenly become "quite concerned" about drunk driving in his state, particularly on I-30, one of the most heavily traveled highways in the nation.

The Arkansas state troopers required drivers and passengers to exit their stopped vehicles and perform sobriety tests, the famous finger-to-nose exercise among them. Of course, the real reason why people were forced to exit was in order to get them out from behind the metal shield of their cars and trucks. Using recently acquired terahertz imaging detectors, technicians were able to measure the natural radiation emitted by people and detect when the energy flow was impeded by an object, such as a gun. State troopers also ran sniffer dogs and handheld Geiger counters around the vehicles while the drunk tests were being performed. Vehicles occupied by Hispanics were given special attention.

An unmarked panel van was racing along eastbound I-30 at 12:05 a.m. when the driver caught sight of a ten-mile-long string of red brake lights shining in the midst of a great curtain of pines. Traffic was already beginning to slow. The Spanish-language news station broadcasting out of Little Rock announced the traffic delay due to the fact that state troopers were stopping all eastbound vehicles at a sobriety checkpoint.

The Spanish-speaking driver tapped his brakes and eased left into the broad grassy median strip, then made a sharp U-turn and bounded back on the westbound side.

That was exactly the kind of maneuver someone wanting to hide something would do. Two Arkansas State Police officers on big Harley bikes who were lurking in the dark on the westbound shoulder blasted their lights and roared after the van as soon as it had made the illegal median crossing.

When the two motorcycles had pulled within a hundred yards of the van, the two panel doors in back flung open and an AK-47 flashed from inside. The blistering 7.62 rounds shattered the windshield of the first bike and the trooper slid his Harley into the grassy median. The other trooper broke off the chase with bullets gouging the asphalt around her, and threw her body and her bike between the fleeing van and her downed partner to protect him from any more gunfire.

She instantly called in the attack and within minutes a helicopter-based sniper was putting rounds through the van's roof as a dozen squad cars joined the chase. More gunfire erupted from the van, but a second later it ran over a police spike strip that blew out all four tires. The two men in the back of the van were tossed onto the pavement and skidded like hockey pucks across the asphalt, skinning them alive while the van cartwheeled end over end until it slammed into a pine tree just off the shoulder and erupted in flames.

The Arkansas State Police had just killed three Bravos and the fiery explosion had destroyed the weapons they'd been carrying. The identity of the fourth man couldn't be determined, but if they could have run an instant DNA test or found fingerprints on the charred remains, they might have been able to identify him as Hamid Nezhat, Ali's most senior Quds Force commando.

One by one, the Bravos were getting picked off by the relentless efforts of courageous LEOs all over the country. Good police work was winning the day. Broken fingers, cracked skulls, and a couple of unauthorized waterboarding incidents loosened up a few tongues, too, along with the vigilance of ordinary citizens. Even the Russian mob helped out a time or two when it suited their interests.

The Arkansas incident confirmed Donovan's suspicion that the Bravos had broken up into smaller groups, though how many was still unknown. The attacks also were growing less frequent, probably because of the full-court press the DHS was putting on, or so Donovan hoped.

Known Bravo and Castillo drug houses were raided and then later staked out, sometimes by citizen volunteers because there weren't enough uniforms to cover them all. Two Bravos were killed that way, and three more were wounded before they escaped.

There were a few setbacks. A Claymore mine exploded on a popular camping trail in Yosemite, killing a newlywed couple. An empty one-hundred-pound bag of rat poison had been found adjacent to a water reservoir near Birmingham, Alabama. A car racing past Temple Emanuel in St. Louis, Missouri, fired an RPG and hit the building, but fortunately it did little damage and no one was inside at the time of the attack. However, a U.S. Marine private at home on leave from active duty in Afghanistan saw the attack and chased the vehicle as it raced up I-270. St. Louis police units joined the chase and shot out the tires, slamming the car into the guardrail. The three Bravos inside came out shooting and were killed by a river of lead.

The LEO community began to suspect that a significant corner had been turned in the hunt. They didn't know how right they were. But Ali

Abdi knew. His rogue teams were required to report in on a regular basis by means of a covert encrypted cell-phone network that the Iranians had deployed throughout the United States. Fewer and fewer teams reported in, and fewer and fewer media reports about terror acts were going out. That was all Ali needed to know. His latest plan to provoke an American invasion of Mexico had failed.

The Iranian commando had just two more cards to play, then he'd have to resort to last-ditch measures. He prayed it wouldn't come to that, but he was more than willing to pay that price since the reward would be his triumphant entrance into heaven.

Washington, D.C.

Senator Diele hung up the phone, fighting the desire to shout for joy. His Democrat counterpart, Cleeve Gormer from Ohio, the Chairman of the House Armed Services Committee, had eagerly agreed to Diele's proposal and guaranteed he could deliver a majority vote on the Democrat-controlled House Judiciary Committee if they acted quickly.

Gormer hated Myers's guts. She had sided with the Pentagon when the army requested the Lima Army Tank Plant to temporarily quit manufacturing M-1 Abrams tanks that it said it no longer needed for wars it had no intention of fighting anytime soon. Gormer was furious. It didn't matter to him that the army estimated it would save the taxpayers over $3 billion to shutter the facility for just three years. The LATP provided hundreds of highly paid jobs in Gormer's district. Like most politicians, he viewed military spending as another source of constituent employment and, hence, his own source of job security. Luckily, he'd managed to defeat the generals on this issue, but he swore retribution on Myers if he ever got the chance and Diele had just offered it to him.

There was a soft knock on his door.

"Come."

Diele's personal assistant, a pretty young freshman intern from Brown, entered with a tray larded with fried eggs, bacon, hash browns, and coffee, and set it in front of him at his desk. She was a beautiful girl and his eyes raked over the curves of her body. But the era of incriminating Facebook and Twitter posts had curbed Diele's animal appetites for volunteer staff. Instead, he thanked her politely and she left.

Diele's mouth watered. This was a real workingman's breakfast. Not like the prison fare of oatmeal mush and tepid green tea his haggard wife served him at home these days.

Dolores Hidalgo, Mexico

It was a warm September evening in the provincial city, and the night was exceptionally special. September 15 was the eve of Mexico's Independence Day, the night on which the warrior-priest Father Hidalgo uttered the *grito* from his pulpit, declaring Mexico's independence from Spain. Father Hidalgo had called for the abolition of slavery and led a peasant army to its first victories against the ruling Spanish government. He was the George Washington of Mexico, "the Father who fathered a nation."

But tonight President Barraza—ever the showman—would be the one to utter the cry from the pulpit of the Hidalgo church instead of the local priest. The symbolism was as subtle as a *telenovela* romance, but perfectly effective for the bold young president to project his growing defiance and contempt toward the colonial aspirations of *los norteamericanos*. At Hernán's urging, he'd been stoking Mexican nationalism ever since the *Aztec Dream* attack and promoting the conspiracy theory that the Bravo attacks in the U.S. were part of an elaborate plan to justify an American invasion of Mexico.

Antonio was just as glad that Hernán had elected to stay home in Mexico City to enjoy the festivities with his own family this evening. Lately, his brother had become increasingly grim and too unpleasant to be around. The president was thankful, however, that his wise and efficient sibling had arranged for a live national television broadcast of the event tonight.

Traditionally, the president of Mexico uttered the *grito* from the balcony of the National Palace at 11 p.m. on September 15, as would mayors all over Mexico in their respective towns. But this year, instead of occupying the National Palace, President Barraza wanted to stand in the symbolic heart of his people.

Father Hidalgo's church, along with the giant statue and monument towering out front commemorating him, was a big tourist draw, and the town plaza was always crowded on the holiday. But this year, the nation's patriotic fervor had been stoked to a fever pitch by perceived American injustices and carefully orchestrated Barraza jingoism. The spirit of revolution was in the air.

For security reasons, the crowds had been kept far back from the entrance of the church, though there was a standing-room-only audience inside. President Barraza's image was projected on a giant portable Jumbo-Tron erected in the plaza for the event, and stacks of Marshall speakers thundered with his voice as he delivered his patriotic sermon. The plaza rang with the noise of the liquored-up crowd, hundreds of popping firecrackers, blaring patriotic music, and Barraza's ear-busting harangue.

And then the screams.

Two rockets whooshed out of the sky, smashing into the crowd like the fists of an angry god, tearing flesh, shattering bone.

The cries were drowned out by the roar of the Reaper's turbofan engine as it swooped in low over the treetops and dove toward the wide-open doors of the church.

The drone's wide, fragile wings were clipped off as they slammed against the heavy wooden door frame, but the large bulbous nose and slender fuselage shot through like a spear into the sanctuary. The big four-bladed prop sliced into skulls, torsos, and limbs as it raked over a line of pews. The blades finally stopped spinning when the drone ran out of fuel, but the scalding-hot engine pinned a keening middle-aged German tourist to the floor who later died of severe burns on her upper body and face.

Miraculously, the president wasn't killed or even injured when one of the wheels from the landing gear broke loose and slammed against the pulpit where he had been standing seconds before. The members of the audience who hadn't fared as well were wailing with pain. Medics rushed in to treat the wounded. Dozens of cell-phone cameras recorded the carnage, most of them focused on the American flag still visible on the wrecked fuselage. The big television cameras inside the church caught everything in glorious 1080p HD broadcast quality.

Hernán watched the live breaking newscast with keen interest. It was on every channel; the attack was played over and over again. With any luck, he thought, this would become Mexico's Twin Towers moment. Then the people would rally around his brother.

But that wasn't the plan.

Hernán wondered why the missiles weren't fired at the church. If they had been, the church would have exploded in flames and Antonio would have been crushed beneath the smoking rubble.

That was the plan. And then the people would rally around *him*.

Hernán picked up his cell phone to find out what went wrong. He'd give Ali one more chance to kill heaven's favored son.

Ali's phone rang. He answered it with a question.

"What went wrong?"

Mo Mirza was on the other end. "It was the cheap Chinese crap. Missiles wouldn't lock on. Had to improvise. I'm sorry."

Ali shrugged. "It was already written in the Book." He clicked off.

54

Gulf of Mexico

The looming shadow of a Cuban fishing trawler rose and fell in the swelling sea. It was just after midnight.

The ARM *Joaquín* approached cautiously. The Mexican skipper of the Azteca-class patrol boat had spotted the stranded trawler on his radar thirty minutes earlier. No distress signals were flashing on his radio. Lights out on the vessel meant no electricity. *But not even a backup battery?* His radioman tried to raise them, but got no response.

The dark outline of the ship looked familiar through his night-vision binoculars. It was a sturdy East German design built back in the '70s. A limp Cuban flag hung off the stern. His radar man confirmed they were the only vessel within a reasonable distance of the stranded trawler.

A moment later, a red distress flare arced from the trawler deck. That was a good sign. He had been worried he was going to find a murdered crew or an abandoned ship that would be hell to deal with in these conditions.

The skipper gave orders to the radioman to report back to their base at Veracruz that he was lending assistance to the Cuban boat and that he would let them know when the fishing vessel was either secured or the crew rescued.

That was the last time the authorities in Veracruz heard from the captain or crew of the *Joaquín*.

Coronado, California

Pearce was running on the beach. Sunrise wasn't for another twenty minutes. Keeping in shape was one of the few things he had any control of at the moment. His cell phone rang. He clicked on the earpiece but kept running.

"We found Ali." Ian was on the other end.

Pearce stopped in his tracks. "Where?"

"Greyhound bus depot in Stockton, California. Caught him on camera at the ticket counter. Purchased a one-way ride to L.A. just under two hours ago. Bus pulled out at four-twenty this morning. Scheduled to arrive at twelve-thirty."

Pearce marveled at Ali's ingenuity. Security would be lax at a bus terminal compared to the airports.

"Anybody else know about this?"

"No, sir. Not that I can tell." Myers and her team were focused on the Bravos and at this point they had too much information to keep track of even if they wanted to keep tabs on the Iranian. Ian had to create his own data-mining software package in order to sift through the tsunami of intel coming out of the Utah Data Center.

"And he definitely got on the bus?"

"Yes. And the bus is sold out. Packed like a tin of sardines, I'm sure."

Pearce heard the concern in Ian's voice. "Don't worry. He's not going to blow it up. He would've just planted a bomb or ambushed it along the way if that was his target."

"Want me to contact the local gendarmes? Pull him off?"

"No. Can't take the chance they'll lock him away and we won't get a crack at him. Besides, if he gets cornered, he might shoot it out and then there really will be a massacre. Let him come all the way to Los Angeles, and we'll see what he's up to. Good work, Ian."

Pearce clicked off, turned around, then jogged toward his condo two miles back on the beachfront. His mind began racing through checklists, preparing for a showdown with the Iranian.

But a nagging thought dogged his steps. Why did Ali suddenly appear out of nowhere? He was too careful to let himself get caught on a ticket-counter camera, even at a bus station. It was too damn convenient. Ambush? Feint? Or something else?

Washington, D.C.

Congressman Gorman gaveled the House Armed Services Committee hearing into session. The gallery was full. A parade of expert witnesses handpicked by Diele appeared one after another all morning.

Each of the witnesses had impeccable defense and intelligence credentials with prior government service, and each of them currently occupied a prominent position in the defense industry or academia. And each scripted answer they gave was designed to draw the inevitable conclusion that President Myers was incompetent, negligent, and quite possibly dangerous—charges that could easily rise to the standard of "high crimes and misdemeanors."

Myers's defenders on the committee offered up the best arguments they could before the hearing was gaveled to a close, but it was the damning quotes of the anti-Myers experts that lit up the news cycle all day.

No one in the mainstream media either noted or cared that the experts who testified against Myers all had skin in the game if she suddenly found herself impeached.

Gulf of Mexico

In 1950, the American merchant marine fleet comprised nearly half of all shipping vessels at sea, but in the twenty-first century that number fell to the low single digits. The U.S. merchant fleet was probably the first great American industry completely outsourced in the twentieth century.

In 2013, there were fewer than three hundred American-flagged cargo ships, and one of them was the *Star Louisiana*, a fifty-one-thousand-ton Panamax containership hauling Pennsylvania-built high-tech power-generation and transmission equipment destined for Shanghai, China.

The captain of the *Star Louisiana*, Angela Costa, was a third-generation merchant mariner, the child of a Portuguese sailing family with roots in Massachusetts and, generations before that, the Azores. Fifteen minutes earlier, she'd greeted a new day standing on the outer bridge wing sipping hot coffee while watching the great silver disk of the sun rise out of the gray gloom. The long, white foamy trail churning behind her vessel reached straight toward the eastern horizon. Sunrises and coffee were her morning ritual, and she'd performed it on every ocean she'd ever sailed. She savored this morning's sunrise ritual especially. There wouldn't be many more for a while. When she got back to home port, she would inform her husband that she was, indeed, finally pregnant. It was time to exchange the chart table for a changing table, at least until the little skipper started school.

Captain Costa was in the galley securing another cup of freshly brewed dark roast when she was summoned on the intercom by her anxious first mate. A Mexican Azteca-class naval patrol boat was closing fast at twenty-five knots.

The big radar-controlled 40mm Bofors deck gun on the *Joaquín* began firing just as Captain Costa reached the bridge. The first round tore into the thin steel skin of the six-hundred-foot-long freighter ten feet above the waterline. The whole ship shuddered with the strike. Another shell followed five seconds later, slamming into one of the big stacked containers on deck. It tumbled overboard with twenty tons of diesel motor parts inside. The splash leaped thirty feet into the air.

The captain bellowed orders to the radio operator to send out a May-day to the naval air station in New Orleans and report they were under attack.

Minutes later, a pair of F/A-18 Hornets flown by the River Rattler squadron scrambled into action.

Captain Costa ordered the helmsman hard to port, trying to turn her big ship's bow toward the Mexican warship to reduce her target profile. It was a completely futile gesture on her part, but it was better than doing nothing.

The *Joaquín*, traveling at more than twice the speed of the freighter, turned to starboard, drawing out into a wider circle to improve its angle of attack. For a brief moment, the two ships actually were bow on, but the radar-controlled gun continued to fire. The armor-piercing round struck the topmost container on the bow and blew it to pieces, turning the machine parts inside to shrapnel that sprayed the surface of the water like shot pellets.

The two ships were now only a thousand yards apart as their bows separated on the point of axis, and the patrol boat's L70 Oerlikon 20mm cannon opened up, raking the *Star Louisiana*'s superstructure with withering fire at the rate of five rounds per second. The 20mm rounds shattered the thick marine window glass and shredded the bridge like tissue paper. The helmsman standing at his post took a round square in his broad chest. His upper torso disintegrated in a spray of blood and bone as shards of glass and steel pinged around the cabin.

The captain and the first mate had instinctively hit the deck, both barely escaping decapitation by the molten lead scythe roaring above their heads. They were safe for the time being. The Mexican warship was low in the water relative to their position on the deck inside the high bridge superstructure. But that would last only until the Mexicans came full around and could fire on her exposed port side.

Right now, though, Captain Costa's ship was drifting to a halt. Man-size wooden ship wheels and brass-plated engine-order telegraphs had disappeared decades ago, replaced by an array of computer monitors, control sticks, and track balls that looked more like the bridge of a spaceship than a merchant vessel. Now that the helmsman's torso was sprayed over the back wall of the bridge and his station smashed, the engines were cycling down and the ship's rudder returned to neutral position.

Costa belly-crawled toward the helmsman's station. She had to find a way to switch the systems back to manual and get the ship under way. Her elbows bled as they scraped across the razor-sharp glass and metal fragments on the rubberized deck.

Another 40mm round slammed into the sky-blue hull of the *Star Louisiana* and the ship shuddered again. The chief engineering officer's voice shouted over the loudspeakers that the number one engine had just been destroyed. Costa knew that the chief was shouting because the engine room was so damn loud, not because the old salt was panicked. She kept crawling, and wondered what the adrenaline dump into her bloodstream was doing to her baby.

The bridge of the *Joaquín* was in significantly better shape than the bridge of the *Star Lousiana*, though the dried blood from the slaughtered Mexican crew on the steel deck wouldn't have passed the lieutenant's inspection under normal circumstances.

"Two aircraft, closing fast, six hundred knots, lieutenant," said the radar operator in Farsi.

"That's it, then. Helmsman, come hard to starboard. Let's ram the great fat bitch," the lieutenant ordered.

The young Iranian naval officer was surprisingly calm for his first action, the senior helmsman noted. Under normal circumstances, he would have nominated him for a hero's medal. But there was no need now. Martyrs received their rewards from the hand of Allah himself.

"Coming hard to starboard, Lieutenant."

The Iranian naval crew had been brought in for just such a mission.

They had been stationed in Cuba for over three months waiting for an opportunity for naval jihad against the Great Satan and had spent their time studying Mexican naval operations and Spanish. Operating the vessel was simple enough; ship controls were universal in design and function these days. All of the enlisted men selected were veteran sailors and eager for martyrdom.

The ship's bow turned surprisingly fast and soon pointed directly at the giant white letters painted along the side of the enormous hull.

"All ahead flank."

"All ahead flank," the helmsman repeated.

With any luck, the lieutenant hoped, they'd rip the containership in half and sink her before the American fighter bombers pinging on his radar scope could stop them.

The two automatic deck guns continued to boom and roar as they fired their shells. The noise was fearsome even inside the sealed bridge. The air bore the faint copper smell of the explosives despite the air scrubbers. The big white letters on the containership were quickly pockmarked with giant shell holes and the big steel containers on deck practically melted under the stream of lead from the 20mm gun.

"One minute to target, sir!" the helmsman shouted proudly.

"*Inshallah!*" the lieutenant shouted back with a joyous smile.

But the lieutenant had made a tactical error. By maneuvering the *Joaquín* into ramming position, he put himself between the two F/A-18 Hornets and the *Star Louisiana*. That gave the Hornets a clear line of sight to the *Joaquín*. They acquired radar lock on their target, then fired four antiship missiles from twenty miles away.

Too late.

Ten seconds later, the bow of the *Joaquín* tore into the starboard side of the big containership, ripping a twenty-foot-tall hole in the hull and fatally snapping the ship's steel spine.

The Iranians cheered as they were thrown against the bulkheads with the force of impact, but their victory cries caught in their throats as the four inbound missiles struck the *Joaquín*, vaporizing the warship in a cloud of fire and steel.

Thirteen minutes later, the *Star Louisiana* sank with all hands on board.

Inshallah.

55

San Diego, California

The news about the Mexican patrol boat attack on the American freighter and its subsequent sinking by U.S. Navy aircraft jammed the radio and television news broadcasts all day, but Pearce couldn't pay attention to any of it. Pearce knew Myers would have her hands full and she'd be lucky to get out of a full-blown shooting war with Mexico before the day was over.

But that was her problem. Pearce and his team were laser-focused on tracking Ali and hell-bent on setting up a capture with zero civilian casualties, which was growing increasingly unlikely.

After arriving at L.A.'s Union Station by bus, Ali grabbed a couple of *cabrito* tacos from a nearby food truck and washed them down with a grape soda before purchasing a ticket with cash for a shared Prime Time Shuttle ride to the San Diego airport. What made Pearce nervous was that Ali wore a beige windbreaker that he kept zipped up at all times.

Judy Hopper flew Pearce in a company helicopter to the San Diego airport where Pearce Systems maintained a private hangar. The Euro-copter AS350 she was flying was decked out with Pearce Systems corporate logos, which wasn't ideal, but there weren't any other options at the moment.

Pearce grabbed the company car—an unmarked sterling gray 2013

Ford Mustang Shelby GT 500—out of its designated parking spot and
took up station at the shuttle drop-off ten minutes before the shuttle was
due while Hopper waited for him to radio her.

At the San Diego shuttle drop-off, Ali grabbed a taxi that jumped on
southbound I-5. Pearce trailed Ali in his Mustang as Judy kept tabs on
both of them by helicopter. A few minutes into the ride, she called Pearce.

"He's heading for Petco Park. That's got to be his target."

"Agreed," Pearce said.

"We'd better grab him before he gets in. The Padres game is sold out.
I heard it on the radio."

Pearce knew that if Ali really did have access to a bomb or some other
WMD, Petco Park would be the perfect venue to set it off—live on national television. Pearce weighed the arguments raging in his head. Ali
was probably wearing a suicide vest under that zippered jacket and was
probably smart enough to load it up with glass marbles and some kind of
detonator that kept him from being caught by any of the metal detectors
he'd already passed through. If the Iranian had booked his reservation for
the seventy-two-virgin hotel, a mass murder at Petco Park was the perfect
place to check in.

But something still didn't add up. Ali had practically begged to be
discovered and followed. He made no attempt to hide his face with either
a hat or sunglasses, let alone engage in the tricks every junior field operative employs to avoid detection by electronic surveillance. Ali wanted to
be discovered and followed. Why?

"Stay close, Judy. I might need you. How far away are Johnny and
Stella?" Pearce had had Judy contact them as soon as Ali hit the freeway.

"Twelve minutes, tops."

Ali's cab dropped him off at Petco Park just in time for the start of the
second inning. The sellout crowd of over forty-five thousand people roared
as some sort of a play was made inside. He picked up a ticket at the will-
call booth for the sold-out game against the Los Angeles Dodgers and
dashed inside.

Pearce dropped his car off at the valet service and ran up to the only open ticket window, desperate to find a way into the sold-out game without setting off alarm bells. Before he could concoct a cover story, the ticket seller asked, "You Troy Pearce?"

"Yeah."

"Some guy just left this for you."

The ticket seller slid a ticket under the glass. Pearce snatched it up. The Iranian had style.

Pearce raced through the casual stadium security with a flash of a fake CIA identity card and made his way to a third-floor Premier Club suite right behind home plate. He pushed through the unlocked door.

Ali stood at the bar and poured himself a club soda. His windbreaker was off. No suicide vest. Not even a gun or a knife.

Pearce unholstered his .45 caliber Glock and marched straight at the Iranian, shoving the muzzle tip against the side of Ali's head.

Ali didn't flinch. He held up the glass with the fizzy water and said, "Cheers," lifting the drink to his mouth. Pearce batted it away.

"You Americans. No manners."

"I'm two heartbeats away from blasting your brains against the wall. Tell me why I shouldn't?"

"Because if it was a good idea, you would have already done so. Why haven't you, Pearce?"

Hearing the Iranian pronounce his name chilled him. The Quds Force was a serious organization with world-class intelligence-gathering capabilities, but it was more likely that Ali had gotten his name through the torture he'd put Udi through. Pearce's grip tightened on the pistol.

"No answer? Let me help you. Is it A, because you don't know why I went to all the trouble to arrange this little meeting? Or is it B, because you don't know what might happen if I don't come out of this suite alive? Or is it C, because you sense there is something else at work behind the scenes that you still have not figured out?"

"All of the above, ass wipe."

Ali smiled. "Honestly, I'm surprised. Now lower your weapon, or I will signal my man to fire his SA-7 at your helicopter and kill your friend Judy."

Pearce's eyes narrowed. *How does he know about Judy?*

"I've been monitoring your comms since Union Station." Ali pointed at his Bluetooth earpiece. "We have scanners, too."

The SA-7 was the Russian version of an American shoulder-fired Redeye antiaircraft missile, perfectly capable of taking out a thin-skinned civilian helicopter. When Libya fell, dozens of SA-7s fell into Iranian hands, though they had plenty in their arsenal already.

Pearce lowered his pistol. "Start talking."

Ali tapped his earpiece, shutting down the comm link. He didn't want his associates to hear the proposal he was about to make to the American.

"You are a businessman, so let me get down to business." Ali motioned to a chair. Pearce refused. Ali took a seat anyway, putting his feet up on a nearby table.

"I need safe transportation to Tehran."

Pearce laughed. "Oh, really? Well, I have a need, too. A powerful need to throw your ass through that plate-glass window and watch you break your scrawny neck on the dugout railing. You tortured and murdered one of my friends and I mean to pay you back with interest."

"You mean the Israeli spy who came to Mexico to capture me? Don't be such a child. His duty was to capture me; my duty was to kill him. I did my duty, he failed his. For soldiers such as ourselves, it is as simple as that, is it not?"

Pearce clenched his fists. He was definitely going to enjoy beating this cold-blooded bastard to death with his bare hands.

Ali leaped to his feet and kicked his chair aside.

"If you think you have what it takes to kill me, I welcome the battle. In fairness, I should warn you: if I don't win and you emerge from this suite without me, a thousand people will be killed in this stadium by ex-

plosive charges. Is that price too high to pay for you to get your vengeance?"

Pearce inwardly raged. There was no question he could take the Iranian out. But Ali had beaten him at every turn so far. Better let this thing
play out.

"Why don't you let the Mexicans ship you out?"

"We are no longer on friendly terms."

"Because you were the one behind the Bravo attacks here in the States."
Pearce grinned. "The Mexican government must be pretty pissed off at
you."

"You have a gift for stating the obvious. They are as eager to kill me as
you are."

"What do I get in exchange for transporting you in one piece to
Tehran?"

"Information of the highest order. Information that affects the vital
national security of your country. It's far more valuable than my worthless skin."

"What's the information?"

"Do we have a deal?"

"If the information is solid."

"It is, I assure you."

"And if I don't agree to this deal?"

"Then I walk out of here, and when I am in a secure position, I will
remotely disarm the wireless detonators, and no one need die today, and
I will find another way home."

"How do I know you'll actually disarm them?"

"You don't. The only thing you can be certain of is that if I don't leave
here under my own power, the explosives will be detonated."

What would Myers say? Should he try to contact her first? Pearce was
completely off the reservation now—maybe too far off. Letting Ali go
posed significant security risks that he wasn't authorized to incur. But

Pearce was the one who had boarded this runaway train. It was up to him now to decide when and where to get off.

"We have a deal. Now quit jawing me to death and tell me what you know."

Ali nodded, satisfied that he'd finally set the hook. He crossed back over to the bar, opened up the fridge, and found another cold club soda and poured himself one over ice. As he poured, he nodded at Pearce. "You might want to pour yourself a whiskey. You're going to need it."

Pearce finally holstered his gun, then poured himself a drink.

Ali laid everything out. Iran and Russia had forged a secret alliance to dominate their relative spheres of influence—the Middle East and Western Europe. The Russians had engaged the Iranians to provoke the Americans into a ground war in Mexico in order to keep them distracted while the Russians secured the rich oil fields of the Caucasus. A second Mexican-American war would also drive up oil and gas prices, which benefitted both Iran and Russia.

"And who was the brain behind the plan?" Pearce asked.

"Ambassador Britnev formulated the original plan."

Or at least he thought he had, Ali mused.

"Of course, his Kremlin masters had to approve it, and Titov himself signed off on it. The only problem with the plan is that we could never get Myers to comply with it. She is a woman of remarkable resolve, quite unlike any other woman I have ever known. I have had to improvise quite a bit."

"And the Mexican government had no part in this?"

"Did I say that?"

"What role did they play in your scheme?"

"Since you killed both Castillo and Bravo, the Barrazas accepted my offer of protection against your government and the civil war that is about to erupt beneath their feet."

"Then why did you attack the president at the Hidalgo church?"

"Hernán Barraza ordered the attack on his brother."

"Why would he want you to attack his brother?"

"He wanted his brother to think that you Americans were trying to assassinate him."

"But that drone could easily have killed the president."

Ali shrugged. "Hernán wants to be president. He is already making plans for another attempt."

"What proof do I have that you aren't just making all of this up to get your dick out of the wood chipper?"

"It is normal in a business transaction to secure a contract with a deposit in good faith, particularly when one is doing business with a new partner."

Ali reached into his pocket and pulled out a slip of paper and set it on the bar. Pearce read it.

"I don't believe it. The navy would have picked this thing up a long time ago."

"Believe it. There are several Russian subs that operate with impunity in the Gulf of Mexico. You Americans are not as clever as you think you are. This submarine has been assigned exclusively to my unit for supply and transport."

"Then why not use it to get back to Tehran?"

"I made that request. The Russians refused to allow me to 'abandon my post,' as they put it." Ali was lying.

The Iranian pointed at the paper. "GPS coordinates and radio codes are valid for the next seventy-two hours, then they change again. I will not provide new ones." He picked up his windbreaker and pulled it on as he headed for the door.

"Where do you think you're going?" Pearce asked.

"I'm leaving." He pointed at the stadium. "Baseball bores me. I prefer American football. You are welcome to stay, of course. There is excellent room service that has already been paid for."

"You aren't going anywhere." Pearce's hand drifted toward his pistol.

"Of course I am. I told you, if I don't leave here under my own terms, a thousand people will die. Maybe more. If you don't find what I promise on that paper, then you have no need to fulfill your agreement with me. But if you do find that submarine, then you contact me with the cell number also on that paper and we will agree to a meeting place and time."

And with that, Ali left.

The Quds Force officer had him by the short hairs and they both knew it.

Pearce's face darkened.

The Iranian was still running the show.

56

Mexico City, Mexico

U.S. Ambassador Romero sat in the office of his Mexican counterpart, the secretary of foreign affairs, along with the Mexican secretary of defense, a retired general. Heated accusations on both sides finally simmered down to a low boil.

After the meeting, Romero reported back to Myers that he was convinced that the Mexican government had, in fact, *not* ordered the attack on the *Star Louisiana* and that he accepted the Mexican theory that a rogue naval officer had foolishly taken matters into his own hands. Romero further suggested that the matter now be handled by lawyers, insurance companies, and high-level bureaucrats, rather than generals and admirals if war was to be avoided. Myers thanked him.

An emergency cabinet meeting affirmed Romero's recommendation despite Early's concern that it was a Bravo operation. The chief of naval operations, a four-star admiral, assured Myers that operating a modern combat vessel was beyond the skill sets of street thugs. "So is hijacking a Reaper," Early protested. It would be weeks before salvage operations could recover any bodies for identification—if any bodies were still intact. For Myers, the question of identity was academic. All that mattered to her at the moment was that the United States and Mexico had just avoided a shooting war.

But she wasn't out of the woods yet. Myers knew that the House

Armed Services Committee hearings would find a way to forge the tragedy into a weapon against her administration.

Gulf of Mexico

The Russian nuclear attack submarine *Vepr* was cruising at a leisurely five
knots nearly three hundred meters below the surface of the gulf on a
mapping exercise. No American warships were in the area. The nearest
vessel was a small civilian pleasure boat on the surface four hundred meters away, according to its radar signature.

The young but professional crew was performing its duties with affable efficiency when a heavy metallic *clang* sounded against the *Vepr*'s
outer hull. Everybody suddenly shut up, as if a switch had been thrown.
The captain ordered all stop, fearing they'd struck something. According to their charts, an abandoned explosives and ordnance dumping
ground the Americans had used for decades was several kilometers north
of their position, but radar and sonar both indicated nothing of the kind
close by.

Moments later, a puzzled radioman called the captain to his station
and handed him the headphones.

"Hello, Captain!" Yamada's voice blasted in the Russian's ears.

"What's going on? Who are you?" the captain demanded.

"Doesn't matter who I am, *moke*. What matters is that I know who
you are."

The captain frowned in confusion. "What do you want?"

Yamada explained to the sub captain that an underwater drone had
just successfully attached an explosive device to the Akula-class submarine's outer hull and—*clang*—was attaching yet others. *There was no
reason to worry*, Yamada assured the captain, *at least not yet.*

The Russian captain at first expressed doubts, but a visual confirmation by an external video camera confirmed Yamada's claims. Both the

stealth UUV and the magnetic limpet mines attached to the *Vepr's* hull were visually confirmed.

Clang.

The captain resorted to vile threats, but within moments he succumbed to his worst fears as Yamada explained the captain's dire situation.

"The *Vepr* must immediately withdraw from the gulf at full speed and return to the fleet base in Severomorsk or face certain destruction." The *Vepr* was part of the great Northern Fleet that operated out of Murmansk Oblast near the Finnish and Norwegian borders.

"This is an act of war," the captain declared.

"I am a private citizen representing no government. Private citizens cannot wage war," Yamada countered. Pearce had instructed him to use this precise legal language.

"You are a liar. You are an American."

"Actually, I'm your worst nightmare. I'm a Japanese with a long memory."

The captain shuddered. "A terrorist, then?"

"More like a contractor, terrorizing you at the moment. I am tracking your position by satellite. Failure to set course for Severomorsk and follow it immediately will result in detonation of the limpet mines attached to your hull. Once I see that the *Vepr* has returned to Severomorsk, I will contact your base commander, he will arrange to have a great deal of money transferred to an account of my designation, and then I will deactivate the mines."

"I don't trust you."

"Good!" Yamada laughed. "That would be a mistake. My ancestors have been killing Russians since the Battle of Tsushima. So, yes, I want you to worry about the fact that I might change my mind and blow your pig boat to pieces just for the fun of it, and I want you to sweat as you think about my finger on the button for every minute of every kilometer it takes you to get back to Severomorsk."

Yamada laughed again and cut the link.

Sixty seconds later, the *Vepr* powered up to full speed and set a direct course for home.

But Yamada had lied. The robotic arm on his stealthy research UUV had only attached large magnets to the submarine's hull. Pearce promised Yamada that his UUV would never be deployed in a military operation, so it took a while to convince his friend that scaring the Russians with magnets was not the same as blowing them out of the water with mines. Yamada finally yielded the point on the promise of lavish funding for his next round of whale research. Yamada was actually glad to screw with the Russians. He knew that the Soviets had killed whales illegally for over forty years, slaughtering nearly two hundred thousand of them globally and causing several population crashes. Making a Russian sub captain piss his pants seemed like a good start on payback to the idealistic pacifist.

Pearce was just as glad they were only magnets attached to the *Vepr*'s hull. If World War III was about to begin, he preferred it was someone else who started it. But he made sure that one of the magnets featured a GPS tracker with a signal that he would pass on to the U.S. Navy.

Ali had kept his side of the bargain. Galling as it was, now it was Pearce's turn to ante up.

San Diego, California

Two days later, Ali appeared at the Pearce Systems hangar at the San Diego airport, as per Pearce's instructions. One of Pearce's private jets, a Bombardier Global 8000, sat in the cavernous space. Ali could see the two pilots in the cockpit window prepping for takeoff.

Pearce escorted the Iranian up the stairs into the luxurious cabin. On the back end of the passenger compartment was a sliding cantilevered door for privacy. The door was locked open. A rolling medical/surgical bed was in the separate space, along with a heart monitor and IV pump.

"What is that?" Ali asked.

A clean-shaven thirty-year-old Pakistani man in a sport coat and tie stepped into the cabin, carrying a doctor's satchel and a small roll-on travel case. He was out of breath. "Sorry I'm late."

Pearce shook the Pakistani's hand with a smile. "You're fine, Doctor. Take a seat, please."

"Who is that?" Ali asked.

"I promised you safe delivery to Tehran. I didn't promise to reveal my underground network to you so we're going to have to knock you out with drugs."

Ali's eyes narrowed with suspicion.

"Dr. Khan is a professor of anesthesiology at the USC Medical Center. He's also a Muslim."

"Sunni Muslim," Khan corrected.

Ali bristled. "A heretic." The Iranian was a devout Shia.

"That's the best I could do on short notice," Pearce said.

"This was not part of our deal," Ali said.

"If I was going to kill you, you little shit, I promise you I wouldn't do it with tranquilizers."

"And if I leave right now?"

"It means our deal is off. Then I'll put a bullet in your stomach before you reach the exit door, and then the fun times can really begin."

Ali was trapped. Without the threat of the explosives at Petco Park, he didn't have any more leverage.

"I am trusting your honor to deliver me safely," Ali reminded Pearce, mustering as much ferocity as he could.

"You're lucky I value my honor."

"I am surprised you do. Infidel mercenaries have no loyalty to anyone but themselves, and there is no honor in that. Perhaps Allah will indeed be merciful to you on the Day of Judgment."

"I'm curious. Why did you reveal the location of the Petco Park explosives to us? I thought you people enjoyed slaughtering helpless civilians."

Bravos had posed as installers two weeks before and replaced the foam bumper guards that wrapped around the support poles throughout the stadium, but instead of using styrofoam in the replacement job, they had used tubes packed with C4 and steel fléchettes, then reattached the advertising sleeves that covered the bumpers. After Pearce had confirmed the Russian submarine with Ali, the Iranian revealed the location of the bombs. An FBI demolition squad took care of the rest.

"New American civilian deaths would have served no purpose, but they would have incurred the wrath of the United States upon my government. And for the record, I did not install those devices. It was Bravo's men who did it. So, technically, I and my government have assisted the United States in defeating a terrorist attack by the Bravos upon your nation."

"And we're supposed to be grateful?"

"No. That would be presumptuous."

Pearce marveled. Like most Eastern cultures, Iranians had no sense of irony.

Ali continued. "I just want the record to be clear. There must be no false pretext for hostilities between your government and mine."

"We don't need a false pretext to wipe your maniac government off the face of the earth. You've given us plenty of real ones." Pearce checked his watch. "Time to get rolling. Dr. Khan is going to put you to sleep, and when you wake up, you will be in Tehran, alive and safe. The rest is up to you."

"I must warn you that the anesthesia I will be using is quite potent. You will probably have a slight headache when you wake up, but it's nothing to worry about," Khan added.

"And it goes without saying, once you arrive in Tehran, all bets are off. My promise is to deliver you alive and well today. My one goal in life is to make sure you have very few tomorrows. Understood?"

"Understood."

Pearce stepped closer to the smiling Iranian.

"When this mess finally gets cleaned up, don't be surprised if you find me knocking on your door."

Ali didn't flinch. "I shall be waiting with a cup of hot tea."

"Dr. Khan will take care of you from here. And the two pilots up front? Both are armed, and both know who you are."

Dr. Khan slipped back his sport coat, revealing a pistol on his hip. "Don't worry, Mr. Pearce. There won't be any trouble." He glared at Ali.

"One more thing." Pearce held out his smartphone for Ali to read. It had a text message on it for Ali from President Myers to Mehdi Sadr, the volatile president of the Iranian regime.

"Have you memorized her message?"

Ali nodded.

"It's for President Sadr's ears only. If he doesn't contact her within twenty-four hours after your arrival, her offer is withdrawn. Understood?"

Ali nodded again. "I will deliver it as soon as I arrive."

"Roll up your sleeve," Khan ordered.

Pearce remained in the cabin until Ali was safely knocked out and tucked into bed with an IV drip in his arm.

"Thanks, Doc. I owe you one."

"I'm just paying it forward, Mr. Pearce. My family owes you everything."

Pearce stepped off the jet stairs just as a van rolled up to the hangar. Three men and two women swiftly exited the vehicle and began unloading the crates of high-tech gear they'd brought with them for the long flight to Tehran.

Washington, D.C.

After several days of testimony by experts hostile to the president's agenda, the House Armed Services Committee hearing finally invited a Myers ally: Mike Early. As the president's special assistant on security affairs, he was both appropriate and relevant to the hearing's subject matter.

"Invited" was a term of art; the administration intended to fight any sort of summons on the grounds of separation of powers. But Early eagerly agreed to answer any questions put to him. He wasn't even sworn in.

The first questions from the committee Republicans were personal, detailing Early's extensive and heroic national service, and the next questions they asked were pure softballs that allowed him the chance to crow about the great successes of the national security structure in the past few weeks rounding up drug kingpins and wiping out the Bravo terrorists.

Representative Gormer let them ask all of the questions they needed to. Early's smile got wider and wider as the morning went on, Gormer noted. Early relaxed, dropping his guard. He even cracked a few jokes.

Until Gormer dropped the bomb.

Gormer pulled his microphone closer. "Tell us, Mr. Early, exactly who is Troy Pearce?"

Early was caught short. In a million years, he wouldn't have guessed that Gormer had any clue about Troy, let alone the balls to ask about him in the middle of an ongoing classified operation. The more he thought about the question, the angrier he became, but also the more confused. He hadn't been briefed for this possibility.

"Troy Pearce is a friend of mine, and the CEO of Pearce Systems, a registered federal defense contractor."

"And is it true that President Myers hired Mr. Pearce and Pearce Systems to conduct the targeted assassination of Mr. Aquiles Castillo, a private citizen of Mexico?"

Early couldn't hear himself think as dozens of digital cameras whirred and flashed in front of him. A crowd of news photographers was squatting directly in front of his table, blasting away with their cameras like frenzied paparazzi.

"No comment, Mr. Chairman," Early finally blurted out.

"Is it true this administration hired Mr. Pearce to murder other foreign nationals and to carry out its other clandestine foreign-policy objectives?"

"No comment."

"Is it true that this administration has engaged the services of Pearce Systems to perform espionage operations against foreign governments, including Mexico, a respected ally?"

"No comment."

And so it went.

The shit storm had begun and Early had forgotten to bring his umbrella.

The chairman of the House Judiciary Committee, Sandra Quinn (D-GA), watched the live hearings seated on a couch in Senator Diele's office. In the chair next to her was Vice President Greyhill.

"Just like I promised," Diele said. He wanted to see her reaction when Gormer dropped the bomb.

"Too bad Early's not under oath," Quinn said.

"The next time he's on camera, he will be," Greyhill assured her. "Just let him try and hide behind 'executive privilege.'"

"I trust this means you'll be moving forward with the impeachment resolution?" Diele asked.

"He delivered the goods, didn't he?" Quinn was referring to the fact that Diele had spilled the beans to Gormer about Pearce and his operation.

"He sure did. And wrapped it all up in a pink bow."

Quinn hoped that the Pearce revelation would be enough to throw Myers out of office and, with any luck, straight into a federal prison. During her election campaign, Myers ran a humiliating campaign ad featuring a Quinn quote that "Guam would capsize if too many U.S. Marines were stationed there" as proof of the idiocy of Congress. Quinn had barely won reelection and privately vowed revenge at the first possible opportunity.

What neither Quinn nor Greyhill realized was that Diele's source for the Pearce revelation was Ambassador Britnev, and Britnev's source was Ali, who had tortured it out of Udi just before feeding him to the pigs while he was still alive.

OCTOBER

57

Washington, D.C.

Myers stood alone in the secured media room at the White House, video conferencing with the Kremlin. Not even Strasburg had been allowed into the room with her.

On the other hand, Titov had several advisors in the room with him, including a half dozen scowling generals and admirals with chests full of gleaming service medals. The oldest was Colonel General Petrov, commander of the Strategic Rocket Forces, with enough nuclear ICBMs at his disposal to destroy the United States a dozen times over. Two stern-faced women sat around the long table as well. Even Ambassador Britnev was there, perched on Titov's left.

"You've seen and heard the video and audio files I've forwarded to you?" Myers asked. She was referring to the conversation Pearce had secretly recorded with Ali in the Padres luxury suite along with the video recordings that Yamada had made of the *Vepr* lurking in the gulf. On Pearce's orders, however, Yamada didn't pass along to Myers the conversation with the Russian captain.

"Yes, of course." Titov had a bulldog face but his voice was surprisingly gentle, even calming. His English was excellent as well.

"My intelligence services are analyzing the files now. The first reports are that they are fabrications. Everybody knows how skilled your Hollywood technicians are at manipulating sounds and images. But I am waiting for the final analysis, of course."

"Mr. Titov, we are far beyond the point of playing games. I'm standing here alone for a reason. As far as I'm concerned, this conversation is completely private. As you can see, none of my advisors are here with me, and I assure you none of them is listening in on this conversation. I have no desire to embarrass you or your government, nor do I wish to provoke a war with you. But the actions you have taken against my government are, in fact, acts of aggression, and I will not stand for them."

Titov turned his head slightly to the general sitting next to him and grinned. The general whispered something to Titov that made Titov chuckle, and that set off a chain reaction of controlled laughter.

"Forgive me, Mr. President, but my Russian is terrible. Do you mind letting me in on the joke?"

"My colleague, Colonel General Petrov, said that you remind him of his ex-wife, a very unpleasant lady. Beyond that, I do not wish to repeat."

Again, the Russians rumbled with laughter, including the women.

Myers smiled. "Perhaps the old missile general had an unhappy wife because his rocket was no longer able to launch."

The old general's face turned beet red. The Russians instantly roared with laughter, Titov most of all. Myers was alone in the room but she had been thoroughly briefed on the Russian high command.

"Forgive me, Madame President," Titov said, wiping a tear from his eye. "I have clearly underestimated you."

"In more ways than you can possibly know, Mr. President."

That sobered him up.

"Then let us be frank. What is the purpose of this pleasant chat? To discuss the electronic fictions you have sent to us?" Titov asked.

"We are far beyond discussions, Mr. President. Here is my proposal. In twenty-four hours, you will announce to the world that your cross-border antiterror operations in Azerbaijan have been a success and that you will begin withdrawing your forces within seventy-two hours, abandoning the country entirely within seven days. My government will publicly commend you for your decision to withdraw, and privately you will negotiate with the Azerbaijanis over monetary compensation for the damages you have caused that nation."

Titov glowered at Myers. "And why would we do such a thing? Because you simply order it?"

Myers pressed a button on her console. A live feed appeared as a picture within a picture on both of their screens. It showed a giant steel pipeline.

"Do you recognize this, Mr. Titov?"

"It looks like an oil pipeline."

"It is. It's the BTC pipeline. As I'm sure you know, it's over a thousand miles long and pumps a million gallons of oil per day from Baku all the way to the Mediterranean. Right now, it's the only viable means you have of transporting all of that Azeri oil you're stealing out of the Caspian Sea into the European markets."

Titov's advisors murmured among themselves.

Myers pressed another button. Yet another live picture-in-picture image appeared, also of a pipeline.

"This is the 2,500-mile-long Druzhba pipeline, which your nation operates. It supplies 1.4 million barrels of oil per day from Siberian and Kazakh oil fields to end users all over Europe. This is your main oil artery to the West, Mr. President.

"In both cases, armed drones under my control are flying over these extremely vulnerable pipelines. On my order, they will destroy a section of each pipeline. No matter how quickly you are able to repair them, I will be able to destroy another section with the push of a button. Besides the environmental damage and financial cost these attacks will incur, the most important thing they will accomplish is to convince the Europeans that you are no longer able to deliver a reliable supply of oil. My nation, however, is prepared to step in and fill that void. Oh, and for what it's worth, I have your natural gas pipelines targeted as well."

Titov's face hardened. "One moment." He slammed a button that muted the sound on his end. Myers watched the room erupt into a frenzied conference. A minute later, he snapped the sound back on.

"You're bluffing, Madame President. Your nation is not prepared to engage in a ground war with us. Your military has exhausted itself with its misadventures in Iraq and Afghanistan, and you yourself are about to be impeached for your war crimes against the people and government of Mexico."

"Do not underestimate my nation's capacity for war, Mr. President. But I concede your point. My nation does not desire war at this time, and my nation makes no threat to you."

Titov pointed at the screen where the video images still played. "That is no threat?"

"I said, my *nation* makes no threat. Right now, I am the one making the threat. Those unmanned drones are flown by a private contractor under my employ. The American government has no part in this now. This is a personal matter between me and you, Mr. Titov. Not our governments. And you are absolutely right. I am about to be impeached, but that hardly means I will be thrown out of office, especially if our two nations are suddenly at war. But even if I was to be thrown out of office, I still control these drones and will still pose a threat to your pipelines, even from prison, if it comes to that."

Again, Titov snapped off the sound and conferred with his advisors. Britnev bent Titov's ear the most.

Myers wondered if she had overplayed her hand. She essentially called him out in front of his peers, just like in a schoolyard brawl. If Titov was like most men, he'd give himself over to his anger and pride, and her gamble would fail. The sound came back on.

"Your criminal mercenary Pearce is behind this, isn't he?" Titov demanded.

"Troy Pearce is an honorable man, and he's the best in the world at what he does. But he's not the only resource available to me. I can always release the audio and video files I sent to you to Congress. Senator Diele would beg for war. Ask Britnev if I'm telling the truth or not."

Titov didn't have to. He'd been intimately familiar with Diele for years, dating back to when he was a KGB officer.

"Mr. President, the choice here is very simple. If you stay in Azerbaijan, you will never be able to exploit the oil resources available there anyway once I destroy your pipeline, and you will lose all of your capacity to transport your nation's legitimate oil and gas reserves. At the very least, you'll lose the European markets. We both know that the only thing propping up your economy is your oil and gas exports. Are you willing to start World War III knowing that you will begin that war in a state of economic collapse?"

Titov drummed his fingers on the table. He was dancing on the knife's edge.

Myers wondered, *Have I pushed him too far?*

Titov finally spoke. "If we withdraw from Azerbaijan and you release these files, your Congress may still declare war on us, so perhaps it is best for us to stay where we are and see what happens?"

"If you withdraw from Azerbaijan, I guarantee that I will destroy those files. I'm no fool, either, Mr. President. A shooting war between your country and mine would be a disaster for both of us, and a nightmare for the whole world. There is nothing to be gained, except to advance the interests of our mutual competitors, especially China and Iran."

"And what is to keep you from threatening our pipelines in the future? Even holding them for ransom?"

"You have my word."

"That's not good enough," Titov said.

"What else can I offer?" Myers asked.

Britnev leaned into Titov and whispered something. Titov nodded, smiled.

"One thing in order to prove your sincere desire to avoid war."

"Name it."

Titov did. It was an outrageous suggestion.

To his astonishment, Myers agreed to it instantly.

58

Los Pinos, Mexico D.F.

President Barraza's security detail stood alert around the office. Antonio sat behind his desk in an elegantly cut light blue suit, while Hernán took up his usual position, slouched on the couch with a glass of liquor in his hands.

Cruzalta sat opposite the president, and next to him, Senator Madero, a silver-haired elder statesman. Both men had been checked for weapons when they entered the building and again when they entered the president's office. Madero kept a hand-stitched brown leather attaché case on his lap.

"What we have to say might be better said in private," Cruzalta suggested.

Antonio shot a glance at Hernán, who nodded his approval.

Antonio turned to the security chief. "Dismissed."

"But, Mr. President—"

Antonio's glowering eyes cut him off.

"Yes, Mr. President."

The security chief nodded to his men and they left the room.

"Say what you're going to say, traitor."

"Traitor?" Cruzalta could barely contain his rage.

"What my brother means to say is, what is it that you are proposing?" Hernán asked.

Madero opened his attaché case and handed Antonio a sheet of paper. He read it.

"There are 425 signatures on that list requesting that you vacate the office of president," Madero said with great solemnity. "Enough to satisfy the constitutional requirements to elect an interim president."

Antonio laughed. "I have no reason to step down."

"You have over a one hundred fourteen million reasons to resign. Our nation is about to collapse into a civil war. We need new leadership, now," Cruzalta said.

Antonio laughed again. "You?"

"No. Senator Madero is my choice, and the choice of the majority on that list, and of many of the governors." Cruzalta was right. Madero was the most respected politician in Mexico. For decades, Madero had displayed courage, honesty, and integrity in his public service.

"If this nation is on the brink of revolution, as you think it is, then it's of your own making. You're the one who partnered with the Americans to kill poor Bravo and wage war on our people," Hernán said.

"Our people? You're talking about the animals who butchered tens of thousands of innocents—those are the people *you* partnered with. The greed, the corruption, the violence—all of it must end if our nation is to have any hope of real democracy."

"A dreamer's dream, Cruzalta. This is Mexico," Hernán laughed. "You can't change a whole culture by changing a few names on the office door."

"Perhaps not. But we can at least try, and if we fail, we can fail as *men*, rather than living like a pack of vicious dogs."

Madero trembled with rage. "How dare you speak so poorly of your own people, Barraza. It's the politicians who corrupt the people, not the other way around."

"You have many enemies, Barraza. Some closer than you think. Get out while you can," Cruzalta said.

"I have no fear of enemies. The people love me, especially after the attempt on my life," Antonio said.

Cruzalta reached into his pocket and pulled out a digital player. He explained that it was a portion of the conversation Pearce had secretly recorded with Ali in San Diego.

> *"Then why did you attack the president at the Hidalgo church?"*
> *"Hernán Barraza ordered the attack on his brother."*
> *"Why would he want you to attack his brother?"*
> *"He wanted his brother to think that you Americans were trying to as-sassinate him."*
> *"But that drone could easily have killed the president."*
> *"Hernán wants to be president. He is already making plans for another attempt."*

Antonio turned toward his brother. He was on the verge of tears. "Hernán?"

"What is that recording supposed to prove?" Hernán protested. "Americans can doctor anything on digital." He knew Antonio thought the moon landings were staged.

Antonio turned back to Cruzalta. "You are a dangerous man and a traitor. You make me sick." Antonio nodded at Madero. "And you, old man, are a fool."

Hernán slumped in his chair, visibly relieved.

"So give me one good reason why I should resign in disgrace and let you traitors take over the government?" Antonio demanded.

Madero pulled out another document and set it carefully in front of Antonio. "On this resignation letter, you are guaranteed a full and complete pardon and total immunity for all crimes you may have committed, and you may keep all of the money you currently possess by whatever means you acquired it, up to and including the moment you sign the document."

Antonio read the resignation and the pardon, then handed it to Hernán. "You're the lawyer. What do you think?"

Hernán took the paper from his brother and scanned it.

"What about my brother? Is he included in this pardon?" Antonio asked.

"We are prepared to extend that offer."

Hernán nodded, smiling with approval. "It appears to be legitimate to me." He handed back the paper to Antonio, who set it on his desk.

"What's to keep the new government from changing its mind? What about lawsuits?" Antonio asked.

Madero's kind brown eyes narrowed. A faint smile appeared beneath his elegantly trimmed silver mustache.

"You have my word, señor. But of course, for a wretch like you, honor is no virtue. So I suggest that you leave the country. Take everything with you. Find a place that does not permit extradition. We will not violate our agreement, but take every precaution if that lets you sleep at night. Whatever it takes to get you to sign that paper."

"I need seventy-two hours to settle my affairs before I can leave the country. After that, you can have your government. Is that acceptable?"

"We agree," Cruzalta said.

Antonio opened a drawer. "And I am completely pardoned and immune from all prosecutions for any crimes I have committed up until the time I sign this paper, correct?"

"That is exactly correct," Madero said.

Antonio pulled out a big chromed Smith & Wesson .44 Magnum and stood up with it. He held it up in front of his face.

"Even if I kill the two of you?"

Madero didn't flinch. "Yes. The agreement is ironclad."

Antonio rubbed the big silver barrel against his cheek. "I love this gun. Have you ever seen what a slug from one of these can do to a bear's skull?"

Guns didn't bother Cruzalta. He'd had too many of them pointed at him over the years to care anymore.

Antonio whipped around, pointed the pistol at Hernán, and fired.

The giant hand cannon roared, but the kick was enormous. The slug tore into the wall six inches above Hernán's head. Everybody's ears rang from the deafening gun blast.

Antonio lowered the barrel directly at Hernán's furrowed forehead.

Hernán fell to his knees, begging for his life, wrapping his arms around his brother's waist.

To Cruzalta's ruined ears, it sounded like Hernán was crying underwater.

BOOM!

Hernán's head exploded like a ripe melon.

The security team broke through the door, guns drawn. They aimed their weapons at Cruzalta and Madero.

"Mr. President! Are you all right?"

Hernán's blood and brain tissue stained the front of Antonio's elegant blue suit.

"I'm fine. Leave," Antonio ordered, waving them away with the pistol.

Confused, the security detail holstered their weapons. Blood was still pumping out of what was left of Hernán's cranium onto the finely woven Persian carpet.

"I said leave. Now!"

The security detail left, tails tucked between their legs. "We'll be outside if you need us, Mr. President."

Antonio tossed the heavy gun onto the desk, then picked up a Montblanc pen and unscrewed the top. He flashed his signature smile at Madero and Cruzalta. Flecks of his brother's gore were still on his face.

"Now, gentlemen, where do I sign?"

59

Tehran, Iran

The policeman nudged the bum in the gutter with his shoe.

"Drunkard! Get up, or I'll have you whipped."

The man moaned, barely stirring.

The policeman kicked him harder. The bum groaned, sat up, rubbed his face. He seemed too well dressed to be a drunk.

"Where am I?" His voice sounded strange, like he had a cold.

"You're going to jail if you don't stand up and start walking, now." The policeman grabbed him by the nape of the neck and yanked him to his feet.

"Let go of me, fool. Do you know who I am?" The man blinked hard against the harsh morning light. His head ached, and his sinuses were packed. Was he sick?

"You are Mohammad Reza Shah Pahlavi back from the dead for all I care." The policeman grabbed the man by his rock-hard bicep. The policeman frowned. What kind of derelict had an arm like that?

Ali broke the policeman's grip and shattered his jaw in a lightning-fast strike. The cop crumpled to the alley pavement, knocked out cold.

Ali checked his watch. He needed to reach President Sadr with Myers's amazing offer as quickly as possible. He just hoped he could find some aspirin before then. That Sunni pig Khan said the headache would only be mild, but the effects of the anesthetic were excruciating. *If I ever find him, I'll cut off his hands,* Ali promised himself.

Two hours later, Ali sat in a chair in the president's office, the headache roaring in his head. He rubbed his temples with the tips of his fingers to try to alleviate the pressure.

A male aide rushed in with a glass of water and a couple of Tylenols and set them on the president's desk.

"That will be all," the president told his aide. The man departed quickly and silently.

Sadr crossed from behind his desk, picked up the glass of water and the two tablets, and handed them to his most trusted Quds officer. He leaned in close.

"Here, my friend. Take these. They will help."

Sitting at his tiny metal desk just outside of Sadr's door, the aide heard a sharp crack, like a firecracker inside of a tin can. He flinched, then leaped to his feet and dashed into the office. A dozen armed guards thundered in close behind him.

Ali's headless corpse still sat in its chair, slumped slightly to one side.

Sadr lay on his back on top of his desk, his arms extended like a crucifix. A bone shard from Ali's skull had driven itself through Sadr's left eye socket into his brain, killing him instantly.

Tamar had been able to time the detonation visually through one of Dr. Rao's micro cameras attached to Ali's numbed scalp. Unfortunately, the camera was destroyed in the blast.

Pearce knew that if Sadr was dead, the secretive mullahs wouldn't confirm it for weeks, but he sensed that the gamble would pay off. Dr. Khan and his surgical team had implanted four ounces of CL-20 in Ali's sinus cavity while he was knocked out on the jet ride over, enough high explosive to blow up a car. The average human skull was an excellent source of organic shrapnel containing twenty-five separate bones. Pearce savored the irony. He had turned Iran's most dangerous terrorist into a living IED. It wasn't as satisfying as killing the bastard Ali with his own hands, but letting Tamar take him out along with the maniac Sadr was at least some small measure of retribution for his murdered friend.

"Thank you, Troy," Tamar said from her Tel Aviv apartment. Pearce had arranged for her to remotely detonate the charge he'd so carefully arranged.

"It doesn't bring Udi back," he said.

"I know. But it was a gift. Udi would be glad that I was the one to push the button."

Washington, D.C.

The rotors on *Marine One* cycled up slowly as the engine spun to life. Myers climbed the steps for the last time. As always, she wore smart but sensible shoes. She stood at the top of the steps and waved good-bye to Jeffers and the other loyal members of her cabinet who had gathered to watch her go.

Only Jeffers, Pearce, and Myers knew the real reason she had resigned. Her enemies on the Hill assumed it was because she was afraid that she would have lost the impeachment battle. They were wrong. Politics was the last thing on her mind now. Her soul ached. Everyone she had ever loved had been taken from her. What was there to be afraid of anymore?

Myers's prayer now was that no one on Titov's side of the table would leak the details of their deal. Otherwise, everything was back in play and the country she loved so deeply would fall into harm's way. The Russians had withdrawn from Azerbaijan on schedule, and Myers had resigned as promised—Titov's proof of her sincere desire to avoid a shooting war—but not before securing blanket amnesty for Pearce and his team, along with Mike Early and all the others who had participated in her scheme. It had been a classic queen sacrifice, a device that more than one chess master had used to win a desperate game.

The press cameras whirred and flashed as the chopper gently lifted off. She hoped that President Greyhill was up to the job.

She, for one, was glad to give it up. It was time to go home to Colorado and grieve for her son properly.

FEBRUARY

EPILOGUE

Moscow, Russian Federation

It was a particularly miserable February in Moscow. Heavy wet flakes of snow swirled in a freezing arctic wind. Thick ice blanketed everything. In this punishing environment, exposed human flesh blistered instantly; moments later, it began to die.

It was the kind of weather that had beaten the invincible German Wehrmacht, Britnev reminded himself as he stared out of the sliding glass door of his penthouse suite. Ironically, his towering high-rise was kept deliciously warm by an HVAC unit manufactured in Frankfurt.

Now retired from the diplomatic service, Britnev was the newest board member of the third-largest oil and gas conglomerate in his country, a newly formed joint Russian-European venture. He was thoroughly enjoying the perks of his largely ceremonial position this evening and reveling in his good fortune after the debacle of the Myers affair. In the old days, he would have been marched down to one of the basement cells in the Kremlin, tortured, and then eventually shot in the base of the neck with a small-caliber pistol.

But the new Russia was full of surprises. Connections, bribes, and useful information greatly enhanced life expectancy these days. He was still of some use to Titov, as it turned out. His connection to Vice President Diele had proven to be the ultimate life-saving grace.

Britnev admired the sparkling skyline as he took another long drag on his beloved Gauloises. He relished the burn of the harsh tobacco. Britnev first learned to love the thick filterless cigarettes as a young diplomat in Paris.

Vivaldi played on the surround-sound stereo. Britnev checked his Movado watch. It wouldn't be long before the girls he'd ordered earlier from his favorite escort service would be arriving, a pair of Eurasian sisters he'd had his eye on for a while.

His cell phone rang. The number was unlisted. It was probably the girls trying to get past the airtight building security. He crushed the cigarette butt in a crowded ashtray and picked up the phone.

"Yes?"

"Konstantin Britnev. Do you know who I am?"

The Russian paused. He could scarce believe it.

"Pearce. How did you get my number?"

"Turn on your television set."

"What?"

"I'm doing you a favor. Trust me."

Britnev crossed over to his glass-top desk and picked up a remote control. A big eighty-inch Samsung LCD popped on. Pearce's face filled the screen.

"I should ask 'how' you are able to do this, but I wouldn't understand the technical aspects anyway. And 'why' probably won't bring me any satisfaction, either," Britnev said.

"You already know 'why.' The only question you should be asking is 'when'?" Pearce's voice boomed through the television speakers.

"Soon, I imagine." Britnev felt the sweat running down his back. How did this maniac find him?

"There are two ways to play this. The first way is for you to walk back over to that sliding glass door, step out onto the balcony, and throw yourself off the building. If the asphalt doesn't kill you, the traffic will. That would be the easy way."

"What's the other option?"

"I kill you with my bare hands."

"There's a third option. I call security and leave." Britnev punched in the three-digit emergency number on his phone. It rang twice. Someone picked up.

"Hello, scumbag," Pearce answered on the other end.

Britnev glanced up at the television. Pearce wagged his cell phone at the screen. "Your security team isn't available tonight. Neither are the hookers. It's just you and me, babe."

Britnev killed the call and marched toward the front door.

"You're making a big mistake, Britnev. I'd take the balcony option if I were you."

Britnev turned around and faced the television.

"What are you being paid to do this? I'll triple it."

"This isn't about business. It's personal. A favor for a friend of mine."

"I don't want to die."

"Neither did Ryan Martinez or those kids your men slaughtered."

"I didn't pull the trigger. There's no blood on my hands."

"Take the jump, Britnev. You'll be glad you did."

Britnev turned on his heel again and raced for the door. His leather shoes clopped on the polished marble floor. He reached the door, unbolted the locks, and flung it open.

Pearce stood there, smiling.

Pearce jabbed a laser-pulsed drug injector against Britnev's neck before he could scream, paralyzing him. He pushed the Russian back inside the apartment, kicked the door shut, and guided the whimpering, gurgling man onto a modular white leather sofa.

Pearce snicked open a spring-loaded blade. The razor-sharp steel gleamed in the light.

Terror flooded the Russian's face, his eyes bulging wide like dinner plates.

Pearce had been right, Britnev realized.

Perhaps even kind.

The balcony would have been a much better option.

ACKNOWLEDGMENTS

A tumultuous sea stands between a first draft and a published novel, but my journey was eased by the sure hands and stout hearts at G. P. Putnam's Sons. My amazing editor, Nita Taublib, steered a wise but gentle rudder; her dexterous assistant editor, Meaghan Wagner, showed me the ropes, literally; and eagle-eyed copy editor David Hough spied out the hazards of my own folly. Thank you all. I can't wait for our next adventure together.

David Hale Smith at InkWell Management is both my agent and my secret weapon, and his team over there has kept a careful watch. Thank you.

I couldn't have made it this far in life without comrades-in-arms like Martin Hironaga, Mark Okada, Steve Miller, and Scott Werntz, along with too many others to name. My oldest friends, Vaughn Heppner and B. V. Larson, first suggested I take up the challenge of writing a book not too long ago, something they each do more often than anybody else I know, and they do it well.

This past year Anthony V., my reading/math study buddy at Wilson Elementary School, reminded me what hard work really looks like and why books matter. And a shout-out to Ivan Sanchez and the other 'tenders at the tequila bar at Mi Dia in Grapevine, Texas. Research never tasted so good.

I am constantly inspired by my family in ways they will never fully realize, but my wife, Angela, is the person I most want to be like in the world. She is a fixed and constant grace to those around her, me most of all.

ADDENDA

Nikola Tesla was both a scientific genius and a humanistic visionary, perhaps one of the greatest minds in human history. His technical achievements were both prodigious and unprecedented and yet his accomplishments remain largely unknown to the general public. I'll refer you to the work of Tesla scholars and advocates for further explication of this tragic conundrum.

In 1898 Nikola Tesla won the world's first patent for a radio-controlled device, which he termed a "teleautomaton." In my book, that makes him the father of all remotely piloted and autonomous vehicles, which would surely include drones but also missile and robotic systems. Even the Mars rover "Curiosity" bears the *imago Tesla*.

Now nineteenth-century observations about the teleautomaton's possible twenty-first-century applications are, typically, both anachronistic and prescient. Here is an excerpt from his patent:

> Be it known that I, Nikola Tesla a citizen of the United States, residing at New York, in the county and State of New York, have invented certain new and useful improvements in methods of and apparatus for control-ling from a distance the operation of the propelling-engines, the steering apparatus, and other mechanism carried by moving bodies or floating vessels, of which the following is a specification, reference being had to the drawings accompanying and forming part of the same . . . The inven-tion which I have described will prove useful in many ways. Vessels or vehicles of any suitable kind may be used, as life, dispatch, or pilot boats

or the like, or for carrying letters, packages, provisions, instruments, objects, or materials of any description, for establishing communication with inaccessible regions and exploring the conditions existing in the same, for killing or capturing whales or other animals of the sea, and for many other scientific, engineering, or commercial purposes; but the greatest value of my invention will result from its effect upon warfare and armaments, for by reason of its certain and unlimited destructiveness it will tend to bring about and maintain permanent peace among nations.

From: "Specification forming part of Letters Patent No. 613,809, dated November 8, 1898." The full original text and diagrams can be found at the U.S. Patent and Trademark Office website: http://patimg1.uspto.gov/.piw?docid=00613809&SectionNum=1&IDKey=CC2FD2DDACBB&HomeUrl=http://pimg-piw.uspto.gov/ If you use a Mac, however, you're out of luck. You can still view it through another fantastic website, Free Patents Online: http://www.freepatentsonline.com/0613809.pdf

In an article published thirteen days later in *The Sun* (New York) newspaper, Tesla expanded upon his thoughts concerning both the fascinating origins and unexpected ramifications of his marvelous invention. Here's an excerpt:

Referring to my latest invention, I wish to bring out a point which has been overlooked. I arrived, as has been stated, at the idea through entirely abstract speculations on the human organism, which I conceived to be a self-propelling machine, the motions of which are governed by impressions received through the eye. Endeavoring to construct a mechanical model resembling in its essential, material features of the human body, I was led to combine a controlling device, or organ sensitive to certain waves, with a body provided with propelling and directing mechanism, and the rest naturally followed. Originally the idea interested me only from the scientific point of view, but soon I saw that I had made a departure which sooner or later must produce a profound change in things and conditions presently existing. I hope this change will be for the good only, for, if it were otherwise, I wish that I had never made the invention.

The future may or may not bear out my present convictions, but I cannot refrain from saying that it is difficult for me to see at present how, with such a principle brought to perfection, as it undoubtedly will be in the course of time, guns can maintain themselves as weapons. We shall be able, by availing ourselves of this advance, to send a projectile at much greater distance, it will not be limited in any way by weight or amount of explosive charge, we shall be able to submerge it at command, to arrest it in its flight, and call it back, and to send it out again and explode it at will, and, more than this, it will never make a miss, since all chance in this regard, if hitting the object of attack were at all required, is eliminated. But the chief feature of such a weapon is still to be told, namely, it may be made to respond only to a certain note or tune, it may be endowed with selective power. Directly such an arm is produced, it becomes almost impossible to meet it with a corresponding development. It is in this feature, perhaps, more than its power of destruction, that its tendency to arrest the development of arms and to stop warfare will reside.

From: *The Sun*, November 21, 1898, page 6. You can read the entire article online at the Library of Congress: http://chroniclingamerica.loc.gov/lccn/sn83030272/1898-11-21/ed-1/seq-6/